TOMMY AND GRIZEL

AND CLUNG TO IT, HIS TEETH SET

TOMMY AND GRIZEL

BY
J. M. BARRIE

ILLUSTRATED BY
BERNARD PARTRIDGE

NEW YORK
CHARLES SCRIBNER'S SONS
1912

Copyright, 1900, by
CHARLES SCRIBNER'S SONS

CONTENTS

PART I

CHAPTER		PAGE
I	How Tommy Found a Way	3
II	The Search for the Treasure	16
III	Sandys on Woman	36
IV	Grizel of the Crooked Smile	52
V	The Tommy Myth	69
VI	Ghosts That Haunt the Den	87
VII	The Beginning of the Duel	101
VIII	What Grizel's Eyes Said	119
IX	Gallant Behaviour of T. Sandys	132
X	Gavinia on the Track	147
XI	The Tea-Party	153
XII	In Which a Comedian Challenges Tragedy to Bowls	175
XIII	Little Wells of Gladness	194
XIV	Elspeth	210
XV	By Prosen Water	220
XVI	"How Could You Hurt Your Grizel So!"	232
XVII	How Tommy Saved the Flag	246

CONTENTS

PART II

CHAPTER		PAGE
XVIII	THE GIRL SHE HAD BEEN	1
XIX	OF THE CHANGE IN THOMAS	13
XX	A LOVE-LETTER	30
XXI	THE ATTEMPT TO CARRY ELSPETH BY NUMBERS	54
XXII	GRIZEL'S GLORIOUS HOUR	70
XXIII	TOMMY LOSES GRIZEL	80
XXIV	THE MONSTER	95
XXV	MR. T. SANDYS HAS RETURNED TO TOWN	114
XXVI	GRIZEL ALL ALONE	133
XXVII	GRIZEL'S JOURNEY	152
XXVIII	TWO OF THEM	164
XXIX	THE RED LIGHT	181
XXX	THE LITTLE GODS DESERT HIM	192
XXXI	"THE MAN WITH THE GREETIN' EYES"	211
XXXII	TOMMY'S BEST WORK	229
XXXIII	THE LITTLE GODS RETURN WITH A LADY	241
XXXIV	A WAY IS FOUND FOR TOMMY	254
XXXV	THE PERFECT LOVER	276

ILLUSTRATIONS

PART I

And clung to it, his teeth set . . . . . *Frontispiece*

                                              FACING PAGE

"She is standing behind that tree looking at us" . 200

She did not look up, she waited 220

PART II

"I sit still by his arm-chair and tell him what is happening to his Grizel" 6

They told Aaron something 68

"But my friends still call me Mrs. Jerry," she said softly 118

"I woke up," she said 190

He heard their seductive voices, they danced around him in numbers. 250

TOMMY AND GRIZEL

PART I

TOMMY AND GRIZEL

CHAPTER I

HOW TOMMY FOUND A WAY

O. P. PYM, the colossal Pym, that vast and rolling figure, who never knew what he was to write about until he dipped grandly, an author in such demand that on the foggy evening which starts our story his publishers have had his boots removed lest he slip thoughtlessly round the corner before his work is done, as was the great man's way — shall we begin with him, or with Tommy, who has just arrived in London, carrying his little box and leading a lady by the hand? It was Pym, as we are about to see, who in the beginning held Tommy up to the public gaze, Pym who first noticed his remarkable indifference to female society, Pym who gave him —— But alack! does no one remember Pym for himself? Is the king of the *Penny Number* already no more than a button that once upon a time kept Tommy's person together? And we are at the night when they first met! Let us hasten into Marylebone before little Tommy arrives and Pym is swallowed like an oyster.

This is the house, 22 Little Owlet Street, Marylebone, but which were his rooms it is less easy to determine, for he was a lodger who flitted placidly from floor to floor according to the state of his finances, carrying his apparel and other belongings in one great armful, and spilling by the way. On this particular evening he was on the second floor front, which had a fireplace in the corner, furniture all his landlady's and mostly horsehair, little to suggest his calling save a noble saucerful of ink, and nothing to draw attention from Pym, who lolled, gross and massive, on a sofa, one leg over the back of it, the other drooping, his arms extended, and his pipe, which he could find nowhere, thrust between the buttons of his waistcoat, an agreeable pipe-rack. He wore a yellow dressing-gown, or could scarcely be said to wear it, for such of it as was not round his neck he had converted into a cushion for his head, which is perhaps the part of him we should have turned to first. It was a big round head, the plentiful gray hair in tangles, possibly because in Pym's last flitting the comb had dropped over the banisters; the features were ugly and beyond life-size, yet the forehead had al-

HOW TOMMY FOUND A WAY

tered little except in colour since the day when he was near being made a fellow of his college; there was sensitiveness left in the thick nose, humour in the eyes, though they so often watered; the face had gone to flabbiness at last, but not without some lines and dents, as if the head had resisted the body for a space before the whole man rolled contentedly downhill.

He had no beard. "Young man, let your beard grow." Those who have forgotten all else about Pym may recall him in these words. They were his one counsel to literary aspirants, who, according as they took it, are now bearded and prosperous or shaven and on the rates. To shave costs threepence, another threepence for loss of time — nearly ten pounds a year, three hundred pounds since Pym's chin first bristled. With his beard he could have bought an annuity or a cottage in the country, he could have had a wife and children, and driven his dog-cart, and been made a church-warden. All gone, all shaved, and for what? When he asked this question he would move his hand across his chin with a sigh, and so, bravely to the barber's.

Pym was at present suffering from an ailment that had spread him out on that sofa again and again — acute disinclination to work.

Meanwhile all the world was waiting for his new tale; so the publishers, two little round men, have told him. They have blustered, they have fawned, they have asked each other out to talk it over behind the door.

Has he any idea of what the story is to be about? He has no idea.

Then at least, Pym—excellent Pym—sit down and dip, and let us see what will happen.

He declined to do even that. While all the world waited, this was Pym's ultimatum:

"I shall begin the damned thing at eight o'clock."

Outside, the fog kept changing at intervals from black to white, as lazily from white to black (the monster blinking); there was not a sound from the street save of pedestrians tapping with their sticks on the pavement as they moved forward warily, afraid of an embrace with the unknown; it might have been a city of blind beggars, one of them a boy.

At eight o'clock Pym rose with a groan and sat down in his stocking-soles to write his delicious tale. He was now alone. But though his legs were wound round his waste-paper basket, and he dipped often and loudly in the saucer, like one ringing at the door of Fancy, he could not get the idea that would set him going. He was still dipping for inspiration when T. Sandys, who had been told to find the second floor for himself, knocked at the door, and entered, quaking.

HOW TOMMY FOUND A WAY

"I remember it vividly," Pym used to say when questioned in the after years about this his first sight of Tommy, "and I hesitate to decide which impressed me more, the richness of his voice, so remarkable in a boy of sixteen, or his serene countenance, with its noble forehead, behind which nothing base could lurk."

Pym, Pym! it is such as you that makes the writing of biography difficult. The richness of Tommy's voice could not have struck you, for at that time it was a somewhat squeaky voice; and as for the noble forehead behind which nothing base could lurk, how could you say that, Pym, you who had a noble forehead yourself?

No; all that Pym saw was a pasty-faced boy sixteen years old, and of an appearance mysteriously plain; hair light brown, and waving defiance to the brush; nothing startling about him but the expression of his face, which was almost fearsomely solemn and apparently unchangeable. He wore his Sunday blacks, of which the trousers might with advantage have borrowed from the sleeves; and he was so nervous that he had to wet his lips before he could speak. He had left the door ajar for a private reason; but Pym, misunderstanding, thought he did it to fly the more readily if anything was flung at him, and so concluded that he must be a printer's devil.

Pym had a voice that shook his mantelpiece

ornaments; he was all on the same scale as his ink-pot. "Your Christian name, boy?" he roared hopefully, for it was thus he sometimes got the idea that started him.

"Thomas," replied the boy.

Pym gave him a look of disgust. "You may go," he said. But when he looked up presently, Thomas was still there. He was not only there, but whistling — a short, encouraging whistle that seemed to be directed at the door. He stopped quickly when Pym looked up, but during the remainder of the interview he emitted this whistle at intervals, always with that anxious glance at his friend the door; and its strained joviality was in odd contrast with his solemn face, like a cheery tune played on the church organ.

"Begone!" cried Pym.

"My full name," explained Tommy, who was speaking the English correctly, but with a Scots accent, "is Thomas Sandys. And fine you know who that is," he added, exasperated by Pym's indifference. "I'm the T. Sandys that answered your advertisement."

Pym knew who he was now. "You young ruffian," he gasped, "I never dreamt that you would come!"

"I have your letter engaging me in my pocket," said Tommy, boldly, and he laid it on the table. Pym surveyed it and him in comic dismay, then

HOW TOMMY FOUND A WAY

with a sudden thought produced nearly a dozen letters from a drawer, and dumped them down beside the other. It was now his turn to look triumphant and Tommy aghast.

Pym's letters were all addressed from the Dubb of Prosen Farm, near Thrums, N. B., to different advertisers, care of a London agency, and were Tommy's answers to the "wants" in a London newspaper which had found its way to the far North. "X Y Z" was in need of a chemist's assistant, and from his earliest years, said one of the letters, chemistry had been the study of studies for T. Sandys. He was glad to read, was T. Sandys, that one who did not object to long hours would be preferred, for it seemed to him that those who objected to long hours did not really love their work, their heart was not in it, and only where the heart is can the treasure be found.

"123" had a vacancy for a page-boy, "Glasgow Man" for a photographer; page-boy must not be over fourteen, photographer must not be under twenty. "I am a little over fourteen, but I look less," wrote T. Sandys to "123"; "I am a little under twenty," he wrote to "Glasgow Man," "but I look more." His heart was in the work.

To be a political organizer! If "H and H," who advertised for one, only knew how eagerly the undersigned desired to devote his life to political organizing!

TOMMY AND GRIZEL

In answer to "Scholastic's" advertisement for janitor in a boys' school, T. Sandys begged to submit his name for consideration.

Undoubtedly the noblest letter was the one applying for the secretaryship of a charitable society, salary to begin at once, but the candidate selected must deposit one hundred pounds. The application was noble in its offer to make the work a labour of love, and almost nobler in its argument that the hundred pounds was unnecessary.

"Rex" had a vacancy in his drapery department. T. Sandys had made a unique study of drapery.

Lastly, "Anon" wanted an amanuensis. "Salary," said "Anon," who seemed to be a humourist, "salary large but uncertain." He added with equal candour: "Drudgery great, but to an intelligent man the pickings may be considerable." Pickings! Is there a finer word in the language? T. Sandys had felt that he was particularly good at pickings. But amanuensis? The thing was unknown to him; no one on the farm could tell him what it was. But never mind; his heart was in it.

All this correspondence had produced one reply, the letter on which Tommy's hand still rested. It was a brief note, signed "O. P. Pym," and engaging Mr. Sandys on his own recommendation, "if he really felt quite certain that his heart (treasure included) was in the work." So far good, Tommy had thought when he received this answer, but

HOW TOMMY FOUND A WAY

there was nothing in it to indicate the nature of the work, nothing to show whether O. P. Pym was "Scholastic," or "123," or "Rex," or any other advertiser in particular. Stop, there was a postscript: "I need not go into details about your duties, as you assure me you are so well acquainted with them, but before you join me please send (in writing) a full statement of what you think they are."

There were delicate reasons why Mr. Sandys could not do that, but oh, he was anxious to be done with farm labour, so he decided to pack and risk it. The letter said plainly that he was engaged; what for he must find out slyly when he came to London. So he had put his letter firmly on Pym's table; but it was a staggerer to find that gentleman in possession of the others.

One of these was Pym's by right; the remainder were a humourous gift from the agent who was accustomed to sift the correspondence of his clients. Pym had chuckled over them, and written a reply that he flattered himself would stump the boy; then he had unexpectedly come into funds (he found a forgotten check while searching his old pockets for tobacco-crumbs), and in that glory T. Sandys escaped his memory. Result, that they were now face to face.

A tiny red spot, not noticeable before, now appeared in Tommy's eyes. It was never there except when he was determined to have his way. Pym, my friend, yes, and everyone of you who is destined to challenge Tommy, 'ware that red light!

"Well, which am I?" demanded Pym, almost amused, Tommy was so obviously in a struggle with the problem.

The saucer and the blank pages told nothing. "Whichever you are," the boy answered heavily, "it's not herding nor foddering cattle, and so long as it's not that, I'll put my heart in it, and where the heart is, there the treasure ——"

He suddenly remembered that his host must be acquainted with the sentiment.

Easy-going Pym laughed, then said irritably, "Of what use could a mere boy be to me?"

"Then it's not the page-boy!" exclaimed Tommy, thankfully.

"Perhaps I am 'Scholastic,'" suggested Pym.

"No," said Tommy, after a long study of his face.

Pym followed this reasoning, and said touchily, "Many a schoolmaster has a red face."

"Not that kind of redness," explained Tommy, without delicacy.

"I am 'H and H,'" said Pym.

"You forget you wrote to me as one person," replied Tommy.

"So I did. That was because I am the chemist;

HOW TOMMY FOUND A WAY

and I must ask you, Thomas, for your certificate."

Tommy believed him this time, and Pym triumphantly poured himself a glass of whisky, spilling some of it on his dressing-gown.

"Not you," said Tommy, quickly; "a chemist has a steady hand."

"Confound you!" cried Pym, "what sort of a boy is this?"

"If you had been the draper you would have wiped the drink off your gown," continued Tommy, thoughtfully, "and if you had been 'Glasgow Man' you would have sucked it off, and if you had been the charitable society you would n't swear in company." He flung out his hand. "I'll tell you who you are," he said sternly, "you're 'Anon.'"

Under this broadside Pym succumbed. He sat down feebly. "Right," he said, with a humourous groan, "and I shall tell you who you are. I am afraid you are my amanuensis!"

Tommy immediately whistled, a louder and more glorious note than before.

"Don't be so cocky," cried Pym, in sudden rebellion. "You are only my amanuensis if you can tell me what that is. If you can't — out you go!"

He had him at last!

Not he!

"An amanuensis," said Tommy, calmly, "is one who writes to dictation. Am I to bring in my box? It's at the door."

This made Pym sit down again. "You didn't know what an amanuensis was when you answered my advertisement," he said.

"As soon as I got to London," Tommy answered, "I went into a bookseller's shop, pretending I wanted to buy a dictionary, and I looked the word up."

"Bring in your box," Pym said, with a groan.

But it was now Tommy's turn to hesitate. "Have you noticed," he asked awkwardly, "that I sometimes whistle?"

"Don't tell me," said Pym, "that you have a dog out there."

"It's not a dog," Tommy replied cautiously.

Pym had resumed his seat at the table and was once more toying with his pen. "Open the door," he commanded, "and let me see what you have brought with you."

Tommy obeyed gingerly, and then Pym gaped, for what the open door revealed to him was a tiny roped box with a girl of twelve sitting on it. She was dressed in some dull-coloured wincey, and looked cold and patient and lonely, and as she saw the big man staring at her she struggled in alarm to her feet, and could scarce stand on them. Tommy was looking apprehensively from her to Pym.

HOW TOMMY FOUND A WAY

"Good God, boy!" roared Pym, "are you married?"

"No," cried Tommy, in agony, "she's my sister, and we're orphans, and did you think I could have the heart to leave Elspeth behind?" He took her stoutly by the hand.

"And he never will marry," said little Elspeth, almost fiercely; "will you, Tommy?"

"Never!" said Tommy, patting her and glaring at Pym.

But Pym would not have it. "Married!" he shouted. "Magnificent!" And he dipped exultantly, for he had got his idea at last. Forgetting even that he had an amanuensis, he wrote on and on and on.

"He smells o' drink," Elspeth whispered.

"All the better," replied Tommy, cheerily. "Make yourself at home, Elspeth; he's the kind I can manage. Was there ever a kind I couldna manage?" he whispered, top-heavy with conceit.

"There was Grizel," Elspeth said, rather thoughtlessly; and then Tommy frowned.

CHAPTER II

THE SEARCH FOR THE TREASURE

SIX years afterwards Tommy was a famous man, as I hope you do not need to be told; but you may be wondering how it came about. The whole question, in Pym's words, resolves itself into how the solemn little devil got to know so much about women. It made the world marvel when they learned his age, but no one was quite so staggered as Pym, who had seen him daily for all those years, and been damning him for his indifference to the sex during the greater part of them.

It began while he was still no more than an amanuensis, sitting with his feet in the waste-paper basket, Pym dictating from the sofa, and swearing when the words would not come unless he was perpendicular. Among the duties of this amanuensis was to remember the name of the heroine, her appearance, and other personal details; for Pym constantly forgot them in the night, and he had to go searching back through his pages for them, cursing her so horribly that Tommy signed to Elspeth to retire to her tiny bedroom at the top of the

THE SEARCH FOR THE TREASURE

house. He was always most careful of Elspeth, and with the first pound he earned he insured his life, leaving all to her, but told her nothing about it, lest she should think it meant his early death. As she grew older he also got good dull books for her from a library, and gave her a piano on the hire system, and taught her many things about life, very carefully selected from his own discoveries.

Elspeth out of the way, he could give Pym all the information wanted. "Her name is Felicity," he would say at the right moment; "she has curly brown hair in which the sun strays, and a blushing neck, and her eyes are like blue lakes."

"Height!" roared Pym. "Have I mentioned it?"

"No; but she is about five feet six."

"How the —— could you know that?"

"You tell Percy's height in his stocking-soles, and when she reached to his mouth and kissed him she had to stand on her tiptoes so to do."

Tommy said this in a most businesslike tone, but could not help smacking his lips. He smacked them again when he had to write: "Have no fear, little woman; I am by your side." Or, "What a sweet child you are!"

Pym had probably fallen into the way of making the Percys revel in such epithets because he could not remember the girl's name; but this delicious use of the diminutive, as addressed to full-grown ladies, went to Tommy's head. His solemn face kept his secret, but he had some narrow escapes; as once, when saying good-night to Elspeth, he kissed her on mouth, eyes, nose, and ears, and said: "Shall I tuck you in, little woman?" He came to himself with a start.

"I forgot," he said hurriedly, and got out of the room without telling her what he had forgotten.

Pym's publishers knew their man, and their arrangement with him was that he was paid on completion of the tale. But always before he reached the middle he struck for what they called his honorarium; and this troubled them, for the tale was appearing week by week as it was written. If they were obdurate, he suddenly concluded his story in such words as these:

"Several years have passed since these events took place, and the scene changes to a lovely garden by the bank of old Father Thames. A young man sits by the soft-flowing stream, and he is calm as the scene itself; for the storm has passed away, and Percy (for it is no other) has found an anchorage. As he sits musing over the past, Felicity steals out by the French window and puts her soft arms around his neck. 'My little wife!' he murmurs. *The End — unless you pay up by messenger.*"

This last line, which was not meant for the world (but little would Pym have cared though it had been printed), usually brought his employers to their knees; and then, as Tommy advanced in experience, came the pickings — for Pym, with money in his pockets, had important engagements round the corner, and risked intrusting his amanuensis with the writing of the next instalment, "all except the bang at the end."

Smaller people, in Tommy's state of mind, would have hurried straight to the love-passages; but he saw the danger, and forced his Pegasus away from them. "Do your day's toil first," he may be conceived saying to that animal, "and at evenfall I shall let you out to browse." So, with this reward in front, he devoted many pages to the dreary adventures of pretentious males, and even found a certain pleasure in keeping the lady waiting. But as soon as he reached her he lost his head again.

"Oh, you beauty! oh, you small pet!" he said to himself, with solemn transport.

As the artist in him was stirred, great problems presented themselves; for instance, in certain circumstances was "darling" or "little one" the better phrase? "Darling" in solitary grandeur is more pregnant of meaning than "little one," but "little" has a flavour of the patronizing which "darling" perhaps lacks. He wasted many sheets over such questions; but they were in his pocket when Pym or Elspeth opened the door. It is wonderful how much you can conceal between the touch on the handle and the opening of the door, if your heart is in it.

Despite this fine practice, however, he was the shyest of mankind in the presence of women, and this shyness grew upon him with the years. Was it because he never tried to uncork himself? Oh, no! It was about this time that he, one day, put his arm round Clara, the servant—not passionately, but with deliberation, as if he were making an experiment with machinery. He then listened, as if to hear Clara ticking. He wrote an admirable love-letter — warm, dignified, sincere — to nobody in particular, and carried it about in his pocket in readiness. But in love-making, as in the other arts, those do it best who cannot tell how it is done; and he was always stricken with a palsy when about to present that letter. It seemed that he was only able to speak to ladies when they were not there. Well, if he could not speak, he thought the more; he thought so profoundly that in time the heroines of Pym ceased to thrill him.

This was because he had found out that they were not flesh and blood. But he did not delight in his discovery: it horrified him; for what he wanted was the old thrill. To make them human so that they could be his little friends again — nothing less was called for. This meant slaughter here and there of the great Pym's brain-work, and Tommy tried to keep his hands off; but his heart was in it. In

THE SEARCH FOR THE TREASURE

Pym's pages the ladies were the most virtuous and proper of their sex (though dreadfully persecuted), but he merely told you so at the beginning, and now and again afterwards to fill up, and then allowed them to act with what may be called rashness, so that the story did not really suffer. Before Tommy was nineteen he changed all that. Out went this because she would not have done it, and that because she could not have done it. Fathers might now have taken a lesson from T. Sandys in the upbringing of their daughters. He even sternly struck out the diminutives. With a pen in his hand and woman in his head, he had such noble thoughts that his tears of exaltation damped the pages as he wrote, and the ladies must have been astounded as well as proud to see what they were turning into.

That was Tommy with a pen in his hand and a handkerchief hard by; but it was another Tommy who, when the finest bursts were over, sat back in his chair and mused. The lady was consistent now, and he would think about her, and think and think, until concentration, which is a pair of blazing eyes, seemed to draw her out of the pages to his side, and then he and she sported in a way forbidden in the tale. While he sat there with eyes riveted, he had her to dinner at a restaurant, and took her up the river, and called her " little woman "; and when she held up her mouth he said tantalizingly that she must wait until he had finished his cigar. This queer delight enjoyed, back he popped her into the story, where she was again the vehicle for such glorious sentiments that Elspeth, to whom he read the best of them, feared he was becoming too good to live.

In the meantime the great penny public were slowly growing restive, and at last the two little round men called on Pym to complain that he was falling off; and Pym turned them out of doors, and then sat down heroically to do what he had not done for two decades — to read his latest work.

"Elspeth, go upstairs to your room," whispered Tommy, and then he folded his arms proudly. He should have been in a tremble, but latterly he had often felt that he must burst if he did not soon read some of his bits to Pym, more especially the passages about the hereafter; also the opening of Chapter Seventeen.

At first Pym's only comment was, "It is the same old drivel as before; what more can they want?"

But presently he looked up, puzzled. "Is this chapter yours or mine?" he demanded.

"It is about half and half," said Tommy.

"Is mine the first half? Where does yours begin?"

"That is not exactly what I mean," explained

THE SEARCH FOR THE TREASURE

Tommy, in a glow, but backing a little; "you wrote that chapter first, and then I — I ——"

"You rewrote it!" roared Pym. "You dared to meddle with ——" He was speechless with fury.

"I tried to keep my hand off," Tommy said, with dignity, "but the thing had to be done, and they are human now."

"Human! who wants them to be human? The fiends seize you, boy! you have even been tinkering with my heroine's personal appearance; what is this you have been doing to her nose?"

"I turned it up slightly, that's all," said Tommy.

"I like them down," roared Pym.

"I prefer them up," said Tommy, stiffly.

"Where," cried Pym, turning over the leaves in a panic, "where is the scene in the burning house?"

"It's out," Tommy explained, "but there is a chapter in its place about — it's mostly about the beauty of the soul being everything, and mere physical beauty nothing. Oh, Mr. Pym, sit down and let me read it to you."

But Pym read it, and a great deal more, for himself. No wonder he stormed, for the impossible had been made not only consistent, but unreadable. The plot was lost for chapters. The characters no longer did anything, and then went and did something else: you were told instead how they did it. You were not allowed to make up your own mind about them: you had to listen to the mind of T. Sandys; he described and he analyzed; the road he had tried to clear through the thicket was impassable for chips.

"A few more weeks of this," said Pym, "and we should all three be turned out into the streets."

Tommy went to bed in an agony of mortification, but presently to his side came Pym.

"Where did you copy this from?" he asked. "'It is when we are thinking of those we love that our noblest thoughts come to us, and the more worthy they are of our love the nobler the thought; hence it is that no one has done the greatest work who did not love God.'"

"I copied it from nowhere," replied Tommy, fiercely; "it's my own."

"Well, it has nothing to do with the story, and so is only a blot on it, and I have no doubt the thing has been said much better before. Still, I suppose it is true."

"It's true," said Tommy; "and yet —— "

"Go on. I want to know all about it."

"And yet," Tommy said, puzzled, "I've known noble thoughts come to me when I was listening to a brass band."

Pym chuckled. "Funny things, noble thoughts," he agreed. He read another passage:

"'It was the last half-hour of day when I was

THE SEARCH FOR THE TREASURE

admitted, with several others, to look upon my friend's dead face. A handkerchief had been laid over it. I raised the handkerchief. I know not what the others were thinking, but the last time we met he had told me something, it was not much — only that no woman had ever kissed him. It seemed to me that, as I gazed, the wistfulness came back to his face. I whispered to a woman who was present, and stooping over him, she was about to — but her eyes were dry, and I stopped her. The handkerchief was replaced, and all left the room save myself. Again I raised the handkerchief. I cannot tell you how innocent he looked.'"

"Who was he?" asked Pym.

"Nobody," said Tommy, with some awe; "it just came to me. Do you notice how simple the wording is? It took me some time to make it so simple."

"You are just nineteen, I think?"

"Yes."

Pym looked at him wonderingly.

"Thomas," he said, "you are a very queer little devil."

He also said: "And it is possible you may find the treasure you are always talking about. Don't jump to the ceiling, my friend, because I say that. I was once after the treasure, myself; and you can see whether I found it."

From about that time, on the chances that this mysterious treasure might spring up in the form of a new kind of flower, Pym zealously cultivated the ground, and Tommy had an industrious time of it. He was taken off his stories, which at once regained their elasticity, and put on to exercises.

"If you have nothing to say on the subject, say nothing," was one of the new rules, which few would have expected from Pym. Another was: "As soon as you can say what you think, and not what some other person has thought for you, you are on the way to being a remarkable man."

"Without concentration, Thomas, you are lost; concentrate, though your coat-tails be on fire.

"Try your hand at description, and when you have done chortling over the result, reduce the whole by half without missing anything out.

"Analyze your characters and their motives at the prodigious length in which you revel, and then, my sonny, cut your analysis out. It is for your own guidance, not the reader's.

"'I have often noticed,' you are always saying. The story has nothing to do with you. Obliterate yourself. I see that will be your stiffest job.

"Stop preaching. It seems to me the pulpit is where you should look for the treasure. Nineteen, and you are already as didactic as seventy."

And so on.

Over his exercises Tommy was now engrossed

THE SEARCH FOR THE TREASURE

for so long a period that, as he sits there, you may observe his legs slowly lengthening and the coming of his beard. No, his legs lengthened as he sat with his feet in the basket; but I feel sure that his beard burst through prematurely some night when he was thinking too hard about the ladies.

There were no ladies in the exercises, for, despite their altercation about noses, Pym knew that on this subject Tommy's mind was a blank. But he recognized the sex's importance, and becoming possessed once more of a black coat, marched his pupil into the somewhat shoddy drawing-rooms that were still open to him, and there ordered Tommy to be fascinated for his future good. But it was as it had always been. Tommy sat white and speechless and apparently bored; could not even say, "You sing with so much expression!" when the lady at the pianoforte had finished.

"Shyness I could pardon," the exasperated Pym would roar; "but want of interest is almost immoral. At your age the blood would have been coursing through my veins. Love! You are incapable of it. There is not a drop of sentiment in your frozen carcass."

"Can I help that?" growled Tommy. It was an agony to him even to speak about women.

"If you can't," said Pym, "all is over with you. An artist without sentiment is a painter without colours. Young man, I fear you are doomed."

And Tommy believed him, and quaked. He had the most gallant struggles with himself. He even set his teeth and joined a dancing-class; though neither Pym nor Elspeth knew of it, and it never showed afterwards in his legs. In appearance he was now beginning to be the Sandys of the photographs: a little over the middle height and rather heavily built; nothing to make you uncomfortable until you saw his face. That solemn countenance never responded when he laughed, and stood coldly by when he was on fire; he might have winked for an eternity, and still the onlooker must have thought himself mistaken. In his boyhood the mask had descended scarce below his mouth, for there was a dimple in the chin to put you at ease; but now the short brown beard had come, and he was for ever hidden from the world.

He had the dandy's tastes for superb neckties, velvet jackets, and he got the ties instead of dining; he panted for the jacket, knew all the shop-windows it was in, but for years denied himself, with a moan, so that he might buy pretty things for Elspeth. When eventually he got it, Pym's friends ridiculed him. When he saw how ill his face matched it he ridiculed himself. Often when Tommy was feeling that now at last the ladies must come to heel, he saw his face suddenly in a mirror, and all the spirit went out of him. But still he clung to his velvet jacket.

THE SEARCH FOR THE TREASURE

I see him in it, stalking through the terrible dances, a heroic figure at last. He shuddered every time he found himself on one leg; he got sternly into everybody's way; he was the butt of the little noodle of an instructor. All the social tortures he endured grimly, in the hope that at last the cork would come out. Then, though there were all kinds of girls in the class, merry, sentimental, practical, coquettish, prudes, there was no kind, he felt, whose heart he could not touch. In love-making, as in the favourite Thrums game of the dambrod, there are sixty-one openings, and he knew them all. Yet at the last dance, as at the first, the universal opinion of his partners (shop-girls, mostly, from the large millinery establishments, who had to fly like Cinderellas when the clock struck a certain hour) was that he kept himself to himself, and they were too much the lady to make up to a gentleman who so obviously did not want them.

Pym encouraged his friends to jeer at Tommy's want of interest in the sex, thinking it a way of goading him to action. One evening, the bottles circulating, they mentioned one Dolly, goddess at some bar, as a fit instructress for him. Coarse pleasantries passed, but for a time he writhed in silence, then burst upon them indignantly for their unmanly smirching of a woman's character, and swept out, leaving them a little ashamed. That was very like Tommy.

But presently a desire came over him to see this girl, and it came because they had hinted such dark things about her. That was like him also.

There was probably no harm in Dolly, though it is man's proud right to question it in exchange for his bitters. She was tall and willowy, and stretched her neck like a swan, and returned you your change with disdainful languor; to call such a haughty beauty Dolly was one of the minor triumphs for man, and Dolly they all called her, except the only one who could have given an artistic justification for it.

This one was a bearded stranger who, when he knew that Pym and his friends were elsewhere, would enter the bar with a cigar in his mouth, and ask for a whisky-and-water, which was heroism again, for smoking was ever detestable to him, and whisky more offensive than quinine. But these things are expected of you, and by asking for the whisky you get into talk with Dolly; that is to say, you tell her several times what you want, and when she has served every other body you get it. The commercial must be served first; in the barroom he blocks the way like royalty in the street. There is a crown for us all somewhere.

Dolly seldom heard the bearded one's "good-evening"; she could not possibly have heard the "dear," for though it was there, it remained behind his teeth. She knew him only as the stiff

THE SEARCH FOR THE TREASURE

man who got separated from his glass without complaining, and at first she put this down to forgetfulness, and did nothing, so that he could go away without drinking; but by and by, wherever he left his tumbler, cunningly concealed behind a water-bottle, or temptingly in front of a commercial, she restored it to him, and there was a twinkle in her eye.

"You little rogue, so you see through me!" Surely it was an easy thing to say; but what he did say was "Thank you." Then to himself he said, "Ass, ass, ass!"

Sitting on the padded seat that ran the length of the room, and surreptitiously breaking his cigar against the cushions to help it on its way to an end, he brought his intellect to bear on Dolly at a distance, and soon had a better knowledge of her than could be claimed by those who had Dollied her for years. He also wove romances about her, some of them of too lively a character, and others so noble and sad and beautiful that the tears came to his eyes, and Dolly thought he had been drinking. He could not have said whether he would prefer her to be good or bad.

These were but his leisure moments, for during the long working hours he was still at the exercises, toiling fondly, and right willing to tear himself asunder to get at the trick of writing. So he passed from exercises to the grand experiment.

TOMMY AND GRIZEL

It was to be a tale, for there, they had taken for granted, lay the treasure. Pym was most considerate at this time, and mentioned woman with an apology.

"I have kept away from them in the exercises," he said in effect, "because it would have been useless (as well as cruel) to force you to labour on a subject so uncongenial to you; and for the same reason I have decided that it is to be a tale of adventure, in which the heroine need be little more than a beautiful sack of coals which your cavalier carries about with him on his left shoulder. I am afraid we must have her to that extent, Thomas, but I am not asking much of you; dump her down as often as you like."

And Thomas did his dogged best, the red light in his eye; though he had not, and never could have had, the smallest instinct for story-writing, he knew to the finger-tips how it is done; but for ever he would have gone on breaking all the rules of the game. How he wrestled with himself! Sublime thoughts came to him (nearly all about that girl), and he drove them away, for he knew they beat only against the march of his story, and, whatever befall, the story must march. Relentlessly he followed in the track of his men, pushing the dreary dogs on to deeds of valour. He tried making the lady human, and then she would not march; she sat still, and he talked about her;

THE SEARCH FOR THE TREASURE

he dumped her down, and soon he was yawning. This weariness was what alarmed him most, for well he understood that there could be no treasure where the work was not engrossing play, and he doubted no more than Pym that for him the treasure was in the tale or nowhere. Had he not been sharpening his tools in this belief for years? Strange to reflect now that all the time he was hacking and sweating at that novel (the last he ever attempted) it was only marching towards the waste-paper basket!

He had a fine capacity, as has been hinted, for self-deception, and in time, of course, he found a way of dodging the disquieting truth. This, equally of course, was by yielding to his impulses. He allowed himself an hour a day, when Pym was absent, in which he wrote the story as it seemed to want to write itself, and then he cut this piece out, which could be done quite easily, as it consisted only of moralizings. Thus was his day brightened, and with this relaxation to look forward to he plodded on at his proper work, delving so hard that he could avoid asking himself why he was still delving. What shall we say? He was digging for the treasure in an orchard, and every now and again he came out of his hole to pluck an apple; but though the apple was so sweet to the mouth, it never struck him that the treasure might be growing overhead. At first he destroyed the fruit of his stolen hour, and even after he took to carrying it about fondly in his pocket, and to rewriting it in a splendid new form that had come to him just as he was stepping into bed, he continued to conceal it from his overseer's eyes. And still he thought all was over with him when Pym said the story did not march.

"It is a dead thing," Pym would roar, flinging down the manuscript,—"a dead thing because the stakes your man is playing for, a woman's love, is less than a wooden counter to you. You are a fine piece of mechanism, my solemn-faced don, but you are a watch that won't go because you are not wound up. Nobody can wind the artist up except a chit of a girl; and how you are ever to get one to take pity on you, only the gods who look after men with a want can tell.

"It becomes more impenetrable every day," he said. "No use your sitting there tearing yourself to bits. Out into the street with you! I suspend these sittings until you can tell me you have kissed a girl."

He was still saying this sort of thing when the famous "Letters" were published — T. Sandys, author. "Letters to a Young Man About to be Married" was the full title, and another almost as applicable would have been "Bits Cut Out of a Story because They Prevented its Marching." If you have any memory you do not need to be told

THE SEARCH FOR THE TREASURE

how that splendid study, so ennobling, so penetrating, of woman at her best, took the town. Tommy woke a famous man, and, except Elspeth, no one was more pleased than big-hearted, hopeless, bleary Pym.

"But how the —— has it all come about!" he kept roaring.

"A woman can be anything that the man who loves her would have her be," says the "Letters"; and "Oh," said woman everywhere, "if all men had the same idea of us as Mr. Sandys!"

"To meet Mr. T. Sandys." Leaders of society wrote it on their invitation cards. Their daughters, athirst for a new sensation, thrilled at the thought, "Will he talk to us as nobly as he writes?" And oh, how willing he was to do it, especially if their noses were slightly tilted!

CHAPTER III

SANDYS ON WOMAN

"Can you kindly tell me the name of the book I want?"

It is the commonest question asked at the circulating library by dainty ladies just out of the carriage; and the librarian, after looking them over, can usually tell. In the days we have now to speak of, however, he answered, without looking them over:

"Sandys's 'Letters.'"

"Ah, yes, of course. May I have it, please?"

"I regret to find that it is out."

Then the lady looked naughty. "Why don't you have two copies?" she pouted.

"Madam," said the librarian, "we have a thousand."

A small and very timid girl of eighteen, with a neat figure that shrank from observation, although it was already aware that it looked best in gray, was there to drink in this music, and carried it home in her heart. She was Elspeth, and that dear heart was almost too full at this time. I hesitate whether to tell or to conceal how it even created a disturbance in no less a place than the House of Commons. She was there with Mrs. Jerry, and the thing was recorded in the papers of the period in these blasting words: "The Home Secretary was understood to be quoting a passage from 'Letters to a Young Man,' but we failed to catch its drift, owing to an unseemly interruption from the ladies' gallery."

"But what was it you cried out?" Tommy asked Elspeth, when she thought she had told him everything. (Like all true women, she always began in the middle.)

"Oh, Tommy, have I not told you? I cried out, 'I'm his sister.'"

Thus, owing to Elspeth's behaviour, it can never be known which was the passage quoted in the House; but we may be sure of one thing — that it did the House good. That book did everybody good. Even Pym could only throw off its beneficent effects by a tremendous effort, and young men about to be married used to ask at the bookshops, not for the "Letters," but simply for "Sandys on Woman," acknowledging Tommy as the authority on the subject, like Mill on Jurisprudence, or Thomson and Tait on the Differential Calculus. Controversies raged about it. Some thought he asked too much of man, some thought he saw too much in women; there was a fear that young people, knowing at last how far short they fell of what they ought to be, might shrink from the matrimony that must expose them to each other, now that they had Sandys to guide them, and the persons who had simply married and risked it (and it was astounding what a number of them there proved to be) wrote to the papers suggesting that he might yield a little in the next edition. But Sandys remained firm.

At first they took for granted that he was a very aged gentleman; he had, indeed, hinted at this in the text; and when the truth came out ("And just fancy, he is not even married!") the enthusiasm was doubled. "Not engaged!" they cried. "Don't tell that to me. No unmarried man could have written such a eulogy of marriage without being on the brink of it." Perhaps she was dead? It ran through the town that she was dead. Some knew which cemetery.

The very first lady Mr. Sandys ever took in to dinner mentioned this rumour to him, not with vulgar curiosity, but delicately, with a hint of sympathy in waiting, and it must be remembered, in fairness to Tommy, that all artists love sympathy. This sympathy uncorked him, and our Tommy could flow comparatively freely at last. Observe the delicious change.

"Has that story got abroad?" he said simply. "The matter is one which, I need not say, I have never mentioned to a soul."

SANDYS ON WOMAN

"Of course not," the lady said, and waited eagerly.

If Tommy had been an expert he might have turned the conversation to brighter topics, but he was not; there had already been long pauses, and in dinner talk it is perhaps allowable to fling on any faggot rather than let the fire go out. "It is odd that I should be talking of it now," he said musingly.

"I suppose," she said gently, to bring him out of the reverie into which he had sunk, "I suppose it happened some time ago?"

"Long, long ago," he answered. (Having written as an aged person, he often found difficulty in remembering suddenly that he was two and twenty.)

"But you are still a very young man."

"It seems long ago to me," he said with a sigh.

"Was she beautiful?"

"She was beautiful to my eyes."

"And as good, I am sure, as she was beautiful."

"Ah me!" said Tommy.

His confidante was burning to know more, and hoping they were being observed across the table; but she was a kind, sentimental creature, though stout, or because of it, and she said, "I am so afraid that my questions pain you."

"No, no," said Tommy, who was very, very happy.

"Was it very sudden?"

"Fever."

"Ah! but I meant your attachment."

"We met and we loved," he said with gentle dignity.

"That is the true way," said the lady.

"It is the only way," he said decisively.

"Mr. Sandys, you have been so good, I wonder if you would tell me her name?"

"Felicity," he said, with emotion. Presently he looked up. "It is very strange to me," he said wonderingly, "to find myself saying these things to you who an hour ago were a complete stranger to me. But you are not like other women."

"No, indeed!" said the lady, warmly.

"That," he said, "must be why I tell you what I have never told to another human being. How mysterious are the workings of the heart!"

"Mr. Sandys," said the lady, quite carried away, "no words of mine can convey to you the pride with which I hear you say that. Be assured that I shall respect your confidences." She missed his next remark because she was wondering whether she dare ask him to come to dinner on the twenty-fifth, and then the ladies had to retire, and by the time he rejoined her he was as tongue-tied as at the beginning. The cork had not been extracted; it had been knocked into the bottle, where it still often barred the way, and there was always, as we shall see, a flavour of it in the wine.

"You will get over it yet; the summer and the flowers will come to you again," she managed to whisper to him kind-heartedly, as she was going.

"Thank you," he said, with that inscrutable face. It was far from his design to play a part. He had, indeed, had no design at all, but an opportunity for sentiment having presented itself, his mouth had opened as at a cherry. He did not laugh afterwards, even when he reflected how unexpectedly Felicity had come into his life; he thought of her rather with affectionate regard, and pictured her as a tall, slim girl in white. When he took a tall, slim girl in white in to dinner, he could not help saying huskily:

"You remind me of one who was a very dear friend of mine. I was much startled when you came into the room."

"You mean some one who is dead?" she asked in awe-struck tones.

"Fever," he said.

"You think I am like her in appearance?"

"In every way," he said dreamily; "the same sweet — pardon me, but it is very remarkable. Even the tones of the voice are the same. I suppose I ought not to ask your age?"

"I shall be twenty-one in August."

"She would have been twenty-one in August

had she lived," Tommy said with fervour. "My dear young lady——"

This was the aged gentleman again, but she did not wince; he soon found out that they expect authors to say the oddest things, and this proved to be a great help to him.

"My dear young lady, I feel that I know you very well."

"That," she said, "is only because I resemble your friend outwardly. The real me (she was a bit of philosopher also) you cannot know at all."

He smiled sadly. "Has it ever struck you," he asked, "that you are very unlike other women?"

"Oh, how ever could you have found that out?" she exclaimed, amazed.

Almost before he knew how it came about, he was on terms of very pleasant sentiment with this girl, for they now shared between them a secret that he had confided to no other. His face, which had been so much against him hitherto, was at last in his favour; it showed so plainly that when he looked at her more softly or held her hand longer than is customary, he was really thinking of that other of whom she was the image. Or if it did not precisely show that, it suggested something or other of that nature which did just as well. There was a sweet something between them which brought them together and also kept them apart;

it allowed them to go a certain length, while it was also a reason why they could never, never exceed that distance; and this was an ideal state for Tommy, who could be most loyal and tender so long as it was understood that he meant nothing in particular. She was the right kind of girl, too, and admired him the more (and perhaps went a step further) because he remained so true to Felicity's memory.

You must not think him calculating and cold-blooded, for nothing could be less true to the fact. When not engaged, indeed, on his new work, he might waste some time planning scenes with exquisite ladies, in which he sparkled or had a hidden sorrow (he cared not which); but these scenes seldom came to life. He preferred very pretty girls to be rather stupid (oh, the artistic instinct of the man!), but instead of keeping them stupid, as he wanted to do, he found himself trying to improve their minds. They screwed up their noses in the effort. Meaning to thrill the celebrated beauty who had been specially invited to meet him, he devoted himself to a plain woman for whose plainness a sudden pity had mastered him (for, like all true worshippers of beauty in women, he always showed best in the presence of plain ones). With the intention of being a gallant knight to Lady I-Won't-Tell-the-Name, a whim of the moment made him so stiff to her that

TOMMY AND GRIZEL

she ultimately asked the reason; and such a charmingly sad reason presented itself to him that she immediately invited him to her riverside party on Thursday week. He had the conversations and incidents for that party ready long before the day arrived; he altered them and polished them as other young gentlemen in the same circumstances overhaul their boating costumes; but when he joined the party there was among them the children's governess, and seeing her slighted, his blood boiled, and he was her attendant for the afternoon.

Elspeth was not at this pleasant jink in high life. She had been invited, but her ladyship had once let Tommy kiss her hand for the first and last time, so he decided sternly that this was no place for Elspeth. When temptation was nigh, he first locked Elspeth up, and then walked into it.

With two in every three women he was still as shy as ever, but the third he escorted triumphantly to the conservatory. She did no harm to his work—rather sent him back to it refreshed. It was as if he were shooting the sentiment which other young men get rid of more gradually by beginning earlier, and there were such accumulations of it that I don't know whether he ever made up on them. Punishment sought him in the night, when he dreamed constantly that he was married—to whom scarcely mattered; he saw himself coming out of a church a married man, and the fright woke him up. But with the daylight came again his talent for dodging thoughts that were lying in wait, and he yielded as recklessly as before to every sentimental impulse. As illustration, take his humourous passage with Mrs. Jerry. Geraldine Something was her name, but her friends called her Mrs. Jerry.

She was a wealthy widow, buxom, not a day over thirty when she was merry, which might be at inappropriate moments, as immediately after she had expressed a desire to lead the higher life. "But I have a theory, my dear," she said solemnly to Elspeth, "that no woman is able to do it who cannot see her own nose without the help of a mirror." She had taken a great fancy to Elspeth, and made many engagements with her, and kept some of them, and the understanding was that she apprenticed herself to Tommy through Elspeth, he being too terrible to face by himself, or, as Mrs. Jerry expressed it, "all nose." So Tommy had seen very little of her, and thought less, until one day he called by passionate request to sign her birthday-book, and heard himself proposing to her instead!

For one thing, it was twilight, and she had forgotten to ring for the lamps. That might have been enough, but there was more: she read to him part of a letter in which her hand was solicited in marriage. "And, for the life of me," said Mrs. Jerry, almost in tears, "I cannot decide whether to say yes or no."

This put Tommy in a most awkward position. There are probably men who could have got out of it without proposing; but to him there seemed at the moment no other way open. The letter complicated matters also by beginning "Dear Jerry," and saying "little Jerry" further on — expressions which stirred him strangely.

"Why do you read this to me?" he asked, in a voice that broke a little.

"Because you are so wise," she said. "Do you mind?"

"Do I mind!" he exclaimed bitterly. ("Take care, you idiot!" he said to himself.)

"I was asking your advice only. Is it too much?"

"Not at all. I am quite the right man to consult at such a moment, am I not?"

It was said with profound meaning; but his face was as usual.

"That is what I thought," she said, in all good faith.

"You do not even understand!" he cried, and he was also looking longingly at his hat.

"Understand what?"

"Jerry," he said, and tried to stop himself, with the result that he added, "dear little Jerry!" ("What am I doing!" he groaned.)

She understood now. "You don't mean—" she began, in amazement.

"Yes," he cried passionately. "I love you. Will you be my wife?" ("I am lost!")

"Gracious!" exclaimed Mrs. Jerry; and then, on reflection, she became indignant. "I would not have believed it of you," she said scornfully. "Is it my money, or what? I am not at all clever, so you must tell me."

With Tommy, of course, it was not her money. Except when he had Elspeth to consider, he was as much a Quixote about money as Pym himself; and at no moment of his life was he a snob.

"I am sorry you should think so meanly of me," he said with dignity, lifting his hat; and he would have got away then (which, when you come to think of it, was what he wanted) had he been able to resist an impulse to heave a broken-hearted sigh at the door.

"Don't go yet, Mr. Sandys," she begged. "I may have been hasty. And yet—why, we are merely acquaintances!"

He had meant to be very careful now, but that word sent him off again. "Acquaintances!" he cried. "No, we were never that."

"It almost seemed to me that you avoided me."

"You noticed it!" he said eagerly. "At least, you do me that justice. Oh, how I tried to avoid you!"

"It was because—"

"Alas!"

She was touched, of course, but still puzzled. "We know so little of each other," she said.

"I see," he replied, "that you know me very little, Mrs. Jerry; but you—oh, Jerry, Jerry! I know you as no other man has ever known you!"

"I wish I had proof of it," she said helplessly.

Proof! She should not have asked Tommy for proof. "I know," he cried, "how unlike all other women you are. To the world you are like the rest, but in your heart you know that you are different; you know it, and I know it, and no other person knows it."

Yes, Mrs. Jerry knew it, and had often marvelled over it in the seclusion of her boudoir; but that another should have found it out was strange and almost terrifying.

"I know you love me now," she said softly. "Only love could have shown you that. But—oh, let me go away for a minute to think!" And she ran out of the room.

Other suitors have been left for a space in Tommy's state of doubt, but never, it may be hoped, with the same emotions. Oh, heavens! if she should accept him! He saw Elspeth sickening and dying of the news.

His guardian angel, however, was very good to Tommy at this time; or perhaps, like cannibals

SANDYS ON WOMAN

with their prisoner, the god of sentiment (who has a tail) was fattening him for a future feast; and Mrs. Jerry's answer was that it could never be.

Tommy bowed his head.

But she hoped he would let her be his very dear friend. It would be the proudest recollection of her life that Mr. Sandys had entertained such feelings for her.

Nothing could have been better, and he should have found difficulty in concealing his delight; but this strange Tommy was really feeling his part again. It was an unforced tear that came to his eye. Quite naturally he looked long and wistfully at her.

"Jerry, Jerry!" he articulated huskily, and whatever the words mean in these circumstances he really meant; then he put his lips to her hand for the first and last time, and so was gone, broken but brave. He was in splendid fettle for writing that evening. Wild animals sleep after gorging, but it sent this monster, refreshed, to his work.

Nevertheless, the incident gave him some uneasy reflections. Was he, indeed, a monster? was one that he could dodge, as yet; but suppose Mrs. Jerry told his dear Elspeth of what had happened? She had said that she would not, but a secret in Mrs. Jerry's breast was like her pug in her arms, always kicking to get free.

"Elspeth," said Tommy, "what do you say

to going north and having a sight of Thrums again?"

He knew what she would say. They had been talking for years of going back; it was the great day that all her correspondence with old friends in Thrums looked forward to.

"They made little of you, Tommy," she said, "when we left; but I 'm thinking they will all be at their windows when you go back."

"Oh," replied Thomas, "that's nothing. But I should like to shake Corp by the hand again."

"And Aaron," said Elspeth. She was knitting stockings for Aaron at that moment.

"And Gavinia," Tommy said, "and the Dominie."

"And Ailie."

And then came an awkward pause, for they were both thinking of that independent girl called Grizel. She was seldom discussed. Tommy was oddly shy about mentioning her name; he would have preferred Elspeth to mention it: and Elspeth had misgivings that this was so, with the result that neither could say "Grizel" without wondering what was in the other's mind. Tommy had written twice to Grizel, the first time unknown to Elspeth, but that was in the days when the ladies of the penny numbers were disturbing him, and, against his better judgment (for well he knew she would never stand it), he had begun his letter with these mad words: "Dear Little Woman." She did not answer this, but soon afterwards she wrote to Elspeth, and he was not mentioned in the letter proper, but it carried a sting in its tail. "P. S.," it said. "How is Sentimental Tommy?"

None but a fiend in human shape could have written thus, and Elspeth put her protecting arms round her brother. "Now we know what Grizel is," she said. "I am done with her now."

But when Tommy had got back his wind he said nobly: "I'll call her no names. If this is how she likes to repay me for — for all my kindnesses, let her. But, Elspeth, if I have the chance, I shall go on being good to her just the same."

Elspeth adored him for it, but Grizel would have stamped had she known. He had that comfort.

The second letter he never posted. It was written a few months before he became a celebrity, and had very fine things indeed in it, for old Dr. McQueen, Grizel's dear friend, had just died at his post, and it was a letter of condolence. While Tommy wrote it he was in a quiver of genuine emotion, as he was very pleased to feel, and it had a specially satisfying bit about death, and the world never being the same again. He knew it was good, but he did not send it to her, for no reason I can discover save that postscripts jarred on him.

CHAPTER IV

GRIZEL OF THE CROOKED SMILE

To expose Tommy for what he was, to appear to be scrupulously fair to him so that I might really damage him the more, that is what I set out to do in this book, and always when he seemed to be finding a way of getting round me (as I had a secret dread he might do) I was to remember Grizel and be obdurate. But if I have so far got past some of his virtues without even mentioning them (and I have), I know how many opportunities for discrediting him have been missed, and that would not greatly matter, there are so many more to come, if Grizel were on my side. But she is not; throughout those first chapters a voice has been crying to me, "Take care; if you hurt him you will hurt me"; and I know it to be the voice of Grizel, and I seem to see her, rocking her arms as she used to rock them when excited in the days of her innocent childhood. "Don't, don't, don't!" she cried at every cruel word I gave him, and she, to whom it was ever such agony to weep, dropped a tear upon each word, so that they were obliterated; and "Surely I knew him best," she said, "and I always loved him"; and she stood there defending him, with her hand on her heart to conceal the gaping wound that Tommy had made.

Well, if Grizel had always loved him there was surely something fine and rare about Tommy. But what was it, Grizel? Why did you always love him, you who saw into him so well and demanded so much of men? When I ask that question the spirit that hovers round my desk to protect Tommy from me rocks her arms mournfully, as if she did not know the answer; it is only when I seem to see her as she so often was in life, before she got that wound and after, bending over some little child and looking up radiant, that I think I suddenly know why she always loved Tommy. It was because he had such need of her.

I don't know whether you remember, but there were once some children who played at Jacobites in the Thrums Den under Tommy's leadership. Elspeth, of course, was one of them, and there were Corp Shiach, and Gavinia, and lastly, there was Grizel. Had Tommy's parents been alive she would not have been allowed to join, for she was a painted lady's child; but Tommy insisted on having her, and Grizel thought it was just sweet of him. He also chatted with her in public places, as if she were a respectable character; and oh, how she longed to be respectable! but, on the other hand, he was the first to point out how superbly he was behaving, and his ways were masterful, so the independent girl would not be captain's wife; if he said she was captain's wife he had to apologize, and if he merely looked it he had to apologize just the same.

One night the Painted Lady died in the Den, and then it would have gone hard with the lonely girl had not Dr. McQueen made her his little housekeeper, not out of pity, he vowed (she was so anxious to be told that), but because he was an old bachelor sorely in need of someone to take care of him. And how she took care of him! But though she was so happy now, she knew that she must be very careful, for there was something in her blood that might waken and prevent her being a good woman. She thought it would be sweet to be good.

She told all this to Tommy, and he was profoundly interested, and consulted a wise man, whose advice was that when she grew up she should be wary of any man whom she liked and mistrusted in one breath. Meaning to do her a service, Tommy communicated this to her; and then, what do you think? Grizel would have no more dealings with him! By and by the gods, in a sportive mood, sent him to labour on a farm, whence, as we have seen, he found a way to Lon-

GRIZEL OF THE CROOKED SMILE

don, and while he was growing into a man Grizel became a woman. At the time of the doctor's death she was nineteen, tall and graceful, and very dark and pale. When the winds of the day flushed her cheek she was beautiful; but it was a beauty that hid the mystery of her face. The sun made her merry, but she looked more noble when it had set; then her pallor shone with a soft, radiant light, as though the mystery and sadness and serenity of the moon were in it. The full beauty of Grizel came out only at night, like the stars.

I had made up my mind that when the time came to describe Grizel's mere outward appearance I should refuse her that word "beautiful" because of her tilted nose; but now that the time has come, I wonder at myself. Probably when I am chapters ahead I shall return to this one and strike out the word "beautiful," and then, as likely as not, I shall come back afterwards and put it in again. Whether it will be there at the end, God knows. Her eyes, at least, were beautiful. They were unusually far apart, and let you look straight into them, and never quivered; they were such clear, gray, searching eyes, they seemed always to be asking for the truth. And she had an adorable mouth. In repose it was, perhaps, hard, because it shut so decisively; but often it screwed up provokingly at one side, as when she smiled, or was sorry, or for no particular reason; for she seemed unable to control this vagary, which was perhaps a little bit of babyhood that had forgotten to grow up with the rest of her. At those moments the essence of all that was characteristic and delicious about her seemed to have run to her mouth; so that to kiss Grizel on her crooked smile would have been to kiss the whole of her at once. She had a quaint way of nodding her head at you when she was talking. It made you forget what she was saying, though it was really meant to have precisely the opposite effect. Her voice was rich, with many inflections. When she had much to say it gurgled like a stream in a hurry; but its cooing note was best worth remembering at the end of the day. There were times when she looked like a boy. Her almost gallant bearing, the poise of her head, her noble frankness — they all had something in them of a princely boy who had never known fear.

I have no wish to hide her defects; I would rather linger over them, because they were part of Grizel, and I am sorry to see them go one by one. Thrums had not taken her to its heart. She was a proud-purse, they said, meaning that she had a haughty walk. Her sense of justice was too great. She scorned frailties that she should have pitied. (How strange to think that there was a time when pity was not the feeling that leaped to Grizel's

GRIZEL OF THE CROOKED SMILE

bosom first!) She did not care for study. She learned French and the pianoforte to please the doctor; but she preferred to be sewing or dusting. When she might have been reading, she was perhaps making for herself one of those costumes that annoyed every lady of Thrums who employed a dressmaker; or, more probably, it was a delicious garment for a baby; for as soon as Grizel heard that there was a new baby anywhere, all her intellect deserted her, and she became a slave. Books often irritated her because she disagreed with the author; and it was a torment to her to find other people holding to their views when she was so certain that hers were right. In church she sometimes rocked her arms; and the old doctor by her side knew that it was because she could not get up and contradict the minister. She was, I presume, the only young lady who ever dared to say that she hated Sunday because there was so much sitting still in it.

Sitting still did not suit Grizel. At all other times she was happy; but then her mind wandered back to the thoughts that had lived too closely with her in the old days, and she was troubled. What woke her from these reveries was probably the doctor's hand placed very tenderly on her shoulder, and then she would start, and wonder how long he had been watching her, and what were the grave thoughts behind his cheerful face; for the doctor never looked more cheerful than when he was drawing Grizel away from the ugly past, and he talked to her as if he had noticed nothing; but after he went upstairs he would pace his bedroom for a long time; and Grizel listened, and knew that he was thinking about her. Then, perhaps, she would run up to him, and put her arms around his neck. These scenes brought the doctor and Grizel very close together; but they became rarer as she grew up, and then for once that she was troubled she was a hundred times irresponsible with glee, and "Oh, you dearest, darlingest," she would cry to him, "I must dance,— I must, I must!— though it is a fast-day; and you must dance with your mother this instant— I am so happy, so happy!" "Mother" was his nickname for her, and she delighted in the word. She lorded it over him as if he were her troublesome boy.

How could she be other than glorious when there was so much to do? The work inside the house she made for herself, and outside the doctor made it for her. At last he had found for nurse a woman who could follow his instructions literally, who understood that if he said five o'clock for the medicine the chap of six would not do as well, who did not in her heart despise the thermometer, and who resolutely prevented the patient from skipping out of bed to change her pillow-

GRIZEL OF THE CROOKED SMILE

slips because the minister was expected. Such tyranny enraged every sufferer who had been ill before and got better; but what they chiefly complained of to the doctor (and he agreed with a humourous sigh) was her masterfulness about fresh air and cold water. Windows were opened that had never been opened before (they yielded to her pressure with a groan); and as for cold water, it might have been said that a bath followed her wherever she went—not, mark me, for putting your hands and face in, not even for your feet; but in you must go, the whole of you, "as if," they said indignantly, "there was something the matter with our skin."

She could not gossip, not even with the doctor, who liked it of an evening when he had got into his carpet shoes. There was no use telling her a secret, for she kept it to herself for evermore. She had ideas about how men should serve a woman, even the humblest, that made the men gaze with wonder, and the women (curiously enough) with irritation. Her greatest scorn was for girls who made themselves cheap with men; and she could not hide it. It was a physical pain to Grizel to hide her feelings; they popped out in her face, if not in words, and were always in advance of her self-control. To the doctor this impulsiveness was pathetic; he loved her for it, but it sometimes made him uneasy.

TOMMY AND GRIZEL

He died in the scarlet-fever year. "I'm smitten," he suddenly said at a bedside; and a week afterwards he was gone.

"We must speak of it now, Grizel," he said, when he knew that he was dying.

She pressed his hand. She knew to what he was referring. "Yes," she said, "I should love you to speak of it now."

"You and I have always fought shy of it," he said, "making a pretence that it had altogether passed away. I thought that was best for you."

"Dearest, darlingest," she said, "I know — I have always known."

"And you," he said, "you pretended because you thought it was best for me."

She nodded. "And we saw through each other all the time," she said.

"Grizel, has it passed away altogether now?"

Her grip upon his hand did not tighten in the least. "Yes," she could say honestly, "it has altogether passed away."

"And you have no more fear?"

"No, none."

It was his great reward for all that he had done for Grizel.

"I know what you are thinking of," she said, when he did not speak. "You are thinking of the haunted little girl you rescued seven years ago."

GRIZEL OF THE CROOKED SMILE

"No," he answered; "I was thanking God for the brave, wholesome woman she has grown into; and for something else, Grizel — for letting me live to see it."

"To do *it*," she said, pressing his hand to her breast.

She was a strange girl, and she had to speak her mind. "I don't think God has done it all," she said. "I don't even think that He told you to do it. I think He just said to you, 'There is a painted lady's child at your door. You can save her if you like.'

"No," she went on, when he would have interposed; "I am sure He did not want to do it all. He even left a little bit of it to me to do myself. I love to think that I have done a tiny bit of it myself. I think it is the sweetest thing about God that He lets us do some of it ourselves. Do I hurt you, darling?"

No, she did not hurt him, for he understood her. "But you are naturally so impulsive," he said, "it has often been a sharp pain to me to see you so careful."

"It was not a pain to me to be careful; it was a joy. Oh, the thousand dear, delightful joys I have had with you!"

"It has made you strong, Grizel, and I rejoice in that; but sometimes I fear that it has made you too difficult to win."

"I don't want to be won," she told him.

"You don't quite mean that, Grizel."

"No," she said at once. She whispered to him impulsively: "It is the only thing I am at all afraid of now."

"What?"

"Love."

"You will not be afraid of it when it comes."

"But I want to be afraid," she said.

"You need not," he answered. "The man on whom those clear eyes rest lovingly will be worthy of it all. If he were not, they would be the first to find him out."

"But need that make any difference?" she asked. "Perhaps though I found him out I should love him just the same."

"Not unless you loved him first, Grizel."

"No," she said at once again. "I am not really afraid of love," she whispered to him. "You have made me so happy that I am afraid of nothing."

Yet she wondered a little that he was not afraid to die, but when she told him this he smiled and said: "Everybody fears death except those who are dying." And when she asked if he had anything on his mind, he said: "I leave the world without a care. Not that I have seen all I would fain have seen. Many a time, especially this last year, when I have seen the mother in you crooning

GRIZEL OF THE CROOKED SMILE

to some neighbour's child, I have thought to myself, 'I don't know my Grizel yet; I have seen her in the bud only,' and I would fain —" He broke off. "But I have no fears," he said. "As I lie here, with you sitting by my side, looking so serene, I can say, for the first time for half a century, that I have nothing on my mind.

"But, Grizel, I should have married," he told her. "The chief lesson my life has taught me is that they are poor critturs — the men who don't marry."

"If you had married," she said, "you might never have been able to help me."

"It is you who have helped me," he replied. "God sent the child; He is most reluctant to give any of us up. Ay, Grizel, that's what my life has taught me, and it's all I can leave to you." The last he saw of her, she was holding his hand, and her eyes were dry, her teeth were clenched; but there was a brave smile upon her face, for he had told her that it was thus he would like to see her at the end. After his death, she continued to live at the old house; he had left it to her ("I want it to remain in the family," he said), with all his savings, which were quite sufficient for the needs of such a manager. He had also left her plenty to do, and that was a still sweeter legacy.

And the other Jacobites, what of them? Hi, where are you, Corp? Here he comes, grinning, in his spleet new uniform, to demand our tickets of us. He is now the railway porter. Since Tommy left Thrums "steam" had arrived in it, and Corp had by nature such a gift for giving luggage the twist which breaks everything inside as you dump it down that he was inevitably appointed porter. There was no travelling to Thrums without a ticket. At Tilliedrum, which was the junction for Thrums, you showed your ticket and were then locked in. A hundred yards from Thrums Corp leaped upon the train and fiercely demanded your ticket. At the station he asked you threateningly whether you had given up your ticket. Even his wife was afraid of him at such times, and had her ticket ready in her hand.

His wife was one Gavinia, and she had no fear of him except when she was travelling. To his face she referred to him as a doited sumph, but to Grizel pleading for him she admitted that despite his warts and quarrelsome legs he was a great big muckle sonsy, stout, buirdly well set up, wise-like, havering man. When first Corp had proposed to her, she gave him a clout on the head; and so little did he know of the sex that this discouraged him. He continued, however, to propose and she to clout him until he heard, accidentally (he woke up in church), of a man in the Bible who had wooed a woman for seven years, and this example he determined to emulate; but when Gavinia heard of it

GRIZEL OF THE CROOKED SMILE

she was so furious that she took him at once. Dazed by his good fortune, he rushed off with it to his aunt, whom he wearied with his repetition of the great news.

"To your bed wi' you," she said, yawning.

"Bed!" cried Corp, indignantly. "And so, auntie, says Gavinia, 'Yes,' says she, 'I'll hae you.' Those were her never-to-be-forgotten words."

"You pitiful object," answered his aunt. "Men hae been married afore now without making sic a stramash."

"I daursay," retorted Corp; "but they hinna married Gavinia." And this is the best known answer to the sneer of the cynic.

He was a public nuisance that night, and knocked various people up after they had gone to bed, to tell them that Gavinia was to have him. He was eventually led home by kindly though indignant neighbours; but early morning found him in the country, carrying the news from farm to farm.

"No, I winna sit down," he said; "I just cried in to tell you Gavinia is to hae me." Six miles from home he saw a mud house on the top of a hill, and ascended genially. He found at their porridge a very old lady with a nut-cracker face, and a small boy. We shall see them again. "Auld wifie," said Corp, "I dinna ken you, but I've just stepped up to tell you that Gavinia is to hae me."

It made him the butt of the sportive. If he or Gavinia were nigh, they gathered their fowls round them and then said: "Hens, I didna bring you here to feed you, but just to tell you that Gavinia is to hae me." This flustered Gavinia; but Grizel, who enjoyed her own jokes too heartily to have more than a polite interest in those of other people, said to her: "How can you be angry! I think it was just sweet of him."

"But was it no vulgar?"

"Vulgar!" said Grizel. "Why, Gavinia, that is how every lady would like a man to love her."

And then Gavinia beamed. "I'm glad you say that," she said; "for, though I wouldna tell Corp for worlds, I fell likit it."

But Grizel told Corp that Gavinia liked it.

"It was the proof," she said, smiling, "that you have the right to marry her. You have shown your ticket. Never give it up, Corp."

About a year afterwards Corp, armed in his Sunday stand, rushed to Grizel's house, occasionally stopping to slap his shiny knees. "Grizel," he cried, "there's somebody come to Thrums without a ticket!" Then he remembered Gavinia's instructions. "Mrs. Shiach's compliments," he said ponderously, "and it's a boy."

"Oh, Corp!" exclaimed Grizel, and immediately began to put on her hat and jacket.

Corp watched her uneasily. "Mrs. Shiach's

compliments," he said firmly, "and he's ower young to be bathed yet; but she's awid to show him off to you," he hastened to add. "'Tell Grizel,' was her first words."

"Tell Grizel"! They were among the first words of many mothers. None, they were aware, would receive the news with quite such glee as she. They might think her cold and reserved with themselves, but to see the look on her face as she bent over a baby, and to know that the baby was yours! What a way she had with them! She always welcomed them as if in coming they had performed a great feat. That is what babies are agape for from the beginning. Had they been able to speak they would have said "Tell Grizel" themselves.

"And Mrs. Shiach's compliments," Corp remembered, "and she would be windy if you would carry the bairn at the christening."

"I should love it, Corp! Have you decided on the name?"

"Lang syne. Gin it were a lassie we were to call her Grizel——"

"Oh, how sweet of you!"

"After the finest lassie we ever kent," continued Corp, stoutly. "But I was sure it would be a laddie."

"Why?"

"Because if it was a laddie it was to be called

after Him," he said, with emphasis on the last word; "and thinks I to mysel', 'He'll find a way.' What a crittur he was for finding a way, Grizel! And he lookit so holy a' the time. Do you mind that swear word o' his—'stroke'? It just meant 'damn'; but he could make even 'damn' look holy."

"You are to call the baby Tommy?"

"He'll be christened Thomas Sandys Shiach," said Corp. "I hankered after putting something out o' the Jacobites intil his name; and I says to Gavinia, 'Let's call him Thomas Sandys Stroke Shiach,' says I, 'and the minister'll be nane the wiser'; but Gavinia was scandalized."

Grizel reflected. "Corp," she said, "I am sure Gavinia's sister will expect to be asked to carry the baby. I don't think I want to do it."

"After you promised!" cried Corp, much hurt. "I never kent you to break a promise afore."

"I will do it, Corp," she said, at once.

She did not know then that Tommy would be in church to witness the ceremony, but she knew before she walked down the aisle with T. S Shiach in her arms. It was the first time that Tommy and she had seen each other for seven years. That day he almost rivalled his namesake in the interests of the congregation, who, however, took prodigious care that he should not see it—all except Grizel; she smiled a welcome to him, and he knew that her serene gray eyes were watching him.

CHAPTER V

THE TOMMY MYTH

On the evening before the christening, Aaron Latta, his head sunk farther into his shoulders, his beard gone grayer, no other perceptible difference in a dreary man since we last saw him in the book of Tommy's boyhood, had met the brother and sister at the station, a barrow with him for their luggage. It was a great hour for him as he wheeled the barrow homeward, Elspeth once more by his side; but he could say nothing heartsome in Tommy's presence, and Tommy was as uncomfortable in his. The old strained relations between these two seemed to begin again at once. They were as self-conscious as two mastiffs meeting in the street; and both breathed a sigh of relief when Tommy fell behind.

"You're bonny, Elspeth," Aaron then said eagerly. "I'm glad, glad to see you again."

"And him too, Aaron?" Elspeth pleaded.

"He took you away frae me."

"He has brought me back."

"Ay, and he has but to whistle to you and away

you go wi' him again. He's ower grand to bide lang here now."

"You don't know him, Aaron. We are to stay a long time. Do you know Mrs. McLean invited us to stay with her? I suppose she thought your house was so small. But Tommy said, 'The house of the man who befriended us when we were children shall never be too small for us.'"

"Did he say that? Ay, but, Elspeth, I would rather hear what you said."

"I said it was to dear, good Aaron Latta I was going back, and to no one else."

"God bless you for that, Elspeth."

"And Tommy," she went on, "must have his old garret room again, to write as well as sleep in, and the little room you partitioned off the kitchen will do nicely for me."

"There's no a window in it," replied Aaron; "but it will do fine for you, Elspeth." He was almost chuckling, for he had a surprise in waiting for her. "This way," he said excitedly, when she would have gone into the kitchen, and he flung open the door of what had been his warping-room. The warping-mill was gone — everything that had been there was gone. What met the delighted eyes of Elspeth and Tommy was a cozy parlour, which became a bedroom when you opened that other door.

"You are a leddy now, Elspeth," Aaron said,

THE TOMMY MYTH

husky with pride, "and you have a leddy's room. Do you see the piano?"

He had given up the warping, having at last "twa three hunder'" in the bank, and all the work he did now was at a loom which he had put into the kitchen to keep him out of languor. "I have sorted up the garret, too, for you," he said to Tommy, "but this is Elspeth's room."

"As if Tommy would take it from me!" said Elspeth, running into the kitchen to hug this dear Aaron.

"You may laugh," Aaron replied vindictively, "but he is taking it frae you already"; and later, when Tommy was out of the way, he explained his meaning. "I did it all for you, Elspeth; 'Elspeth's room,' I called it. When I bought the mahogany arm-chair, 'That's Elspeth's chair,' I said to mysel'; and when I bought the bed, 'It's hers,' I said. Ay; but I was soon disannulled o' that thait, for, in spite of me, they were all got for him. Not a rissom in that room is yours or mine, Elspeth; every muhlen belongs to him."

"But who says so, Aaron? I am sure he won't."

"I dinna ken them. They are leddies that come here in their carriages to see the house where Thomas Sandys was born."

"But, Aaron, he was born in London!"

"They think he was born in this house," Aaron

replied doggedly, "and it's no for me to cheapen him."

"Oh, Aaron, you pretend——"

"I was never very fond o' him," Aaron admitted, "but I winna cheapen Jean Myles's bairn, and when they chap at my door and say they would like to see the room Thomas Sandys was born in, I let them see the best room I have. So that's how he has laid hands on your parlor, Elspeth. Afore I can get rid o' them they gie a squeak and cry, 'Was that Thomas Sandys's bed?' and I says it was. That's him taking the very bed frae you, Elspeth."

"You might at least have shown them his bed in the garret," she said.

"It's a shilpit bit thing," he answered, "and I winna cheapen him. They're curious, too, to see his favourite seat."

"It was the fender," she declared.

"It was," he assented, "but it's no for me to cheapen him, so I let them see your new mahogany chair. 'Thomas Sandys's chair,' they call it, and they sit down in it reverently. They winna even leave you the piano. 'Was this Thomas Sandys's piano?' they speir. 'It was,' says I, and syne they gowp at it." His under lip shot out, a sure sign that he was angry. "I dinna blame him," he said, "but he had the same masterful way of scooping everything into his lap when he was a

THE TOMMY MYTH

laddie, and I like him none the mair for it"; and from this position Aaron would not budge.

"Quite right, too," Tommy said, when he heard of it. "But you can tell him, Elspeth, that we shall allow no more of those prying women to come in." And he really meant this, for he was a modest man that day, was Tommy. Nevertheless, he was, perhaps, a little annoyed to find, as the days went on, that no more ladies came to be turned away.

He heard that they had also been unable to resist the desire to shake hands with Thomas Sandys's schoolmaster. "It must have been a pleasure to teach him," they said to Cathro.

"Ah me, ah me!" Cathro replied enigmatically. It had so often been a pleasure to Cathro to thrash him!

"Genius is odd," they said. "Did he ever give you any trouble?"

"We were like father and son," he assured them. With natural pride he showed them the ink-pot into which Thomas Sandys had dipped as a boy. They were very grateful for his interesting reminiscence that when the pot was too full Thomas inked his fingers. He presented several of them with the ink-pot.

Two ladies, who came together, bothered him by asking what the Hugh Blackadder competition was. They had been advised to inquire of him about Thomas Sandys's connection therewith by another schoolmaster, a Mr. Ogilvy, whom they had met in one of the glens.

Mr. Cathro winced, and then explained with emphasis that the Hugh Blackadder was a competition in which the local ministers were the sole judges; he therefore referred the ladies to them. The ladies did go to a local minister for enlightenment, to Mr. Dishart; but, after reflecting, Mr. Dishart said that it was too long a story, and this answer seemed to amuse Mr. Ogilvy, who happened to be present.

It was Mr. McLean who retailed this news to Tommy. He and Ailie had walked home from church with the newcomers on the day after their arrival, the day of the christening. They had not gone into Aaron's house, for you are looked askance at in Thrums if you pay visits on Sundays, but they had stood for a long time gossiping at the door, which is permitted by the strictest. Ailie was in a twitter, as of old, and not able even yet to speak of her husband without an apologetic look to the ladies who had none. And oh, how proud she was of Tommy's fame! Her eyes were an offering to him.

"Don't take her as a sample of the place, though," Mr. McLean warned him, "for Thrums does not catch fire so readily as London." It was quite true. "I was at the school wi' him," they

THE TOMMY MYTH

said up there, and implied that this damned his book.

But there were two faithful souls, or, more strictly, one, for Corp could never have carried it through without Gavinia's help. Tommy called on them promptly at their house in the Bellies Brae (four rooms, but a lodger), and said, almost before he had time to look, that the baby had Corp's chin and Gavinia's eyes. He had made this up on the way. He also wanted to say, so desirous was he of pleasing his old friends, that he should like to hold the baby in his arms; but it was such a thundering lie that even an author could not say it.

Tommy sat down in that house with a very warm heart for its inmates; but they chilled him — Gavinia with her stiff words, and Corp by looking miserable instead of joyous.

"I expected you to come to me first, Corp," said Tommy, reproachfully. "I had scarcely a word with you at the station."

"He couldna hae presumed," replied Gavinia, primly.

"I couldna hae presumed," said Corp, with a groan.

"Fudge!" Tommy said. "You were my greatest friend, and I like you as much as ever, Corp."

Corp's face shone, but Gavinia said at once,

"You werena sic great friends as that; were you, man?"

"No," Corp replied gloomily.

"Whatever has come over you both?" asked Tommy, in surprise. "You will be saying next, Gavinia, that we never played at Jacobites in the Den!"

"I dinna deny that Corp and me played," Gavinia answered determinedly, "but you didna. You said to us, 'Think shame,' you said, 'to be playing vulgar games when you could be reading superior books.' They were his very words, were they no, man?" she demanded of her unhappy husband, with a threatening look.

"They were," said Corp, in deepest gloom.

"I must get to the bottom of this," said Tommy, rising, "and as you are too great a coward, Corp, to tell the truth with that shameless woman glowering at you, out you go, Gavinia, and take your disgraced bairn with you. Do as you are told, you besom, for I am Captain Stroke again."

Corp was choking with delight as Gavinia withdrew haughtily. "I was sure you would sort her," he said, rubbing his hands, "I was sure you wasna the kind to be ashamed o' auld friends."

"But what does it mean?"

"She has a notion," Corp explained, growing grave again, "that it wouldna do for you to own the like o' us. 'We mauna cheapen him,' she said.

THE TOMMY MYTH

She wanted you to see that we hinna been cheapening you." He said, in a sepulchral voice, "There has been leddies here, and they want to ken what Thomas Sandys was like as a boy. It's me they speir for, but Gavinia she just shoves me out o' sight, and says she, 'Leave them to me.'"

Corp told Tommy some of the things Gavinia said about Thomas Sandys as a boy: how he sat rapt in church, and, instead of going bird-nesting, lay on the ground listening to the beautiful little warblers overhead, and gave all his pennies to poorer children, and could repeat the Shorter Catechism, beginning at either end, and was very respectful to the aged and infirm, and of a yielding disposition, and said, from his earliest years, "I don't want to be great; I just want to be good."

"How can she make them all up?" Tommy asked, with respectful homage to Gavinia.

Corp, with his eye on the door, produced from beneath the bed a little book with coloured pictures. It was entitled "Great Boyhoods," by "Aunt Martha." "She doesna make them up," he whispered; "she gets them out o' this."

"And you back her up, Corp, even when she says I was not your friend!"

"It was like a t' knife intil me," replied loyal Corp; "every time I forswore you it was like a t' knife, but I did it, ay, and I'll go on doing it if you think my friendship cheapens you."

Tommy was much moved, and gripped his old lieutenant by the hand. He also called Gavinia ben, and, before she could ward him off, the masterful rogue had saluted her on the cheek. "That," said Tommy, "is to show you that I am as fond of the old times and my old friends as ever, and the moment you deny it I shall take you to mean, Gavinia, that you want another kiss."

"He's just the same!" Corp remarked ecstatically, when Tommy had gone.

"I dinna deny," Gavinia said, "but what he's fell taking"; and for a time they ruminated.

"Gavinia," said Corp, suddenly, "I wouldna wonder but what he's a gey lad wi' the women!"

"What makes you think that?" she replied coldly, and he had the prudence not to say. He should have followed his hero home to be disabused of this monstrous notion, for even while it was being propounded Tommy was sitting in such an agony of silence in a woman's presence that she could not resist smiling a crooked smile at him. His want of words did not displease Grizel; she was of opinion that young men should always be a little awed by young ladies.

He had found her with Elspeth on his return home. Would Grizel call and be friendly? he had asked himself many times since he saw her in church yesterday, and Elspeth was as curious. Each wanted to know what the other thought of

THE TOMMY MYTH

her, but neither had the courage to inquire, they both wanted to know so much. Her name had been mentioned but casually, not a word to indicate that she had grown up since they saw her last. The longer Tommy remained silent, the more, he knew, did Elspeth suspect him. He would have liked to say, in a careless voice, "Rather pretty, isn't she?" but he felt that this little Elspeth would see through him at once.

For at the first glance he had seen what Grizel was, and a thrill of joy passed through him as he drank her in; it was but the joy of the eyes for the first moment, but it ran to his heart to say, "This is the little hunted girl that was!" and Tommy was moved with a manly gladness that the girl who once was so fearful of the future had grown into this. The same unselfish delight in her for her own sake came over him again when he shook hands with her in Aaron's parlor. This glorious creature with the serene eyes and the noble shoulders had been the hunted child of the Double Dykes! He would have liked to race back into the past and bring little Grizel here to look. How many boyish memories he recalled! and she was in every one of them. His heart held nothing but honest joy in this meeting after so many years; he longed to tell her how sincerely he was still her friend. Well, why don't you tell her, Tommy? It is a thing you are good at, and you have been polishing up the phrases ever since she passed down the aisle with Master Shiach in her arms; you have even planned out a way of putting Grizel at her ease, and behold, she is the only one of the three who is at ease. What has come over you? Does the reader think it was love? No, it was only that pall of shyness; he tried to fling it off, but could not. Behold Tommy being buried alive!

Elspeth showed less contemptibly than her brother, but it was Grizel who did most of the talking. She nodded her head and smiled crookedly at Tommy, but she was watching him all the time. She wore a dress in which brown and yellow mingled as in woods on an autumn day, and the jacket had a high collar of fur, over which she watched him. Let us say that she was watching to see whether any of the old Tommy was left in him. Yet, with this problem confronting her, she also had time to study the outer man, Tommy the dandy — his velvet jacket (a new one), his brazen waistcoat, his poetic neckerchief, his spotless linen. His velvet jacket was to become the derision of Thrums, but Tommy took his bonneting haughtily, like one who was glad to suffer for a Cause. There were to be meetings here and there where people told with awe how many shirts he sent weekly to the wash. Grizel disdained his dandy tastes; why did not Elspeth strip him of them? And oh, if he must wear that absurd waistcoat, could she not see that it would look another thing if the second button was put half an inch farther back? How sinful of him to spoil the shape of his silly velvet jacket by carrying so many letters in the pockets! She learned afterwards that he carried all those letters because there was a check in one of them, he did not know which, and her sense of orderliness was outraged. Elspeth did not notice these things. She helped Tommy by her helplessness. There is reason to believe that once in London, when she had need of a new hat, but money there was none, Tommy, looking very defiant, studied ladies' hats in the shop-windows, brought all his intellect to bear on them, with the result that he did concoct out of Elspeth's old hat a new one which was the admired of O. P. Pym and friends, who never knew the name of the artist. But obviously he could not take proper care of himself, and there is a kind of woman, of whom Grizel was one, to whose breasts this helplessness makes an unfair appeal. Oh, to dress him properly! She could not help liking to be a mother to men; she wanted them to be the most noble characters, but completely dependent on her.

Tommy walked home with her, and it seemed at first as if Elspeth's absence was to be no help to him. He could not even plagiarize from "Sandys on Woman." No one knew so well the kind of thing he should be saying, and no one could have been more anxious to say it, but a weight of shyness sat on the lid of Tommy. Having for half an hour raged internally at his misfortune, he now sullenly embraced it. "If I am this sort of an ass, let me be it in the superlative degree," he may be conceived saying bitterly to himself. He addressed Grizel coldly as "Miss McQueen," a name she had taken by the doctor's wish soon after she went to live with him.

"There is no reason why you should call me that," she said. "Call me Grizel, as you used to do."

"May I?" replied Tommy, idiotically. He knew it was idiotic, but that mood now had grip of him.

"But I mean to call you Mr. Sandys," she said decisively.

He was really glad to hear it, for to be called Tommy by anyone was now detestable to him (which is why I always call him Tommy in these pages). So it was like him to say, with a sigh, "I had hoped to hear you use the old name."

That sigh made her look at him sharply. He knew that he must be careful with Grizel, and that she was irritated, but he had to go on.

"It is strange to me," said Sentimental Tommy, "to be back here after all those years, walking this familiar road once more with you. I thought it

THE TOMMY MYTH

would make me feel myself a boy again, but, heigh-ho, it has just the opposite effect: I never felt so old as I do to-day."

His voice trembled a little, I don't know why. Grizel frowned.

"But you never were as old as you are to-day, were you?" she inquired politely. It whisked Tommy out of dangerous waters and laid him at her feet. He laughed, not perceptibly or audibly, of course, but somewhere inside him the bell rang. No one could laugh more heartily at himself than Tommy, and none bore less malice to those who brought him to land.

"That, at any rate, makes me feel younger," he said candidly; and now the shyness was in full flight.

"Why?" asked Grizel, still watchful.

"It is so like the kind of thing you used to say to me when we were boy and girl. I used to enrage you very much, I fear," he said, half gleefully.

"Yes," she admitted, with a smile, "you did."

"And then how you rocked your arms at me, Grizel! Do you remember?"

She remembered it all so well! This rocking of the arms, as they called it, was a trick of hers that signified sudden joy or pain. They hung rigid by her side, and then shook violently with emotion.

"Do you ever rock them now when people annoy you?" he asked.

"There has been no one to annoy me," she replied demurely, "since you went away."

"But I have come back," Tommy said, looking hopefully at her arms.

"You see they take no notice of you."

"They don't remember me yet. As soon as they do they will cry out."

Grizel shook her head confidently, and in this she was pitting herself against Tommy, always a bold thing to do.

"I have been to see Corp's baby," he said suddenly; and this was so important that she stopped in the middle of the road.

"What do you think of him?" she asked, quite anxiously.

"I thought," replied Tommy, gravely, and making use of one of Grizel's pet phrases, "I thought he was just sweet."

"Isn't he!" she cried; and then she knew that he was making fun of her. Her arms rocked.

"Hurray!" cried Tommy, "they recognize me now! Don't be angry, Grizel," he begged her. "You taught me, long ago, what was the right thing to say about babies, and how could I be sure it was you until I saw your arms rocking?"

"It was so like you," she said reproachfully, "to try to make me do it."

THE TOMMY MYTH

"It was so unlike you," he replied craftily, "to let me succeed. And, after all, Grizel, if I was horrid in the old days I always apologized."

"Never!" she insisted.

"Well, then," said Tommy, handsomely, "I do so now"; and then they both laughed gaily, and I think Grizel was not sorry that there was a little of the boy who had been horrid left in Tommy — just enough to know him by.

"He'll be vain," her aged maid, Maggy Ann, said curiously to her that evening. They were all curious about Tommy.

"I don't know that he is vain," Grizel replied guardedly.

"If he's no vain," Maggy Ann retorted, "he's the first son of Adam it could be said o'. I jalouse it's his bit book."

"He scarcely mentioned it."

"Ay, then, it's his beard."

Grizel was sure it was not that.

"Then it'll be the women," said Maggy Ann.

"Who knows!" said Grizel of the watchful eyes; but she smiled to herself. She thought not incorrectly that she knew one woman of whom Mr. Sandys was a little afraid.

About the same time Tommy and Elspeth were discussing her. Elspeth was in bed, and Tommy had come into the room to kiss her good-night — he had never once omitted doing it since they

TOMMY AND GRIZEL

went to London, and he was always to do it, for neither of them was ever to marry.

"What do you think of her?" Elspeth asked. This was their great time for confidences.

"Of whom?" Tommy inquired lightly.

"Grizel."

He must be careful.

"Rather pretty, don't you think?" he said, gazing at the ceiling.

She was looking at him keenly, but he managed to deceive her. She was much relieved, and could say what was in her heart. "Tommy," she said, "I think she is the most noble-looking girl I ever saw, and if she were not so masterful in her manner she would be beautiful." It was nice of Elspeth to say it, for she and Grizel were never very great friends.

Tommy brought down his eyes. "Did you think as much of her as that?" he said. "It struck me that her features were not quite classic. Her nose is a little tilted, is it not?"

"Some people like that kind of nose," replied Elspeth.

"It is not classic," Tommy said sternly.

CHAPTER VI

GHOSTS THAT HAUNT THE DEN

LOOKING through the Tommy papers of this period, like a conscientious biographer, I find among them manuscripts that remind me how diligently he set to work at his new book the moment he went North, and also letters which, if printed, would show you what a wise and good man Tommy was. But while I was fingering those, there floated from them to the floor a loose page, and when I saw that it was a chemist's bill for oil and liniment I remembered something I had nigh forgotten. "Eureka!" I cried. "I shall tell the story of the chemist's bill, and some other biographer may print the letters."

Well, well! but to think that this scrap of paper should flutter into view to damn him after all those years!

The date is Saturday, May 28, by which time Tommy had been a week in Thrums without doing anything very reprehensible, so far as Grizel knew. She watched for telltales as for a mouse to show at its hole, and at the worst, I think, she saw only its little head. That was when Tommy was talking beautifully to her about her dear doctor. He would have done wisely to avoid this subject; but he was so notoriously good at condolences that he had to say it. He had thought it out, you may remember, a year ago, but hesitated to post it; and since then it had lain heavily within him, as if it knew it was a good thing and pined to be up and strutting.

He said it with emotion; evidently Dr. McQueen had been very dear to him, and any other girl would have been touched; but Grizel stiffened, and when he had finished, this is what she said, quite snappily:

"He never liked you."

Tommy was taken aback, but replied, with gentle dignity, "Do you think, Grizel, I would let that make any difference in my estimate of him?"

"But you never liked him," said she; and now that he thought of it, this was true also. It was useless to say anything about the artistic instinct to her; she did not know what it was, and would have had plain words for it as soon as he told her. Please to picture Tommy picking up his beautiful speech and ramming it back into his pocket as if it were a rejected manuscript.

"I am sorry you should think so meanly of me, Grizel," he said with manly forbearance, and when she thought it all out carefully that night she

GHOSTS THAT HAUNT THE DEN

decided that she had been hasty. She could not help watching Tommy for backslidings, but oh, it was sweet to her to decide that she had not found any.

"It was I who was horrid," she announced to him frankly, and Tommy forgave her at once. She offered him a present: "When the doctor died I gave some of his things to his friends; it is the Scotch custom, you know. He had a new overcoat; it had been worn but two or three times. I should be so glad if you would let me give it to you for saying such sweet things about him. I think it will need very little alteration."

Thus very simply came into Tommy's possession the coat that was to play so odd a part in his history. "But oh, Grizel," said he, with mock reproach, "you need not think that I don't see through you! Your deep design is to cover me up. You despise my velvet jacket!"

"It does not——" Grizel began, and stopped.

"It is not in keeping with my doleful countenance," said Tommy, candidly; "that was what you were to say. Let me tell you a secret, Grizel: I wear it to spite my face. Sha'n't give up my velvet jacket for anybody, Grizel; not even for you." He was in gay spirits, because he knew she liked him again; and she saw that was the reason, and it warmed her. She was least able to resist Tommy when he was most a boy, and it was actually watch-

TOMMY AND GRIZEL

ful Grizel who proposed that he and she and Elspeth should revisit the Den together. How often since the days of their childhood had Grizel wandered it alone, thinking of those dear times, making up her mind that if ever Tommy asked her to go into the Den again with him she would not go, the place was so much sweeter to her than it could be to him. And yet it was Grizel herself who was saying now, " Let us go back to the Den."

Tommy caught fire. " We sha'n't go back," he cried defiantly, " as men and women. Let us be boy and girl again, Grizel. Let us have that Saturday we missed long ago. I missed a Saturday on purpose, Grizel, so that we should have it now."

She shook her head wistfully, but she was glad that Tommy would fain have had one of the Saturdays back. Had he waxed sentimental she would not have gone a step of the way with him into the past, but when he was so full of glee she could take his hand and run back into it.

" But we must wait until evening," Tommy said, " until Corp is unharnessed; we must not hurt the feelings of Corp by going back to the Den without him."

" How mean of me not to think of Corp!" Grizel cried; but the next moment she was glad she had not thought of him, it was so delicious to have proof that Tommy was more loyal.

" But we can't turn back the clock, can we,

GHOSTS THAT HAUNT THE DEN

Corp?" she said to the fourth of the conspirators, to which Corp replied, with his old sublime confidence, "He'll find a wy."

And at first it really seemed as if Tommy had found a way. They did not go to the Den four in a line or two abreast — nothing so common as that. In the wild spirits that mastered him he seemed to be the boy incarnate, and it was always said of Tommy by those who knew him best that if he leaped back into boyhood they had to jump with him. Those who knew him best were with him now. He took command of them in the old way. He whispered, as if Black Cathro were still on the prowl for him. Corp of Corp had to steal upon the Den by way of the Silent Pool, Grizel by the Queen's Bower, Elspeth up the burn-side, Captain Stroke down the Reekie Brothpot. Grizel's arms rocked with delight in the dark, and she was on her way to the Cuttle Well, the trysting-place, before she came to and saw with consternation that Tommy had been ordering her about.

She was quite a sedate young lady by the time she joined them at the well, and Tommy was the first to feel the change. "Don't you think this is all rather silly?" she said, when he addressed her as the Lady Griselda, and it broke the spell. Two girls shot up into women, a beard grew on Tommy's chin, and Corp became a father. Grizel had blown Tommy's pretty project to dust just when

TOMMY AND GRIZEL

he was most gleeful over it; yet, instead of bearing resentment, he pretended not even to know that she was the culprit.

"Corp," he said ruefully, "the game is up!" And "Listen," he said, when they had sat down, crushed, by the old Cuttle Well, "do you hear anything?"

It was a very still evening. "I hear nocht," said Corp, "but the trickle o' the burn. What did you hear?"

"I thought I heard a baby cry," replied Tommy, with a groan. "I think it was your baby, Corp. Did you hear it, Grizel?"

She understood, and nodded.

"And you, Elspeth?"

"Yes."

"My bairn!" cried the astounded Corp.

"Yours," said Tommy, reproachfully; "and he has done for us. Ladies and gentlemen, the game is up."

Yes, the game was up, and she was glad, Grizel said to herself, as they made their melancholy pilgrimage of what had once been an enchanted land. But she felt that Tommy had been very forbearing to her, and that she did not deserve it. Undoubtedly he had ordered her about, but in so doing had he not been making half-pathetic sport of his old self — and was it with him that she was annoyed for ordering, or with herself for obeying? And

GHOSTS THAT HAUNT THE DEN

why should she not obey, when it was all a jest? It was as if she still had some lingering fear of Tommy. Oh, she was ashamed of herself. She must say something nice to him at once. About what? About his book, of course. How base of her not to have done so already! but how good of him to have overlooked her silence on that great topic!

It was not ignorance of its contents that had kept her silent. To confess the horrid truth, Grizel had read the book suspiciously, looking as through a microscope for something wrong—hoping not to find it, but peering minutely. The book, she knew, was beautiful; but it was the writer of the book she was peering for — the Tommy she had known so well, what had he grown into? In her heart she had exulted from the first in his success, and she should have been still more glad (should she not?) to learn that his subject was woman; but no, that had irritated her. What was perhaps even worse, she had been still more irritated on hearing that the work was rich in sublime thoughts. As a boy, he had maddened her most in his grandest moments. I can think of no other excuse for her.

She would not accept it as an excuse for herself now. What she saw with scorn was that she was always suspecting the worst of Tommy. Very probably there was not a thought in the book that had been put in with his old complacent waggle of the head. "Oh, am I not a wonder!" he used to cry, when he did anything big; but that was no reason why she should suspect him of being conceited still. Very probably he really and truly felt what he wrote — felt it not only at the time, but also next morning. In his boyhood Mr. Cathro had christened him Sentimental Tommy; but he was a man now, and surely the sentimentalities in which he had dressed himself were flung aside for ever, like old suits of clothes. So Grizel decided eagerly, and she was on the point of telling him how proud she was of his book, when Tommy, who had thus far behaved so well, of a sudden went to pieces.

He and Grizel were together. Elspeth was a little in front of them, walking with a gentleman who still wondered what they meant by saying that they had heard his baby cry. "For he's no here," Corp had said earnestly to them all; "though I'm awid for the time to come when I'll be able to bring him to the Den and let him see the Jacobites' Lair."

There was nothing startling in this remark, so far as Grizel could discover; but she saw that it had an immediate and incomprehensible effect on Tommy. First, he blundered in his talk as if he was thinking deeply of something else; then his face shone as it had been wont to light up in his boyhood when he was suddenly enraptured with

GHOSTS THAT HAUNT THE DEN

himself; and lastly, down his cheek and into his beard there stole a tear of agony. Obviously, Tommy was in deep woe for somebody or something.

It was a chance for a true lady to show that womanly sympathy of which such exquisite things are said in the first work of T. Sandys; but it merely infuriated Grizel, who knew that Tommy did not feel nearly so deeply as she this return to the Den, and, therefore, what was he in such distress about? It was silly sentiment of some sort, she was sure of that. In the old days she would have asked him imperiously to tell her what was the matter with him; but she must not do that now — she dare not even rock her indignant arms; she could only walk silently by his side, longing fervently to shake him.

He had quite forgotten her presence; indeed, she was not really there, for a number of years had passed, and he was Corp Shiach, walking the Den alone. To-morrow he was to bring his boy to show him the old Lair and other fondly remembered spots; to-night he must revisit them alone. So he set out blithely, but, to his bewilderment, he could not find the Lair. It had not been a tiny hollow where muddy water gathered; he remembered an impregnable fortress full of men whose armour rattled as they came and went; so this could not be the Lair. He had taken the wrong way to it, for the way was across a lagoon, up a deep-flowing river, then by horse till the rocky ledge terrified all four-footed things; no, up a grassy slope had never been the way. He came night after night, trying different ways; but he could not find the golden ladder, though all the time he knew that the Lair lay somewhere over there. When he stood still and listened he could hear the friends of his youth at play, and they seemed to be calling: "Are you coming, Corp? Why does not Corp come back?" but he could never see them, and when he pressed forward their voices died away. Then at last he said sadly to his boy: "I shall never be able to show you the Lair, for I cannot find the way to it." And the boy was touched, and he said: "Take my hand, father, and I will lead you to the Lair; I found the way long ago for myself."

It took Tommy about two seconds to see all this, and perhaps another half-minute was spent in sad but satisfactory contemplation of it. Then he felt that, for the best effect, Corp's home life was too comfortable; so Gavinia ran away with a soldier. He was now so sorry for Corp that the tear rolled down. But at the same moment he saw how the effect could be still further heightened by doing away with his friend's rude state of health, and he immediately jammed him between the buffers of two railway carriages, and gave him a wooden leg.

GHOSTS THAT HAUNT THE DEN

It was at this point that a lady who had kept her arms still too long rocked them frantically, then said, with cutting satire: "Are you not feeling well, or have you hurt yourself? You seem to be very lame." And Tommy woke with a start, to see that he was hobbling as if one of his legs were timber to the knee.

"It is nothing," he said modestly. "Something Corp said set me thinking; that is all."

He had told the truth, and if what he imagined was twenty times more real to him than what was really there, how could Tommy help it? Indignant Grizel, however, who kept such a grip of facts, would make no such excuse for him.

"Elspeth!" she called.

"There is no need to tell her," said Tommy. But Grizel was obdurate.

"Come here, Elspeth," she cried vindictively. "Something Corp said a moment ago has made your brother lame."

Tommy was lame; that was all Elspeth and Corp heard or could think of as they ran back to him. When did it happen? Was he in great pain? Had he fallen? Oh, why had he not told Elspeth at once?

"It is nothing," Tommy insisted, a little fiercely.

"He says so," Grizel explained, "not to alarm us. But he is suffering horribly. Just before I called to you his face was all drawn up in pain."

This made the sufferer wince. "That was another twinge," she said promptly. "What is to be done, Elspeth?"

"I think I could carry him," suggested Corp, with a forward movement that made Tommy stamp his foot — the wooden one.

"I am all right," he told them testily, and looking uneasily at Grizel.

"How brave of you to say so!" said she.

"It is just like him," Elspeth said, pleased with Grizel's remark.

"I am sure it is," Grizel said, so graciously.

It was very naughty of her. Had she given him a chance he would have explained that it was all a mistake of Grizel's. That had been his intention; but now a devil entered into Tommy and spoke for him.

"I must have slipped and sprained my ankle," he said. "It is slightly painful; but I shall be able to walk home all right, Corp, if you let me use you as a staff."

I think he was a little surprised to hear himself saying this; but, as soon as it was said, he liked it. He was Captain Stroke playing in the Den again, after all, and playing as well as ever. Nothing being so real to Tommy as pretence, I daresay he even began to feel his ankle hurting him. "Gently," he begged of Corp, with a gallant smile, and clenching his teeth so that the pain should not make him

GHOSTS THAT HAUNT THE DEN

cry out before the ladies. Thus, with his lieutenant's help, did Stroke manage to reach Aaron's house, making light of his mishap, assuring them cheerily that he should be all right to-morrow, and carefully avoiding Grizel's eye, though he wanted very much to know what she thought of him (and of herself) now.

There were moments when she did not know what to think, and that always distressed Grizel, though it was a state of mind with which Tommy could keep on very friendly terms. The truth seemed too monstrous for belief. Was it possible she had misjudged him? Perhaps he really had sprained his ankle. But he had made no pretence of that at first, and besides, — yes, she could not be mistaken, — it was the other leg.

She soon let him see what she was thinking. "I am afraid it is too serious a case for me," she said, in answer to a suggestion from Corp, who had a profound faith in her medical skill, "but, if you like,"—she was addressing Tommy now,—"I shall call at Dr. Gemmell's, on my way home, and ask him to come to you."

"There is no necessity; a night's rest is all I need," he answered hastily.

"Well, you know best," she said, and there was a look on her face which Thomas Sandys could endure from no woman.

"On second thoughts," he said, "I think it

would be advisable to have a doctor. Thank you very much, Grizel. Corp, can you help me to lift my foot on to that chair? Softly — ah! — ugh!"

His eyes did not fall before hers. " And would you mind asking him to come at once, Grizel?" he said sweetly.

She went straight to the doctor.

CHAPTER VII

THE BEGINNING OF THE DUEL

It was among old Dr. McQueen's sayings that when he met a man who was certified to be in no way remarkable he wanted to give three cheers. There are few of them, even in a little place like Thrums; but David Gemmell was one.

So McQueen had always said, but Grizel was not so sure. "He is very good-looking, and he does not know it," she would point out. "Oh, what a remarkable man!"

She had known him intimately for nearly six years now, ever since he became the old doctor's assistant on the day when, in the tail of some others, he came to Thrums, aged twenty-one, to apply for the post. Grizel had even helped to choose him; she had a quaint recollection of his being submitted to her by McQueen, who told her to look him over and say whether he would do — an odd position in which to place a fourteen-year-old girl, but Grizel had taken it most seriously, and, indeed, of the two men only Gemmell dared to laugh.

"You should not laugh when it is so important," she said gravely; and he stood abashed, although I believe he chuckled again when he retired to his room for the night. She was in that room next morning as soon as he had left it, to smell the curtains (he smoked), and see whether he folded his things up neatly and used both the brush and the comb, but did not use pomade, and slept with his window open, and really took a bath instead of merely pouring the water into it and laying the sponge on top (oh, she knew them!) — and her decision, after some days, was that, though far from perfect, he would do, if he loved her dear darling doctor sufficiently. By this time David was openly afraid of her, which Grizel noticed, and took to be, in the circumstances, a satisfactory sign.

She watched him narrowly for the next year, and after that she ceased to watch him at all. She was like a congregation become so sure of its minister's soundness that it can risk going to sleep. To begin with, he was quite incapable of pretending to be anything he was not. Oh, how unlike a boy she had once known! His manner, like his voice, was quiet. Being himself the son of a doctor, he did not dodder through life amazed at the splendid eminence he had climbed to, which is the weakness of Scottish students when they graduate, and often for fifty years afterwards. How sweet

THE BEGINNING OF THE DUEL

he was to Dr. McQueen, never forgetting the respect due to gray hairs, never hinting that the new school of medicine knew many things that were hidden from the old, and always having the sense to support McQueen when she was scolding him for his numerous naughty ways. When the old doctor came home now on cold nights it was not with his cravat in his pocket, and Grizel knew very well who had put it round his neck. McQueen never had the humiliation, so distressing to an old doctor, of being asked by patients to send his assistant instead of coming himself. He thought they preferred him, and twitted David about it; but Grizel knew that David had sometimes to order them to prefer the old man. She knew that when he said good-night and was supposed to have gone to his lodgings, he was probably off to some poor house where, if not he, a tired woman must sit the long night through by a sufferer's bedside, and she realized with joy that his chief reason for not speaking of such things was that he took them as part of his natural work and never even knew that he was kind. He was not specially skilful, he had taken no honours either at school or college, and he considered himself to be a very ordinary young man. If you had said that on this point you disagreed with him, his manner probably would have implied that he thought you a bit of an ass.

TOMMY AND GRIZEL

When a new man arrives in Thrums, the women come to their doors to see whether he is good-looking. They said No of Tommy when he came back, but it had been an emphatic Yes for Dr. Gemmell. He was tall and very slight, and at twenty-seven, as at twenty-one, despite the growth of a heavy moustache, there was a boyishness about his appearance, which is, I think, what women love in a man more than anything else. They are drawn to him by it, and they love him out of pity when it goes. I suppose it brings back to them some early, beautiful stage in the world's history when men and women played together without fear. Perhaps it lay in his smile, which was so winning that wrinkled old dames spoke of it, who had never met the word before, smiles being little known in Thrums, where in a workaday world we find it sufficient either to laugh or to look thrawn. His dark curly hair was what Grizel was most suspicious of; he must be vain of that, she thought, until she discovered that he was quite sensitive to its being mentioned, having ever detested his curls as an eyesore, and in his boyhood clipped them savagely to the roots. He had such a firm chin, if there had been another such chin going a-begging, I should have liked to clap it on to Tommy Sandys.

Tommy Sandys! All this time we have been neglecting that brave sufferer, and while we talk his ankle is swelling and swelling. Well, Grizel

THE BEGINNING OF THE DUEL

was not so inconsiderate, for she walked very fast and with an exceedingly determined mouth to Dr. Gemmell's lodgings. He was still in lodgings, having refused to turn Grizel out of her house, though she had offered to let it to him. She left word, the doctor not being in, that he was wanted at once by Mr. Sandys, who had sprained his ankle.

Now, then, Tommy!

For an hour, perhaps until she went to bed, she remained merciless. She saw the quiet doctor with the penetrating eyes examining that ankle, asking a few questions, and looking curiously at his patient; then she saw him lift his hat and walk out of the house.

It gave her pleasure; no, it did not. While she thought of this Tommy she despised, there came in front of him a boy who had played with her long ago when no other child would play with her, and now he said, "You have grown cold to me, Grizel," and she nodded assent, and little wells of water rose to her eyes and lay there because she had nodded assent.

She had never liked Dr. Gemmell so little as when she saw him approaching her house next morning. The surgery was still attached to it, and very often he came from there, his visiting-book in his hand, to tell her of his patients, even to consult her; indeed, to talk to Grizel about his work without consulting her would have been difficult, for it was natural to her to decide what was best for everybody. These consultations were very unprofessional, but from her first coming to the old doctor's house she had taken it as a matter of course that in his practice, as in affairs relating to his boots and buttons, she should tell him what to do and he should do it. McQueen had introduced his assistant to this partnership half-shamefacedly and with a cautious wink over the little girl's head; and Gemmell fell into line at once, showing her his new stethoscope as gravely as if he must abandon it at once should not she approve, which fine behaviour, however, was quite thrown away on Grizel, who, had he conducted himself otherwise, would merely have wondered what was the matter with the man; and as she was eighteen or more before she saw that she had exceeded her duties, it was then, of course, too late to cease doing it.

She knew now how good, how forbearing, he had been to the little girl, and that it was partly because he was acquainted with her touching history. The grave courtesy with which he had always treated her—and which had sometimes given her as a girl a secret thrill of delight, it was so sweet to Grizel to be respected—she knew now to be less his natural manner to women than something that came to him in her presence because he who knew her so well thought her worthy of deference; and

THE BEGINNING OF THE DUEL

it helped her more, far more, than if she had seen it turn to love. Yet as she received him in her parlor now — her too spotless parlor, for not even the ashes in the grate were visible, which is a mistake — she was not very friendly. He had discovered what Tommy was, and as she had been the medium she could not blame him for that, but how could he look as calm as ever when such a deplorable thing had happened?

"What you say is true; I knew it before I asked you to go to him, and I knew you would find it out; but please to remember that he is a man of genius, whom it is not for such as you to judge."

That was the sort of haughty remark she held ready for him while they talked of other cases; but it was never uttered, for by and by he said:

"And then, there is Mr. Sandys's ankle. A nasty accident, I am afraid."

Was he jesting? She looked at him sharply. "Have you not been to see him yet?" she asked.

He thought she had misunderstood him. He had been to see Mr. Sandys twice, both last night and this morning.

And he was sure it was a sprain?

Unfortunately it was something worse — dislocation; further mischief might show itself presently.

"Hæmorrhage into the neighbouring joint on inflammation?" she asked scientifically and with scorn.

"Yes."

Grizel turned away from him. "I think not," she said.

Well, possibly not, if Mr. Sandys was careful and kept his foot from the ground for the next week. The doctor did not know that she was despising him, and he proceeded to pay Tommy a compliment. "I had to reduce the dislocation, of course," he told her, "and he bore the wrench splendidly, though there is almost no pain more acute."

"Did he ask you to tell me that?" Grizel was thirsting to inquire, but she forbore. Unwittingly, however, the doctor answered the question. "I could see," he said, "that Mr. Sandys made light of his sufferings to save his sister pain. I cannot recall ever having seen a brother and sister so attached."

That was quite true, Grizel admitted to herself. In all her recollections of Tommy she could not remember one critical moment in which Elspeth had not been foremost in his thoughts. It passed through her head, "Even now he must make sure that Elspeth is in peace of mind before he can care to triumph over me," and she would perhaps have felt less bitter had he put his triumph first.

His triumph! Oh, she would show him whether it was a triumph. He had destroyed for ever her faith in David Gemmell. The quiet, observant doc-

THE BEGINNING OF THE DUEL

tor, who had such an eye for the false, had been deceived as easily as all the others, and it made her feel very lonely. But never mind; Tommy should find out, and that within the hour, that there was one whom he could not cheat. Her first impulse, always her first impulse, was to go straight to his side and tell him what she thought of him. Her second, which was neater, was to send by messenger her compliments to Mr. and Miss Sandys, and would they, if not otherwise engaged, come and have tea with her that afternoon? Not a word in the note about the ankle, but a careful sentence to the effect that she had seen Dr. Gemmell to-day, and proposed asking him to meet them.

Maggy Ann, who had conveyed the message, came back with the reply. Elspeth regretted that they could not accept Grizel's invitation, owing to the accident to her brother being *very much more* serious than Grizel seemed to think. "I can't understand," Elspeth added, "why Dr. Gemmell did not tell you this when he saw you."

"Is it a polite letter?" asked inquisitive Maggy Ann, and Grizel assured her that it was most polite. "I hardly expected it," said the plain-spoken dame, "for I'm thinking by their manner it's more than can be said of yours."

"I merely invited them to come to tea."

"And him wi' his leg broke! Did you no ken he was lying on chairs?"

TOMMY AND GRIZEL

"I did not know it was so bad as that, Maggy Ann. So my letter seemed to annoy him, did it?" said Grizel, eagerly, and, I fear, well pleased.

"It angered her most terrible," said Maggy Ann, "but no him. He gave a sort of a laugh when he read it."

"A laugh!"

"Ay, and syne she says, 'It is most heartless of Grizel; she does not even ask how you are to-day; one would think she did not know of the accident'; and she says, 'I have a good mind to write her a very stiff letter.' And says he in a noble, melancholic voice, 'We must not hurt Grizel's feelings,' he says. And she says, 'Grizel thinks it was nothing because you bore it so cheerfully; oh, how little she knows you!' she says; and 'You are too forgiving,' she says. And says he, 'If I have anything to forgive Grizel for, I forgive her willingly.' And syne she quieted down and wrote the letter."

Forgive her! Oh, how it enraged Grizel! How like the Tommy of old to put it in that way. There never had been a boy so good at forgiving people for his own crimes, and he always looked so modest when he did it. He was reclining on his chairs at this moment, she was sure he was, forgiving her in every sentence. She could have endured it more easily had she felt sure that he was seeing himself as he was; but she remembered him too well to have any hope of that.

THE BEGINNING OF THE DUEL

She put on her bonnet, and took it off again; a terrible thing, remember, for Grizel to be in a state of indecision. For the remainder of that day she was not wholly inactive. Meeting Dr. Gemmell in the street, she impressed upon him the advisability of not allowing Mr. Sandys to move for at least a week.

"He might take a drive in a day or two," the doctor thought, "with his sister."

"He would be sure to use his foot," Grizel maintained, "if you once let him rise from his chair; you know they all do." And Gemmell agreed that she was right. So she managed to give Tommy as irksome a time as possible.

But next day she called. To go through another day without letting him see how despicable she thought him was beyond her endurance. Elspeth was a little stiff at first, but Tommy received her heartily and with nothing in his manner to show that she had hurt his finer feelings. His leg (the wrong leg, as Grizel remembered at once) was extended on a chair in front of him; but instead of nursing it ostentatiously as so many would have done, he made humourous remarks at its expense. "The fact is," he said cheerily, "that so long as I don't move I never felt better in my life. And I daresay I could walk almost as well as either of you, only my tyrant of a doctor won't let me try."

"He told me you had behaved splendidly," said

Grizel, "while he was reducing the dislocation. How brave you are! You could not have endured more stoically though there had been nothing the matter with it."

"It was soon over," Tommy replied lightly. "I think Elspeth suffered more than I."

Elspeth told the story of his heroism. "I could not stay in the room," she said; "it was too terrible." And Grizel despised too tender-hearted Elspeth for that; she was so courageous at facing pain herself. But Tommy had guessed that Elspeth was trembling behind the door, and he had called out, "Don't cry, Elspeth; I am all right; it is nothing at all."

"How noble!" was Grizel's comment, when she heard of this; and then Elspeth was her friend again, insisted on her staying to tea, and went into the kitchen to prepare it. Aaron was out.

The two were alone now, and in the circumstances some men would have given the lady the opportunity to apologize, if such was her desire. But Tommy's was a more generous nature; his manner was that of one less sorry to be misjudged than anxious that Grizel should not suffer too much from remorse. If she had asked his pardon then and there, I am sure he would have replied, "Right willingly, Grizel," and begged her not to give another thought to the matter. What is of more importance, Grizel was sure of this also, and it was the magnanimity of him that especially annoyed

THE BEGINNING OF THE DUEL

her. There seemed to be no disturbing it. Even when she said, "Which foot is it?" he answered, "The one on the chair," quite graciously, as if she had asked a natural question.

Grizel pointed out that the other foot must be tired of being a foot in waiting. It had got a little exercise, Tommy replied lightly, last night and again this morning, when it had helped to convey him to and from his bed.

Had he hopped? she asked brutally.

No, he said; he had shuffled along. Half rising, he attempted to show her humourously how he walked nowadays — tried not to wince, but had to. Ugh, that was a twinge! Grizel sarcastically offered her assistance, and he took her shoulder gratefully. They crossed the room — a tedious journey. "Now let me see if you can manage alone," she says, and suddenly deserts him.

He looked rather helplessly across the room. Few sights are so pathetic as the strong man of yesterday feeling that the chair by the fire is a distant object to-day. Tommy knew how pathetic it was, but Grizel did not seem to know.

"Try it," she said encouragingly; "it will do you good."

He got as far as the table, and clung to it, his teeth set. Grizel clapped her hands. "Excellently done!" she said, with fell meaning, and recommended him to move up and down the room for a little; he would feel ever so much the better for it afterwards.

The pain — was — considerable, he said. Oh, she saw that, but he had already proved himself so good at bearing pain, and the new school of surgeons held that it was wise to exercise an injured limb.

Even then it was not a reproachful glance that Tommy gave her, though there was some sadness in it. He moved across the room several times, a groan occasionally escaping him. "Admirable!" said his critic. "Bravo! Would you like to stop now?"

"Not until you tell me to," he said determinedly, but with a gasp.

"It must be dreadfully painful," she replied coldly, "but I should like you to go on." And he went on until suddenly he seemed to have lost the power to lift his feet. His body swayed; there was an appealing look on his face. "Don't be afraid; you won't fall," said Grizel. But she had scarcely said it when he fainted dead away, and went down at her feet.

"Oh, how dare you!" she cried in sudden flame, and she drew back from him. But after a moment she knew that he was shamming no longer — or she knew it and yet could not quite believe it; for, hurrying out of the room for water, she had no sooner passed the door than she swiftly put back

THE BEGINNING OF THE DUEL

her head as if to catch him unawares; but he lay motionless.

The sight of her dear brother on the floor paralyzed Elspeth, who could only weep for him, and call to him to look at her and speak to her. But in such an emergency Grizel was as useful as any doctor, and by the time Gemmell arrived in haste the invalid was being brought to. The doctor was a practical man who did not ask questions while there was something better to do. Had he asked any as he came in, Grizel would certainly have said: "He wanted to faint to make me believe he really has a bad ankle, and somehow he managed to do it." And if the doctor had replied that people can't faint by wishing, she would have said that he did not know Mr. Sandys.

But, with few words, Gemmell got his patient back to the chairs, and proceeded to undo the bandages that were round his ankle. Grizel stood by, assisting silently. She had often assisted the doctors, but never before with that scornful curl of her lip. So the bandages were removed and the ankle laid bare. It was very much swollen and discoloured, and when Grizel saw this she gave a little cry, and the ointment she was holding slipped from her hand. For the first time since he came to Thrums, she had failed Gemmell at a patient's side.

"I had not expected it to be — like this," she

said in a quivering voice, when he looked at her in surprise.

"It will look much worse to-morrow," he assured them, grimly. "I can't understand, Miss Sandys, how this came about."

"Miss Sandys was not in the room," said Grizel, abjectly, "but I was, and I ——"

Tommy's face was begging her to stop. He was still faint and in pain, but all thought of himself left him in his desire to screen her. "I owe you an apology, doctor," he said quickly, "for disregarding your instructions. It was entirely my own fault; I would try to walk."

"Every step must have been agony," the doctor rapped out; and Grizel shuddered.

"Not nearly so bad as that," Tommy said, for her sake.

"Agony," insisted the doctor, as if, for once, he enjoyed the word. "It was a mad thing to do, as surely you could guess, Grizel. Why did you not prevent him?"

"She certainly did her best to stop me," Tommy said hastily; "but I suppose I had some insane fit on me, for do it I would. I am very sorry, doctor."

His face was wincing with pain, and he spoke jerkily; but the doctor was still angry. He felt that there was something between these two which he did not understand, and it was strange to him,

THE BEGINNING OF THE DUEL

and unpleasant, to find Grizel unable to speak for herself. I think he doubted Tommy from that hour. All he said in reply, however, was: "It is unnecessary to apologize to me; you yourself are the only sufferer."

But was Tommy the only sufferer? Gemmell left, and Elspeth followed him to listen to those precious words which doctors drop, as from a vial, on the other side of a patient's door; and then Grizel, who had been standing at the window with head averted, turned slowly round and looked at the man she had wronged. Her arms, which had been hanging rigid, the fists closed, went out to him to implore forgiveness. I don't know how she held herself up and remained dry-eyed, her whole being wanted so much to sink by the side of his poor, tortured foot, and bathe it in her tears.

So, you see, he had won; nothing to do now but forgive her beautifully. Go on, Tommy; you are good at it.

But the unexpected only came out of Tommy. Never was there a softer heart. In London the old lady who sold matches at the street corner had got all his pence; had he heard her, or any other, mourning a son sentenced to the gallows, he would immediately have wondered whether he might take the condemned one's place. (What a speech Tommy could have delivered from the scaffold!) There was nothing he would not jump at doing for a woman in distress, except, perhaps, destroy his note-book. And Grizel was in anguish. She was his suppliant, his brave, lonely little playmate of the past, the noble girl of to-day, Grizel whom he liked so much. As through a magnifying-glass he saw her topheavy with remorse for life, unable to sleep of nights, crushed and ——

He was not made of the stuff that could endure it. The truth must out. "Grizel," he said impulsively, "you have nothing to be sorry for. You were quite right. I did not hurt my foot that night in the Den, but afterwards, when I was alone, before the doctor came. I wricked it here intentionally in the door. It sounds incredible; but I set my teeth and did it, Grizel, because you had challenged me to a duel, and I would not give in."

As soon as it was out he was proud of himself for having the generosity to confess it. He looked at Grizel expectantly.

Yes, it sounded incredible, and yet she saw that it was true. As Elspeth returned at that moment, Grizel could say nothing. She stood looking at him only over her high collar of fur. Tommy actually thought that she was admiring him.

CHAPTER VIII

WHAT GRIZEL'S EYES SAID

To be the admired of women — how Tommy had fought for it since first he drank of them in Pym's sparkling pages! To some it seems to be easy, but to him it was a labour of Sisyphus. Everything had been against him. But he concentrated. No labour was too Herculean; he was prepared, if necessary, to walk round the world to get to the other side of the wall across which some men can step. And he did take a roundabout way. It is my opinion, for instance, that he wrote his book in order to make a beginning with the ladies.

That as it may be, at all events he is on the right side of the wall now, and here is even Grizel looking wistfully at him. Had she admired him for something he was not (and a good many of them did that) he would have been ill satisfied. He wanted her to think him splendid because he was splendid, and the more he reflected the more clearly he saw that he had done a big thing. How many men would have had the courage to wrick their foot as he had done? (He shivered when he thought of it.) And even of these Spartans how many would have let the reward slip through their fingers rather than wound the feelings of a girl? These had not been his thoughts when he made confession; he had spoken on an impulse; but now that he could step out and have a look at himself, he saw that this made it a still bigger thing. He was modestly pleased that he had not only got Grizel's admiration, but earned it, and he was very kind to her when next she came to see him. No one could be more kind to them than he when they admired him. He had the most grateful heart, had our Tommy.

When next she came to see him! That was while his ankle still nailed him to the chair, a fortnight or so during which Tommy was at his best, sending gracious messages by Elspeth to the many who called to inquire, and writing hard at his new work, pad on knee, so like a brave soul whom no unmerited misfortune could subdue that it would have done you good merely to peep at him through the window. Grizel came several times, and the three talked very ordinary things, mostly reminiscences; she was as much a plain-spoken princess as ever, but often he found her eyes fixed on him wistfully, and he knew what they were saying; they spoke so eloquently that he was a little nervous lest Elspeth should notice. It was delicious to Tommy to feel that there was this little

WHAT GRIZEL'S EYES SAID

unspoken something between him and Grizel; he half regretted that the time could not be far distant when she must put it into words—as soon, say, as Elspeth left the room; an exquisite moment, no doubt, but it would be the plucking of the flower.

Don't think that Tommy conceived Grizel to be in love with him. On my sacred honour, that would have horrified him.

Curiously enough, she did not take the first opportunity Elspeth gave her of telling him in words how much she admired his brave confession. She was so honest that he expected her to begin the moment the door closed, and now that the artistic time had come for it, he wanted it; but no. He was not hurt, but he wondered at her shyness, and cast about for the reason. He cast far back into the past, and caught a little girl who had worn this same wistful face when she admired him most. He compared those two faces of the anxious girl and the serene woman, and in the wistfulness that sometimes lay on them both they looked alike. Was it possible that the fear of him which the years had driven out of the girl still lived a ghost's life to haunt the woman?

At once he overflowed with pity. As a boy he had exulted in Grizel's fear of him; as a man he could feel only the pain of it. There was no one, he thought, less to be dreaded of a woman than he; oh, so sure Tommy was of that! And he must lay this ghost; he gave his whole heart to the laying of it.

Few men, and never a woman, could do a fine thing so delicately as he; but of course it included a divergence from the truth, for to Tommy afloat on a generous scheme the truth was a buoy marking sunken rocks. She had feared him in her childhood, as he knew well; he therefore proceeded to prove to her that she had never feared him. She had thought him masterful, and all his reminiscences now went to show that it was she who had been the masterful one.

"You must often laugh now," he said, "to remember how I feared you. The memory of it makes me afraid of you still. I assure you, I joukit back, as Corp would say, that day I saw you in church. It was the instinct of self-preservation. 'Here comes Grizel to lord it over me again,' I heard something inside me saying. You called me masterful, and yet I had always to give in to you. That shows what a gentle, yielding girl you were, and what a masterful character I was!"

His intention, you see, was, without letting Grizel know what he was at, to make her think he had forgotten certain unpleasant incidents in their past, so that, seeing they were no longer anything to him, they might the sooner become nothing to her. And she believed that he had forgotten, and she was glad. She smiled when he told her to go on being masterful, for old acquaintance had made him like it. Hers, indeed, was a masterful nature; she could not help it; and if the time ever came when she must help it, the glee of living would be gone from her.

She did continue to be masterful — to a greater extent than Tommy, thus nobly behaving, was prepared for; and his shock came to him at the very moment when he was modestly expecting to receive the prize. She had called when Elspeth happened to be out; and though now able to move about the room with the help of a staff, he was still an interesting object. He saw that she thought so, and perhaps it made him hobble slightly more, not vaingloriously, but because he was such an artist. He ceased to be an artist suddenly, however, when Grizel made this unexpected remark:

"How vain you are!"

Tommy sat down, quite pale. "Did you come here to say that to me, Grizel?" he inquired, and she nodded frankly over her high collar of fur. He knew it was true as Grizel said it, but though taken aback, he could bear it, for she was looking wistfully at him, and he knew well what Grizel's wistful look meant; so long as women admired him Tommy could bear anything from them. "God knows I have little to be vain of," he said humbly.

"Those are the people who are most vain," she

replied; and he laughed a short laugh, which surprised her, she was so very serious.

"Your methods are so direct," he explained. "But of what am I vain, Grizel? Is it my book?"

"No," she answered, "not about your book, but about meaner things. What else could have made you dislocate your ankle rather than admit that you had been rather silly?"

Now "silly" is no word to apply to a gentleman, and, despite his forgiving nature, Tommy was a little disappointed in Grizel.

"I suppose it was a silly thing to do," he said, with just a touch of stiffness.

"It was an ignoble thing," said she, sadly.

"I see. And I myself am the meaner thing than the book, am I?"

"Are you not?" she asked, so eagerly that he laughed again.

"It is the first compliment you have paid my book," he pointed out.

"I like the book very much," she answered gravely. "No one can be more proud of your fame than I. You are hurting me very much by pretending to think that it is a pleasure to me to find fault with you."

There was no getting past the honesty of her, and he was touched by it. Besides, she did admire him, and that, after all, is the great thing.

WHAT GRIZEL'S EYES SAID

"Then why say such things, Grizel?" he replied good-naturedly.

"But if they are true?"

"Still let us avoid them," said he; and at that she was most distressed.

"It is so like what you used to say when you were a boy!" she cried.

"You are so anxious to have me grow up," he replied, with proper dolefulness. "If you like the book, Grizel, you must have patience with the kind of thing that produced it. That night in the Den, when I won your scorn, I was in the preliminary stages of composition. At such times an author should be locked up; but I had got out, you see. I was so enamoured of my little fancies that I forgot I was with you. No wonder you were angry."

"I was not angry with you for forgetting me," she said sharply. (There was no catching Grizel, however artful you were.) "But you were sighing to yourself, you were looking as tragic as if some dreadful calamity had occurred——"

"The idea that had suddenly come to me was a touching one," he said.

"But you looked triumphant, too."

"That was because I saw I could make something of it."

"Why did you walk as if you were lame?"

"The man I was thinking of," Tommy explained, "had broken his leg. I don't mind telling you that it was Corp."

He ought to have minded telling her, for it could only add to her indignation; but he was too conceited to give weight to that.

"Corp's leg was not broken," said practical Grizel.

"I broke it for him," replied Tommy; and when he had explained, her eyes accused him of heartlessness.

"If it had been my own," he said, in self-defence, "it should have gone crack just the same."

"Poor Gavinia! Had you no feeling for her?"

"Gavinia was not there," Tommy replied triumphantly. "She had run off with a soldier."

"You dared to conceive that?"

"It helped."

Grizel stamped her foot. "You could take away dear Gavinia's character with a smile!"

"On the contrary," said Tommy, "my heart bled for her. Did you not notice that I was crying?" But he could not make Grizel smile; so, to please her, he said, with a smile that was not very sincere: "I wish I were different, but that is how ideas come to me—at least, all those that are of any value."

"Surely you could fight against them and drive them away?"

This to Tommy, who held out sugar to them to

WHAT GRIZEL'S EYES SAID

lure them to him! But still he treated her with consideration.

"That would mean my giving up writing altogether, Grizel," he said kindly.

"Then why not give it up?"

Really! But she admired him, and still he bore with her.

"I don't like the book," she said, "if it is written at such a cost."

"People say the book has done them good, Grizel."

"What does that matter, if it does you harm?" In her eagerness to persuade him, her words came pell-mell. "If writing makes you live in such an unreal world, it must do you harm. I see now what Mr. Cathro meant, long ago, when he called you Senti——"

Tommy winced. "I remember what Mr. Cathro called me," he said, with surprising hauteur for such a good-natured man. "But he does not call me that now. No one calls me that now, except you, Grizel."

"What does that matter," she replied distressfully, "if it is true? In the definition of sentimentality in the dictionary——"

He rose indignantly. "You have been looking me up in the dictionary, have you, Grizel?"

"Yes, the night you told me you had hurt your ankle intentionally."

TOMMY AND GRIZEL

He laughed, without mirth now. "I thought you had put that down to vanity."

"I think," she said, "it was vanity that gave you the courage to do it." And he liked one word in this remark.

"Then you do give me credit for a little courage?"

"I think you could do the most courageous things," she told him, "so long as there was no real reason why you should do them."

It was a shot that rang the bell. Oh, our Tommy heard it ringing. But, to do him justice, he bore no malice; he was proud, rather, of Grizel's marksmanship. "At least," he said meekly, "it was courageous of me to tell you the truth in the end?" But, to his surprise, she shook her head.

"No," she replied; "it was sweet of you. You did it impulsively, because you were sorry for me, and I think it was sweet. But impulse is not courage."

So now Tommy knew all about it. His plain-spoken critic had been examining him with a candle, and had paid particular attention to his defects; but against them she set the fact that he had done something chivalrous for her, and it held her heart, though the others were in possession of the head. "How like a woman!" he thought, with a pleased smile. He knew them!

Still he was chagrined that she made so little of

WHAT GRIZEL'S EYES SAID

his courage, and it was to stab her that he said, with subdued bitterness: "I always had a suspicion that I was that sort of person, and it is pleasant to have it pointed out by one's oldest friend. No one will ever accuse you of want of courage, Grizel."

She was looking straight at him, and her eyes did not drop, but they looked still more wistful. Tommy did not understand the courage that made her say what she had said, but he knew he was hurting her; he knew that if she was too plain-spoken it was out of loyalty, and that to wound Grizel because she had to speak her mind was a shame — yes, he always knew that.

But he could do it; he could even go on: "And it is satisfactory that you have thought me out so thoroughly, because you will not need to think me out any more. You know me now, Grizel, and can have no more fear of me."

"When was I ever afraid of you?" she demanded. She was looking at him suspiciously now.

"Never as a girl?" he asked. It jumped out of him. He was sorry as soon as he had said it.

There was a long pause. "So you remembered it all the time," she said quietly. "You have been making pretence — again!"

He asked her to forgive him, and she nodded her head at once. "But why did you pretend to have forgotten?"

"I thought it would please you, Grizel."

"Why should pretence please me?" She rose suddenly, in a white heat. "You don't mean to say that you think I am afraid of you still?"

He said No a moment too late. He knew it was too late.

"Don't be angry with me, Grizel," he begged her, earnestly. "I am so glad I was mistaken. It made me miserable. I have been a terrible blunderer, but I mean well; I misread your eyes."

"My eyes?"

"They have always seemed to be watching me, and often there was such a wistful look in them—it reminded me of the past."

"You thought I was still afraid of you! Say it," said Grizel, stamping her foot. But he would not say it. It was not merely fear that he thought he had seen in her eyes, you remember. This was still his comfort, and, I suppose, it gave the touch of complacency to his face that made Grizel merciless. She did not mean to be merciless, but only to tell the truth. If some of her words were scornful, there was sadness in her voice all the time, instead of triumph. "For years and years," she said, standing straight as an elvint, "I have been able to laugh at all the ignorant fears of my childhood; and if you don't know why I have watched you and been unable to help watching you since you came back, I shall tell you. But I think

WHAT GRIZEL'S EYES SAID

you might have guessed, you who write books about women. It is because I liked you when you were a boy. You were often horrid, but you were my first friend when every other person was against me. You let me play with you when no other boy or girl would let me play. And so, all the time you have been away, I have been hoping that you were growing into a noble man; and when you came back, I watched to see whether you were the noble man I wanted you so much to be, and you are not. Do you see now why my eyes look wistful? It is because I wanted to admire you, and I can't."

She went away, and the great authority on women raged about the room. Oh, but he was galled! There had been five feet nine of him, but he was shrinking. By and by the red light came into his eyes.

CHAPTER IX

GALLANT BEHAVIOUR OF T. SANDYS

THERE were now no fewer than three men engaged, each in his own way, in the siege of Grizel, nothing in common between them except insulted vanity. One was a broken fellow who took for granted that she preferred to pass him by in the street. His bow was also an apology to her for his existence. He not only knew that she thought him wholly despicable, but agreed with her. In the long ago (yesterday, for instance) he had been happy, courted, esteemed; he had even esteemed himself, and so done useful work in the world. But she had flung him to earth so heavily that he had made a hole in it out of which he could never climb. There he lay damned, hers the glory of destroying him — he hoped she was proud of her handiwork. That was one Thomas Sandys, the one, perhaps, who put on the velvet jacket in the morning. But it might be number two who took that jacket off at night. He was a good-natured cynic, vastly amused by the airs this little girl put on before a man of note, and he took a malicious

GALLANT BEHAVIOUR OF T. SANDYS

pleasure in letting her see that they entertained him. He goaded her intentionally into expressions of temper, because she looked prettiest then, and trifled with her hair (but this was in imagination only), and called her a quaint child (but this was beneath his breath). The third — he might be the one who wore the jacket — was a haughty boy who was not only done with her for ever, but meant to let her see it. (His soul cried, Oh, oh, for a conservatory and some of society's darlings, and Grizel at the window to watch how he got on with them!) And now that I think of it, there was also a fourth: Sandys, the grave author, whose life (in two vols. 8vo.) I ought at this moment to be writing, without a word about the other Tommies. They amused him a good deal. When they were doing something big he would suddenly appear and take a note of it.

The boy, who was stiffly polite to her (when Tommy was angry he became very polite), told her that he had been invited to the Spittal, the seat of the Rintoul family, and that he understood there were some charming girls there.

"I hope you will like them," Grizel said pleasantly.

"If you could see how they will like me!" he wanted to reply; but of course he could not, and unfortunately there was no one by to say it for him. Tommy often felt this want of a secretary.

The abject one found a glove of Grizel's, that she did not know she had lost, and put it in his pocket. There it lay, unknown to her. He knew that he must not even ask them to bury it with him in his grave. This was a little thing to ask, but too much for him. He saw his effects being examined after all that was mortal of T. Sandys had been consigned to earth, and this pathetic little glove coming to light. Ah, then, then Grizel would know! By the way, what would she have known? I am sure I cannot tell you. Nor could Tommy, forced to face the question in this vulgar way, have told you. Yet, whatever it was, it gave him some moist moments. If Grizel saw him in this mood, her reproachful look implied that he was sentimentalizing again. How little this chit understood him!

The man of the world sometimes came upon the glove in his pocket, and laughed at it, as such men do when they recall their callow youth. He took walks with Grizel without her knowing that she accompanied him; or rather, he let her come, she was so eager. In his imagination (for bright were the dreams of Thomas!) he saw her looking longingly after him, just as the dog looks; and then, not being really a cruel man, he would call over his shoulder, "Put on your hat, little woman; you can come." Then he conceived her wandering with him through the Den and Caddam Wood, clinging

GALLANT BEHAVIOUR OF T. SANDYS

to his arm and looking up adoringly at him. "What a loving little soul it is!" he said, and pinched her ear, whereat she glowed with pleasure. "But I forgot," he would add, bantering her; "you don't admire me. Heigh-ho! Grizel wants to admire me, but she can't!" He got some satisfaction out of these flights of fancy, but it had a scurvy way of deserting him in the hour of greatest need; where was it, for instance, when the real Grizel appeared and fixed that inquiring eye on him?

He went to the Spittal several times, Elspeth with him when she cared to go; for Lady Rintoul and all the others had to learn and remember that, unless they made much of Elspeth, there could be no T. Sandys for them. He glared at anyone, male or female, who, on being introduced to Elspeth, did not remain, obviously impressed, by her side. "Give pleasure to Elspeth or away I go," was written all over him. And it had to be the right kind of pleasure, too. The ladies must feel that she was more innocent than they, and talk accordingly. He would walk the flower-garden with none of them until he knew for certain that the man walking it with little Elspeth was a person to be trusted. Once he was convinced of this, however, he was very much at their service, and so little to be trusted himself that perhaps they should have had careful brothers also. He told them, one at a time, that they were strangely unlike all the other women he had known, and held their hands a moment longer than was absolutely necessary, and then went away, leaving them and him a prey to conflicting and puzzling emotions.

Lord Rintoul, whose hair was so like his skin that in the family portraits he might have been painted in one colour, could never rid himself of the feeling that it must be a great thing to a writing chap to get a good dinner; but her ladyship always explained him away with an apologetic smile which went over his remarks like a piece of india-rubber, so that in the end he had never said anything. She was a slight, pretty woman of nearly forty, and liked Tommy because he remembered so vividly her coming to the Spittal as a bride. He even remembered how she had been dressed — her white bonnet, for instance.

"For long," Tommy said, musing, "I resented other women in white bonnets; it seemed profanation."

"How absurd!" she told him, laughing. "You must have been quite a small boy at the time."

"But with a lonely boy's passionate admiration for beautiful things," he answered; and his gravity was a gentle rebuke to her. "It was all a long time ago," he said, taking both her hands in his, "but I never forget, and, dear lady, I have often wanted to thank you." What he was thanking her for is not precisely clear, but she knew that the

GALLANT BEHAVIOUR OF T. SANDYS

artistic temperament is an odd sort of thing, and from this time Lady Rintoul liked Tommy, and even tried to find the right wife for him among the families of the surrounding clergy. His step was sometimes quite springy when he left the Spittal; but Grizel's shadow was always waiting for him somewhere on the way home, to take the life out of him, and after that it was again, oh, sorrowful disillusion! oh, world gone gray! Grizel did not admire him. T. Sandys was no longer a wonder to Grizel. He went home to that as surely as the labourer to his evening platter.

And now we come to the affair of the Slugs. Corp had got a holiday, and they were off together fishing the Drumly Water, by Lord Rintoul's permission. They had fished the Drumly many a time without it, and this was to be another such day as those of old. The one who woke at four was to rouse the other. Never had either waked at four; but one of them was married now, and any woman can wake at any hour she chooses, so at four Corp was pushed out of bed, and soon thereafter they took the road. Grizel's blinds were already up. "Do you mind," Corp said, "how often, when we had boasted we were to start at four and didna get roaded till six, we wriggled by that window so that Grizel shouldna see us?"

"She usually did see us," Tommy replied ruefully. "Grizel always spotted us, Corp, when we had anything to hide, and missed us when we were anxious to be seen."

"There was no jouking her," said Corp. "Do you mind how that used to bother you?" a senseless remark to a man whom it was bothering still — or shall we say to a boy? For the boy came back to Tommy when he heard the Drumly singing; it was as if he had suddenly seen his mother looking young again. There had been a thunder-shower as they drew near, followed by a rush of wind that pinned them to a dike, swept the road bare, banged every door in the glen, and then sank suddenly as if it had never been, like a mole in the sand. But now the sun was out, every fence and farm-yard rope was a string of diamond drops. There was one to every blade of grass; they lurked among the wild roses; larks, drunken with song, shook them from their wings. The whole earth shone so gloriously with them that for a time Tommy ceased to care whether he was admired. We can pay nature no higher compliment.

But when they came to the Slugs! The Slugs of Kenny is a wild crevice through which the Drumly cuts its way, black and treacherous, into a lovely glade where it gambols for the rest of its short life; you would not believe, to see it laughing, that it had so lately escaped from prison. To the Slugs they made their way — not to fish, for any trout that are there are thinking for ever of the

GALLANT BEHAVIOUR OF T. SANDYS

way out and of nothing else, but to eat their luncheon, and they ate it sitting on the mossy stones their persons had long ago helped to smooth, and looking at a roan-branch, which now, as then, was trailing in the water.

There were no fish to catch, but there was a boy trying to catch them. He was on the opposite bank; had crawled down it, only other boys can tell how, a barefooted urchin of ten or twelve, with an enormous bagful of worms hanging from his jacket button. To put a new worm on the hook without coming to destruction, he first twisted his legs about a young birch, and put his arms round it. He was after a big one, he informed Corp, though he might as well have been fishing in a treatise on the art of angling.

Corp exchanged pleasantries with him; told him that Tommy was Captain Ure, and that he was his faithful servant Alexander Bett, both of Edinburgh. Since the birth of his child, Corp had become something of a humourist. Tommy was not listening. As he lolled in the sun he was turning, without his knowledge, into one of the other Tommies. Let us watch the process.

He had found a half-fledged mavis lying dead in the grass. Remember also how the larks had sung after rain.

Tommy lost sight and sound of Corp and the boy. What he seemed to see was a baby lark that had got out of its nest sideways, a fall of half a foot only, but a dreadful drop for a baby. "You can get back this way," its mother said, and showed it the way, which was quite easy, but when the baby tried to leap, it fell on its back. Then the mother marked out lines on the ground, from one to the other of which it was to practise hopping, and soon it could hop beautifully so long as its mother was there to say every moment, "How beautifully you hop!" "Now teach me to hop up," the little lark said, meaning that it wanted to fly; and the mother tried to do that also, but in vain; she could soar up, up, up bravely, but could not explain how she did it. This distressed her very much, and she thought hard about how she had learned to fly long ago last year, but all she could recall for certain was that you suddenly do it. "Wait till the sun comes out after rain," she said, half remembering. "What is sun? What is rain?" the little bird asked. "If you cannot teach me to fly, teach me to sing." "When the sun comes out after rain," the mother replied, "then you will know how to sing." The rain came, and glued the little bird's wings together. "I shall never be able to fly nor to sing," it wailed. Then, of a sudden, it had to blink its eyes; for a glorious light had spread over the world, catching every leaf and twig and blade of grass in tears, and putting a smile into every tear. The baby bird's

GALLANT BEHAVIOUR OF T. SANDYS

breast swelled, it did not know why; and it fluttered from the ground, it did not know how. "The sun has come out after the rain," it trilled. "Thank you, sun; thank you, thank you! Oh, mother, did you hear me? I can sing!" And it floated up, up, up, crying, "Thank you, thank you, thank you!" to the sun. "Oh, mother, do you see me? I am flying!" And being but a baby, it soon was gasping, but still it trilled the same ecstasy, and when it fell panting to earth it still trilled, and the distracted mother called to it to take breath or it would die, but it could not stop. "Thank you, thank you, thank you!" it sang to the sun till its little heart burst.

With filmy eyes Tommy searched himself for the little pocket-book in which he took notes of such sad thoughts as these, and in place of the book he found a glove wrapped in silk paper. He sat there with it in his hand, nodding his head over it so broken-heartedly you could not have believed that he had forgotten it for several days.

Death was still his subject; but it was no longer a bird he saw: it was a very noble young man, and his white, dead face stared at the sky from the bottom of a deep pool. I don't know how he got there, but a woman who would not admire him had something to do with it. No sun after rain had come into that tragic life. To the water that had ended it his white face seemed to be saying,

"Thank you, thank you, thank you." It was the old story of a faithless woman. He had given her his heart, and she had played with it. For her sake he had striven to be famous; for her alone had he toiled through dreary years in London, the goal her lap, in which he should one day place his book — a poor, trivial little work, he knew (yet much admired by the best critics). Never had his thoughts wandered for one instant of that time to another woman; he had been as faithful in life as in death; and now she came to the edge of the pool and peered down at his staring eyes and laughed.

He had got thus far when a shout from Corp brought him, dazed, to his feet. It had been preceded by another cry, as the boy and the sapling he was twisted round toppled into the river together, uprooted stones and clods pounding after them and discolouring the pool into which the torrent rushes between rocks, to swirl frantically before it dives down a narrow channel and leaps into another caldron.

There was no climbing down those precipitous rocks. Corp was shouting, gesticulating, impotent. "How can you stand so still?" he roared.

For Tommy was standing quite still, like one not yet thoroughly awake. The boy's head was visible now and again as he was carried round in the seething water; when he came to the outer

GALLANT BEHAVIOUR OF T. SANDYS

ring down that channel he must infallibly go, and every second or two he was in a wider circle.

Tommy was awake now, and he could not stand still and see a boy drown before his eyes. He knew that to attempt to save him was to face a terrible danger, especially as he could not swim; but he kicked off his boots. There was some gallantry in the man.

"You wouldna dare!" Corp cried, aghast.

Tommy hesitated for a moment, but he had abundance of physical courage. He clenched his teeth and jumped. But before he jumped he pushed the glove into Corp's hand, saying, "Give her that, and tell her it never left my heart." He did not say who she was; he scarcely knew that he was saying it. It was his dream intruding on reality, as a wheel may revolve for a moment longer after the spring breaks.

Corp saw him strike the water and disappear. He tore along the bank as he had never run before, until he got to the water's edge below the Slugs, and climbed and fought his way to the scene of the disaster. Before he reached it, however, we should have had no hero had not the sapling, the cause of all this pother, made amends by barring the way down the narrow channel. Tommy was clinging to it, and the boy to him, and, at some risk, Corp got them both ashore, where they lay gasping like fish in a creel.

The boy was the first to rise to look for his fishing-rod, and he was surprised to find no six-pounder at the end of it. "She has broke the line again!" he said; for he was sure then and ever afterwards that a big one had pulled him in.

Corp slapped him for his ingratitude; but the man who had saved this boy's life wanted no thanks. "Off to your home with you, wherever it is," he said to the boy, who obeyed silently; and then to Corp: "He is a little fool, Corp, but not such a fool as I am." He lay on his face, shivering, not from cold, not from shock, but in a horror of himself. I think it may fairly be said that he had done a brave if foolhardy thing; it was certainly to save the boy that he had jumped, and he had given himself a moment's time in which to draw back if he chose, which vastly enhances the merit of the deed. But sentimentality had been there also, and he was now shivering with a presentiment of the length to which it might one day carry him.

They lit a fire among the rocks, at which he dried his clothes, and then they set out for home, Corp doing all the talking. "What a town there will be about this in Thrums!" was his text; and he was surprised when Tommy at last broke silence by saying passionately: "Never speak about this to me again, Corp, as long as you live. Promise me that. Promise never to mention it to anyone. I

GALLANT BEHAVIOUR OF T. SANDYS

want no one to know what I did to-day, and no one will ever know unless you tell; the boy can't tell, for we are strangers to him."

"He thinks you are a Captain Ure, and that I'm Alexander Bett, his servant," said Corp. "I telled him that for a divert."

"Then let him continue to think that."

Of course Corp promised. "And I'll go to the stake afore I break my promise," he swore, happily remembering one of the Jacobite oaths. But he was puzzled. They would make so much of Tommy if they knew. They would think him a wonder. Did he not want that?

"No," Tommy replied.

"You used to like it; you used to like it most michty."

"I have changed."

"Ay, you have; but since when? Since you took to making printed books?"

Tommy did not say, but it was more recently than that. What he was surrendering no one could have needed to be told less than he; the magnitude of the sacrifice was what enabled him to make it. He was always at home among the superlatives; it was the little things that bothered him. In his present fear of the ride that sentimentality might yet goad him to, he craved for mastery over self; he knew that his struggles with his Familiar usually ended in an embrace, and he had made a passionate vow that it should be so no longer. The best beginning of the new man was to deny himself the glory that would be his if his deed were advertised to the world. Even Grizel must never know of it — Grizel, whose admiration was so dear to him. Thus he punished himself, and again I think he deserves respect.

CHAPTER X

GAVINIA ON THE TRACK

CORP, you remember, had said that he would go to the stake rather than break his promise; and he meant it, too, though what the stake was, and why such a pother about going to it, he did not know. He was to learn now, however, for to the stake he had to go. This was because Gavinia, when folding up his clothes, found in one of the pockets a glove wrapped in silk paper.

Tommy had forgotten it until too late, for when he asked Corp for the glove it was already in Gavinia's possession, and she had declined to return it without an explanation. "You must tell her nothing," Tommy said sternly. He was uneasy, but relieved to find that Corp did not know whose glove it was, nor even why gentlemen carry a lady's glove in their pocket.

At first Gavinia was mildly curious only, but her husband's refusal to answer any questions roused her dander. She tried cajolery, fried his take of trout deliciously for him, and he sat down to them sniffing. They were small, and the remainder of their brief career was in two parts. First he lifted them by the tail, then he laid down the tail. But not a word about the glove.

She tried tears. "Dinna greet, woman," he said in distress. "What would the bairn say if he kent I made you greet?"

Gavinia went on greeting, and the baby, waking up, promptly took her side.

"D—n the thing!" said Corp.

"Your ain bairn!"

"I meant the glove!" he roared.

It was curiosity only that troubled Gavinia. A reader of romance, as you may remember, she had encountered in the printed page a score of ladies who, on finding such parcels in their husbands' pockets, left their homes at once and for ever, and she had never doubted but that it was the only course to follow; such is the power of the writer of fiction. But when the case was her own she was merely curious; such are the limitations of the writer of fiction. That there was a woman in it she did not believe for a moment. This, of course, did not prevent her saying, with a sob, "Wha is the woman?"

With great earnestness Corp assured her that there was no woman. He even proved it: "Just listen to reason, Gavinia. If I was sich a black as to be chief wi' ony woman, and she wanted to gie me a present, weel, she might gie me a pair o'

GAVINIA ON THE TRACK

gloves, but one glove, what use would one glove be to me? I tell you, if a woman had the impidence to gie me one glove, I would fling it in her face."

Nothing could have been clearer, and he had put it thus considerately because when a woman, even the shrewdest of them, is excited (any man knows this), one has to explain matters to her as simply and patiently as if she were a four-year-old; yet Gavinia affected to be unconvinced, and for several days she led Corp the life of a lodger in his own house.

"Hands off that poor innocent," she said when he approached the baby.

If he reproved her, she replied meekly, "What can you expect frae a woman that doesna wear gloves?"

To the baby she said: "He despises you, my bonny, because you hae no gloves. Ay, that's what maks him turn up his nose at you. But your mother is fond o' you, gloves or no gloves."

She told the baby the story of the glove daily, with many monstrous additions.

When Corp came home from his work, she said that a poor, love-lorn female had called with a boot for him, and a request that he should carry it in the pocket of his Sabbath breeks.

Worst of all, she listened to what he said in the night. Corp had a habit of talking in his sleep.

TOMMY AND GRIZEL

He was usually taking tickets at such times, and it had been her custom to stop him violently; but now she changed her tactics: she encouraged him. "I would be lying in my bed," he said to Tommy, "dreaming that a man had fallen into the Slugs, and instead o' trying to save him I cried out, 'Tickets there, all tickets ready,' and first he hands me a glove and neist he hands me a boot and havers o' that kind sich as onybody dreams. But in the middle o' my dream it comes ower me that I had better waken up to see what Gavinia's doing, and I open my een, and there she is, sitting up, hearkening avidly to my every word, and putting sly questions to me about the glove."

"What glove?" Tommy asked coldly.

"The glove in silk paper."

"I never heard of it," said Tommy.

Corp sighed. "No," he said loyally, "neither did I"; and he went back to the station and sat gloomily in a wagon. He got no help from Tommy, not even when rumours of the incident at the Slugs became noised abroad.

"A'body kens about the laddie now," he said.

"What laddie?" Tommy inquired.

"Him that fell into the Slugs."

"Ah, yes," Tommy said; "I have just been reading about it in the paper. A plucky fellow, this Captain Ure who saved him. I wonder who he is."

GAVINIA ON THE TRACK

"I wonder!" Corp said with a groan.

"There was an Alexander Bett with him, according to the papers," Tommy went on. "Do you know any Bett?"

"It's no a Thrums name," Corp replied thankfully. "I just made it up."

"What do you mean?" Tommy asked blankly.

Corp sighed, and went back again to the wagon. He was particularly truculent that evening when the six-o'clock train came in. "Tickets, there; look slippy wi' your tickets." His head bobbed up at the window of another compartment. "Tick——" he began, and then he ducked.

The compartment contained a boy looking as scared as if he had just had his face washed, and an old woman who was clutching a large linen bag as if expecting some scoundrel to appear through the floor and grip it. With her other hand she held on to the boy, and being unused to travel, they were both sitting very self-conscious, humble, and defiant, like persons in church who have forgotten to bring their Bible. The general effect, however, was lost on Corp, for whom it was enough that in one of them he recognized the boy of the Slugs. He thought he had seen the old lady before, also, but he could not give her a name. It was quite a relief to him to notice that she was not wearing gloves.

He heard her inquiring for one Alexander Bett, and being told that there was no such person in Thrums, "He's married on a woman of the name of Gavinia," said the old lady; and then they directed her to the house of the only Gavinia in the place. With dark forebodings Corp skulked after her. He remembered who she was now. She was the old woman with the nutcracker face on whom he had cried in, more than a year ago, to say that Gavinia was to have him. Her mud cottage had been near the Slugs. Yes, and this was the boy who had been supping porridge with her. Corp guessed rightly that the boy had remembered his unlucky visit. "I'm doomed!" Corp muttered to himself—pronouncing it in another way.

The woman, the boy, and the bag entered the house of Gavinia, and presently she came out with them. She was looking very important and terrible. They went straight to Ailie's cottage, and Corp was wondering why, when he suddenly remembered that Tommy was to be there at tea to-day.

CHAPTER XI

THE TEA-PARTY

It was quite a large tea-party, and was held in what had been the school-room; nothing there now, however, to recall an academic past, for even the space against which a map of the world (Mercator's projection) had once hung was gone the colour of the rest of the walls, and with it had faded away the last relic of the Hanky School.

"It will not fade so quickly from my memory," Tommy said, to please Mrs. McLean. His affection for his old schoolmistress was as sincere as hers for him. I could tell you of scores of pretty things he had done to give her pleasure since his return, all carried out, too, with a delicacy which few men could rival, and never a woman; but they might make you like him, so we shall pass them by.

Ailie said, blushing, that she had taught him very little. "Everything I know," he replied, and then, with a courteous bow to the gentleman opposite, "except what I learned from Mr. Cathro."

"Thank you," Cathro said shortly. Tommy had

behaved splendidly to him, and called him his dear preceptor, and yet the Dominie still itched to be at him with the tawse as of old. "And fine he knows I'm itching," he reflected, which made him itch the more.

It should have been a most successful party, for in the rehearsals between the hostess and her maid Christina every conceivable difficulty had been ironed out. Ailie was wearing her black silk, but without the Honiton lace, so that Miss Sophia Innes need not become depressed; and she had herself taken the chair with the weak back. Mr. Cathro, who, though a lean man, needed a great deal of room at table, had been seated far away from the spinet, to allow Christina to pass him without climbing. Miss Sophia and Grizel had the doctor between them, and there was also a bachelor, but an older one, for Elspeth. Mr. McLean, as stout and humoursome as of yore, had solemnly promised his wife to be jocular but not too jocular. Neither minister could complain, for if Mr. Dishart had been asked to say grace, Mr. Gloag knew that he was to be called on for the benediction. Christina, obeying strict orders, glided round the table leisurely, as if she were not in the least excited, though she could be heard rushing along the passage like one who had entered for a race. And, lastly, there was, as chief guest, the celebrated Thomas Sandys. It should have been

THE TEA-PARTY

a triumph of a tea-party, and yet it was not. Mrs. McLean could not tell why.

Grizel could have told why; her eyes told why every time they rested scornfully on Mr. Sandys. It was he, they said, who was spoiling the entertainment, and for the pitiful reason that the company were not making enough of him. He was the guest of the evening, but they were talking admiringly of another man, and so he sulked. Oh, how she scorned Tommy!

That other man was, of course, the unknown Captain Ure, gallant rescuer of boys, hero of all who admire brave actions except the jealous Sandys. Tommy had pooh-poohed him from the first, to Grizel's unutterable woe.

"Have you not one word of praise for such a splendid deed?" she had asked in despair.

"I see nothing splendid about it," he replied coldly.

"I advise you in your own interests not to talk in that way to others," she said. "Don't you see what they will say?"

"I can't help that," answered Tommy the just. "If they ask my opinion, I must give them the truth. I thought you were fond of the truth, Grizel."

To that she could only wring her hands and say nothing; but it had never struck her that the truth could be so bitter.

And now he was giving his opinion at Mrs. McLean's party, and they were all against him, except, in a measure, Elspeth's bachelor, who said cheerily, "We should all have done it if we had been in Captain Ure's place; I would have done it myself, Miss Elspeth, though not fond of the water." He addressed all single ladies by their Christian name with a Miss in front of it. This is the mark of the confirmed bachelor, and comes upon him at one-and-twenty.

"I could not have done it," Grizel replied decisively, though she was much the bravest person present, and he explained that he meant the men only. His name was James Bonthron; let us call him Mr. James.

"Men are so brave!" she responded, with her eyes on Tommy, and he received the stab in silence. Had the blood spouted from the wound, it would have been an additional gratification to him. Tommy was like those superb characters of romance who bare their breast to the enemy and say, "Strike!"

"Well, well," Mr. Cathro observed, "none of us was on the spot, and so we had no opportunity of showing our heroism. But you were near by, Mr. Sandys, and if you had fished up the water that day, instead of down, you might have been called upon. I wonder what you would have done?"

Yes, Tommy was exasperating to him still as

THE TEA-PARTY

in the long ago, and Cathro said this maliciously, yet feeling that he did a risky thing, so convinced was he by old experience that you were getting in the way of a road-machine when you opposed Thomas Sandys.

"I wonder," Tommy replied quietly.

The answer made a poor impression, and Cathro longed to go on. "But he was always most dangerous when he was quiet," he reflected uneasily, and checked himself in sheer funk.

Mr. Gloag came, as he thought, to Tommy's defence. "If Mr. Sandys questions," he said heavily, "whether courage would have been vouchsafed to him at that trying hour, it is right and fitting that he should admit it with Christian humility."

"Quite so, quite so," Mr. James agreed, with heartiness. He had begun to look solemn at the word "vouchsafed."

"For we are differently gifted," continued Mr. Gloag, now addressing his congregation. "To some is given courage, to some learning, to some grace. Each has his strong point," he ended abruptly, and tucked reverently into the jam, which seemed to be his.

"If he would not have risked his life to save the boy," Elspeth interposed hotly, "it would have been because he was thinking of me."

"I should like to believe that thought of you would have checked me," Tommy said.

"I am sure it would," said Grizel.

Mr. Cathro was rubbing his hands together covertly, yet half wishing he could take her aside and whisper: "Be canny; it's grand to hear you, but be canny; he is looking most extraordinar meek, and unless he has cast his skin since he was a laddie, it's not chancey to meddle with him when he is meek."

The doctor also noticed that Grizel was pressing Tommy too hard, and though he did not like the man, he was surprised — he had always thought her so fair-minded.

"For my part," he said, "I don't admire the unknown half so much for what he did as for his behaviour afterwards. To risk his life was something, but to disappear quietly without taking any credit for it was finer and I should say much more difficult."

"I think it was sweet of him," Grizel said.

"I don't see it," said Tommy, and the silence that followed should have been unpleasant to him; but he went on calmly: "Doubtless it was a mere impulse that made him jump into the pool, and impulse is not courage." He was quoting Grizel now, you observe, and though he did not look at her, he knew her eyes were fixed on him reproachfully. "And so," he concluded, "I suppose Captain Ure knew he had done no great thing, and preferred to avoid exaggerated applause."

THE TEA-PARTY

Even Elspeth was troubled; but she must defend her dear brother. "He would have avoided it himself," she explained quickly. "He dislikes praise so much that he does not understand how sweet it is to smaller people."

This made Tommy wince. He was always distressed when timid Elspeth blurted out things of this sort in company, and not the least of his merits was that he usually forbore from chiding her for it afterwards, so reluctant was he to hurt her. In a world where there were no women except Elspeths, Tommy would have been a saint. He saw the doctor smiling now, and at once his annoyance with her changed to wrath against him for daring to smile at little Elspeth. She saw the smile, too, and blushed; but she was not angry: she knew that the people who smiled at her liked her, and that no one smiled so much at her as Dr. Gemmell.

The Dominie said fearfully: "I have no doubt that explains it, Miss Sandys. Even as a boy I remember your brother had a horror of vulgar applause."

"Now," he said to himself, "he will rise up and smite me." But no; Tommy replied quietly;

"I am afraid that was not my character, Mr. Cathro; but I hope I have changed since then, and that I could pull a boy out of the water without wanting to be extolled for it."

That he could say such things before her was terrible to Grizel. It was perhaps conceivable that he might pull the boy out of the water, as he so ungenerously expressed it; but that he could refrain from basking in the glory thereof, that, she knew, was quite impossible. Her eyes begged him to take back those shameful words, but he bravely declined; not even to please Grizel could he pretend that what was not was. No more sentiment for T. Sandys.

"The spirit has all gone out of him; what am I afraid of?" reflected the Dominie, and he rose suddenly to make a speech, tea-cup in hand. "Cathro, Cathro, you tattie-doolie, you are riding to destruction," said a warning voice within him, but against his better judgment he stifled it and began. He begged to propose the health of Captain Ure. He was sure they would all join with him cordially in drinking it, including Mr. Sandys, who unfortunately differed from them in his estimation of the hero; that was only, however, as had been conclusively shown, because he was a hero himself, and so could make light of heroic deeds — with other sly hits at Mr. Sandys. But when all the others rose to drink the toast, Tommy remained seated. The Dominie coughed.

"Perhaps Mr. Sandys means to reply," Grizel suggested icily. And it was at this uncomfortable moment that Christina appeared suddenly, and in

THE TEA-PARTY

a state of suppressed excitement requested her mistress to speak with her behind the door. All the knowing ones were aware that something terrible must have happened in the kitchen. Miss Sophia thought it might be the china tea-pot. She smiled reassuringly to signify that, whatever it was, she would help Mrs. McLean through, and so did Mr. James. He was a perfect lady.

How dramatic it all was, as Ailie said frequently afterwards. She was back in a moment, with her hand on her heart. "Mr. Sandys," were her astounding words, "a lady wants to see you."

Tommy rose in surprise, as did several of the others.

"Was it really you?" Ailie cried. "She says it was you!"

"I don't understand, Mrs. McLean," he answered; "I have done nothing."

"But she says — and she is at the door!"

All eyes turned on the door so longingly that it opened under their pressure, and a boy who had been at the keyhole stumbled forward.

"That's him!" he announced, pointing a stern finger at Mr. Sandys.

"But he says he did not do it," Ailie said.

"He's a liar," said the boy.

His manner was that of the police, and it had come so sharply upon Tommy that he looked not unlike a detected criminal.

Most of them thought he was being accused of something vile, and the Dominie demanded, with a light heart, "Who is the woman?" while Mr. James had a pleasant feeling that the ladies should be requested to retire. But just then the woman came in, and she was much older than they had expected.

"That's him, granny," the boy said, still severely; "that's the man as saved my life at the Slugs." And then, when the truth was dawning on them all, and there were exclamations of wonder, a pretty scene suddenly presented itself, for the old lady, who had entered with the timidest courtesy, slipped down on her knees before Tommy and kissed his hand. That young rascal of a boy was all she had.

They were all moved by her simplicity, but none quite so much as Tommy. He gulped with genuine emotion, and saw her through a maze of beautiful thoughts that delayed all sense of triumph and even made him forget, for a little while, to wonder what Grizel was thinking of him now. As the old lady poured out her thanks tremblingly, he was excitedly planning her future. He was a poor man, but she was to be brought by him into Thrums to a little cottage overgrown with roses. No more hard work for these dear old hands. She could sell scones, perhaps. She should have a cow. He would send the boy to college and

THE TEA-PARTY

make a minister of him; she should yet hear her grandson preach in the church to which as a boy——

But here the old lady somewhat imperilled the picture by rising actively and dumping upon the table the contents of the bag — a fowl for Tommy.

She was as poor an old lady as ever put a halfpenny into the church plate on Sundays; but that she should present a hen to the preserver of her grandson, her mind had been made up from the moment she had reason to think she could find him, and it was to be the finest hen in all the country round. She was an old lady of infinite spirit, and daily, dragging the boy with her lest he again went a-fishing, she trudged to farms near and far to examine and feel their hens. She was a brittle old lady who creaked as she walked, and cracked like a whin-pod in the heat, but she did her dozen miles or more a day, and passed all the fowls in review, and could not be deceived by the craftiest of farmers' wives; and in the tail of the day she became possessor, and did herself thraw the neck of the stoutest and toughest hen that ever entered a linen bag head foremost. By this time the boy had given way in the legs, and hence the railway journey, its cost defrayed by admiring friends.

With careful handling he should get a week out of her gift, she explained complacently, besides two makes of broth; and she and the boy looked as if they would like dearly to sit opposite Tommy during those seven days and watch him gorging.

If you look at the matter aright it was a handsomer present than many a tiara, but if you are of the same stuff as Mr. James it was only a hen. Mr. James tittered, and one or two others made ready to titter. It was a moment to try Tommy, for there are doubtless heroes as gallant as he who do not know how to receive a present of a hen. Grizel, who had been holding back, moved a little nearer. If he hurt that sweet old woman's feelings, she could never forgive him — never!

He heard the titter, and ridicule was terrible to him; but he also knew why Grizel had come closer, and what she wanted of him. Our Tommy, in short, had emerged from his emotion, and once more knew what was what. It was not his fault that he stood revealed a hero: the little gods had done it; therefore let him do credit to the chosen of the little gods. The way he took that old lady's wrinkled hand, and bowed over it, and thanked her, was an ode to manhood. Everyone was touched. Those who had been about to titter wondered what on earth Mr. James had seen to titter at, and Grizel almost clapped her hands with joy; she would have done it altogether had not Tommy just then made the mistake of looking at

THE TEA-PARTY

her for approval. She fell back, and, intoxicated with himself, he thought it was because her heart was too full for utterance. Tommy was now splendid, and described the affair at the Slugs with an adorable modesty.

"I assure you, it was a much smaller thing to do than you imagine; it was all over in a few minutes; I knew that in your good nature you would make too much of it, and so—foolishly, I can see now—I tried to keep it from you. As for the name Captain Ure, it was an invention of that humourous dog, Corp."

And so on, with the most considerate remarks when they insisted on shaking hands with him: "I beseech you, don't apologize to me; I see clearly that the fault was entirely my own. Had I been in your place, Mr. James, I should have behaved precisely as you have done, and had you been at the Slugs you would have jumped in as I did. Mr. Cathro, you pain me by holding back; I assure you I esteem my old Dominie more than ever for the way in which you stuck up for Captain Ure, though you must see why I could not drink that gentleman's health."

And Mr. Cathro made the best of it, wringing Tommy's hand effusively, while muttering, "Fool, donnard stirk, gowk!" He was addressing himself and any other person who might be so presumptuous as to try to get the better of Thomas

Sandys. Cathro never tried it again. Had Tommy died that week his old Dominie would have been very chary of what he said at the funeral.

They were in the garden now, the gentlemen without their hats. "Have you made your peace with him?" Cathro asked Grizel, in a cautious voice. "He is a devil's buckie, and I advise you to follow my example, Miss McQueen, and capitulate. I have always found him reasonable so long as you bend the knee to him."

"I am not his enemy," replied Grizel, loftily, "and if he has done a noble thing I am proud of him and will tell him so."

"I would tell him so," said the Dominie, "whether he had done it or not."

"Do you mean," she asked indignantly, "that you think he did not do it?"

"No, no, no," he answered hurriedly; "for mercy's sake, don't tell him I think that." And then, as Tommy was out of ear-shot: "But I see there is no necessity for my warning you against standing in his way again, Miss McQueen, for you are up in arms for him now."

"I admire brave men," she replied, "and he is one, is he not?"

"You'll find him reasonable," said the Dominie, drily.

But though it was thus that she defended

THE TEA-PARTY

Tommy when others hinted doubts, she had not yet said she was proud of him to the man who wanted most to hear it. For one brief moment Grizel had exulted on learning that he and Captain Ure were one, and then suddenly, to all the emotions now running within her, a voice seemed to cry, "Halt!" and she fell to watching sharply the doer of noble deeds. Her eyes were not wistful, nor were they contemptuous, but had Tommy been less elated with himself he might have seen that they were puzzled and suspicious. To mistrust him in face of such evidence seemed half a shame; she was indignant with herself even while she did it; but she could not help doing it, the truth about Tommy was such a vital thing to Grizel. She had known him so well, too well, up to a minute ago, and this was not the man she had known.

How unfair she was to Tommy while she watched! When the old lady was on her knees thanking him, and every other lady was impressed by the feeling he showed, it seemed to Grizel that he was again in the arms of some such absurd sentiment as had mastered him in the Den. When he behaved so charmingly about the gift she was almost sure he looked at her as he had looked in the old days before striding his legs and screaming out, "Oh, am I not a wonder? I see by your face that you think me a wonder!" All the time he was so considerately putting those who had misjudged him at their ease she believed he did it considerately that they might say to each other, "How considerate he is!" When she misread Tommy in such comparative trifles as these, is it to be wondered that she went into the garden still tortured by a doubt about the essential? It was nothing less than torture to her; when you discover what is in her mind, Tommy, you may console yourself with that.

He discovered what was in her mind as Mr. Cathro left her. She felt shy, he thought, of coming to him after what had taken place, and, with the generous intention of showing that she was forgiven, he crossed good-naturedly to her.

"You were very severe, Grizel," he said, "but don't let that distress you for a moment; it served me right for not telling the truth at once."

She did not flinch. "Do we know the truth now?" she asked, looking at him steadfastly. "I don't want to hurt you—you know that; but please tell me, did you really do it? I mean, did you do it in the way we have been led to suppose?"

It was a great shock to Tommy. He had not forgotten his vows to change his nature, and had she been sympathetic now he would have confessed to her the real reason of his silence. He wanted boyishly to tell her, though of course without mention of the glove; but her words hardened him.

THE TEA-PARTY

"Grizel!" he cried reproachfully, and then in a husky voice: "Can you really think so badly of me as that?"

"I don't know what to think," she answered, pressing her hands together. "I know you are very clever."

He bowed slightly.

"Did you?" she asked again. She was no longer chiding herself for being over-careful; she must know the truth.

He was silent for a moment. Then, "Grizel," he said, "I am about to pain you very much, but you give me no option. I did do it precisely as you have heard. And may God forgive you for doubting me," he added with a quiver, "as freely as I do."

You will scarcely believe this, but a few minutes afterwards, Grizel having been the first to leave, he saw her from the garden going, not home, but in the direction of Corp's house, obviously to ask him whether Tommy had done it. Tommy guessed her intention at once, and he laughed a bitter ho-ho-ha, and wiped her from his memory.

"Farewell, woman; I am done with you," are the terrible words you may conceive Tommy saying. Next moment, however, he was hurriedly bidding his hostess good-night, could not even wait for Elspeth, clapped his hat on his head, and was off after Grizel. It had suddenly struck him that, now the rest of the story was out, Corp might tell her about the glove. Suppose Gavinia showed it to her!

Sometimes he had kissed that glove passionately, sometimes pressed his lips upon it with the long tenderness that is less intoxicating but makes you a better man; but now, for the first time, he asked himself bluntly why he had done those things, with the result that he was striding to Corp's house. It was not only for his own sake that he hurried; let us do him that justice. It was chiefly to save Grizel the pain of thinking that he whom she had been flouting loved her, as she must think if she heard the story of the glove. That it could be nothing but pain to her he was boyishly certain, for assuredly this scornful girl wanted none of his love. And though she was scornful, she was still the dear companion of his boyhood. Tommy was honestly anxious to save Grizel the pain of thinking that she had flouted a man who loved her.

He took a different road from hers, but, to his annoyance, they met at Couthie's corner. He would have passed her with a distant bow, but she would have none of that.

"You have followed me," said Grizel, with the hateful directness that was no part of Tommy's character.

THE TEA-PARTY

"Grizel!"

"You followed me to see whether I was going to question Corp. You were afraid he would tell me what really happened. You wanted to see him first to tell him what to say."

"Really, Grizel ——"

"Is it not true?"

There are no questions so offensive to the artistic nature as those that demand a Yes or No for answer. "It is useless for me to say it is not true," he replied haughtily, "for you won't believe me."

"Say it and I shall believe you," said she.

Tommy tried standing on the other foot, but it was no help. "I presume I may have reasons for wanting to see Corp that you are unacquainted with," he said.

"Oh, I am sure of it!" replied Grizel, scornfully. She had been hoping until now, but there was no more hope left in her.

"May I ask what it is that my oldest friend accuses me of? Perhaps you don't even believe that I was Captain Ure?"

"I am no longer sure of it."

"How you read me, Grizel! I could hoodwink the others, but never you. I suppose it is because you have such an eye for the worst in anyone."

It was not the first time he had said something

of this kind to her; for he knew that she suspected herself of being too ready to find blemishes in others, to the neglect of their better qualities, and that this made her uneasy and also very sensitive to the charge. To-day, however, her own imperfections did not matter to her; she was as nothing to herself just now, and scarcely felt his insinuations.

"I think you were Captain Ure," she said slowly, "and I think you did it, but not as the boy imagines."

"You may be quite sure," he replied, "that I would not have done it had there been the least risk. That, I flatter myself, is how you reason it out."

"It does not explain," she said, "why you kept the matter secret."

"Thank you, Grizel! Well, at least I have not boasted of it."

"No, and that is what makes me ——" She paused.

"Go on," said he, "though I can guess what agreeable thing you were going to say."

But she said something else: "You may have noticed that I took the boy aside and questioned him privately."

"I little thought then, Grizel, that you suspected me of being an impostor."

She clenched her hands again; it was all so hard to say, and yet she must say it! "I did not. I

THE TEA-PARTY

saw he believed his story. I was asking him whether you had planned his coming with it to Mrs. McLean's house at that dramatic moment."

"You actually thought me capable of that!"

"It makes me horrid to myself," she replied wofully, "but if I thought you had done that I could more readily believe the rest."

"Very well, Grizel," he said, "go on thinking the worst of me; I would not deprive you of that pleasure if I could."

"Oh, cruel, cruel!" she could have replied; "you know it is no pleasure; you know it is a great pain." But she did not speak.

"I have already told you that the boy's story is true," he said, "and now you ask me why I did not shout it from the housetops myself. Perhaps it was for your sake, Grizel; perhaps it was to save you the distress of knowing that in a momentary impulse I could so far forget myself as to act the part of a man."

She pressed her hands more tightly. "I may be wronging you," she answered; "I should love to think so; but—you have something you want to say to Corp before I see him."

"Not at all," Tommy said; "if you still want to see Corp, let us go together."

She hesitated, but she knew how clever he was. "I prefer to go alone," she replied. "Forgive me if I ask you to turn back."

"Don't go," he entreated her. "Grizel, I give you my word of honour it is to save you acute pain that I want to see Corp first."

She smiled wanly at that, for though, as we know, it was true, she misunderstood him. He had to let her go on alone.

CHAPTER XII

IN WHICH A COMEDIAN CHALLENGES TRAGEDY TO BOWLS

WHEN Grizel opened the door of Corp's house she found husband and wife at home, the baby in his father's arms; what is more, Gavinia was looking on smiling and saying, "You bonny litlin, you're windy to have him dandling you; and no wonder, for he's a father to be proud o'." Corp was accepting it all with a complacent smirk. Oh, agreeable change since last we were in this house! oh, happy picture of domestic bliss! oh — but no, these are not the words; what we meant to say was, "Gavinia, you limmer, so you have got the better of that man of yours at last."

How had she contrived it? We have seen her escorting the old lady to the Dovecot, Corp skulking behind. Our next peep at them shows Gavinia back at her house, Corp peering through the window and wondering whether he dare venture in. Gavinia was still bothered, for though she knew now the story of Tommy's heroism, there was no glove in it, and it was the glove that maddened her.

"No, I ken nothing about a glove," the old lady had assured her.

"Not a sylup was said about a glove," maintained Christina, who had given her a highly coloured narrative of what took place in Mrs. McLean's parlour.

"And yet there's a glove in't as sure as there's a quirk in't," Gavinia kept muttering to herself. She rose to have another look at the hoddy-place in which she had concealed the glove from her husband, and as she did so she caught sight of him at the window. He bobbed at once, but she hastened to the door to scarify him. The clock had given only two ticks when she was upon him, but in that time she had completely changed her plan of action. She welcomed him with smiles of pride. Thus is the nimbleness of women's wit measured once and for all. They need two seconds if they are to do the thing comfortably.

"Never to have telled me, and you behaved so grandly!" she cried, with adoring glances that were as a carpet on which he strode pompously into the house.

"It wasna me that did it; it was him," said Corp, and even then he feared that he had told too much. "I kenna what you're speaking about," he added loyally.

A COMEDIAN CHALLENGES TRAGEDY

"Corp," she answered, "you needna be so canny, for the laddie is in the town, and Mr. Sandys has confessed all."

"The whole o't?"

"Every risson."

"About the glove, too?"

"Glove and all," said wicked Gavinia, and she continued to feast her eyes so admiringly on her deceived husband that he passed quickly from the gratified to the dictatorial.

"Let this be a lesson to you, woman," he said sternly; and Gavinia intimated with humility that she hoped to profit by it.

"Having got the glove in so solemn a way," he went on, "it would have been ill done of me to blab to you about it. Do you see that now, woman?"

She said it was as clear as day to her. "And a solemn way it was," she added, and then waited eagerly.

"My opinion," continued Corp, lowering his voice as if this were not matter for the child, "is that it's a love-token frae some London woman."

"Behear's!" cried Gavinia.

"Else what," he asked, "would make him hand it to me so solemn-like, and tell me to pass it on to her if he was drowned? I didna think o' that at the time, but it has come to me, Gavinia; it has come."

This was a mouthful indeed to Gavinia. So the glove was the property of Mr. Sandys, and he was in love with a London lady, and — no, this is too slow for Gavinia; she saw these things in passing, as one who jumps from the top of a house may have lightning glimpses through many windows on the way down. What she jumped to was the vital question, Who was the woman?

But she was too cunning to ask a leading question.

"Ay, she's his lady-love," she said, controlling herself, "but I forget her name. It was a very wise-like thing o' you to speir the woman's name."

"But I didna."

"You didna!"

"He was in the water in a klink."

Had Gavinia been in Corp's place she would have had the name out of Tommy, water or no water; but she did not tell her husband what she thought of him.

"Ay, of course," she said pleasantly. "It was after you helped him out that he telled you her name."

"Did he say he telled me her name?"

"He did."

"Well, then, I've fair forgot it."

Instead of boxing his ears she begged him to reflect. Result of reflection, that if the name had

A COMEDIAN CHALLENGES TRAGEDY

been mentioned to Corp, which he doubted, it began with M.

Was it Mary?

That was the name.

Or was it Martha?

It had a taste of Martha about it.

It was not Margaret?

It might have been Margaret.

Or Matilda?

It was fell like Matilda.

And so on. "But wi' a' your wheedling," Corp reminded his wife, bantering her from aloft, "you couldna get a scraping out o' me till I was free to speak."

He thought it a good opportunity for showing Gavinia her place once and for all. "In small matters," he said, "I gie you your ain way, for though you may be wrang, thinks I to mysel', 'She's but a woman'; but in important things, Gavinia, if I humoured you I would spoil you, so let this be a telling to you that there's no diddling a determined man"; to which she replied by informing the baby that he had a father to be proud of.

A father to be proud of! They were the words heard by Grizel as she entered. She also saw Gavinia looking admiringly at her man, and in that doleful moment she thought she understood all. It was Corp who had done it, and Tommy had been the looker-on. He had sought to keep the incident secret because, though he was in it, the glory had been won by another (oh, how base!), and now, profiting by the boy's mistake, he was swaggering in that other's clothes (oh, baser still!). Everything was revealed to her in a flash, and she stooped over the baby to hide a sudden tear. She did not want to hear any more.

The baby cried. Babies are aware that they can't do very much; but all of them who knew Grizel were almost contemptuously confident of their power over her, and when this one saw (they are very sharp) that in his presence she could actually think of something else, he was so hurt that he cried.

Was she to be blamed for thinking so meanly of Tommy? You can blame her with that tear in her eye if you choose; but I can think only of the gladness that came afterwards when she knew she had been unjust to him. "Thank you, thank you, thank you!" the bird sang to its Creator when the sun came out after rain, and it was Grizel's song as she listened to Corp's story of heroic Tommy. There was no room in her exultant heart for remorse. It would have shown littleness to be able to think of herself at all when she could think so gloriously of him. She was more than beautiful now; she was radiant; and it was because Tommy was the man she wanted him to be. As those who are cold hold out their hands to the fire did she warm her heart at what Corp had to tell, and the great joy that was

A COMEDIAN CHALLENGES TRAGEDY

lit within her made her radiant. Now the baby was in her lap, smiling back to her. He thought he had done it all. "So you thought you could resist me!" the baby crowed.

The glove had not been mentioned yet. "The sweetest thing of all to me," Grizel said, "is that he did not want me to hear the story from you, Corp, because he knew you would sing his praise so loudly."

"I'm thinking," said Gavinia, archly, "he had another reason for no wanting you to question Corp. Maybe he didna want you to ken about the London lady and her glove. Will you tell her, man, or will I?"

They told her together, and what had been conjectures were now put forward as facts. Tommy had certainly said a London lady, and as certainly he had given her name, but what it was Corp could not remember. But "Give her this and tell her it never left my heart"—he could swear to these words.

"And no words could be stronger," Gavinia said triumphantly. She produced the glove, and was about to take off its paper wrapping when Grizel stopped her.

"We have no right, Gavinia."

"I suppose we hinna, and I'm thinking the pocket it came out o' is feeling gey toom without it. Will you take it back to him?"

TOMMY AND GRIZEL

"It was very wrong of you to keep it," Grizel answered, "but I can't take it to him, for I see now that his reason for wanting me not to come here was to prevent my hearing about it. I am sorry you told me. Corp must take it back." But when she saw it being crushed in Corp's rough hand, a pity for the helpless glove came over her. She said: "After all, I do know about it, so I can't pretend to him that I don't. I will give it to him, Corp"; and she put the little package in her pocket with a brave smile.

Do you think the radiance had gone from her face now? Do you think the joy that had been lit in her heart was dead? Oh, no, no! Grizel had never asked that Tommy should love her; she had asked only that he should be a fine man. She did not ask it for herself, only for him. She could not think of herself now, only of him. She did not think she loved him. She thought a woman should not love any man until she knew he wanted her to love him.

But if Tommy had wanted it she would have been very glad. She knew, oh, she knew so well, that she could have helped him best. Many a noble woman has known it as she stood aside.

In the meantime Tommy had gone home in several states of mind — reckless, humble, sentimental, most practical, defiant, apprehensive. At one moment he was crying, "Now, Grizel, now,

A COMEDIAN CHALLENGES TRAGEDY

when it is too late, you will see what you have lost." At the next he quaked and implored the gods to help him out of his predicament. It was apprehension that, on the whole, played most of the tunes, for he was by no means sure that Grizel would not look upon the affair of the glove as an offer of his hand, and accept him. They would show her the glove, and she would, of course, know it to be her own. "Give her this and tell her it never left my heart." The words thumped within him now. How was Grizel to understand that he had meant nothing in particular by them?

I wonder if you misread him so utterly as to believe that he thought himself something of a prize? That is a vulgar way of looking at things of which our fastidious Tommy was incapable. As much as Grizel herself, he loathed the notion that women have a thirsty eye on man; when he saw them cheapening themselves before the sex that should hold them beyond price, he turned his head and would not let his mind dwell on the subject. He was a sort of gentleman, was Tommy. And he knew Grizel so well that had all the other women in the world been of this kind, it would not have persuaded him that there was a drop of such blood in her.

Then, if he feared that she was willing to be his, it must have been because he thought she loved him? Not a bit of it. As already stated, he thought he had abundant reason to think otherwise. It was remorse that he feared might bring her to his feet, the discovery that while she had been gibing at him he had been a heroic figure, suffering in silence, eating his heart for love of her. Undoubtedly that was how Grizel must see things now; he must seem to her to be an angel rather than a mere man; and in sheer remorse she might cry, "I am yours!" Vain though Tommy was, the picture gave him not a moment's pleasure. Alarm was what he felt.

Of course he was exaggerating Grizel's feelings. She had too much self-respect and too little sentiment to be willing to marry any man because she had unintentionally wronged him. But this was how Tommy would have acted had he happened to be a lady. Remorse, pity, no one was so good at them as Tommy.

In his perturbation he was also good at maidenly reserve. He felt strongly that the proper course for Grizel was not to refer to the glove — to treat that incident as closed, unless he chose to reopen it. This was so obviously the correct procedure that he seemed to see her adopting it like a sensible girl, and relief would have come to him had he not remembered that Grizel usually took her own way, and that it was seldom his way.

There were other ways of escape. For instance, if she would only let him love her hopelessly.

A COMEDIAN CHALLENGES TRAGEDY

Oh, Grizel had but to tell him there was no hope, and then how finely he would behave! It would bring out all that was best in him. He saw himself passing through life as her very perfect knight. "Is there no hope for me?" He heard himself begging for hope, and he heard also her firm answer: "None!" How he had always admired the outspokenness of Grizel. Her "None!" was as splendidly decisive as of yore.

The conversation thus begun ran on in him, Tommy doing the speaking for both (though his lips never moved), and feeling the scene as vividly as if Grizel had really been present and Elspeth was not. Elspeth was sitting opposite him.

"At least let me wait, Grizel," he implored. "I don't care for how long; fix a time yourself, and I shall keep to it, and I promise never to speak one word of love to you until that time comes, and then if you bid me go I shall go. Give me something to live for. It binds you to nothing, and oh, it would make such a difference to me."

Then Grizel seemed to reply gently, but with the firmness he adored: "I know I cannot change, and it would be mistaken kindness to do as you suggest. No, I can give you no hope; but though I can never marry you, I will watch your future with warm regard, for you have to-day paid me the highest compliment a man can pay a woman."

(How charmingly it was all working out!)

TOMMY AND GRIZEL

Tommy bowed with dignity and touched her hand with his lips. What is it they do next in Pym and even more expensive authors? Oh, yes! "If at any time in your life, dear Grizel," he said, "you are in need of a friend, I hope you will turn first to me. It does not matter where your message reaches me, I will come to you without delay."

In his enthusiasm he saw the letter being delivered to him in Central Africa, and immediately he wheeled round on his way to Thrums.

"There is one other little request I should like to make of you," he said huskily. "Perhaps I ask too much, but it is this: may I keep your glove?"

She nodded her head; she was so touched that she could scarcely trust herself to speak. "But you will soon get over this," she said at last; "another glove will take the place of mine; the time will come when you will be glad that I said I could not marry you."

"Grizel!" he cried in agony. He was so carried away by his feelings that he said the word aloud.

"Where?" asked Elspeth, looking at the window.

"Was it not she who passed just now?" he replied promptly; and they were still discussing his mistake when Grizel did pass, but only to stop at the door. She came in.

A COMEDIAN CHALLENGES TRAGEDY

"My brother must have the second sight," declared Elspeth, gaily, "for he saw you coming before you came"; and she told what had happened, while Grizel looked happily at Tommy, and Tommy looked apprehensively at her. Grizel, he might have seen, was not wearing the tragic face of sacrifice; it was a face shining with gladness, a girl still too happy in his nobility to think remorsefully of her own misdeeds. To let him know that she was proud of him, that was what she had come for chiefly, and she was even glad that Elspeth was there to hear. It was an excuse to her to repeat Corp's story, and she told it with defiant looks at Tommy that said, "You are so modest, you want to stop me, but Elspeth will listen; it is nearly as sweet to Elspeth as it is to me, and I shall tell her every word, yes, and tell her a great deal of it twice."

It was not modesty which made Tommy so anxious that she should think less of him, but naturally it had that appearance. The most heroic fellows, I am told, can endure being extolled by pretty girls, but here seemed to be one who could not stand it.

"You need not think it is of you we are proud," she assured him light-heartedly; "it is really of ourselves. I am proud of being your friend. To-morrow, when I hear the town ringing your praises, I shall not say, 'Yes, isn't he wonderful?'

I shall say, 'Talk of me; I, too, am an object of interest, for I am his friend.'"

"I have often been pointed out as his sister," said Elspeth, complacently.

"He did not choose his sister," replied Grizel, "but he chose his friends."

For a time he could suck no sweetness from it. She avoided the glove, he was sure, only because of Elspeth's presence. But anon there arrived to cheer him a fond hope that she had not heard of it, and as this became conviction, exit the Tommy who could not abide himself, and enter another who was highly charmed therewith. Tommy had a notion that certain whimsical little gods protected him in return for the sport he gave them, and he often kissed his hand to them when they came to the rescue. He would have liked to kiss it now, but gave a grateful glance instead to the corner in the ceiling where they sat chuckling at him. Grizel admired him at last. Tra, la, la! What a dear girl she was! Into his manner there crept a certain masterfulness, and instead of resisting it she beamed. Rum-ti-tum!

"If you want to spoil me," he said lazily, "you will bring me that footstool to rest my heroic feet upon."

She smiled and brought it. She even brought a cushion for his heroic head. Adoring little thing that she was, he must be good to her.

A COMEDIAN CHALLENGES TRAGEDY

He was now looking forward eagerly to walking home with her. I can't tell you how delicious he meant to be. When she said she must go, he skipped upstairs for his hat, and wafted the gods their kiss. But it was always the unexpected that lay in wait for Tommy. He and she were no sooner out of the house than Grizel said, " I did not mention the glove, as I was not sure whether Elspeth knew of it."

He had turned stone-cold.

"Corp and Gavinia told me," she went on quietly, "before I had time to stop them. Of course I should have preferred not to know until I heard it from yourself."

Oh, how cold he was!

"But as I do know, I want to tell you that it makes me very happy."

They had stopped, for his legs would carry him no farther. "Get us out of this," every bit of him was crying, but not one word could Tommy say.

"I knew you would want to have it again," Grizel said brightly, producing the little parcel from her pocket, "so I brought it to you."

The frozen man took it and held it passively in his hand. His gods had flown away.

No, they were actually giving him another chance. What was this Grizel was saying? "I have not looked at it, for to take it out of its wrapping would have been profanation. Corp told me she was a London girl; but I know nothing more, not even her name. You are not angry with me for speaking of her, are you? Surely I may wish you and her great happiness."

He was saved. The breath came back quickly to him. He filled like a released ball. Had ever a heart better right to expand? Grizel, looking so bright and pleased, had snatched him from the Slugs. Surely you will be nice to your preserver, Tommy. You will not be less grateful than a country boy?

Ah me! not even yet have we plumed his vanity. But we are to do it now. He could not have believed it of himself, but in the midst of his rejoicings he grew bitter, and for no better reason than that Grizel's face was bright.

"I am glad," he said quite stiffly, "that it is such pleasant news to you."

His tone surprised her; but she was in a humble mood, and answered, without being offended: "It is sweet news to me. How could you think otherwise?"

So it was sweet to her to think that he was another's! He who had been modestly flattering himself a few moments ago that he must take care not to go too far with this admiring little girl! O woman, woman, how difficult it is to know you, and how often, when we think we know you at last, have we to begin again at the beginning! He

A COMEDIAN CHALLENGES TRAGEDY

had never asked an enduring love from her; but surely, after all that had passed between them, he had a right to expect a little more than this. Was it maidenly to bring the glove and hand it to him without a tremor? If she could do no more, she might at least have turned a little pale when Corp told her of it, and then have walked quietly away. Next day she could have referred to it, with just the slightest break in her voice. But to come straight to him, looking delighted ——

"And, after all, I am entitled to know first," Grizel said, "for I am your oldest friend."

Friend! He could not help repeating the word with bitter emphasis. For her sake, as it seemed to him now, he had flung himself into the black waters of the Drumly. He had worn her glove upon his heart. It had been the world to him. And she could stand there and call herself his friend. The cup was full. Tommy nodded his head sorrowfully three times.

"So be it, Grizel," he said huskily; "so be it!" Sentiment could now carry him where it willed. The reins were broken.

"I don't understand."

Neither did he; but, "Why should you? What is it to you!" he cried wildly. "Better not to understand, for it might give you five minutes' pain, Grizel, a whole five minutes, and I should be sorry to give you that."

"What have I said! What have I done!"

"Nothing," he answered her, "nothing. You have been most exemplary; you have not even got any entertainment out of it. The thing never struck you as possible. It was too ludicrous!"

He laughed harshly at the package, which was still in his hand. "Poor little glove," he said; "and she did not even take the trouble to look at you. You might have looked at it, Grizel. I have looked at it a good deal. It meant something to me once upon a time when I was a vain fool. Take it and look at it before you fling it away. It will make you laugh."

Now she knew, and her arms rocked convulsively. Joy surged to her face, and she drove it back. She looked at him steadfastly over the collar of her jacket; she looked long, as if trying to be suspicious of him for the last time. Ah, Grizel, you are saying good-bye to your best friend!

As she looked at him thus there was a mournfulness in her brave face that went to Tommy's heart and almost made a man of him. It was as if he knew that she was doomed.

"Grizel," he cried, "don't look at me in that way!" And he would have taken the package from her, but she pressed it to her heart.

"Don't come with me," she said almost in a whisper, and went away.

He did not go back to the house. He wan-

A COMEDIAN CHALLENGES TRAGEDY

dered into the country, quite objectless when he was walking fastest, seeing nothing when he stood still and stared. Elation and dread were his companions. What elation whispered he could not yet believe; no, he could not believe it. While he listened he knew that he must be making up the words. By and by he found himself among the shadows of the Den. If he had loved Grizel he would have known that it was here she would come, to the sweet Den where he and she had played as children, the spot where she had loved him first. She had always loved him — always, always. He did not know what figure it was by the Cuttle Well until he was quite close to her. She was kissing the glove passionately, and on her eyes lay little wells of gladness.

CHAPTER XIII

LITTLE WELLS OF GLADNESS

It was dusk, and she had not seen him. In the silent Den he stood motionless within a few feet of her, so amazed to find that Grizel really loved him that for the moment self was blotted out of his mind. He remembered he was there only when he heard his heavy breathing, and then he tried to check it that he might steal away undiscovered. Divers emotions fought for the possession of him. He was in the meeting of many waters, each capable of whirling him where it chose, but two only imperious: the one the fierce joy of being loved; the other an agonizing remorse. He would fain have stolen away to think this tremendous thing over, but it tossed him forward. "Grizel," he said in a husky whisper, "Grizel!"

She did not start; she was scarcely surprised to hear his voice: she had been talking to him, and he had answered. Had he not been there she would still have heard him answer. She could not see him more clearly now than she had been seeing

LITTLE WELLS OF GLADNESS

him through those little wells of gladness. Her love for him was the whole of her. He came to her with the opening and the shutting of her eyes; he was the wind that bit her and the sun that nourished her; he was the lowliest object by the Cuttle Well, and he was the wings on which her thoughts soared to eternity. He could never leave her while her mortal frame endured.

When he whispered her name she turned her swimming eyes to him, and a strange birth had come into her face. Her eyes said so openly they were his, and her mouth said it was his, her whole being went out to him; in the radiance of her face could be read immortal designs: the maid kissing her farewell to innocence was there, and the reason why it must be, and the fate of the unborn; it was the first stirring for weal or woe of a movement that has no end on earth, but must roll on, growing lusty on beauty or dishonour till the crack of time. This birth which comes to every woman at that hour is God's gift to her in exchange for what He has taken away, and when He has given it He stands back and watches the man.

To this man she was a woman transformed. The new bloom upon her face entranced him. He knew what it meant. He was looking on the face of love at last, and it was love coming out smiling from its hiding-place because it thought it had heard him call. The artist in him who had done this thing was entranced, as if he had written an immortal page.

But the man was appalled. He knew that he had reached the critical moment in her life and his, and that if he took one step farther forward he could never again draw back. It would be comparatively easy to draw back now. To remain a free man he had but to tell her the truth; and he had a passionate desire to remain free. He heard the voices of his little gods screaming to him to draw back. But it could be done only at her expense, and it seemed to him that to tell this noble girl, who was waiting for him, that he did not need her, would be to spill for ever the happiness with which she overflowed, and sap the pride that had been the marrow of her during her twenty years of life. Not thus would Grizel have argued in his place; but he could not change his nature, and it was Sentimental Tommy, in an agony of remorse for having brought dear Grizel to this pass, who had to decide her future and his in the time you may take to walk up a garden path. Either her mistake must be righted now or kept hidden from her for ever. He was a sentimentalist, but in that hard moment he was trying to be a man. He took her in his arms and kissed her reverently, knowing that after this there could be no drawing back. In that act he gave himself loyally to her as a husband. He knew he was not worthy of

LITTLE WELLS OF GLADNESS

her, but he was determined to try to be a little less unworthy; and as he drew her to him a slight quiver went through her, so that for a second she seemed to be holding back — for a second only, and the quiver was the rustle of wings on which some part of the Grizel we have known so long was taking flight from her. Then she pressed close to him passionately, as if she grudged that pause. I love her more than ever, far more; but she is never again quite the Grizel we have known.

He was not unhappy; in the near hereafter he might be as miserable as the damned — the little gods were waiting to catch him alone and terrify him; but for the time, having sacrificed himself, Tommy was aglow with the passion he had inspired. He so loved the thing he had created that in his exultation he mistook it for her. He believed all he was saying. He looked at her long and adoringly, not, as he thought, because he adored her, but because it was thus that look should answer look; he pressed her wet eyes reverently because thus it was written in his delicious part; his heart throbbed with hers that they might beat in time. He did not love, but he was the perfect lover; he was the artist trying in a mad moment to be as well as to do.

Love was their theme; but how to know what was said when between lovers it is only the loose change of conversation that gets into words? The important matters cannot wait so slow a messenger; while the tongue is being charged with them, a look, a twitch of the mouth, a movement of a finger, transmits the story, and the words arrive, like Blücher, when the engagement is over.

With a sudden pretty gesture — ah, so like her mother's! — she held the glove to his lips. "It is sad because you have forgotten it."

"I have kissed it so often, Grizel, long before I thought I should ever kiss you!"

She pressed it to her innocent breast at that. And had he really done so? and which was the first time, and the second, and the third? Oh, dear glove, you know so much, and your partner lies at home in a drawer knowing nothing. Grizel felt sorry for the other glove. She whispered to Tommy as a terrible thing, "I think I love this glove even more than I love you — just a tiny bit more." She could not part with it. "It told me before you did," she explained, begging him to give it back to her.

"If you knew what it was to me in those unhappy days, Grizel!"

"I want it to tell me," she whispered.

And did he really love her? Yes, she knew he did. but how could he?

"Oh, Grizel, how could I help it!"

He had to say it, for it is the best answer; but he said it with a sigh, for it sounded like a quotation.

LITTLE WELLS OF GLADNESS

But how could she love him? I think her reply disappointed him.

"Because you wanted me to," she said, with shining eyes. It is probably the commonest reason why women love, and perhaps it is the best; but his vanity was wounded—he had expected to hear that he was possessed of an irresistible power.

"Not until I wanted you to?"

"I think I always wanted you to want me to," she replied, naïvely; "but I would never have let myself love you," she continued very seriously, "until I was sure you loved me."

"You could have helped it, Grizel!" He drew a blank face.

"I did help it," she answered. "I was always fighting the desire to love you,—I can see that plainly,—and I always won. I thought God had made a sort of compact with me that I should always be the kind of woman I wanted to be if I resisted the desire to love you until you loved me."

"But you always had the desire!" he said eagerly.

"Always, but it never won. You see, even you did not know of it. You thought I did not even like you! That was why you wanted to prevent Corp's telling me about the glove, was it not? You thought it would pain me only! Do you remember what you said: 'It is to save you acute pain that I want to see Corp first'?"

All that seemed so long ago to Tommy now!

"How could you think it would be a pain to me!" she cried.

"You concealed your feelings so well, Grizel."

"Did I not?" she said joyously. "Oh, I wanted to be so careful, and I was careful. That is why I am so happy now." Her face was glowing. She was full of odd, delightful fancies to-night. She kissed her hand to the gloaming; no, not to the gloaming — to the little hunted, anxious girl she had been.

"She is looking at us," she said. "She is standing behind that tree looking at us. She wanted so much to grow into a dear, good woman that she often comes and looks at me eagerly. Sometimes her face is so fearful! I think she was a little alarmed when she heard you were coming back."

"She never liked me, Grizel."

"Hush!" said Grizel, in a low voice. "She always liked you; she always thought you a wonder. But she would be distressed if she heard me telling you. She thought it would not be safe for you to know. I must tell him now, dearest, darlingest," she suddenly called out boldly to the little self she had been so quaintly fond of because there was no other to love her. "I must tell him everything now, for you are no longer your own. You are his."

"SHE IS STANDING BEHIND THAT TREE LOOKING AT US"

LITTLE WELLS OF GLADNESS

"She has gone away rocking her arms," she said to Tommy.

"No," he replied. "I can hear her. She is singing because you are so happy."

"She never knew how to sing."

"She has learned suddenly. Everybody can sing who has anything to sing about. And do you know what she said about your dear wet eyes, Grizel? She said they were just sweet. And do you know why she left us so suddenly? She ran home gleefully to stitch and dust and beat carpets, and get baths ready, and look after the affairs of everybody, which she is sure must be going to rack and ruin because she has been away for half an hour!"

At his words there sparkled in her face the fond delight with which a woman assures herself that the beloved one knows her little weaknesses, for she does not truly love unless she thirsts to have him understand the whole of her, and to love her in spite of the foibles and for them. If he does not love you a little for the foibles, madam, God help you from the day of the wedding.

But though Grizel was pleased, she was not to be cajoled. She wandered with him through the Den, stopping at the Lair, and the Queen's Bower, and many other places where the little girl used to watch Tommy suspiciously; and she called, half merrily, half plaintively: "Are you there, you foolish girl, and are you wringing your hands over me ? I believe you are jealous because I love him best."

"We have loved each other so long, she and I," she said apologetically to Tommy. "Ah," she said impulsively, when he seemed to be hurt, "don't you see it is because she doubts you that I am so sorry for the poor thing!"

"Dearest, darlingest," she called to the child she had been, "don't think that you can come to me when he is away, and whisper things against him to me. Do you think I will listen to your croakings, you poor, wet-faced thing!"

"You child!" said Tommy.

"Do you think me a child because I blow kisses to her?"

"Do you like me to think you one?" he replied.

"I like you to call me child," she said, "but not to think me one."

"Then I shall think you one," said he, triumphantly. He was so perfect an instrument for love to play upon that he let it play on and on, and listened in a fever of delight. How could Grizel have doubted Tommy? The god of love himself would have sworn that there were a score of arrows in him. He wanted to tell Elspeth and the others at once that he and Grizel were engaged. I am glad to remember that it was he who urged this, and Grizel who insisted on its being deferred. He even pretended to believe that Elspeth would exult in the news; but Grizel smiled at him for saying this to please her. She had never been a great friend of Elspeth's, they were so dissimilar; and she blamed herself for it now, and said she wanted to try to make Elspeth love her before they told her. Tommy begged her to let him tell his sister at once; but she remained obdurate, so anxious was she that her happiness, when revealed, should bring only happiness to others. There had not come to Grizel yet the longing to be recognized as his by the world. This love was so beautiful and precious to her that there was an added joy in sharing the dear secret with him alone; it was a live thing that might escape if she let anyone but him look between the fingers that held it.

The crowning glory of loving and being loved is that the pair make no real progress; however far they have advanced into the enchanted land during the day, they must start again from the frontier next morning. Last night they had dredged the lovers' lexicon for superlatives and not even blushed; to-day is that the heavens cracking or merely someone whispering "dear"? All this was very strange and wonderful to Grizel. She had never been so young in the days when she was a little girl.

"I can never be quite so happy again!" she had said, with a wistful smile, on the night of nights; but early morn, the time of the day that loves maidens best, retold her the delicious secret as it kissed her on the eyes, and her first impulse was to hurry to Tommy. When joy or sorrow came to her now, her first impulse was to hurry with it to him.

Was he still the same, quite the same? She, whom love had made a child of, asked it fearfully, as if to gaze upon him openly just at first might be blinding; and he pretended not to understand. "The same as what, Grizel?"

"Are you still — what I think you?"

"Ah, Grizel, not at all what you think me."

"But you do?"

"Coward! You are afraid to say the word. But I do!"

"You don't ask whether I do!"

"No."

"Why? Is it because you are so sure of me?"

He nodded, and she said it was cruel of him.

"You don't mean that, Grizel."

"Don't I?" She was delighted that he knew it.

"No; you mean that you like me to be sure of it."

"But I want to be sure of it myself."

"You are. That was why you asked me if I loved you. Had you not been sure of it you would not have asked."

"How clever you are!" she said gleefully, and

caressed a button of his velvet coat. "But you don't know what that means! It does not mean that I love you — not merely that."

"No; it means that you are glad I know you so well. It is an ecstasy to you, is it not, to feel that I know you so well?"

"It is sweet," she said. She asked curiously: "What did you do last night, after you left me? I can't guess, though I daresay you can guess what I did."

"You put the glove under your pillow, Grizel." (She had got the precious glove.)

"However could you guess!"

"It has often lain under my own."

"Oh!" said Grizel, breathless.

"Could you not guess even that?"

"I wanted to be sure. Did it do anything strange when you had it there?"

"I used to hear its heart beating."

"Yes, exactly! But this is still more remarkable. I put it away at last in my sweetest drawer, and when I woke in the morning it was under my pillow again. You could never have guessed that."

"Easily. It often did the same thing with me."

"Story-teller! But what did you do when you went home?"

He could not have answered that exhaustively, even if he would, for his actions had been as contradictory as his emotions. He had feared even while he exulted, and exulted when plunged deep in fears. There had been quite a procession of Tommies all through the night; one of them had been a very miserable man, and the only thing he had been sure of was that he must be true to Grizel. But in so far as he did answer he told the truth.

"I went for a stroll among the stars," he said. "I don't know when I got to bed. I have found a way of reaching the stars. I have to say only, 'Grizel loves me,' and I am there."

"Without me!"

"I took you with me."

"What did we see? What did we do?"

"You spoiled everything by thinking the stars were badly managed. You wanted to take the supreme control. They turned you out."

"And when we got back to earth?"

"Then I happened to catch sight of myself in a looking-glass, and I was scared. I did not see how you could possibly love me. A terror came over me that in the Den you must have mistaken me for someone else. It was a darkish night, you know."

"You are wanting me to say you are handsome."

"No, no; I am wanting you to say I am very, very handsome. Tell me you love me, Grizel, because I am beautiful."

LITTLE WELLS OF GLADNESS

"Perhaps," she replied, "I love you because your book is beautiful."

"Then good-bye for ever," he said sternly.

"Would not that please you?"

"It would break my heart."

"But I thought all authors——"

"It is the commonest mistake in the world. We are simple creatures, Grizel, and yearn to be loved for our face alone."

"But I do love the book," she said, when they became more serious, "because it is part of you."

"Rather that," he told her, "than that you should love me because I am part of it. But it is only a little part of me, Grizel; only the best part. It is Tommy on tiptoes. The other part, the part that does not deserve your love, is what needs it most."

"I am so glad!" she said eagerly. "I want to think you need me."

"How I need you!"

"Yes, I think you do—I am sure you do; and it makes me so happy."

"Ah," he said, "now I know why Grizel loves me." And perhaps he did know now.

She loved to think that she was more to him than the new book, but was not always sure of it; and sometimes this saddened her, and again she decided that it was right and fitting. She would hasten to him to say that this saddened her. She would go just as impulsively to say that she thought it right.

Her discoveries about herself were many.

"What is it to-day?" he would say, smiling fondly at her. "I see it is something dreadful by your face."

"It is something that struck me suddenly when I was thinking of you, and I don't know whether to be glad or sorry."

"Then be glad, you child."

"It is this: I used to think a good deal of myself; the people here thought me haughty; they said I had a proud walk."

"You have it still," he assured her; the vitality in her as she moved was ever a delicious thing to him to look upon.

"Yes, I feel I have," she admitted, "but that is only because I am yours; and it used to be because I was nobody's!"

"Do you expect my face to fall at that?"

"No, but I thought so much of myself once, and now I am nobody at all. At first it distressed me, and then I was glad, for it makes you everything and me nothing. Yes, I am glad, but I am just a little bit sorry that I should be so glad!"

"Poor Grizel!" said he.

"Poor Grizel!" she echoed. "You are not angry with me, are you, for being almost sorry for her? She used to be so different. 'Where is your

LITTLE WELLS OF GLADNESS

independence, Grizel?' I say to her, and she shakes her sorrowful head. The little girl I used to be need not look for me any more; if we were to meet in the Den she would not know me now."

Ah, if only Tommy could have loved in this way! He would have done it if he could. If we could love by trying, no one would ever have been more loved than Grizel. "Am I to be condemned because I cannot?" he sometimes said to himself in terrible anguish; for though pretty thoughts came to him to say to her when she was with him, he suffered anguish for her when he was alone. He knew it was tragic that such love as hers should be given to him, but what more could he do than he was doing?

CHAPTER XIV

ELSPETH

EVER since the beginning of the book we have been neglecting Elspeth so pointedly that were she not the most forgiving creature we should be afraid to face her now. You are not angry with us, are you, Elspeth? We have been sitting with you, talking with you, thinking of you between the chapters, and the only reason why you have so seldom got into them is that our pen insisted on running after your fascinating brother.

(That is the way to get round her.)

Tommy, it need not be said, never neglected her. The mere fact of his having an affair of his own at present is a sure sign that she is comfortable, for, unless all were well with Elspeth, no venture could have lured him from her side. "Now I am ready for you," he said to the world when Elspeth had been, figuratively speaking, put to sleep; but until she was nicely tucked up the world had to wait. He was still as in his boyhood, when he had to see her with a good book in her hand before he could set off on deeds of darkness. If this was but

ELSPETH

the story of a brother and sister, there were matter for it that would make the ladies want to kiss Tommy on the brow.

That Dr. Gemmell disliked or at least distrusted him, Tommy knew before their acquaintance was an hour old; yet that same evening he had said cordially to Elspeth:

"This young doctor has a strong face."

She was evidently glad that Tommy had noticed it. "Do you think him handsome?" she inquired.

"Decidedly so," he replied, very handsomely, for it is an indiscreet question to ask of a plain man.

There was nothing small about Tommy, was there? He spoke thus magnanimously because he had seen that the doctor liked Elspeth, and that she liked him for liking her. Elspeth never spoke to him of such things, but he was aware that an extra pleasure in life came to her when she was admired; it gave her a little of the self-confidence she so wofully lacked; the woman in her was stirred. Take such presents as these to Elspeth, and Tommy would let you cast stones at himself for the rest of the day, and shake your hand warmly on parting.

In London Elspeth had always known quickly, almost at the first clash of eyes, whether Tommy's friends were attracted by her, but she had not known sooner than he. Those acquaintanceships had seldom ripened; but perhaps this was because, though he and she avoided talking of them, he was all the time taking such terrifying care of her. She was always little Elspeth to him, for whom he had done everything since the beginning of her, a frail little female counterpart of himself that would never have dared to grow up had he not always been there to show her the way, like a stronger plant in the same pot. It was even pathetic to him that Elspeth should have to become a woman while he was a man, and he set to, undaunted, to help her in this matter also. To be admired of men is a woman's right, and he knew it gratified Elspeth; therefore he brought them in to admire her. But beyond profound respect they could not presume to go, he was watching them so vigilantly. He had done everything for her so far, and it was evident that he was now ready to do the love-making also, or at least to sift it before it reached her. Elspeth saw this, and perhaps it annoyed her once or twice, though on the whole she was deeply touched; and the young gentlemen saw it also: they saw that he would not leave them alone with her for a moment, and that behind his cordial manner sat a Tommy who had his eye on them.

Subjects suitable for conversation before Elspeth seemed in presence of this strict brother to be limited. You had just begun to tell her the plot of the new novel when T. Sandys fixed you with his gleaming orb. You were in the middle of the

ELSPETH

rumour about Mrs. Golightly when he let the poker fall. If the newsboys were yelling the latest horror he quickly closed the window. He made all visitors self-conscious. If she was not in the room few of them dared to ask if she was quite well. They paled before expressing the hope that she would feel stronger to-morrow. Yet when Tommy went up to sit beside her, which was the moment the front door closed, he took care to mention, incidentally, that they had been inquiring after her. One of them ventured on her birthday to bring her flowers, but could not present them, Tommy looked so alarming. A still more daring spirit once went the length of addressing her by her Christian name. She did not start up haughtily (the most timid of women are a surprise at times), but the poker fell with a crash.

He knew Elspeth so well that he could tell exactly how these poor young men should approach her. As an artist as well as a brother, he frowned when they blundered. He would have liked to be the medium through which they talked, so that he could give looks and words their proper force. He had thought it all out so thoroughly for Elspeth's benefit that in an hour he could have drawn out a complete guide for her admirers.

"At the first meeting look at her wistfully when she does not see you. She will see you." It might have been Rule One.

Rule Two: "Don't talk so glibly." How often that was what the poker meant!

Being herself a timid creature, Elspeth showed best among the timid, because her sympathetic heart immediately desired to put them at their ease. The more glibly they could talk, the less, she knew, were they impressed by her. Even a little boorishness was more complimentary than chatter. Sometimes when she played on the piano which Tommy had hired for her, the visitor was so shy that he could not even mutter "Thank you" to his hat; yet she might play to him again, and not to the gallant who remarked briskly: "How very charming! What is that called?"

To talk disparagingly of other women is so common a way among men of penetrating into the favour of one that, of course, some tried it with Elspeth. Tommy could not excuse such blundering, for they were making her despise them. He got them out of the house, and then he and she had a long talk, not about them, but about men and women in general, from which she gathered once again that there was nobody like Tommy.

When they bade each other good-night, she would say to him: "I think you are the one perfect gentleman in the world."

Or he might say: "You expect so much of men, Elspeth."

To which her reply: "You have taught me to

ELSPETH

do it, and now I expect others to be like you." Sometimes she would even say: "When I see you so fond of me, and taking such care of me, I am ashamed. You think me so much better than I am. You consider me so pure and good, while I know that I am often mean, and even have wicked thoughts. It makes me ashamed, but so proud of you, for I see that you are judging me by yourself."

And then this Tommy would put the gas out softly and go to his own room, and, let us hope, blush a little.

One stripling had proposed to Elspeth, and on her agitatedly declining him, had flung out of the room in a pet. It spoiled all her after-thoughts on the subject, and so roused her brother's indignation with the fellow. If the great baby had only left all the arrangements to Tommy, he could so easily have made that final scene one which Elspeth would remember with gratification for the remainder of her days; for, of course, pride in the offer could not be great unless she retained her respect for the man who made it. From the tremulous proposal and the manly acceptance of his fate to his dignified exit ("Don't grieve for me, Miss Sandys; you never gave me the least encouragement, and to have loved you will always make me a better man"), even to a touching way of closing the door with one long, last, lingering look, Tommy could have fitted him like a tailor.

From all which it will be seen that our splendid brother thought exclusively of what was best for Elspeth, and was willing that the gentlemen, having served their purpose, should, if it pleased them, go hang. Also, though he thought out every other possible move for the suitor, it never struck him to compose a successful proposal, for the simple reason that he was quite certain Elspeth would have none of them. Their attentions pleased her; but exchange Tommy for one of them — never! He knew it from her confessions at all stages of her life; he had felt it from the days when he began to be father and mother to her as well as brother. In his heart he believed there was something of his own odd character in Elspeth which made her as incapable of loving as himself, and some of his devotion to her was due to this belief; for perhaps nothing touches us to the quick more than the feeling that another suffers under our own curse; certainly nothing draws two souls so close together in a lonely comradeship. But though Tommy had reflected about these things, he did not trouble Elspeth with his conclusions. He merely gave her to understand that he loved her and she loved him so much that neither of them had any love to give to another. It was very beautiful, Elspeth thought, and a little tragic.

"You are quite sure that you mean that," she might ask timidly, "and that you are not flinging away your life on me?"

ELSPETH

"You are all I need," he answered cheerily, and he believed it. Or, if he was in another mood, he might reflect that perhaps he was abstaining from love for Elspeth's sake, and that made him cheery also.

And now David Gemmell was the man, and Tommy genially forgave him all else for liking Elspeth. He invited the doctor, who so obviously distrusted him, to drop in of an evening for a game at the dambrod (which they both abominated, but it was an easy excuse); he asked him confidentially to come in and see Aaron, who had been coughing last night; he put on all the airs of a hail-fellow-well-met, though they never became him, and sat awkwardly on his face. David always seemed eager to come, and tried to rise above his suspicions of Tommy, as Tommy saw, and failed, as Tommy saw again. Elspeth dosed the doctor with stories of her brother's lovely qualities, and Tommy, the forgiving, honestly pitied the poor man for having to listen to them. He knew that if all went well Gemmell would presently propose, and find that Elspeth (tearful at having to strike a blow) could not accept him; but he did not look forward maliciously to this as his revenge on the doctor; he was thinking merely of what was good for Elspeth.

There was no open talk about David between the brother and sister. Some day, Tommy presumed, she would announce that the doctor had asked her to marry him; and oh, how sorry she was; and oh, what a good man he was; and oh, Tommy knew she had never encouraged him; and oh, she could never leave Tommy! But until that day arrived they avoided talking directly about what brought Gemmell there. That he came to see Elspeth neither of them seemed to conceive as possible. Did Tommy chuckle when he saw David's eyes following her? No; solemn as a cat blinking at the fire; noticed nothing. The most worldly chaperon, the most loving mother, could not have done more for Elspeth. Yet it was not done to find her a husband, but quite the reverse, as we have seen. On reflection Tommy must smile at what he has been doing, but not while he is working the figures. The artist never smiles at himself until afterwards.

And now he not only wondered at times how Elspeth and David were getting on, but whether she noticed how he was getting on with Grizel; for in matters relating to Tommy Elspeth was almost as sharp as he in matters that related to her, and he knew it. When he proposed to Elspeth that they should ask Gemmell to go fishing with them on the morrow ("He has been overworked of late and it would do him good") he wanted to add, in a careless voice, "We might invite Grizel also," but could not · his lips suddenly went dry.

And when Elspeth said the words that were so difficult to him, he wondered, "Did she say that because she knew I wished it?" But he decided that she did not, for she was evidently looking forward to to-morrow, and he knew she would be shuddering if she thought her Tommy was slipping.

"I am so glad it was she who asked me," Grizel said to him when he told her. "Don't you see what it means? It means that she wants to get you out of the way! You are not everything to her now as you used to be. Are you glad, glad?"

"If I could believe it!" Tommy said.

"What else could make her want to be alone with him?"

Nothing else could have made Grizel want to be alone with him, and she must always judge others by herself. But Tommy knew that Elspeth was different, and that a girl with some of himself in her might want to be alone with a man who admired her without wanting to marry him.

CHAPTER XV

BY PROSEN WATER

THAT day by the banks of Prosen Water was one of Grizel's beautiful memories. All the days when she thought he loved her became beautiful memories.

It was the time of reds and whites, for the glory of the broom had passed, except at great heights, and the wild roses were trooping in. When the broom is in flame there seems to be no colour but yellow; but when the wild roses come we remember that the broom was flaunting. It was not quite a lady, for it insisted on being looked at; while these light-hearted things are too innocent to know that there is anyone to look. Grizel was sitting by the side of the stream, adorning her hat fantastically with roses red and white and some that were neither. They were those that cannot decide whether they look best in white or red, and so waver for the whole of their little lives between the two colours; there are many of them, and it is the pathetic thing about wild roses. She did not pay much heed to her handiwork. What she was say-

SHE DID NOT LOOK UP, SHE WAITED

ing to herself was that in another minute he and she would be alone. Nothing else in the world mattered very much. Every bit of her was conscious of it as the supreme event. Her fingers pressed it upon the flowers. It was in her eyes as much as in her heart. He went on casting his line, moving from stone to stone, dropping down the bank, ascending it, as if the hooking of a trout was something to him. Was he feeling to his marrow that as soon as those other two figures rounded the bend in the stream he and she would have the world to themselves? Ah, of course he felt it, but was it quite as much to him as it was to her?

"Not quite so much," she said bravely to herself. "I don't want it to be quite so much — but nearly."

And now they were alone as no two can be except those who love; for when the third person leaves them they have a universe to themselves, and it is closed in by the heavens, and the air of it is the consciousness of each other's presence. She sat motionless now — trembling, exulting. She could no longer hear the talking of the water, but she heard his step. He was coming slowly towards her. She did not look up — she waited; and while she waited time was annihilated.

He was coming to her to treat her as if she were a fond child; that she, of all women, could permit it was still delicious to him, and a marvel. She had let him do it yesterday, but perhaps she had regained her independence in the night. As he hesitated he became another person. In a flood of feeling he had a fierce desire to tell her the truth about himself. But he did not know what it was. He put aside his rod, and sat down very miserably beside her.

"Grizel, I suppose I am a knave." His lips parted to say it, but no words came. She had given him an adorable look that stopped them as if her dear hand had been placed upon his mouth.

Was he a knave? He wanted honestly to know. He had not tried to make her love him. Had he known in time he would even have warned her against it. He would never have said he loved her had she not first, as she thought, found it out; to tell her the truth then would have been brutal. He had made believe in order that she might remain happy. Was it even make-belief? Assuredly he did love her in his own way, in the only way he was capable of. She was far more to him than any other person except Elspeth. He delighted in her, and would have fought till he dropped rather than let any human being injure her. All his feelings for her were pure. He was prepared to marry her; but if she had not made that mistake, oh, what a delight it would have been

BY PROSEN WATER

to him never to marry anyone! He felt keenly miserable.

"Grizel, I seem to be different from all other men. There seems to be some curse upon me that makes me unable to love as they do. I want to love you, dear one; you are the only woman I ever wanted to love; but apparently I can't. I have decided to go on with this thing because it seems best for you; but is it? I would tell you all and leave the decision to you, were it not that I fear you would think I wanted you to let me off."

It would have been an honest speech, and he might have said it had he begun at once, for it was in a passion to be out, so desirous was he that dear Grizel should not be deceived; but he tried its effect first upon himself, and as he went on the tragedy he saw mastered him. He forgot that she was there, except as a figure needed to complete the picture of the man who could not love. He saw himself a splendidly haggard creature with burning eyes standing aside while all the world rolled by in pursuit of the one thing needful. It was a river, and he must stand parched on the bank for ever and ever. Should he keep that sorrowful figure a man or turn it into a woman? He tried a woman. She was on the bank now, her arms outstretched to the flood. Ah! she would be so glad to drink, though she must drown.

Grizel saw how mournful he had become as he

gazed upon her. In his face she had been seeing all the glories that can be given to mortals. Thoughts had come to her that drew her nearer to her God. Her trust in him stretched to eternity. All that was given to her at that moment she thought was also given to him. She seemed to know why, with love lighting up their souls to each other, he could yet grow mournful.

"Oh," she cried, with a movement that was a passionate caress, "do you indeed love me so much as that? I never wanted you to love me quite so much as that!"

It brought him back to himself, but without a start. Those sudden returns to fact had ceased to bewilder him; they were grown so common that he passed between dreams and reality as through tissue-paper.

"I did not mean," she said at last, in a tremor, "that I wanted you to love me less, but I am almost sorry that you love me quite so much."

He dared say nothing, for he did not altogether understand.

"I have those fears, too, sometimes," she went on; "I have had them when I was with you, but more often when I was alone. They come to me suddenly, and I have such eager longings to run to you and tell you of them, and ask you to drive them away. But I never did it; I kept them to myself."

"You could keep something back from me, Grizel?"

"Forgive me," she implored; "I thought they would distress you, and I had such a desire to bring you nothing but happiness. To bear them by myself seemed to be helping you, and I was glad, I was proud, to feel myself of use to you even to that little extent. I did not know you had the same fears; I thought that perhaps they came only to women; have you had them before? Fears," she continued, so wistfully, "that it is too beautiful to end happily? Oh, have you heard a voice crying, 'It is too beautiful; it can never be'?"

He saw clearly now; he saw so clearly that he was torn with emotion. "It is more than I can bear!" he said hoarsely. Surely he loved her.

"Did you see me die?" she asked, in a whisper.

"I have seen you die."

"Don't, Grizel!" he cried.

But she had to go on. "Tell me," she begged; "I have told you."

"No, no, never that," he answered her. "At the worst I have had only the feeling that you could never be mine."

She smiled at that. "I am yours," she said softly; "nothing can take away that — nothing, nothing. I say it to myself a hundred times a day, it is so sweet. Nothing can separate us but death; I have thought of all the other possible things, and none of them is strong enough. But when I think of your dying, oh, when I think of my being left without you!"

She rocked her arms in a frenzy, and called him dearest, darlingest. All the sweet names that had been the child Grizel's and the old doctor's were Tommy's now. He soothed her, ah, surely as only a lover could soothe. She was his Grizel, she was his beloved. No mortal could have been more impassioned than Tommy. He must have loved her. It could not have been merely sympathy, or an exquisite delight in being the man, or the desire to make her happy again in the quickest way, or all three combined? Whatever it was, he did not know; all he knew was that he felt every word he said, or seemed to feel it.

"It is a punishment to me," Grizel said, setting her teeth, "for loving you too much. I know I love you too much. I think I love you more than God."

She felt him shudder.

"But if I feel it," she said, shuddering also, yet unable to deceive herself, "what difference do I make by saying it? He must know it is so, whether I say it or not."

There was a tremendous difference to Tommy, but not of a kind he could explain, and she went on; she must tell him everything now.

"I pray every night and morning; but that is

nothing — everyone does it. I know I thank God sincerely; I thank Him again and again and again. Do you remember how, when I was a child, you used to be horrified because I prayed standing? I often say little prayers standing now; I am always thanking Him for giving me you. But all the time it is a bargain with Him. So long as you are well I love Him, but if you were to die I would never pray again. I have never said it in words until to-day, but He must know it, for it is behind all my prayers. If He does not know, there cannot be a God."

She was watching his face, half wofully, half stubbornly, as if, whatever might be the issue of those words, she had to say them. She saw how pained he was. To admit the possible non-existence of a God when you can so easily leave the subject alone was horrible to Tommy.

"I don't doubt Him," she continued. "I have believed in Him ever since the time when I was such a lonely child that I did not know His name. I shall always believe in Him so long as He does not take you from me. But if He does, then I shall not believe in Him any more. It may be wrong, but that is what I feel.

"It makes you care less for me!" she cried in anguish.

"No, no, dear."

"I don't think it makes God care less for me,"

she said, very seriously. "I think He is pleased that I don't try to cheat Him."

Somehow Tommy felt uncomfortable at that.

"There are people," he said vaguely, like one who thought it best to mention no names, "who would be afraid to challenge God in that way."

"He would not be worth believing in," she answered, "if He could be revengeful. He is too strong, and too loving, and too pitiful for that." But she took hold of Tommy as if to protect him. Had they been in physical danger, her first impulse would have been to get in front of him to protect him. The noblest women probably always love in this way, and yet it is those who would hide behind them that men seem to love the best.

"I always feel — oh, I never can help feeling," she said, "that nothing could happen to you, that God Himself could not take you from me, while I had hold of you."

"Grizel!"

"I mean only that He could not have the heart," she said hastily. "No, I don't," she had to add. "I meant what you thought I meant. That is why I feel it would be so sweet to be married, so that I could be close to you every moment, and then no harm could come to you. I would keep such a grip of you, I should be such a part of you, that you could not die without my dying also.

BY PROSEN WATER

"Oh, do you care less for me now?" she cried. "I can't see things as clearly as you do, dearest, darlingest. I have not a beautiful nature like yours. I am naturally rebellious. I have to struggle even to be as good as I am. There are evil things in my blood. You remember how we found out that. God knew it, too, and He is compassionate. I think He makes many pitying allowances for me. It is not wicked, is it, to think that?"

"You used to know me too well, Grizel, to speak of my beautiful nature," he said humbly.

"I did think you vain," she replied. "How odd to remember that!"

"But I was, and am."

"I love to hear you proving you are not," said she, beaming upon him. "Do you think," she asked, with a sudden change of manner to the childish, like one trying to coax a compliment out of him, "that I have improved at all during those last days? I think I am not quite such a horrid girl as I used to be; and if I am not, I owe it to you. I am so glad to owe it to you." She told him that she was trying to make herself a tiny bit more like him by studying his book. "It is not exactly the things you say of women that help me, for though they are lovely I am not sure that they are quite true. I almost hope they are not true; for if they are, then I am not even an average woman." She buried her face in his coat. "You say women are naturally purer than men, but I don't know. Perhaps we are more cunning only. Perhaps it is not even a thing to wish; for if we were, it would mean that we are good because there is less evil in us to fight against. Dear, forgive me for saying that; it may be all wrong; but I think it is what nearly all women feel in their hearts, though they keep it locked up till they die. I don't even want you to believe me. You think otherwise of us, and it is so sweet of you that we try to be better than we are — to undeceive you would hurt so. It is not the book that makes me a better woman — it is the man I see behind it."

He was too much moved to be able to reply — too much humbled. He vowed to himself that, whether he could love or not, he would be a good husband to this dear woman.

"Ah, Grizel," he declared, by and by, "what a delicious book you are, and how I wish I had written you! With every word you say, something within me is shouting, 'Am I not a wonder!' I warned you it would be so as soon as I felt that I had done anything really big, and I have. I have somehow made you love me. Ladies and gentlemen," he exclaimed, addressing the river and the trees and the roses, "I have somehow made her love me! Am I not a wonder?"

Grizel clapped her hands gaily; she was merry

again. She could always be what Tommy wanted her to be. "Ladies and gentlemen," she cried, "how could I help it?"

David had been coming back for his fly-book, and though he did not hear their words, he saw a light in Grizel's face that suddenly set him thinking. For the rest of the day he paid little attention to Elspeth; some of his answers showed her that he was not even listening to her.

CHAPTER XVI

"HOW COULD YOU HURT YOUR GRIZEL SO!"

To concentrate on Elspeth so that he might find out what was in her mind was, as we have seen, seldom necessary to Tommy; for he had learned her by heart long ago. Yet a time was now come when he had to concentrate, and even then he was doubtful of the result. So often he had put that mind of hers to rights that it was an open box to him, or had been until he conceived the odd notion that perhaps it contained a secret drawer. This would have been resented by most brothers, but Tommy's chagrin was nothing compared to the exhilaration with which he perceived that he might be about to discover something new about woman. He was like the digger whose hand is on the point of closing on a diamond—a certain holiness added.

What puzzled him was the state of affairs now existing between Elspeth and the doctor. A week had elapsed since the fishing excursion, and David had not visited them. Too busy? Tommy knew that it is the busy people who can find time.

"HOW COULD YOU HURT GRIZEL!"

Could it be that David had proposed to her at the waterside?

No, he could not read that in Elspeth's face. He knew that she would be in distress lest her refusal should darken the doctor's life for too long a time; but yet (shake your fist at him, ladies, for so misunderstanding you!) he expected also to note in that sympathetic face a look of subdued triumph, and as it was not there, David could not have proposed.

The fact of her not having told him about it at once did not prove to Tommy that there had been no proposal. His feeling was that she would consider it too sacred a thing to tell even to him, but that it would force its way out in a week or two.

On the other hand, she could not have resisted dropping shyly such remarks as these: "I think Dr. Gemmell is a noble man," or, "How wonderfully good Dr. Gemmell is to the poor!"

Also she would sometimes have given Tommy a glance that said, "I wonder if you guess."

Had they quarrelled? Tommy smiled. If it was but a quarrel he was not merely appeased — he was pleased. Had he had the ordering of the affair, he would certainly have included a lovers' quarrel in it, and had it not been that he wanted to give her the pleasure of finding these things out for herself, he would have taken her aside and addressed her thus: "No need to look tragic, Elspeth; for to a woman this must be really one of the most charming moments in the comedy. You feel that he would not have quarrelled had he had any real caring for you, and yet in your heart you know it is a proof that he has. To a woman, I who know assure you that nothing can be more delicious. Your feeling for him, as you and I well know, is but a sentiment of attraction because he loves you as you are unable to love him, and as you are so pained by this quarrel, consider how much more painful it must be to him. You think you have been slighted; that when a man has seemed to like you so much you have a right to be told so by him, that you may help him with your sympathy. Oh, Elspeth, you think yourself unhappy just now when you are really in the middle of one of the pleasantest bits of it! Love is a series of thrills, the one leading to the other, and, as your careful guardian, I would not have you miss one of them. You will come to the final bang quickly enough, and find it the finest thrill of all, but it is soon over. When you have had to tell him that you are not for him, there are left only the pleasures of memory, and the more of them there were, the more there will be to look back to. I beg you, Elspeth, not to hurry; loiter rather, smelling the flowers and plucking them, for you may never be this way again."

"HOW COULD YOU HURT GRIZEL!"

All these things he might have pointed out to Elspeth had he wanted her to look at the matter rationally, but he had no such wish. He wanted her to enjoy herself as the blessed do, without knowing why. No pity for the man, you see, but no ill will to him. David was having his thrills also, and though the last of them would seem a staggerer to him at the time, it would gradually become a sunny memory. The only tragedy is not to have known love. So long as you have the experiences, it does not greatly matter whether your suit was a failure or successful.

So Tommy decided, but he feared at the same time that there had been no quarrel — that David had simply drawn back.

How he saw through Elspeth's brave attempts to show that she had never for a moment thought of David's having any feeling for her save ordinary friendship — yes, they were brave, but not brave enough for Tommy. At times she would say something bitter about life (not about the doctor, for he was never mentioned), and it was painful to her brother to see gentle Elspeth grown cynical. He suffered even more when her manner indicated that she knew she was too poor a creature to be loved by any man. Tommy was in great woe about Elspeth at this time. He was thinking much more about her than about Grizel; but do not blame him unreservedly for that: the two women who were his dears were pulling him different ways, and he could not accompany both. He had made up his mind to be loyal to Grizel, and so all his pity could go to Elspeth. On the day he had his talk with the doctor, therefore, he had, as it were, put Grizel aside only because she was happy just now, and so had not Elspeth's need of him.

The doctor and he had met on the hill, whence the few who look may see one of the fairest views in Scotland. Tommy was strolling up and down, and the few other persons on the hill were glancing with good-humoured suspicion at him, as we all look at celebrated characters. Had he been happy he would have known that they were watching him, and perhaps have put his hands behind his back to give them more for their money, as the saying is; but he was miserable. His one consolation was that the blow he must strike Elspeth when he told her of his engagement need not be struck just yet. David could not have chosen a worse moment, therefore, for saying so bluntly what he said: "I hear you are to be married. If so, I should like to congratulate you."

Tommy winced like one charged with open cruelty to his sister — charged with it, too, by the real criminal.

"It is not true?" David asked quietly, and Tommy turned from him glaring. "I am sorry I

"HOW COULD YOU HURT GRIZEL!"

spoke of it, as it is not true," the doctor said after a pause, the crow's-feet showing round his eyes as always when he was in mental pain; and presently he went away, after giving Tommy a contemptuous look. Did Tommy deserve that look? We must remember that he had wanted to make the engagement public at once; if he shrank from admitting it for the present, it was because of Elspeth's plight. "Grizel, you might have given her a little time to recover from this man's faithlessness," was what his heart cried. He believed that Grizel had told David, and for the last time in his life he was angry with her. He strode down the hill savagely towards Caddam Wood, where he knew he should find her.

Soon he saw her. She was on one of the many tiny paths that lead the stranger into the middle of the wood and then leave him there maliciously or because they dare not venture any farther themselves. They could play no tricks on Grizel, however, for she knew and was fond of them all. Tommy had said that she loved them because they were such little paths, that they appealed to her like babies; and perhaps there was something in it.

She came up the path with the swing of one who was gleefully happy. Some of the Thrums people, you remember, said that Grizel strutted because she was so satisfied with herself, and if you like an ugly word, we may say that she strutted to-day. It was her whole being giving utterance to the joy within her that love had brought. As Grizel came up the path on that bright afternoon, she could no more have helped strutting than the bud to open on the appointed day. She was obeying one of Nature's laws. I think I promised long ago to tell you of the day when Grizel would strut no more. Well, this is the day. Observe her strutting for the last time. It was very strange and touching to her to remember in the after years that she had once strutted, but it was still more strange and touching to Tommy.

She was like one overfilled with delight when she saw him. How could she know that he was to strike her?

He did not speak. She was not displeased. When anything so tremendous happened as the meeting of these two, how could they find words at once?

She bent and pressed her lips to his sleeve; but he drew away with a gesture that startled her.

"You are not angry?" she said, stopping.

"Yes," he replied doggedly.

"Not with me?" Her hand went to her heart. "With me!" A wounded animal could not have uttered a cry more pathetic. "Not with me!" She clutched his arm.

"Have I no cause to be angry?" he said.

"HOW COULD YOU HURT GRIZEL!"

She looked at him in bewilderment. Could this be he? Oh, could it be she?

"Cause? How could I give you cause?"

It seemed unanswerable to her. How could Grizel do anything that would give him the right to be angry with her? Oh, men, men! will you never understand how absolutely all of her a woman's love can be? If she gives you everything, how can she give you more? She is not another person; she is part of you. Does one finger of your hand plot against another?

He told her sullenly of his scene with the doctor.

"I am very sorry," she said; but her eyes were still searching for the reason why Tommy could be angry with her.

"You made me promise to tell no one," he said, "and I have kept my promise: but you——"

The anguish that was Grizel's then! "You can't think that I told him!" she cried, and she held out her arms as if to remind him of who she was. "You can believe that of your Grizel?"

"I daresay you have not done it wittingly; but this man has guessed, and he could never have guessed it from look or word of mine."

"It must have been I!" she said slowly. "Tell me," she cried like a suppliant, "how have I done it?"

"Your manner, your face," he answered; "it must have been that. I don't blame you. Grizel, but — yes, it must have been that, and it is hard on me."

He was in misery, and these words leaped out. They meant only that it was hard on him if Elspeth had to be told of his engagement in the hour of her dejection. He did not mean to hurt Grizel to the quick. However terrible the loss of his freedom might be to the man who could not love, he always intended to be true to her. But she gave the words a deeper meaning.

She stood so still she seemed to be pondering, and at last she said quietly, as if they had been discussing some problem outside themselves: "Yes, I think it must have been that." She looked long at him. " It is very hard on you," she said.

"I feel sure it was that," she went on; and now her figure was erect, and again it broke, and sometimes there was a noble scorn in her voice, but more often there was only pitiful humility. " I feel sure it was that, for I have often wondered how everybody did not know. I have broken my promise. I used always to be able to keep a promise. I had every other fault,— I was hard and proud and intolerant,— but I was true. I think I was vain of that, though I see now it was only something I could not help; from the moment when I had a difficulty in keeping a promise, I ceased to keep it. I love you so much that I carry my love in my face for all to read. They

"HOW COULD YOU HURT GRIZEL!"

cannot see me meet you without knowing the truth; they cannot hear me say your name but I betray myself; I show how I love you in every movement; I am full of you. How can anyone look at me and not see you? I should have been more careful — oh, I could have been so much more careful had I loved you a little less! It is very hard on you."

The note of satire had died out of her voice; her every look and gesture carried in it nothing but love for him; but all the unhappy dog could say was something about self-respect.

Her mouth opened as if for bitterness; but no sound came. "How much self-respect do you think is left for me after to-day?" she said mournfully at last; and then she quickly took a step nearer her dear one, as if to caress the spot where these words had struck him. But she stopped, and for a moment she was the Grizel of old. "Have no fear," she said, with a trembling, crooked smile; "there is only one thing to be done now, and I shall do it. All the blame is mine. You shall not be deprived of your self-respect."

He had not been asking for his freedom; but he heard it running to him now, and he knew that if he answered nothing he would be whistling it back for ever. A madness to be free at any cost swept over him. He let go his hold on self-respect, and clapped his hand on freedom.

He answered nothing, and the one thing for her to do was to go; and she did it. But it was only for a moment that she could be altogether the Grizel of old. She turned to take a long, last look at him; but the wofulness of herself was what she saw. She cried, with infinite pathos, "Oh, how could you hurt your Grizel so!"

He controlled himself and let her go. His freedom was fawning on him, licking his hands and face, and in that madness he actually let Grizel go. It was not until she was out of sight that he gave utterance to a harsh laugh. He knew what he was at that moment, as you and I shall never be able to know him, eavesdrop how we may.

He flung himself down in a blaeberry-bed, and lay there doggedly, his weak mouth tightly closed. A great silence reigned; no, not a great silence, for he continued to hear the cry: "Oh, how could you hurt your Grizel so!" She scarcely knew that she had said it; but to him who knew what she had been, and what he had changed her into, and for what alone she was to blame, there was an unconscious pathos in it that was terrible. It was the epitome of all that was Grizel, all that was adorable and all that was pitiful in her. It rang in his mind like a bell of doom. He believed its echo would not be quite gone from his ears when he died. If all the wise men in the world had met

"HOW COULD YOU HURT GRIZEL!"

to consider how Grizel could most effectively say farewell to Tommy, they could not have thought out a better sentence. However completely he had put himself emotionally in her place with this same object, he would have been inspired by nothing quite so good.

But they were love's dying words. He knew he could never again, though he tried, be to Grizel what he had been. The water was spilled on the ground. She had thought him all that was glorious in man — that was what her love had meant; and it was spilled. There was only one way in which he could wound her more cruelly than she was already hurt, and that was by daring to ask her to love him still. To imply that he thought her pride so broken, her independence, her maidenly modesty, all that make up the loveliness of a girl, so lost that by entreaties he could persuade her to forgive him, would destroy her altogether. It would reveal to her how low he thought her capable of falling.

I suppose we should all like to think that it would have been thus with Grizel, but our wishes are of small account. It was not many minutes since she left Tommy, to be his no more, his knife still in her heart; but she had not reached the end of the wood when all in front of her seemed a world of goblins, and a future without him not to be faced. He might beat her or scorn her, but not for an hour could she exist without him. She wrung her arms in woe; the horror of what she was doing tore her in pieces; but not all this prevented her turning back. It could not even make her go slowly. She did not walk back; she stole back in little runs. She knew it was her destruction, but her arms were outstretched to the spot where she had left him.

He was no longer there, and he saw her between the firs before she could see him. As he realized what her coming back meant, his frame shook with pity for her. All the dignity had gone from her. She looked as shamed as a dog stealing back after it had been whipped. She knew she was shamed. He saw she knew it: the despairing rocking of her arms proved it; yet she was coming back to him in little runs.

Pity, chivalry, oh, surely love itself, lifted him to his feet, and all else passed out of him save an imperious desire to save her as much humiliation as he could — to give her back a few of those garments of pride and self-respect that had fallen from her. At least she should not think that she had to come all the way to him. With a stifled sob, he rose and ran up the path towards her.

"Grizel! it is you! My beloved! how could you leave me! Oh, Grizel, my love, how could you misunderstand me so!"

"HOW COULD YOU HURT GRIZEL!"

She gave a glad cry. She sought feebly to hold him at arm's length, to look at him watchfully, to read him as in the old days; but the old days were gone. He strained her to him. Oh, surely it was love at last! He thanked God that he loved at last.

CHAPTER XVII

HOW TOMMY SAVED THE FLAG

HE loved at last, but had no time to exult just now, for he could not rejoice with Tommy while his dear one drooped in shame. Ah, so well he understood that she believed she had done the unpardonable thing in woman, and that while she thought so she must remain a broken column. It was a great task he saw before him — nothing less than to make her think that what she had done was not shameful, but exquisite; that she had not tarnished the flag of love, but glorified it. Artfulness, you will see, was needed; but, remember, he was now using all his arts in behalf of the woman he loved.

"You were so long in coming back to me, Grizel. The agony of it!"

"Did it seem long?" She spoke in a trembling voice, hiding her face in him. She listened like one anxious to seize his answer as it left his heart.

"So long," he answered, "that it seemed to me we must be old when we met again. I saw a

HOW TOMMY SAVED THE FLAG

future without you stretching before me to the grave, and I turned and ran from it."

"That is how I felt," she whispered.

"You!" Tommy cried, in excellent amazement.

"What else could have made me come?"

"I thought it was pity that had brought you — pity for me, Grizel. I thought you had perhaps come back to be angry with me——"

"How could I be!" she cried.

"How could you help it, rather?" said he. "I was cruel, Grizel; I spoke like a fool as well as like a dastard. But it was only anxiety for Elspeth that made me do it. Dear one, be angry with me as often as you choose, and whether I deserve it or not; but don't go away from me; never send me from you again. Anything but that."

It was how she had felt again, and her hold on him tightened with sudden joy. So well he knew what that grip meant! He did not tell her that he had not loved her fully until now. He would have liked to tell her how true love had been born in him as he saw her stealing back to him, but it was surely best for her not to know that any transformation had been needed. "I don't say that I love you more now than ever before," he said carefully, "but one thing I do know: that I never admired you quite so much."

She looked up in surprise.

"I mean your character," he said determinedly. "I have always known how strong and noble it was, but I never quite thought you could do anything so beautiful as this."

"Beautiful!" She could only echo the word.

"Many women, even of the best," he told her, "would have resorted to little feminine ways of humbling such a blunderer as I have been: they would have spurned him for weeks; made him come to them on his knees; perhaps have thought that his brutality of a moment outweighed all his love. When I saw you coming to meet me half-way — oh, Grizel, tell me that you were doing that?"

"Yes, yes, yes!" she answered eagerly, so that she might not detain him a moment.

"When I saw you I realized that you were willing to forgive me; that you were coming to say so; that no thought of lowering me first was in your mind; that yours was a love above the littleness of ordinary people: and the adorableness of it filled me with a glorious joy; I saw in that moment what woman in her highest development is capable of, and that the noblest is the most womanly."

She said "Womanly?" with a little cry. It had always been such a sweet word to her, and she thought it could never be hers again!

"It is by watching you," he replied, "that I know the meaning of the word. I thought I

HOW TOMMY SAVED THE FLAG

knew long ago, but every day you give it a nobler meaning."

If she could have believed it! For a second or two she tried to believe it, and then she shook her head.

"How dear of you to think that of me!" she answered. She looked up at him with exquisite approval in her eyes. She had always felt that men should have high ideas about women.

"But it was not to save you pain that I came back," she said bravely. There was something pathetic in the way the truth had always to come out of her. "I did not think you wanted me to come back. I never expected you to be looking for me, and when I saw you doing it, my heart nearly stopped for gladness. I thought you were wearied of me, and would be annoyed when you saw me coming back. I said to myself, 'If I go back I shall be a disgrace to womanhood.' But I came; and now do you know what my heart is saying, and always will be saying? It is that pride and honour and self-respect are gone. And the terrible thing is that I don't seem to care; I, who used to value them so much, am willing to let them go if you don't send me away from you. Oh, if you can't love me any longer, let me still love you! That is what I came back to say."

"Grizel, Grizel!" he cried. It was she who was wielding the knife now.

"But it is true," she said.

"We could so easily pretend that it isn't." That was not what he said, though it was at his heart. He sat down, saying:

"This is a terrible blow, but better you should tell it to me than leave me to find it out." He was determined to save the flag for Grizel, though he had to try all the Tommy ways, one by one.

"Have I hurt you?" she asked anxiously. She could not bear to hurt him for a moment. "What did I say?"

"It amounts to this," he replied huskily: "you love me, but you wish you did not; that is what it means."

He expected her to be appalled by this; but she stood still, thinking it over. There was something pitiful in a Grizel grown undecided.

"Do I wish I did not?" she said helplessly. "I don't know. Perhaps that is what I do wish. Ah, but what are wishes! I know now that they don't matter at all."

"Yes, they matter," he assured her, in the voice of one looking upon death. "If you no longer want to love me, you will cease to do it soon enough." His manner changed to bitterness. "So don't be cast down, Grizel, for the day of your deliverance is at hand."

But again she disappointed him, and as the flag must be saved at whatever cost, he said.

HOW TOMMY SAVED THE FLAG

"It has come already. I see you no longer love me as you did." Her arms rose in anguish; but he went on ruthlessly: "You will never persuade me that you do; I shall never believe it again."

I suppose it was a pitiable thing about Grizel — it was something he had discovered weeks ago and marvelled over — that nothing distressed her so much as the implication that she could love him less. She knew she could not; but that he should think it possible was the strangest woe to her. It seemed to her to be love's only tragedy. We have seen how difficult it was for Grizel to cry. When she said "How could you hurt your Grizel so!" she had not cried, nor when she knew that if she went back to him her self-respect must remain behind. But a painful tear came to her eyes when he said that she loved him less. It almost unmanned him, but he proceeded, for her good:

"I daresay you still care for me a little, as the rank and file of people love. What right had I, of all people, to expect a love so rare and beautiful as yours to last? It had to burn out, like a great fire, as such love always does. The experience of the world has proved it."

"Oh!" she cried, and her body was rocking. If he did not stop, she would weep herself to death.

"Yes, it seems sad," Tommy continued; "but if ever man knew that it served him right, I know it. And they maintain, the wiseacres who have analyzed love, that there is much to be said in favour of a calm affection. The glory has gone, but the material comforts are greater, and in the end ——"

She sank upon the ground. He was bleeding for her, was Tommy. He went on his knees beside her, and it was terrible to him to feel that every part of her was alive with anguish. He called her many sweet names, and she listened for them between her sobs; but still she sobbed. He could bear it no longer; he cried, and called upon God to smite him. She did not look up, but her poor hands pulled him back. "You said I do not love you the same!" she moaned.

"Grizel!" he answered, as if in sad reproof; "it was not I who said that — it was you. I put into words only what you have been telling me for the last ten minutes."

"No, no," she cried. "Oh, how could I!"

He flung up his arms in despair. "Is this only pity for me, Grizel," he implored, looking into her face as if to learn his fate, "or is it love indeed?"

"You know it is love — you know!"

"But what kind of love?" he demanded fiercely. "Is it the same love that it was? Quick, tell me. I can't have less. If it is but a little less, you will kill me."

The first gleam of sunshine swept across her face

HOW TOMMY SAVED THE FLAG

(and oh, how he was looking for it!). "Do you want it to be the same — do you really want it? Oh, it is, it is!"

"And you would not cease to love me if you could?"

"No, no, no!" She would have come closer to him, but he held her back.

"One moment, Grizel," he said in a hard voice that filled her with apprehension. "There must be no second mistake. In saying that love, and love alone, brought you back, you are admitting, are you not, that you were talking wildly about loss of pride and honour? You did the loveliest thing you have ever done when you came back. If I were you, my character would be ruined from this hour — I should feel so proud of myself."

She smiled at that, and fondled his hand. "If you think so," she said, "all is well."

But he would not leave it thus. "You must think so also," he insisted; and when she still shook her head, "Then I am proud of your love no longer," said he, doggedly. "How proud of it I have been! A man cannot love a woman without reverencing her, without being touched to the quick a score of times a day by the revelations she gives of herself — revelations of such beauty and purity that he is abashed in her presence. The unspoken prayers he offers up to God at those times he gives to her to carry. And when such a one returns his love, he is proud indeed. To me you are the embodiment of all that is fair in woman, and it is love that has made you so, that has taken away your little imperfections — love for me. Ah, Grizel, I was so proud to think that somehow I had done it; but even now, in the moment when your love has manifested itself most splendidly, you are ashamed of it, and what I respect and reverence you for most are changes that have come about against your will. If your love makes you sorrowful, how can I be proud of it? Henceforth it will be my greatest curse."

She started up, wringing her hands. It was something to have got her to her feet.

"Surely," he said, like one puzzled as well as pained by her obtuseness, "you see clearly that it must be so. True love, as I conceive it, must be something passing all knowledge, irresistible; something not to be resented for its power, but worshipped for it; something not to fight against, but to glory in. And such is your love; but you give the proof of it with shame, because your ideal of love is a humdrum sort of affection. That is all you would like to feel, Grizel, and because you feel something deeper and nobler you say you have lost your self-respect. I am the man who has taken it from you. Can I ever be proud of your love again?"

He paused, overcome with emotion. "What it

HOW TOMMY SAVED THE FLAG

has been to me!" he cried. "I walked among my fellows as if I were a colossus. It inspired me at my work. I felt that there was nothing great I was not capable of, and all because Grizel loved me."

She stood trembling with delight at what he said, and with apprehension at what he seemed to threaten. His head being bent, he could not see her, and amid his grief he wondered a little what she was doing now.

"But you spoke"— she said it timidly, as if to refer to the matter at all was cruel of her — "you spoke as if I was disgracing you because I could not conceal my love. You said it was hard on you." She pressed her hands together. "Yes, that is what you said."

This was awkward for Tommy. "She believes I meant that," he cried hoarsely. "Grizel believes that of me! I have behaved since then as if that was what I meant, have I? I meant only that it would be hard on me if Elspeth learned of our love at the very moment when this man is treating her basely. I look as if I had meant something worse, do I? I know myself at last! Grizel has shown me what I am."

He covered his face with his hands. Strong man as he was, he could not conceal his agony.

"Don't!" she cried. "If I was wrong——"
"If you were wrong!"

"I was wrong! I know I was wrong. Somehow it was a mistake. I don't know how it arose. But you love me and you want me to love you still. That is all I know. I thought you did not, but you do. If you wanted me to come back ——"

"If I wanted it!"

"I know you wanted it now, and I am no longer ashamed to have come. I am glad I came, and if you can still be proud of my love and respect me ——"

"Oh, Grizel, if!"

"Then I have got back my pride and my self-respect again. I cannot reason about it, but they have come back again."

It was she who was trying to comfort him by this time, caressing his hair and his hands. But he would not be appeased at once; it was good for her to have something to do.

"You are sure you are happy again, Grizel? You are not pretending in order to please me?"

"So happy!"

"But your eyes are still wet."

"That is because I have hurt you so. Oh, how happy I should be if I could see you smile again!"

"How I would smile if I saw you looking happy!"

"Then smile at once, sir," she could say presently, "for see how happy I am looking." And as

HOW TOMMY SAVED THE FLAG

she beamed on him once more he smiled as well as he was able to. Grizel loved him so much that she actually knew when that face of his was smiling, and soon she was saying gaily to his eyes: "Oh, silly eyes that won't sparkle, what is the use of you?" and she pressed her own upon them; and to his mouth she said: "Mouth that does not know how to laugh — poor, tragic mouth!" He let her do nearly all the talking. She sat there crooning over him as if he were her child.

And so the flag was saved. He begged her to let him tell their little world of his love for her, and especially was he eager to go straight with it to the doctor. But she would not have this. "David and Elspeth shall know in good time," she said, very nobly. "I am sure they are fond of each other, and they shall know of our happiness on the day when they tell us of their own." And until that great day came she was not to look upon herself as engaged to Tommy, and he must never kiss her again until they were engaged. I think it was a pleasure to her to insist on this. It was her punishment to herself for ever having doubted Tommy.

TOMMY AND GRIZEL

PART II

CHAPTER XVIII

THE GIRL SHE HAD BEEN

AS they sat amid the smell of rosin on that summer day, she told him, with a glance that said, "Now you will laugh at me," what had brought her into Caddam Wood.

"I came to rub something out."

He reflected. "A memory?"

"Yes."

"Of me?"

She nodded.

"An unhappy memory?"

"Not to me," she replied, leaning on him. "I have no memory of you I would rub out, no, not the unhappiest one, for it was you, and that makes it dear. All memories, however sad, of loved ones become sweet, don't they, when we get far enough away from them?"

"But to whom, then, is this memory painful, Grizel?"

Again she cast that glance at him. "To her," she whispered.

"'That little girl'!"

TOMMY AND GRIZEL

"Yes; the child I used to be. You see, she never grew up, and so they are not distant memories to her. I try to rub them out of her mind by giving her prettier things to think of. I go to the places where she was most unhappy, and tell her sweet things about you. I am not morbid, am I, in thinking of her still as some one apart from myself? You know how it began, in the lonely days when I used to look at her in mamma's mirror, and pity her, and fancy that she was pitying me and entreating me to be careful. Always when I think I see her now, she seems to be looking anxiously at me and saying, 'Oh, do be careful!' And the sweet things I tell her about you are meant to show her how careful I have become. Are you laughing at me for this? I sometimes laugh at it myself."

"No, it is delicious," he answered her, speaking more lightly than he felt. "What a numskull you make, Grizel, of any man who presumes to write about women! I am at school again, and you are Miss Ailie teaching me the alphabet. But I thought you lost that serious little girl on the doleful day when she heard you say that you loved me best."

"She came back. She has no one but me."

"And she still warns you against me?"

Grizel laughed gleefully. "I am too clever for her," she said. "I do all the talking. I allow her

THE GIRL SHE HAD BEEN

to listen only. And you must not blame her for distrusting you; I have said such things against you to her! Oh, the things I said! On the first day I saw you, for instance, after you came back to Thrums. It was in church. Do you remember?"

"I should like to know what you said to her about me that day."

"Would you?" Grizel asked merrily. "Well, let me see. She was not at church — she never went there, you remember; but of course she was curious to hear about you, and I had no sooner got home than she came to me and said, 'Was he there?' 'Yes,' I said. 'Is he much changed?' she asked. 'He has a beard,' I said. 'You know that is not what I really mean,' she said, and then I said, 'I don't think he is so much changed that it is impossible to recognize him again.'"

Tommy interrupted her: "Now what did you mean by that?"

"I meant that I thought you were a little annoyed to find the congregation looking at Gavinia's baby more than at you!"

"Grizel, you are a wretch, but perhaps you were right. Well, what more did the little inquisitor want to know?"

"She asked me if I felt any of my old fear of you, and I said No, and then she clapped her hands with joy. And she asked whether you looked at me as if you were begging me to say I still thought you a wonder, and I said I thought you did ———"

"Grizel!"

"Oh, I told her ever so many dreadful things as soon as I found them out. I told her the whole story of your ankle, sir, for instance."

"On my word, Grizel, you seem to have omitted nothing!"

"Ah, but I did," she cried. "I never told her how much I wanted you to be admirable; I pretended that I despised you merely, and in reality I was wringing my hands with woe every time you did not behave like a god."

"They will be worn away, Grizel, if you go on doing that."

"I don't think so," she replied, "nor can she think so if she believes half of what I have told her about you since. She knows how you saved the boy's life. I told her that in the old Lair because she had some harsh memories of you there; and it was at the Cuttle Well that I told her about the glove."

"And where," asked Tommy, severely, "did you tell her that you had been mistaken in thinking me jealous of a baby and anxious to be considered a wonder?"

She hid her face for a moment, and then looked up roguishly into his. "I have not told her that yet!" she replied. It was so audacious of her that he took her by the ears.

"If I were vain," Tommy said reflectively, "I would certainly shake you now. You show a painful want of tact, Grizel, in implying that I am not perfect. Nothing annoys men so much. We can stand anything except that."

His merriness gladdened her. "They are only little things," she said, "and I have grown to love them. I know they are flaws; but I love them because———"

"Say because they are mine. You owe me that."

"No; but because they are weaknesses I don't have. I have others, but not those, and it is sweet to me to know that you are weak in some matters in which I am strong. It makes me feel that I can be of use to you."

"Are you insinuating that there are more of them?" Tommy demanded, sitting up.

"You are not very practical," she responded, "and I am."

"Go on."

"And you are — just a little — inclined to be senti———"

"Hush! I don't allow that word; but you may say, if you choose, that I am sometimes carried away by a too generous impulse."

"And that it will be my part," said she, "to

seize you by the arm and hold you back. Oh, you will give me a great deal to do! That is one of the things I love you for. It was one of the things I loved my dear Dr. McQueen for." She looked up suddenly. "I have told him also about you."

"Lately, Grizel?"

"Yes, in my parlour. It was his parlour, you know, and I had kept nothing from him while he was alive; that is to say, he always knew what I was thinking of, and I like to fancy that he knows still. In the evenings he used to sit in the arm-chair by the fire, and I sat talking or knitting at his feet, and if I ceased to do anything except sit still, looking straight before me, he knew I was thinking the morbid thoughts that had troubled me in the old days at Double Dykes. Without knowing it I sometimes shuddered at those times, and he was distressed. It reminded him of my mamma."

"I understand," Tommy said hurriedly. He meant: "Let us avoid painful subjects."

"It is years," she went on, "since those thoughts have troubled me, and it was he who drove them away. He was so kind! He thought so much of my future that I still sit by his arm-chair and tell him what is happening to his Grizel. I don't speak aloud, of course; I scarcely say the words to myself even; and yet we seem to have long talks together. I told him I had given you his coat."

"I SIT STILL BY HIS ARM-CHAIR AND TELL HIM WHAT IS HAPPENING TO HIS GRIZEL"

THE GIRL SHE HAD BEEN

"Well, I don't think he was pleased at that, Grizel. I have had a feeling for some time that the coat dislikes me. It scratched my hand the first time I put it on. My hand caught in the hook of the collar, you will say; but no, that is not what I think. In my opinion, the deed was maliciously done. McQueen always distrusted me, you know, and I expect his coat was saying, 'Hands off my Grizel.'"

She took it as quite a jest. "He does not distrust you now," she said, smiling. "I have told him what I think of you, and though he was surprised at first, in the end his opinion was the same as mine."

"Ah, you saw to that, Grizel!"

"I had nothing to do with it. I merely told him everything, and he had to agree with me. How could he doubt when he saw that you had made me so happy! Even mamma does not doubt."

"You have told her! All this is rather eerie, Grizel."

"You are not sorry, are you?" she asked, looking at him anxiously. "Dr. McQueen wanted me to forget her. He thought that would be best for me. It was the only matter on which we differed. I gave up speaking of her to him. You are the only person I have mentioned her to since I became a woman; but I often think of her. I am sure there was a time, before I was old enough to understand, when she was very fond of me. I was her baby, and women can't help being fond of their babies, even though they should never have had them. I think she often hugged me tight."

"Need we speak of this, Grizel?"

"For this once," she entreated. "You must remember that mamma often looked at me with hatred, and said I was the cause of all her woe; but sometimes in her last months she would give me such sad looks that I trembled, and I felt that she was picturing me growing into the kind of woman she wished so much she had not become herself, and that she longed to save me. That is why I have told her that a good man loves me. She is so glad, my poor dear mamma, that I tell her again and again, and she loves to hear it as much as I to tell it. What she loves to hear most is that you really do want to marry me. She is so fond of hearing that because it is what my father would never say to her."

Tommy was so much moved that he could not speak, but in his heart he gave thanks that what Grizel said of him to her mamma was true at last.

"It makes her so happy," Grizel said, "that when I seem to see her now she looks as sweet and pure as she must have been in the days when she was an innocent girl. I think she can enter into my feelings more than any other person could ever do.

THE GIRL SHE HAD BEEN

Is that because she was my mother? She understands how I feel just as I can understand how in the end she was willing to be bad because he wanted it so much."

"No, no, Grizel," Tommy cried passionately, "you don't understand that!"

She rocked her arms. "Yes, I do," she said; "I do. I could never have cared for such a man; but I can understand how mamma yielded to him, and I have no feeling for her except pity, and I have told her so, and it is what she loves to hear her daughter tell her best of all."

They put the subject from them, and she told him what it was that she had come to rub out in Caddam. If you have read of Tommy's boyhood you may remember the day it ended with his departure for the farm, and that he and Elspeth walked through Caddam to the cart that was to take him from her, and how, to comfort her, he swore that he loved her with his whole heart, and Grizel not at all, and that Grizel was in the wood and heard. And how Elspeth had promised to wave to Tommy in the cart as long as it was visible, but broke down and went home sobbing, and how Grizel took her place and waved, pretending to be Elspeth, so that he might think she was bearing up bravely. Tommy had not known what Grizel did for him that day, and when he heard it now for the first time from her own lips, he realized afresh what a glorious girl she was and had always been.

"You may try to rub that memory out of little Grizel's head," he declared, looking very proudly at her, "but you shall never rub it out of mine."

It was by his wish that they went together to the spot where she had heard him say that he loved Elspeth only—"if you can find it," Tommy said, "after all these years"; and she smiled at his mannish words—she had found it so often since! There was the very clump of whin.

And here was the boy to match. Oh, who by striving could make himself a boy again as Tommy could! I tell you he was always irresistible then. What is genius? It is the power to be a boy again at will. When I think of him flinging off the years and whistling childhood back, not to himself only, but to all who heard, distributing it among them gaily, imperiously calling on them to dance, dance, for they are boys and girls again until they stop — when to recall him in those wild moods is to myself to grasp for a moment at the dear dead days that were so much the best, I cannot wonder that Grizel loved him. I am his slave myself; I see that all that was wrong with Tommy was that he could not always be a boy.

"Hide there again, Grizel," he cried to her, little Tommy cried to her, Stroke the Jacobite, her captain, cried to the Lady Griselda; and he disappeared,

THE GIRL SHE HAD BEEN

and presently marched down the path with an imaginary Elspeth by his side. "I love you both, Elspeth," he was going to say, "and my love for the one does not make me love the other less"; but he glanced at Grizel, and she was leaning forward to catch his words as if this were no play, but life or death, and he knew what she longed to hear him say, and he said it: "I love you very much, Elspeth, but however much I love you, it would be idle to pretend that I don't love Grizel more."

A stifled cry of joy came from a clump of whin hard by, and they were man and woman again.

"Did you not know it, Grizel?"

"No, no; you never told me."

"I never dreamed it was necessary to tell you."

"Oh, if you knew how I have longed that it might be so, yes, and sometimes hated Elspeth because I feared it could not be! I have tried so hard to be content with second place. I have thought it all out, and said to myself it was natural that Elspeth should be first."

"My tragic love," he said, "I can see you arguing in that way, but I don't see you convincing yourself. My passionate Grizel is not the girl to accept second place from anyone. If I know anything of her, I know that."

To his surprise, she answered softly: "You are wrong. I wonder at it myself, but I had made up

TOMMY AND GRIZEL

my mind to be content with second place, and to be grateful for it."

"I could not have believed it!" he cried.

"I could not have believed it myself," said she.

"Are you the Grizel —— " he began.

"No," she said, "I have changed a little," and she looked pathetically at him.

"It stabs me," he said, "to see you so humble."

"I am humbler than I was," she answered huskily, but she was looking at him with the fondest love.

"Don't look at me so, Grizel," he implored. "I am unworthy of it. I am the man who has made you so humble."

"Yes," she answered, and still she looked at him with the fondest love. A film came over his eyes, and she touched them softly with her handkerchief.

"Those eyes that but a little while ago were looking so coldly at you!" he said.

"Dear eyes!" said she.

"Though I were to strike you——" he cried, raising his hand.

She took the hand in hers and kissed it.

"Has it come to this!" he said, and as she could not speak, she nodded. He fell upon his knees before her.

"I am glad you are a little sorry," she said; "I am a little sorry myself."

CHAPTER XIX

OF THE CHANGE IN THOMAS

To find ways of making David propose to Elspeth, of making Elspeth willing to exchange her brother for David — they were heavy tasks, but Tommy yoked himself to them gallantly and tugged like an Arab steed in the plough. It should be almost as pleasant to us as to him to think that love was what made him do it, for he was sure he loved Grizel at last, and that the one longing of his heart was to marry her; the one marvel to him was that he had ever longed ardently for anything else. Well, as you know, she longed for it also, but she was firm in her resolve that until Elspeth was engaged Tommy should be a single man. She even made him promise not to kiss her again so long as their love had to be kept secret. "It will be so sweet to wait," she said bravely. As we shall see presently, his efforts to put Elspeth into the hands of David were apparently of no avail, but though this would have embittered many men, it drew only to the surface some of Tommy's noblest attributes; as he suffered in silence he became gentler, more considerate, and acquired a new command over himself. To conquer self for her sake (this is in the " Letters to a Young Man ") is the highest tribute a man can pay to a woman; it is the only real greatness, and Tommy had done it now. I could give you a score of proofs. Let us take his treatment of Aaron Latta.

One day about this time Tommy found himself alone in the house with Aaron, and had he been the old Tommy he would have waited but a moment to let Aaron decide which of them should go elsewhere. It was thus that these two, ever so uncomfortable in each other's presence, contrived to keep the peace. Now note the change.

"Aaron," said Tommy, in the hush that had fallen on that house since quiet Elspeth left it, "I have never thanked you in words for all that you have done for me and Elspeth."

"Dinna do it now, then," replied the warper, fidgeting.

"I must," Tommy said cheerily, "I must"; and he did, while Aaron scowled.

"It was never done for you," Aaron informed him, "nor for the father you are the marrows o'."

"It was done for my mother," said Tommy, reverently.

"I'm none so sure o't," Aaron rapped out. "I think I brocht you twa here as bairns, that the re-

OF THE CHANGE IN THOMAS

minder of my shame should ever stand before me."

But Tommy shook his head, and sat down sympathetically beside the warper. "You loved her, Aaron," he said simply. "It was an undying love that made you adopt her orphan children." A charming thought came to him. "When you brought us here," he said, with some elation, "Elspeth used to cry at nights because our mother's spirit did not come to us to comfort us, and I invented boyish explanations to appease her. But I have learned since why we did not see that spirit; for though it hovered round this house, its first thought was not for us, but for him who succoured us."

He could have made it much better had he been able to revise it, but surely it was touching, and Aaron need not have said "Damn," which was what he did say.

One knows how most men would have received so harsh an answer to such gentle words, and we can conceive how a very holy man, say a monk, would have bowed to it. Even as the monk did Tommy submit, or say rather with the meekness of a nun.

"I wish I could help you in any way, Aaron," he said, with a sigh.

"You can," replied Aaron, promptly, "by taking yourself off to London, and leaving Elspeth here wi' me. I never made pretence that I wanted you, except because she wouldna come without you. Laddie and man, as weel you ken, you were aye a scunner to me."

"And yet," said Tommy, looking at him admiringly, "you fed and housed and educated us. Ah, Aaron, do you not see that your dislike gives me the more reason only to esteem you?" Carried away by desire to help the old man, he put his hand kindly on his shoulder. "You have never respected yourself," he said, "since the night you and my mother parted at the Cuttle Well, and my heart bleeds to think of it. Many a year ago, by your kindness to two forlorn children, you expiated that sin, and it is blotted out from your account. Forget it, Aaron, as every other person has forgotten it, and let the spirit of Jean Myles see you tranquil once again."

He patted Aaron affectionately; he seemed to be the older of the two.

"Tak' your hand off my shuther," Aaron cried fiercely.

Tommy removed his hand, but he continued to look yearningly at the warper. Another beautiful thought came to him.

"What are you looking so holy about?" asked Aaron, with misgivings.

"Aaron," cried Tommy, suddenly inspired, "you are not always the gloomy man you pass for being.

OF THE CHANGE IN THOMAS

You have glorious moments still. You wake in the morning, and for a second of time you are in the heyday of your youth, and you and Jean Myles are to walk out to-night. As you sit by this fire you think you hear her hand on the latch of the door; as you pass down the street you seem to see her coming towards you. It is for a moment only, and then you are a gray-haired man again, and she has been in her grave for many a year; but you have that moment."

Aaron rose, amazed and wrathful. "The de'il tak' you," he cried, "how did you find out that?"

Perhaps Tommy's nose turned up rapturously in reply, for the best of us cannot command ourselves altogether at great moments, but when he spoke he was modest again.

"It was sympathy that told me," he explained; "and, Aaron, if you will only believe me, it tells me also that a little of the man you were still clings to you. Come out of the moroseness in which you have enveloped yourself so long. Think what a joy it would be to Elspeth."

"It's little she would care."

"If you want to hurt her, tell her so."

"I'm no denying but what she's fell fond o' me."

"Then for her sake," Tommy pleaded.

But the warper turned on him with baleful eyes. "She likes me," he said in a grating voice, "and yet I'm as nothing to her; we are all as nothing to her beside you. If there hadna been you I should hae become the father to her I craved to be; but you had mesmerized her; she had eyes for none but you. I sent you to the herding, meaning to break your power over her, and all she could think o' was my cruelty in sindering you. Syne you ran aff wi' her to London, stealing her frae me. I was without her while she was growing frae lassie to woman, the years when maybe she could hae made o' me what she willed. Magerful Tam took the mother frae me, and he lived again in you to tak' the dochter."

"You really think me masterful—me!" Tommy said, smiling.

"I suppose you never were!" Aaron replied ironically.

"Yes," Tommy admitted frankly, "I was masterful as a boy, ah, and even quite lately. How we change!" he said musingly.

"How we dinna change!" retorted Aaron, bitterly. He had learned the truer philosophy.

"Man," he continued, looking Tommy over, "there's times when I see mair o' your mother than your father in you. She was a wonder at making believe. The letters about her grandeur that she wrote to Thrums when she was starving! Even you couldna hae wrote them better. But she never managed to cheat hersel'. That's whaur you sail away frae her."

OF THE CHANGE IN THOMAS

"I used to make believe, Aaron, as you say," Tommy replied sadly. "If you knew how I feel the folly of it now, perhaps even you would wish that I felt it less.

"But we must each of us dree his own weird," he proceeded, with wonderful sweetness, when Aaron did not answer. "And so far, at least, as Elspeth is concerned, surely I have done my duty. I had the bringing up of her from the days when she was learning to speak."

"She got into the way o' letting you do everything for her," the warper responded sourly. "You thought for her, you acted for her, frae the first; you toomed her, and then filled her up wi' yoursel'."

"She always needed some one to lean on."

"Ay, because you had maimed her. She grew up in the notion that you were all the earth and the wonder o' the world."

"Could I help that?"

"Help it! Did you try? It was the one thing you were sure o' yoursel'; it was the one thing you thought worth anybody's learning. You stood before her crowing the whole day. I said the now I wished you would go and leave her wi' me: but I wouldna dare to keep her; she's helpless without you; if you took your arm awa frae her now, she would tumble to the ground."

"I fear it is true, Aaron," Tommy said, with bent

head. "Whether she is so by nature, or whether I have made her so, I cannot tell, but I fear that what you say is true."

"It's true," said Aaron, "and yours is the wite. There's no life for her now except what you mak'; she canna see beyond you. Go on thinking yoursel' a wonder if you like, but mind this: if you were to cast her off frae you now, she would die like an amputated hand."

To Tommy it was like listening to his doom. Ah, Aaron, even you could not withhold your pity, did you know how this man is being punished now for having made Elspeth so dependent on him! Some such thought passed through Tommy's head, but he was too brave to appeal for pity. "If that is so," he said firmly, "I take the responsibility for it. But I began this talk, Aaron, not to intrude my troubles on you, but hoping to lighten yours. If I could see you smile, Aaron ——"

"Drop it!" cried the warper; and then, going closer to him: "You would hae seen me smile, ay, and heard me laugh, gin you had been here when Mrs. McLean came yont to read your book to me. She fair insistit on reading the terrible noble bits to me, and she grat they were so sublime; but the sublimer they were, the mair I laughed, for I ken you, Tommy, my man, I ken you."

He spoke with much vehemence, and, after all, our hero was not perfect. He withdrew stiffly to

OF THE CHANGE IN THOMAS

the other room. I think it was the use of the word Tommy that enraged him.

But in a very few minutes he scorned himself, and was possessed by a pensive wonder that one so tragically fated as he could resent an old man's gibe. Aaron misunderstood him. Was that any reason why he should not feel sorry for Aaron? He crossed the hallan to the kitchen door, and stopped there, overcome with pity. The warper was still crouching by the fire, but his head rested on his chest; he was a weary, desolate figure, and at the other side of the hearth stood an empty chair. The picture was the epitome of his life, or so it seemed to the sympathetic soul at the door, who saw him passing from youth to old age, staring at the chair that must always be empty. At the same moment Tommy saw his own future, and in it, too, an empty chair. Yet, hard as was his own case, at least he knew that he was loved; if her chair must be empty, the fault was as little hers as his, while Aaron ——

A noble compassion drew him forward, and he put his hand determinedly on the dear old man's shoulder.

"Aaron," he said, in a tremble of pity, "I know what is the real sorrow of your life, and I rejoice because I can put an end to it. You think that Jean Myles never cared for you; but you are strangely wrong. I was with my mother to the last, Aaron, and I can tell you, she asked me with her dying breath to say to you that she loved you all the time."

Aaron tried to rise, but was pushed back into his chair. "Love cannot die," cried Tommy, triumphantly, like the fairy in the pantomime; "love is always young —— "

He stopped in mid-career at sight of Aaron's disappointing face. "Are you done?" the warper inquired. "When you and me are alane in this house there's no room for the both o' us, and as I'll never hae it said that I made Jean Myles's bairn munt, I'll go out mysel'."

And out he went, and sat on the dyke till Elspeth came home. It did not turn Tommy sulky. He nodded kindly to Aaron from the window in token of forgiveness, and next day he spent a valuable hour in making a cushion for the old man's chair. "He must be left with the impression that you made it," Tommy explained to Elspeth, "for he would not take it from me."

"Oh, Tommy, how good you are!"

"I am far from it, Elspeth."

"There is a serenity about you nowadays," she said, "that I don't seem to have noticed before," and indeed this was true; it was the serenity that comes to those who, having a mortal wound, can no more be troubled by the pin-pricks.

OF THE CHANGE IN THOMAS

"There has been nothing to cause it, has there?" Elspeth asked timidly.

"Only the feeling that I have much to be grateful for," he replied. "I have you, Elspeth."

"And I have you," she said, "and I want no more. I could never care for anyone as I care for you, Tommy."

She was speaking unselfishly; she meant to imply delicately that the doctor's defection need not make Tommy think her unhappy. "Are you glad?" she asked.

He said Yes bravely. Elspeth, he was determined, should never have the distress of knowing that for her sake he was giving up the one great joy which life contains. He was a grander character than most. Men have often in the world's history made a splendid sacrifice for women, but if you turn up the annals you will find that the woman nearly always knew of it.

He told Grizel what Aaron had said and what Elspeth had said. He could keep nothing from her now; he was done with the world of make-believe for ever. And it seemed wicked of him to hope, he declared, or to let her hope. "I ought to give you up, Grizel," he said, with a groan.

"I won't let you," she replied adorably.

"Gemmell has not come near us for a week. I ask him in, but he avoids the house."

TOMMY AND GRIZEL

"I don't understand it," Grizel had to admit; "but I think he is fond of her, I do indeed."

"Even if that were so, I fear she would not accept him. I know Elspeth so well that I feel I am deceiving you if I say there is any hope."

"Nevertheless you must say it," she answered brightly; "you must say it and leave me to think it. And I do think it. I believe that Elspeth, despite her timidity and her dependence on you, is like other girls at heart, and not more difficult to win.

"And even if it all comes to nothing," she told him, a little faintly, "I shall not be unhappy. You don't really know me if you think I should love to be married so — so much as all that."

"It is you, Grizel," he replied, "who don't see that it is myself I am pitying. It is I who want to be married as much as all that."

Her eyes shone with a soft light, for of course it was what she wanted him to say. These two seemed to have changed places. That people could love each other, and there the end, had been his fond philosophy and her torment. Now, it was she who argued for it and Tommy who shook his head.

"They can be very, very happy."

"No," he said.

"But one of them is."

OF THE CHANGE IN THOMAS

"Not the other," he insisted; and of course it was again what she wanted him to say.

And he was not always despairing. He tried hard to find a way of bringing David to Elspeth's feet, and once, at least, the apparently reluctant suitor almost succumbed. Tommy had met him near Aaron's house, and invited him to come in and hear Elspeth singing. "I did not know she sang," David said, hesitating.

"She is so shy about it," Tommy replied lightly, "that we can hear her by stealth only. Aaron and I listen at the door. Come and listen at the door."

And David had yielded and listened at the door, and afterwards gone in and remained like one who could not tear himself away. What was more, he and Elspeth had touched upon the subject of love in their conversation, Tommy sitting at the window so engrossed in a letter to Pym that he seemed to hear nothing, though he could repeat everything afterwards to Grizel.

Elspeth had said, in her shrinking way, that if she were a man she could love only a woman who was strong and courageous and helpful — such a woman as Grizel, she had said.

"And yet," David replied, "women have been loved who had none of those qualities."

"In spite of the want of them?" Elspeth asked.

"Perhaps because of it," said he.

"They are noble qualities," Elspeth maintained a little sadly, and he assented. "And one of them, at least, is essential," she said. "A woman has no right to be loved who is not helpful."

"She is helpful to the man who loves her," David replied.

"He would have to do for her," Elspeth said, "the very things she should be doing for him."

"He may want very much to do them," said David.

"Then it is her weakness that appeals to him. Is not that loving her for the wrong thing?"

"It may be the right thing," David insisted, "for him."

"And at that point," Tommy said, boyishly, to Grizel, "I ceased to hear them, I was so elated; I felt that everything was coming right. I could not give another thought to their future, I was so busy mapping out my own. I heard a hammering. Do you know what it was? It was our house going up — your house and mine; our home, Grizel! It was not here, nor in London. It was near the Thames. I wanted it to be upon the bank, but you said No, you were afraid of floods. I wanted to superintend the building, but you conducted me contemptuously to my desk. You intimated that I did not know how to build — that no one knew except yourself. You instructed the architect, and bullied the workmen, and cried

OF THE CHANGE IN THOMAS

for more store-closets. Grizel, I saw the house go up; I saw you the adoration and terror of your servants; I heard you singing from room to room."

He was touched by this; all beautiful thoughts touched him.

But as a rule, though Tommy tried to be brave for her sake, it was usually she who was the comforter now, and he the comforted, and this was the arrangement that suited Grizel best. Her one thought need no longer be that she loved him too much, but how much he loved her. It was not her self-respect that must be humoured back, but his. If hers lagged, what did it matter? What are her own troubles to a woman when there is something to do for the man she loves?

"You are too anxious about the future," she said to him, if he had grown gloomy again. "Can we not be happy in the present, and leave the future to take care of itself?" How strange to know that it was Grizel who said this to Tommy, and not Tommy who said it to Grizel!

She delighted in playing the mother to him. "Now you must go back to your desk," she would say masterfully. "You have three hours' work to do to-night yet."

"It can wait. Let me stay a little longer with you, Grizel," he answered humbly. Ha! it was Tommy who was humble now. Not so long ago he would not have allowed his work to wait for anyone, and Grizel knew it, and exulted.

"To work, sir," she ordered. "And you must put on your old coat before you sit down to write, and pull up your cuffs so that they don't scrape on the desk. Also, you must not think too much about me."

She tried to look businesslike, but she could scarce resist rocking her arms with delight when she heard herself saying such things to him. It was as if she had the old doctor once more in her hands.

"What more, Grizel? I like you to order me about."

"Only this. Good afternoon."

"But I am to walk home with you," he entreated.

"No," she said decisively; but she smiled: once upon a time it had been she who asked for this.

"If you are good," she said, "you shall perhaps see me to-morrow."

"Perhaps only?" He was scared; but she smiled happily again: it had once been she who had to beg that there should be no perhaps.

"If you are good," she replied,—"and you are not good when you have such a long face. Smile, you silly boy; smile when I order you. If you don't I shall not so much as look out at my window to-morrow."

OF THE CHANGE IN THOMAS

He was the man who had caused her so much agony, and she was looking at him with the eternally forgiving smile of the mother. "Ah, Grizel," Tommy cried passionately, "how brave and unselfish and noble you are, and what a glorious wife God intended you to be!"

She broke from him with a little cry, but when she turned round again it was to nod and smile to him.

CHAPTER XX

A LOVE-LETTER

Some beautiful days followed, so beautiful to Grizel that as they passed away she kissed her hand to them. Do you see her standing on tiptoe to see the last of them? They lit a fire in the chamber of her soul which is the home of all pure maids, and the fagots that warmed Grizel were every fond look that had been on her lover's face and every sweet word he had let fall. She counted and fondled them, and pretended that one was lost that she might hug it more than all the others when it was found. To sit by that fire was almost better than having the days that lit it; sometimes she could scarcely wait for the day to go.

Tommy's fond looks and sweet words! There was also a letter in those days, and, now that I remember, a little garnet ring; and there were a few other fagots, but all so trifling it must seem incredible to you that they could have made so great a blaze — nothing else in it, on my honour, except a girl's heart added by herself that the fire might burn a moment longer.

A LOVE-LETTER

And now, what so chilly as the fire that has gone out! Gone out long ago, dear Grizel, while you crouched over it. You may put your hand in the ashes; they will not burn you now. Ah, Grizel, why do you sit there in the cold?

The day of the letter! It began in dread, but ended so joyfully, do you think Grizel grudged the dread? It became dear to her; she loved to return to it and gaze at the joy it glorified, as one sees the sunshine from a murky room. When she heard the postman's knock she was not even curious; so few letters came to her, she thought this must be Maggy Ann's monthly one from Aberdeen, and went on placidly dusting. At last she lifted it from the floor, for it had been slipped beneath the door, and then Grizel was standing in her little lobby, panting as if at the end of a race. The letter lay in both her hands, and they rose slowly until they were pressed against her breast.

She uttered some faint cries (it was the only moment in which I have known Grizel to be hysterical), and then she ran to her room and locked herself in—herself and it. Do you know why that look of elation had come suddenly to her face? It was because he had not even written the address in a disguised hand to deceive the postmistress. So much of the old Grizel was gone that the pathos of her elation over this was lost to her.

Several times she almost opened it. Why did she

pause? why had that frightened look come into her eyes? She put the letter on her table and drew away from it. If she took a step nearer, her hands went behind her back as if saying, "Grizel, don't ask us to open it; we are afraid."

Perhaps it really did say the dear things that love writes. Perhaps it was aghast at the way she was treating it. Dear letter! Her mouth smiled to it, but her hands remained afraid. As she stood irresolute, smiling, and afraid, she was a little like her mother. I have put off as long as possible saying that Grizel was ever like her mother. The Painted Lady had never got any letters while she was in Thrums, but she looked wistfully at those of other people. "They are so pretty," she had said; "but don't open them: when you open them they break your heart." Grizel remembered what her mother had said.

Had the old Grizel feared what might be inside, it would have made her open the letter more quickly. Two minds to one person were unendurable to her. But she seemed to be a coward now. It was pitiable.

Perhaps it was quite a common little letter, beginning "Dear Grizel," and saying nothing more delicious or more terrible than that he wanted her to lend him one of the doctor's books. She thought of a score of trivialities it might be about; but the letter was still unopened when David Gemmell

A LOVE-LETTER

called to talk over some cases in which he required her counsel. He found her sitting listlessly, something in her lap which she at once concealed. She failed to follow his arguments, and he went away puckering his brows, some of the old doctor's sayings about her ringing loud in his ears.

One of them was: "Things will be far wrong with Grizel when she is able to sit idle with her hands in her lap."

Another: "She is almost pitifully straightforward, man. Everything that is in Grizel must out. She can hide nothing."

Yet how cunningly she had concealed what was in her hands. Cunning applied to Grizel! David shuddered. He thought of Tommy, and shut his mouth tight. He could do this easily. Tommy could not do it without feeling breathless. They were types of two kinds of men.

David also remembered a promise he had given McQueen, and wondered, as he had wondered a good deal of late, whether the time had come to keep it.

But Grizel sat on with her unopened letter. She was to meet Tommy presently on the croquet lawn of the Dovecot, when Ailie was to play Mr. James (the champion), and she decided that she must wait till then. She would know what sort of letter it was the moment she saw his face. And then! She pressed her hands together.

Oh, how base of her to doubt him! She said it to herself then and often afterwards. She looked mournfully in her mother's long mirror at this disloyal Grizel, as if the capacity to doubt him was the saddest of all the changes that had come to her. He had been so true yesterday; oh, how could she tremble to-day? Beautiful yesterday! but yesterday may seem so long ago. How little a time had passed between the moment when she was greeting him joyously in Caddam Wood and that cry of the heart, "How could you hurt your Grizel so!" No, she could not open her letter. She could kiss it, but she could not open it.

Foolish fears! for before she had shaken hands with Tommy in Mrs. McLean's garden she knew he loved her still, and that the letter proved it. She was properly punished, yet surely in excess, for when she might have been reading her first loveletter, she had to join in discussions with various ladies about Berlin wool and the like, and to applaud the prowess of Mr. James with the loathly croquet mallet. It seemed quite a long time before Tommy could get a private word with her. Then he began about the letter at once.

"You are not angry with me for writing it?" he asked anxiously. "I should not have done it; I had no right: but such a desire to do it came over me, I had to; it was such a glory to me to say in writing what you are to me."

A LOVE-LETTER

She smiled happily. Oh, exquisite day! "I have so long wanted to have a letter from you," she said. "I have almost wished you would go away for a little time, so that I might have a letter from you."

He had guessed this. He had written to give her delight.

"Did you like the first words of it, Grizel?" he asked eagerly.

The lover and the artist spoke together.

Could she admit that the letter was unopened, and why? Oh, the pain to him! She nodded assent. It was not really an untruth, she told herself. She did like them — oh, how she liked them, though she did not know what they were!

"I nearly began 'My beloved,'" he said solemnly.

Somehow she had expected it to be this. "Why did n't you?" she asked, a little disappointed.

"I like the other so much better," he replied. "To write it was so delicious to me, I thought you would not mind."

"I don't mind," she said hastily. (What could it be?)

"But you would have preferred 'beloved'?"

"It is such a sweet name."

"Surely not so sweet as the other, Grizel?"

"No," she said, "no." (Oh, what could it be!)

"Have you destroyed it?" he asked, and the question was a shock to her. Her hand rose instinctively to defend something that lay near her heart.

"I could not," she whispered.

"Do you mean you wanted to?" he asked dolefully.

"I thought you wanted it," she murmured.

"I!" he cried, aghast, and she was joyous again.

"Can't you guess where it is?" she said.

He understood. "Grizel! You carry my letter there!"

She was full of glee; but she puzzled him presently.

"Do you think I could go now?" she inquired eagerly.

"And leave me?"

It was dreadful of her, but she nodded.

"I want to go home."

"Is it not home, Grizel, when you are with me?"

"I want to go away from home, then." She said it as if she loved to tantalize him.

"But why?"

"I won't tell you." She was looking wistfully at the door. "I have something to do."

"It can wait."

"It has waited too long." He might have heard an assenting rustle from beneath her bodice.

A LOVE-LETTER

"Do let me go," she said coaxingly, as if he held her.

"I can't understand——" he began, and broke off. She was facing him demurely but exultantly, challenging him, he could see, to read her now. "Just when I am flattering myself that I know everything about you, Grizel," he said, with a long face, "I suddenly wonder whether I know anything."

She would have liked to clap her hands. "You must remember that we have changed places," she told him. "It is I who understand you now."

"And I am devoutly glad," he made answer, with humble thankfulness. "And I must ask you, Grizel, why you want to run away from me."

"But you think you know," she retorted smartly. "You think I want to read my letter again!"

Her cleverness staggered him. "But I am right, am I not, Grizel?"

"No," she said triumphantly, "you are quite wrong. Oh, if you knew how wrong you are!" And having thus again unhorsed him, she made her excuses to Ailie and slipped away. Dr. Gemmell, who was present and had been watching her narrowly, misread the flush on her face and her restless desire to be gone.

"Is there anything between those two, do you think?" Mrs. McLean had said in a twitter to him while Tommy and Grizel were talking, and he had answered No almost sharply.

"People are beginning to think there is," she said in self-defence.

"They are mistaken," he told her curtly, and it was about this time that Grizel left. David followed her to her home soon afterwards, and Maggy Ann, who answered his summons, did not accompany him upstairs. He was in the house daily, and she left him to find Grizel for himself. He opened the parlour door almost as he knocked, and she was there, but had not heard him. He stopped short, like one who had blundered unawares on what was not for him.

She was on her knees on the hearth-rug, with her head buried in what had been Dr. McQueen's chair. Ragged had been the seat of it on the day when she first went to live with him, but very early on the following morning, or, to be precise, five minutes after daybreak, he had risen to see if there were burglars in the parlour, and behold, it was his grateful little maid repadding the old arm-chair. How a situation repeats itself! Without disturbing her, the old doctor had slipped away with a full heart. It was what the young doctor did now.

But the situation was not quite the same. She had been bubbling over with glee then; she was sobbing now. David could not know that it was a sob of joy; he knew only that he had never seen her crying before, and that it was the letter in her hands that had brought tears at last to those once tranquil and steadfast eyes.

In an odd conversation which had once taken place in that room between the two doctors, Gemmell had said: "But the time may come without my knowing it." And McQueen's reply was: "I don't think so, for she is so open; but I'll tell you this, David, as a guide. I never saw her eyes wet. It is one of the touching things about her that she has the eyes of a man, to whom it is a shame to cry. If you ever see her greeting, David, I'm sore doubting that the time will have come."

As David Gemmell let himself softly out of the house, to return to it presently, he thought the time had come. What he conceived he had to do was a hard thing, but he never thought of not doing it. He had kept himself in readiness to do it for many days now, and he walked to it as firmly as if he were on his professional rounds. He did not know that the skin round his eyes had contracted, giving them the look of pain which always came there when he was sorry or pitiful or indignant. He was not well acquainted with his eyes, and, had he glanced at them now in a glass, would have presumed that this was their usual expression.

Grizel herself opened the door to him this time, and "Maggy Ann, he is found!" she cried victoriously. Evidently she had heard of his previous visit. "We have searched every room in the house for you," she said gaily, "and had you disappeared for much longer, Maggy Ann would have had the carpets up."

He excused himself on the ground that he had forgotten something, and she chided him merrily for being forgetful. As he sat with her David could have groaned aloud. How vivacious she had become! but she was sparkling in false colours. After what he knew had been her distress of a few minutes ago, it was a painted face to him. She was trying to deceive him. Perhaps she suspected that he had seen her crying, and now, attired in all a woman's wiles, she was defying him to believe his eyes.

Grizel garbed in wiles! Alack the day! She was shielding the man, and Gemmell could have driven her away roughly to get at him. But she was also standing over her own pride, lest anyone should see that it had fallen; and do you think that David would have made her budge an inch?

Of course she saw that he had something on his mind. She knew those puckered eyes so well, and had so often smoothed them for him.

"What is it, David?" she asked sympathetically. "I see you have come as a patient to-night."

"As one of those patients," he rejoined, "who feel better at mere sight of the doctor."

"Fear of the prescription?" said she.

"Not if you prescribe yourself, Grizel."

A LOVE-LETTER

"David!" she cried. He had been paying compliments!

"I mean it."

"So I can see by your face. Oh, David, how stern you look!"

"Dr. McQueen and I," he retorted, "used to hold private meetings after you had gone to bed, at which we agreed that you should no longer be allowed to make fun of us. They came to nothing. Do you know why?"

"Because I continued to do it?"

"No; but because we missed it so much if you stopped."

"You are nice to-night, David," she said, dropping him a courtesy.

"We liked all your bullying ways," he went on. "We were children in your masterful hands."

"I was a tyrant, David," she said, looking properly ashamed. "I wonder you did not marry, just to get rid of me."

"Have you ever seriously wondered why I don't marry?" he asked quickly.

"Oh, David," she exclaimed, "what else do you think your patients and I talk of when I am trying to nurse them? It has agitated the town ever since you first walked up the Marrywellbrae, and we can't get on with our work for thinking of it."

"Seriously, Grizel?"

She became grave at once. "If you could find the right woman," she said wistfully.

"I have found her," he answered; and then she pressed her hands together, too excited to speak.

"If she would only care a little for me," he said.

Grizel rocked her arms. "I am sure she does," she cried. "David, I am so glad!"

He saw what her mistake was, but pretended not to know that she had made one. "Are you really glad that I love you, Grizel?" he asked.

It seemed to daze her for a moment. "Not me, David," she said softly, as if correcting him. "You don't mean that it is me?" she said coaxingly. "David," she cried, "say it is not me!"

He drooped his head, but not before he had seen all the brightness die out of her face. "Is it so painful to you even to hear me say it?" he asked gravely.

Her joy had been selfish as her sorrow was. For nigh a minute she had been thinking of herself alone, it meant so much to her; but now she jumped up and took his hand in hers.

"Poor David!" she said, making much of his hand as if she had hurt it. But David Gemmell's was too simple a face to oppose to her pitying eyes, and presently she let his hand slip from her and stood regarding him curiously. He had to look another way, and then she even smiled, a little forlornly.

A LOVE-LETTER

"Do you mind talking it over with me, Grizel?" he asked. "I have always been well aware that you did not care for me in that way, but nevertheless I believe you might do worse."

"No woman could do better," she answered gravely. "I should like you to talk it over, David, if you begin at the beginning"; and she sat down with her hands crossed.

"I won't say what a good thing it would be for me," was his beginning; "we may take that for granted."

"I don't think we can," she remarked; "but it scarcely matters at present. That is not the beginning, David."

He was very anxious to make it the beginning.

"I am weary of living in lodgings," he said. "The practice suffers by my not being married. Many patients dislike being attended by a single man. I ought to be in McQueen's house; it has been so long known as the doctor's house. And you should be a doctor's wife—you who could almost be the doctor. It would be a shame, Grizel, if you who are so much to patients were to marry out of the profession. Don't you follow me?"

"I follow you," she replied; "but what does it matter? You have not begun at the beginning." He looked at her inquiringly. "You must begin," she informed him, "by saying why you ask me to marry you when you don't love me." She added, in answer to another look from him: "You know you don't." There was a little reproach in it. "Oh, David, what made you think I could be so easily taken in!"

He looked so miserable that by and by she smiled, not so tremulously as before.

"How bad at it you are, David!" she said.

And how good at it she was! he thought gloomily.

"Shall I help you out?" she asked gently, but speaking with dignity. "You think I am unhappy; you believe I am in the position in which you placed yourself, of caring for someone who does not care for me."

"Grizel, I mistrust him."

She flushed; she was not quite so gentle now. "And so you offer me your hand to save me! It was a great self-sacrifice, David, but you used not to be fond of doing showy things."

"I did not mean it to be showy," he answered.

She was well aware of that, but—— "Oh, David," she cried, "that you should believe I needed it! How little you must think of me!"

"Does it look as if I thought little of you?" he said.

"Little of my strength, David, little of my pride."

"I think so much of them that how could I stand by silently and watch them go?"

A LOVE-LETTER

"You think you have seen that!" She was agitated now.

He hesitated. "Yes," he said courageously.

Her eyes cried, "David, how could you be so cruel!" but they did not daunt him.

"Have you not seen it yourself, Grizel?" he said.

She pressed her hands together. "I was so happy," she said, "until you came!"

"Have you not seen it yourself?" he asked again.

"There may be better things," she retorted, "than those you rate so highly."

"Not for you," he said.

"If they are gone," she told him, with a flush of resentment, "it is not you who can bring them back."

"But let me try, Grizel," said he.

"David, can I not even make you angry with me?"

"No, Grizel, you can't. I am very sorry that I can make you angry with me."

"I am not," she said dispiritedly. "It would be contemptible in me." And then, eagerly: "But, David, you have made a great mistake, indeed you have. You — you are a dreadful bungler, sir!" She was trying to make his face relax, with a tremulous smile from herself to encourage him; but the effort was not successful. "You see, I can't even bully you now!" she said. "Did that capacity go with the others, David?"

"Try a little harder," he replied. "I think you will find that I submit to it still."

"Very well." She forced some gaiety to her aid. After all, how could she let his monstrous stupidity wound a heart protected by such a letter?

"You have been a very foolish and presumptuous boy," she began. She was standing up, smiling, wagging a reproachful but nervous finger at him. "If it were not that I have a weakness for seeing medical men making themselves ridiculous so that I may put them right, I should be very indignant with you, sir."

"Put me right, Grizel," he said. He was sure she was trying to blind him again.

"Know, then, David, that I am not the poor-spirited, humble creature you seem to have come here in search of——"

"But you admitted——"

"How dare you interrupt me, sir! Yes, I admit that I am not quite as I was, but I glory in it. I used to be ostentatiously independent; now I am only independent enough. My pride made me walk on air; now I walk on the earth, where there is less chance of falling. I have still confidence in myself; but I begin to see that ways are not necessarily right because they are my ways. In short,

A LOVE-LETTER

David, I am evidently on the road to being a model character!"

They were gay words, but she ended somewhat faintly.

"I was satisfied with you as you were," was the doctor's comment.

"I wanted to excel!"

"You explain nothing, Grizel," he said reproachfully. "Why have you changed so?"

"Because I am so happy. Do you remember how, in the old days, I sometimes danced for joy? I could do it now."

"Are you engaged to be married, Grizel?"

She took a quiet breath. "You have no right to question me in this way," she said. "I think I have been very good in bearing with you so long."

But she laid aside her indignation at once; he was so old a friend, the sincerity of him had been so often tried. "If you must know, David," she said, with a girlish frankness that became her better, "I am not engaged to be married. And I must tell you nothing more," she added, shutting her mouth decisively. She must be faithful to her promise.

"He forbids it?" Gemmell asked mercilessly.

She stamped her foot, not in rage, but in hopelessness. "How incapable you are of doing him justice!" she cried. "If you only knew ——"

"Tell me. I want to do him justice."

She sat down again, sighing. "My attempt to regain my old power over you has not been very successful, has it, David? We must not quarrel, though"— holding out her hand, which he grasped. "And you won't question me any more?" She said it appealingly.

"Never again," he answered. "I never wanted to question you, Grizel. I wanted only to marry you."

"And that can't be."

"I don't see it," he said, so stoutly that she was almost amused. But he would not be pushed aside. He had something more to say.

"Dr. McQueen wished it," he said; "above all else in the world he wished it. He often told me so."

"He never said that to me," Grizel replied quickly.

"Because he thought that to press you was no way to make you care for me. He hoped that it would come about."

"It has not come about, David, with either of us," she said gently. "I am sure that would have been sufficient answer to him."

"No, Grizel, it would not, not now."

He had risen, and his face was whiter than she had ever seen it.

"I am going to hurt you, Grizel," he said, and

A LOVE-LETTER

every word was a pang to him. "I see no other way. It has got to be done. Dr. McQueen often talked to me about the things that troubled you when you were a little girl — the morbid fears you had then, and that had all been swept away years before I knew you. But though they had been long gone, you were so much to him that he tried to think of everything that might happen to you in the future, and he foresaw that they might possibly come back. 'If she were ever to care for some false loon!' he has said to me, and then, Grizel, he could not go on."

Grizel beat her hands. "If he could not go on," she said, "it was not because he feared what I should do."

"No, no," David answered eagerly, "he never feared for that, but for your happiness. He told me of a boy who used to torment you, oh, all so long ago, and of such little account that he had forgotten his name. But that boy has come back, and you care for him, and he is a false loon, Grizel."

She had risen too, and was flashing fire on David; but he went on.

"'If the time ever comes,' he said to me, 'when you see her in torture from such a cause, speak to her openly about it. Tell her it is I who am speaking through you. It will be a hard task to you, but wrestle through with it, David, in memory of any little kindness I may have done you, and the great love I bore my Grizel.'"

She was standing rigid now. "Is there any more, David?" she said in a low voice.

"Only this. I admired you then as I admire you now. I may not love you, Grizel, but of this I am very sure"—he was speaking steadily, he was forgetting no one—"that you are the noblest and bravest woman I have ever known, and I promised—he did not draw the promise from me, I gave it to him—that if I was a free man and could help you in any way without paining you by telling you these things, I would try that way first."

"And this is the way?"

"I could think of no other. Is it of no avail?"

She shook her head. "You have made such a dreadful mistake," she cried miserably, "and you won't see it. Oh, how you wrong him! I am the happiest girl in the world, and it is he who makes me so happy. But I can't explain. You need not ask me; I promised, and I won't."

"You used not to be so fond of mystery, Grizel."

"I am not fond of it now."

"Ah, it is he," David said bitterly, and he lifted his hat. "Is there nothing you will let me do for you, Grizel?" he cried.

"I thought you were to do so much for me when

A LOVE-LETTER

you came into this room," she admitted wistfully, "and said that you were in love. I thought it was with another woman."

He remembered that her face had brightened. "How could that have helped you?" he asked.

She saw that she had but to tell him, and for her sake he would do it at once. But she could not be so selfish.

"We need not speak of that now," she said.

"We must speak of it," he answered. "Grizel, it is but fair to me. It may be so important to me."

"You have shown that you don't care for her, David, and that ends it."

"Who is it?" He was much stirred.

"If you don't know——"

"Is it Elspeth?"

The question came out of him like a confession, and hope turned Grizel giddy.

"Do you love her, David?" she cried.

But he hesitated. "Is what you have told me true, that it would help you?" he asked, looking her full in the eyes.

"Do you love her?" she implored, but he was determined to have her answer first.

"Is it, Grizel?"

"Yes, yes. Do you, David?"

And then he admitted that he did, and she rocked her arms in joy.

"But oh, David, to say such things to me when you were not a free man! How badly you have treated Elspeth to-day!"

"She does not care for me," he said.

"Have you asked her?"—in alarm.

"No; but could she?"

"How could she help it?" She would not tell him what Tommy thought. Oh, she must do everything to encourage David.

"And still," said he, puzzling, "I don't see how it can affect you."

"And I can't tell you," she moaned. "Oh, David, do, do find out. Why are you so blind?" She could have shaken him. "Don't you see that once Elspeth was willing to be taken care of by some other person —— I must not tell you!"

"Then he would marry you?"

She cried in anxiety: "Have I told you, or did you find out?"

"I found out," he said. "Is it possible he is so fond of her as that?"

"There never was such a brother," she answered. She could not help adding, "But he is still fonder of me."

The doctor pulled his arm over his eyes and sat down again. Presently he was saying with a long face: "I came here to denounce the cause of your unhappiness, and I begin to see it is myself."

"Of course it is, you stupid David," she said

A LOVE-LETTER

gleefully. She was very kind to the man who had been willing to do so much for her; but as the door closed on him she forgot him. She even ceased to hear the warning voice he had brought with him from the dead. She was re-reading the letter that began by calling her wife.

CHAPTER XXI

THE ATTEMPT TO CARRY ELSPETH BY NUMBERS

THAT was one of Grizel's beautiful days, but there were others to follow as sweet, if not so exciting; she could travel back through the long length of them without coming once to a moment when she had held her breath in sudden fear; and this was so delicious that she sometimes thought these were the best days of all.

Of course she had little anxieties, but they were nearly all about David. He was often at Aaron's house now, and what exercised her was this—that she could not be certain that he was approaching Elspeth in the right way. The masterful Grizel seemed to have come to life again, for, evidently, she was convinced that she alone knew the right way.

"Oh, David, I would not have said that to her!" she told him, when he reported progress; and now she would warn him, "You are too humble," and again, "You were over-bold." The doctor, to his bewilderment, frequently discovered, on laying re-

THE ATTEMPT TO CARRY ELSPETH

sults before her, that what he had looked upon as encouraging signs were really bad, and that, on the other hand, he had often left the cottage disconsolately when he ought to have been strutting. The issue was that he lost all faith in his own judgment, and if Grizel said that he was getting on well, his face became foolishly triumphant, but if she frowned, it cried, "All is over!"

Of the proposal Tommy did not know; it seemed to her that she had no right to tell even him of that; but the rest she did tell him: that David, by his own confession, was in love with Elspeth; and so pleased was Tommy that his delight made another day for her to cherish.

So now everything depended on Elspeth. "Oh, if she only would!" Grizel cried, and for her sake Tommy tried to look bright, but his head shook in spite of him.

"Do you mean that we should discourage David?" she asked dolefully; but he said No to that.

"I was afraid," she confessed, "that as you are so hopeless, you might think it your duty to discourage him so as to save him the pain of a refusal."

"Not at all," Tommy said, with some hastiness.

"Then you do really have a tiny bit of hope?"

"While there is life there is hope," he answered.

She said: "I have been thinking it over, for it is so important to us, and I see various ways in which you could help David, if you would."

"What would I not do, Grizel! You have to name them only."

"Well, for instance, you might show her that you have a very high opinion of him."

"Agreed. But she knows that already."

"Then, David is an only child. Don't you think you could say that men who have never had a sister are peculiarly gentle and considerate to women?"

"Oh, Grizel! But I think I can say that."

"And — and that having been so long accustomed to doing everything for themselves, they don't need managing wives as men brought up among women need them."

"Yes. But how cunning you are, Grizel! Who would have believed it?"

"And then——" She hesitated.

"Go on. I see by your manner that this is to be a big one."

"It would be such a help," she said eagerly, "if you could be just a little less attentive to her. I know you do ever so much of the housework because she is not fond of it; and if she has a headache you sit with her all day; and you beg her to play and sing to you, though you really dislike music. Oh, there are scores of things you do for

THE ATTEMPT TO CARRY ELSPETH

her, and if you were to do them a little less willingly, in such a way as to show her that they interrupt your work and are a slight trial to you, I — I am sure that would help!"

"She would see through me, Grizel. Elspeth is sharper than you think her."

"Not if you did it very skilfully."

"Then she would believe I had grown cold to her, and it would break her heart."

"One of your failings," replied Grizel, giving him her hand for a moment as recompense for what she was about to say, "is that you think women's hearts break so easily. If, at the slightest sign that she notices any change in you, you think her heart is breaking, and seize her in your arms, crying, 'Elspeth, dear little Elspeth!' — and that is what your first impulse would be ——"

"How well you know me, Grizel!" groaned Sentimental Tommy.

"If that would be the result," she went on, "better not do it at all. But if you were to restrain yourself, then she could not but reflect that many of the things you did for her with a sigh David did for pleasure, and she would compare him and you ——"

"To my disadvantage?" Tommy exclaimed, with sad incredulity. "Do you really think she could, Grizel?"

"Give her the chance," Grizel continued, "and

if you find it hard, you must remember that what you are doing is for her good."

"And for ours," Tommy cried fervently.

Every promise he made her at this time he fulfilled, and more; he was hopeless, but all a man could do to make Elspeth love David he did.

The doctor was quite unaware of it. "Fortunately, her brother had a headache yesterday and was lying down," he told Grizel, with calm brutality, "so I saw her alone for a few minutes."

"The fibs I have to invent," said Tommy, to the same confidante, "to get myself out of their way!"

"Luckily he does not care for music," David said, "so when she is at the piano he sometimes remains in the kitchen talking to Aaron."

Tommy and Aaron left together! Tommy described those scenes with much good humour. "I was amazed at first," he said to Grizel, "to find Aaron determinedly enduring me, but now I understand. He wants what we want. He says not a word about it, but he is watching those two courting like a born match-maker. Aaron has several reasons for hoping that Elspeth will get our friend (as he would express it): one, that this would keep her in Thrums; another, that to be the wife of a doctor is second only in worldly grandeur to marrying the manse; and thirdly and lastly, because he is convinced that it would be

THE ATTEMPT TO CARRY ELSPETH

such a staggerer to me. For he thinks I have not a notion of what is going on, and that, if I had, I would whisk her away to London."

He gave Grizel the most graphic, solemn pictures of those evenings in the cottage. "Conceive the four of us gathered round the kitchen fire — three men and a maid; the three men yearning to know what is in the maid's mind, and each concealing his anxiety from the others. Elspeth gives the doctor a look which may mean much or nothing, and he glares at me as if I were in the way, and I glance at Aaron, and he is on tenterhooks lest I have noticed anything. Next minute, perhaps, David gives utterance to a plaintive sigh, and Aaron and I pounce upon Elspeth (with our eyes) to observe its effect on her, and Elspeth wonders why Aaron is staring, and he looks apprehensively at me, and I am gazing absent-mindedly at the fender.

"You may smile, Grizel," Tommy would say, "and now that I think of it, I can smile myself, but we are an eerie quartet at the time. When the strain becomes unendurable, one of us rises and mends the fire with his foot, and then I think the rest of us could say 'Thank you.' We talk desperately for a little after that, but soon again the awful pall creeps down."

"If I were there," cried Grizel, "I would not have the parlour standing empty all this time."

"We are coming to the parlour," Tommy replies impressively. "The parlour, Grizel, now begins to stir. Elspeth has disappeared from the kitchen, we three men know not whither. We did not notice her go; we don't even observe that she has gone — we are too busy looking at the fire. By and by the tremulous tinkling of an aged piano reaches us from an adjoining chamber, and Aaron looks at me through his fingers, and I take a lightning glance at Mr. David, and he uncrosses his legs and rises, and sits down again. Aaron, in the most unconcerned way, proceeds to cut tobacco and rub it between his fingers, and I stretch out my legs and contemplate them with passionate approval. While we are thus occupied David has risen, and he is so thoroughly at his ease that he has begun to hum. He strolls round the kitchen, looking with sudden interest at the mantelpiece ornaments; he reads, for the hundredth time, the sampler on the wall. Next the clock engages his attention; it is ticking, and that seems to impress him as novel and curious. By this time he has reached the door; it opens to his touch, and in a fit of abstraction he leaves the room."

"You don't follow him into the parlour?" asks Grizel, anxiously.

"Follow whom?" Tommy replies severely. "I don't even know that he has gone to the parlour; now that I think of it, I have not even noticed

THE ATTEMPT TO CARRY ELSPETH

that he has left the kitchen; nor has Aaron noticed it. Aaron and I are not in a condition to notice such things; we are conscious only that at last we have the opportunity for the quiet social chat we so much enjoy in each other's company. That, at least, is Aaron's way of looking at it, and he keeps me there with talk of the most varied and absorbing character; one topic down, another up; when very hard put to it, he even questions me about my next book, as if he would like to read the proof-sheets, and when I seem to be listening, a little restively, for sounds from the parlour (the piano has stopped), he has the face of one who would bar the door rather than lose my society. Aaron appreciates me at my true value at last, Grizel. I had begun to despair almost of ever bringing him under my charm."

"I should be very angry with you," Grizel said warningly, "if I thought you teased the poor old man."

"Tease him! The consideration I show that poor old man, Grizel, while I know all the time that he is plotting to diddle me! You should see me when it is he who is fidgeting to know why the piano has stopped. He stretches his head to listen, and does something to his ear that sends it another inch nearer the door; he chuckles and groans on the sly; and I—I notice nothing. Oh, he is becoming quite fond of me; he thinks me an idiot."

"Why not tell him that you want it as much as he?"

"He would not believe me. Aaron is firmly convinced that I am too jealous of Elspeth's affection to give away a thimbleful of it. He blames me for preventing her caring much even for him."

"At any rate," said Grizel, "he is on our side, and it is because he sees it would be so much the best thing for her."

"And, at the same time, such a shock to me. That poor old man, Grizel! I have seen him rubbing his hands together with glee and looking quite leery as he thought of what was coming to me."

But Grizel could not laugh now. When Tommy saw so well through Aaron and David, through everyone he came in contact with, indeed, what hope could there be that he was deceived in Elspeth?

"And yet she knows what takes him there; she must know it!" she cried.

"A woman," Tommy said, "is never sure that a man is in love with her until he proposes. She may fancy—but it is never safe to fancy, as so many have discovered."

"She has no right," declared Grizel, "to wait until she is sure, if she does not care for him. If she fears that he is falling in love with her, she

THE ATTEMPT TO CARRY ELSPETH

knows how to discourage him; there are surely a hundred easy, kind ways of doing that."

"Fears he is falling in love with her!" Tommy repeated. "Is any woman ever afraid of that?"

He really bewildered her. "No woman would like it," Grizel answered promptly for them all, because she would not have liked it. "She must see that it would result only in pain to him."

"Still——" said Tommy.

"Oh, but how dense you are!" she said, in surprise. "Don't you understand that she would stop him, though it were for no better reasons than selfish ones? Consider her shame if, in thinking it over afterwards, she saw that she might have stopped him sooner! Why," she cried, with a sudden smile, "it is in your book! You say: 'Every maiden carries secretly in her heart an idea of love so pure and sacred that, if by any act she is once false to that conception, her punishment is that she never dares to look at it again.' And this is one of the acts you mean."

"I had not thought of it, though," he said humbly. He was never prouder of Grizel than at that moment. "If Elspeth's outlook," he went on, "is different——"

"It can't be different."

"If it is, the fault is mine; yes, though I wrote the passage that you interpret so nobly, Grizel. Shall I tell you," he said gently, "what I believe is Elspeth's outlook exactly, just now? She knows that the doctor is attracted by her, and it gives her little thrills of exultation; but that it can be love — she puts that question in such a low voice, as if to prevent herself hearing it. And yet she listens, Grizel, like one who would like to know! Elspeth is pitifully distrustful of anyone's really loving her, and she will never admit to herself that he does until he tells her."

"And then?"

Tommy had to droop his head.

"I see you have still no hope!" she said.

"It would be so easy to pretend I have," he replied, with longing, "in order to cheer you for the moment. Oh, it would even be easy to me to deceive myself; but should I do it?"

"No, no," she said; "anything but that; I can bear anything but that," and she shuddered. "But we seem to be treating David cruelly."

"I don't think so," he assured her. "Men like to have these things to look back to. But, if you want it, Grizel, I have to say only a word to Elspeth to bring it to an end. She is as tender as she is innocent, and — but it would be a hard task to me," he admitted, his heart suddenly going out to Elspeth; he had never deprived her of any gratification before. "Still, I am willing to do it."

"No!" Grizel cried, restraining him with her hand. "I am a coward, I suppose, but I can't help

THE ATTEMPT TO CARRY ELSPETH

wanting to hope for a little longer, and David won't grudge it to me."

It was but a very little longer that they had to wait. Tommy, returning home one day from a walk with his old school-friend, Gav Dishart (now M.A.), found Aaron suspiciously near the parlour keyhole.

"There's a better fire in the other end," Aaron said, luring him into the kitchen. So desirous was he of keeping Tommy there, fixed down on a stool, that "I'll play you at the dambrod," he said briskly.

"Anyone with Elspeth?"

"Some women-folk you dinna like," replied Aaron.

Tommy rose. Aaron, with a subdued snarl, got between him and the door.

"I was wondering, merely," Tommy said, pointing pleasantly to something on the dresser, "why one of them wore the doctor's hat."

"I forgot; he's there, too," Aaron said promptly; but he looked at Tommy with misgivings. They sat down to their game.

"You begin," said Tommy; "you're black." And Aaron opened with the Double Corner; but so preoccupied was he that it became a variation of the Ayrshire lassie, without his knowing. His suspicions had to find vent in words: "You dinna speir wha the women-folk are?"

"No."

"Do you think I'm just pretending they're there?" Aaron asked apprehensively.

"Not at all," said Tommy, with much politeness, "but I thought you might be mistaken." He could have "blown" Aaron immediately thereafter, but, with great consideration, forbore. The old man was so troubled that he could not lift a king without its falling in two. His sleeve got in the way of his fingers. At last he sat back in his chair. "Do you ken what is going on, man?" he demanded, "or do you no ken? I can stand this doubt no longer."

A less soft-hearted person might have affected not to understand, but that was not Tommy's way. "I know, Aaron," he admitted. "I have known all the time." It was said in the kindliest manner, but its effect on Aaron was not soothing.

"Curse you!" he cried, with extraordinary vehemence, "you have been playing wi' me a' the time, ay, and wi' him and wi' her!"

What had Aaron been doing with Tommy? But Tommy did not ask that.

"I am sorry you think so badly of me," he said quietly. "I have known all the time, Aaron, but have I interfered?"

"Because you ken she winna take him. I see it plain enough now. You ken your power over her;

THE ATTEMPT TO CARRY ELSPETH

the honest man that thinks he could take her frae you is to you but a divert."

He took a step nearer Tommy. "Listen," he said. "When you came back he was on the point o' speiring her; I saw it in his face as she was playing the piano, and she saw it, too, for her hands began to trem'le and the tune wouldna play. I daursay you think I was keeking, but if I was I stoppit it when the piano stoppit; it was a hard thing to me to do, and it would hae been an easy thing no to do, but I wouldna spy upon Elspeth in her great hour."

"I like you for that, Aaron," Tommy said; but Aaron waved his likes aside.

"The reason I stood at the door," he continued, "was to keep you out o' that room. I offered to play you at the dambrod to keep you out. Ay, you ken that without my telling you, but do you ken what makes me tell you now? It's to see whether you'll go in and stop him; let's see you do that, and I'll hae some hope yet." He waited eagerly.

"You do puzzle me now," Tommy said.

"Ay," replied the old man, bitterly, "you're dull in the uptak' when you like! I dinna ken, I suppose, and you dinna ken, that if you had the least dread o' her taking him you would be into that room full bend to stop it; but you're so sure o' her, you're so michty sure, that you can sit here and lauch instead."

TOMMY AND GRIZEL

"Am I laughing, Aaron? If you but knew, Elspeth's marriage would be a far more joyful thing to me than it could ever be to you."

The old warper laughed unpleasantly at that. "And I'se uphaud," he said, "you're none sure but what she'll tak' him! You're no as sure she'll refuse him as that there's a sun in the heavens, and I'm a broken man."

For a moment sympathy nigh compelled Tommy to say a hopeful thing, but he mastered himself. "It would be weakness," was what he did say, "to pretend that there is any hope."

Aaron gave him an ugly look, and was about to leave the house; but Tommy would not have it. "If one of us must go, Aaron," he said, with much gentleness, "let it be me"; and he went out, passing the parlour door softly, so that he might not disturb poor David. The warper sat on by the fire, his head sunk miserably in his shoulders. The vehemence had passed out of him; you would have hesitated to believe that such a listless, shrunken man could have been vehement that same year. It is a hardy proof of his faith in Tommy that he did not even think it worth while to look up when, by and by, the parlour door opened and the doctor came in for his hat. Elspeth was with him.

They told Aaron something.

It lifted him off his feet and bore him out at the

THEY TOLD AARON SOMETHING

THE ATTEMPT TO CARRY ELSPETH

door. When he made up on himself he knew he was searching everywhere for Tommy. A terror seized him, lest he should not be the first to convey the news.

Had he been left a fortune? neighbours asked, amazed at this unwonted sight; and he replied, as he ran, "I have, and I want to share it wi' him!"

It was his only joke. People came to their doors to see Aaron Latta laughing.

CHAPTER XXII

GRIZEL'S GLORIOUS HOUR

ELSPETH was to be his wife! David had carried the wondrous promise straight to Grizel, and now he was gone and she was alone again.

Oh, foolish Grizel, are you crying, and I thought it was so hard to you to cry!

"Me crying! Oh, no!"

Put your hand to your cheeks, Grizel. Are they not wet?

"They are wet, and I did not know it! It is hard to me to cry in sorrow, but I can cry for joy. I am crying because it has all come right, and I was so much afraid that it never would."

Ah, Grizel, I think you said you wanted nothing else so long as you had his love!

"But God has let it all come right, just the same, and I am thanking Him. That is why I did not know that I was crying."

She was by the fireplace, on the stool that had always been her favourite seat, and of course she sat very straight. When Grizel walked or stood her strong, round figure took a hundred beautiful poses,

GRIZEL'S GLORIOUS HOUR

but when she sat it had but one. The old doctor, in experimenting moods, had sometimes compelled her to recline, and then watched to see her body spring erect the moment he released his hold. "What a dreadful patient I should make!" she said contritely. "I would chloroform you, miss," said he.

She sat thus for a long time; she had so much for which to thank God, though not with her lips, for how could they keep pace with her heart? Her heart was very full; chiefly, I think, with the tears that rolled down unknown to her.

She thanked God, in the name of the little hunted girl who had not been taught how to pray, and so did it standing. "I do so want to be good; oh, how sweet it would be to be good!" she had said in that long ago. She had said it out loud when she was alone on the chance of His hearing, but she had not addressed Him by name because she was not sure that he was really called God. She had not even known that you should end by saying "Amen," which Tommy afterwards told her is the most solemn part of it.

How sweet it would be to be good, but how much sweeter it is to be good! The woman that girl had grown into knew that she was good, and she thanked God for that. She thanked Him for letting her help. If He had said that she had not helped, she would have rocked her arms and replied almost hotly: "You know I have." And He did know: He had seen her many times in the grip of inherited passions, and watched her fighting with them and subduing them; He had seen ugly thoughts stealing upon her, as they crawl towards every child of man; ah, He had seen them leap into the heart of the Painted Lady's daughter, as if a nest already made for them must be there, and still she had driven them away. Grizel had helped. The tears came more quickly now.

She thanked God that she had never worn the ring. But why had she never worn it, when she wanted so much to do so, and it was hers? Why had she watched herself more carefully than ever of late, and forced happiness to her face when it was not in her heart, and denied herself, at fierce moments, the luxuries of grief and despair, and even of rebellion? For she had carried about with her the capacity to rebel, but she had hidden it, and the reason was that she thought God was testing her. If she fell He would not give her the thing she coveted. Unworthy reason for being good, as she knew, but God overlooked it, and she thanked Him for that.

Her hands pressed each other impulsively, as if at the shock of a sudden beautiful thought, and then perhaps she was thanking God for making her the one woman who could be the right wife

GRIZEL'S GLORIOUS HOUR

for Tommy. She was so certain that no other woman could help him as she could; none knew his virtues as she knew them. Had it not been for her, his showy parts only would have been loved; the dear, quiet ones would never have heard how dear they were: the showy ones were open to all the world, but the quiet ones were her private garden. His faults as well as his virtues passed before her, and it is strange to know that it was about this time that Grizel ceased to cry and began to smile instead. I know why she smiled; it was because sentimentality was one of the little monsters that came skipping into her view, and Tommy was so confident that he had got rid at last of it! Grizel knew better! But she could look at it and smile. Perhaps she was not sorry that it was still there with the others, it had so long led the procession. I daresay she saw herself taking the leering, distorted thing in hand and making something gallant of it. She thought that she was too practical, too much given to seeing but one side to a question, too lacking in consideration for others, too impatient, too relentlessly just, and she humbly thanked God for all these faults, because Tommy's excesses were in the opposite direction, and she could thus restore the balance. She was full of humility while she saw how useful she could be to him, but her face did not show this; she had forgotten her face, and elation had spread over it without her knowing. Perhaps God accepted the elation as part of the thanks.

She thanked God for giving Tommy what he wanted so much — herself. Ah, she had thanked Him for that before, but she did it again. And then she went on her knees by her dear doctor's chair, and prayed that she might be a good wife to Tommy.

When she rose the blood was not surging through her veins. Instead of a passion of joy it was a beautiful calm that possessed her, and on noticing this she regarded herself with sudden suspicion, as we put our ear to a watch to see if it has stopped. She found that she was still going, but no longer either fast or slow, and she saw what had happened: her old serene self had come back to her. I think she thanked God for that most of all.

And then she caught sight of her face — oh, oh! Her first practical act as an engaged woman was to wash her face.

Engaged! But was she? Grizel laughed. It is not usually a laughing matter, but she could not help that. Consider her predicament. She could be engaged at once, if she liked, even before she wiped the water from her face, or she might postpone it, to let Tommy share. The careful reader will have noticed that this problem presented itself to her at an awkward moment. She

GRIZEL'S GLORIOUS HOUR

laughed, in short, while her face was still in the basin, with the very proper result that she had to grope for the towel with her eyes shut.

It was still a cold, damp face (Grizel was always in such a hurry) when she opened her most precious drawer and took from it a certain glove which was wrapped in silk paper, but was not perhaps quite so conceited as it had been, for, alas and alack! it was now used as a wrapper itself. The ring was inside it. If Grizel wanted to be engaged, absolutely and at once, all she had to do was to slip that ring upon her finger.

It had been hers for a week or more. Tommy had bought it in a certain Scottish town whose merchant princes are so many, and have risen splendidly from such small beginnings, that after you have been there a short time you beg to be introduced to someone who has not got on. When you look at them they slap their trouser pockets. When they look at you they are wondering if you know how much they are worth. Tommy, one day, roaming their streets (in which he was worth incredibly little), and thinking sadly of what could never be, saw the modest little garnet ring in a jeweller's window, and attached to it was a pathetic story. No other person could have seen the story, but it was as plain to him as though it had been beautifully written on the tag of paper which really contained the price. With his hand on the door he paused, overcome by that horror of entering shops without a lady to do the talking, which all men of genius feel (it is the one sure test), hurried away, came back, went to and fro shyly, until he saw that he was yielding once more to the indecision he thought he had so completely mastered, whereupon he entered bravely (though it was one of those detestable doors that ring a bell as they open), and sternly ordered the jeweller, who could have bought and sold our Tommy with one slap on the trouser leg, to hand the ring over to him.

He had no intention of giving it to Grizel. That, indeed, was part of its great tragedy, for this is the story Tommy read into the ring: There was once a sorrowful man of twenty-three, and forty, and sixty. Ah, how gray the beard has grown as we speak! How thin the locks! But still we know him for the same by that garnet ring. Since it became his no other eye has seen it, and yet it is her engagement ring. Never can he give it to her, but must always carry it about with him as the piteous memory of what had never been. How innocent it looked in his hand, and with an innocence that never wore off, not even when he had reached his threescore years. As it aged it took on another kind of innocence only. It looked pitiable now, for there is but a dishonoured age for a lonely little ring which can never see the finger it was made to span.

GRIZEL'S GLORIOUS HOUR

A hair-shirt! Such it was to him, and he put it on willingly, knowing it could be nothing else. Every smart it gave him pleased, even while it pained. If ever his mind roamed again to the world of make-believe, that ring would jerk him back to facts.

Grizel remembered well her finding of it. She had been in his pockets. She loved to rifle them; to pull out his watch herself, instead of asking him for the time; to exclaim "Oh!" at the many things she found there, when they should have been neatly docketed or in the fire, and from his waistcoat pocket she drew the ring. She seemed to understand all about it at once. She was far ahead while he was explaining. It seemed quite strange to her that there had ever been a time when she did not know of her garnet ring.

How her arms rocked! It was delicious to her to remember now with what agony her arms had rocked. She kissed it; she had not been the first to kiss it.

It was "Oh, how I wish I could have saved you this pain!"

"But I love it," she cried, "and I love the pain."

It was "Am I not to see it on your finger once?"

"No, no; we must not."

"Let me, Grizel!"

"Is it right, oh, is it right?"

"Only this once!"

"Very well!"

"I dare not, Grizel, I can't! What are we to do with it now?"

"Give it to me. It is mine. I will keep it, beside my glove."

"Let me keep it, Grizel."

"No; it is mine."

"Shall I fling it away?"

"How can you be so cruel? It is mine."

"Let me bury it."

"It is mine."

And of course she had got her way. Could he resist her in anything? They had never spoken of it since, it was such a sad little ring. Sad! It was not in the least little bit sad. Grizel wondered as she looked at it now how she could ever have thought it sad.

The object with which she put on her hat was to go to Aaron's cottage, to congratulate Elspeth. So she said to herself. Oh, Grizel!

But first she opened two drawers. They were in a great press and full of beautiful linen woven in Thrums, that had come to Dr. McQueen as a "bad debt." "Your marriage portion, young lady," he had said to Grizel, then but a slip of a girl, whereupon, without waiting to lengthen her frock, she rushed rapturously at her work-basket. "Not at all, miss," he cried ferociously; "you are here to look after this house, not to be preparing

GRIZEL'S GLORIOUS HOUR

for another, and until you are respectably bespoken by some rash crittur of a man, into the drawers with your linen and down with those murderous shears." And she had obeyed; no scissors, the most relentless things in nature when in Grizel's hand, had ever cleaved their way through that snowy expanse; never a stitch had she put into her linen except with her eyes, which became horribly like needles as she looked at it.

And now at last she could begin! Oh, but she was anxious to begin; it is almost a fact that, as she looked at those drawers, she grudged the time that must be given to-day to Tommy and his ring.

Do you see her now, ready to start? She was wearing her brown jacket with the fur collar, over which she used to look so searchingly at Tommy. To think there was a time when that serene face had to look searchingly at him! It nearly made her sad again. She paused to bring out the ring and take another exultant look at it. It was attached now to a ribbon round her neck. Sweet ring! She put it to her eyes. That was her way of letting her eyes kiss it. Then she rubbed them and it, in case the one had left a tear upon the other.

And then she went out, joy surging in her heart. For this was Grizel's glorious hour, the end of it.

CHAPTER XXIII

TOMMY LOSES GRIZEL

It was not Aaron's good fortune to find Tommy. He should have looked for him in the Den.

In that haunt of happier lovers than he, Tommy walked slowly, pondering. He scarce noticed that he had the Den to himself, or that, since he was last here, autumn had slipped away, leaving all her garments on the ground. By this time, undoubtedly, Elspeth had said her gentle No; but he was not railing against Fate, not even for striking the final blow at him through that innocent medium. He had still too much to do for that— to help others. There were three of them at present, and by some sort of sympathetic jugglery he had an arm for each.

"Lean on me, Grizel — dear sister Elspeth, you little know the harm you have done — David, old friend, your hand."

Thus loaded, he bravely returned at the fitting time to the cottage. His head was not even bent.

Had you asked Tommy what Elspeth would probably do when she dismissed David, he might

TOMMY LOSES GRIZEL

have replied that she would go up to his room and lock herself into it, so that no one should disturb her for a time. And this he discovered, on returning home, was actually what had happened. How well he knew her! How distinctly he heard every beat of her tender heart, and how easy to him to tell why it was beating! He did not go up; he waited for little Elspeth to come to him, all in her own good time. And when she came, looking just as he knew she would look, he had a brave, bright face for her.

She was shaking after her excitement, or perhaps she had ceased to shake and begun again as she came down to him. He pretended not to notice it; he would notice it the moment he was sure she wanted him to, but perhaps that would not be until she was in bed and he had come to say good-night and put out her light, for, as we know, she often kept her great confidences till then, when she discovered that he already knew them.

"The doctor has been in."

She began almost at once, and in a quaking voice and from a distance, as if in hope that the bullet might be spent before it reached her brother.

"I am sorry I missed him," he replied cautiously. "What a fine fellow he is!"

"You always liked him," said Elspeth, clinging eagerly to that.

'No one could help liking him, Elspeth, he has such winning ways," said Tommy, perhaps a little in the voice with which at funerals we refer to the departed. She loved his words, but she knew she had a surprise for him this time, and she tried to blurt it out.

"He said something to me. He — oh, what a high opinion he has of you!" (She really thought he had.)

"Was that the something?" Tommy asked, with a smile that helped her, as it was meant to do.

"You understand, don't you?" she said, almost in a whisper.

"Of course I do, Elspeth," he answered reassuringly; but somehow she still thought he didn't.

"No one could have been more manly and gentle and humble," she said beseechingly.

"I am sure of it," said Tommy.

"He thinks nothing of himself," she said.

"We shall always think a great deal of him," replied Tommy.

"Yes, but ——" Elspeth found the strangest difficulty in continuing, for, though it would have surprised him to be told so, Tommy was not helping her nearly as much as he imagined.

"I told him," she said, shaking, "that no one could be to me what you were. I told him ——" and then timid Elspeth altogether broke down.

TOMMY LOSES GRIZEL

Tommy drew her to him, as he had so often done since she was the smallest child, and pressed her head against his breast, and waited. So often he had waited thus upon Elspeth.

"There is nothing to cry about, dear," he said tenderly, when the time to speak came. "You have, instead, the right to be proud that so good a man loves you. I am very proud of it, Elspeth."

"If I could be sure of that!" she gasped.

"Don't you believe me, dear?"

"Yes, but — that is not what makes me cry. Tommy, don't you see?"

"Yes," he assured her, "I see. You are crying because you feel so sorry for him. But I don't feel sorry for him, Elspeth. If I know anything at all, it is this: that no man needs pity who sincerely loves; whether that love be returned or not, he walks in a new and more beautiful world for evermore."

She clutched his hand. "I don't understand how you know those things," she whispered.

Please God, was Tommy's reflection, she should never know. He saw most vividly the pathos of his case, but he did not break down under it; it helped him, rather, to proceed.

"It will be the test of Gemmell," he said, "how he bears this. No man, I am very sure, was ever told that his dream could not come true more kindly and tenderly than you told it to him." He

TOMMY AND GRIZEL

was in the middle of the next sentence (a fine one) before her distress stopped him.

"Tommy," she cried, "you don't understand. That is not what I told him at all!"

It was one of the few occasions on which the expression on the face of T. Sandys perceptibly changed.

"What did you tell him?" he asked, almost sharply.

"I accepted him," she said guiltily, backing away from this alarming face.

"What!"

"If you only knew how manly and gentle and humble he was," she cried quickly, as if something dire might happen if Tommy were not assured of this at once.

"You — said you would marry him, Elspeth?"

"Yes!"

"And leave me?"

"Oh, oh!" She flung her arms around his neck.

"Yes, but that is what you are prepared to do!" said he, and he held her away from him and stared at her, as if he had never seen Elspeth before. "Were you not afraid?" he exclaimed, in amazement.

"I am not the least bit afraid," she answered. "Oh Tommy, if you knew how manly ——" And then she remembered that she had said that already.

TOMMY LOSES GRIZEL

"You did not even say that you would — consult me?"

"Oh, oh!"

"Why didn't you, Elspeth?"

"I — I forgot!" she moaned. "Tommy, you are angry!" She hugged him, and he let her do it, but all the time he was looking over her head fixedly, with his mouth open.

"And I was always so sure of you!" were the words that came to him at last, with a hard little laugh at the end of them.

"Can you think it makes me love you less," she sobbed, "because I love him, too? Oh, Tommy, I thought you would be so glad!"

He kissed her; he put his hand fondly upon her head.

"I am glad," he said, with emotion. "When that which you want has come to you, Elspeth, how can I but be glad? But it takes me aback, and if for a moment I felt forlorn, if, when I should have been rejoicing only in your happiness, the selfish thought passed through my mind, 'What is to become of me?' I hope — I hope ——"
Then he sat down and buried his face in the table.

And he might have been telling her about Grizel! Has the shock stunned you, Tommy? Elspeth thinks it has been a shock of pain. May we lift your head to show her your joyous face?

"I am so proud," she was saying, "that at last,

85

after you have done so much for me, I can do a little thing for you. For it is something to free you, Tommy. You have always pretended, for my sake, that we could not do without each other, but we both knew all the time that it was only I who was unable to do without you. You can't deny it."

He might deny it, but it was true. Ah, Tommy, you bore with her with infinite patience, but did it never strike you that she kept you to the earth? If Elspeth could be happy without you! You were sure she could not, but if she could!—had that thought never made you flap your wings?

"I often had a pain at my heart," she told him, "which I kept from you. It was a feeling that your solicitude for me, perhaps, prevented your caring for any other woman. It seemed terrible and unnatural that I should be a bar to that. I felt that I was starving you, and not you only, but an unknown woman as well."

"So long as I had you, Elspeth," he said reproachfully, "was not that enough?"

"It seemed to be enough," she answered gravely, "but even while I comforted myself with that, I knew that it should not be enough, and still I feared that if it was, the blame was mine. Now I am no longer in the way, and I hope, so ardently, that you will fall in love, like other people. If you never do, I shall always have the fear that

TOMMY LOSES GRIZEL

I am the cause, that you lost the capacity in the days when I let you devote yourself too much to me."

Oh, blind Elspeth! Now is the time to tell her, Tommy, and fill her cup of happiness to the brim.

But it is she who is speaking still, almost gaily now, yet with a full heart. "What a time you have had with me, Tommy! I told David all about it, and what he has to look forward to, but he says he is not afraid. And when you find someone you can love," she continued sweetly, though she had a sigh to stifle, "I hope she will be someone quite unlike me, for oh, my dear, good brother, I know you need a change."

Not a word said Tommy.

She said, timidly, that she had begun to hope of late that Grizel might be the woman, and still he did not speak. He drew Elspeth closer to him, that she might not see his face and the horror of himself that surely sat on it. To the very marrow of him he was in such cold misery that I wonder his arms did not chill her.

This poor devil of a Sentimental Tommy! He had wakened up in the world of facts, where he thought he had been dwelling of late, to discover that he had not been here for weeks, except at meal-times. During those weeks he had most honestly thought that he was in a passion to be married. What do you say to pitying instead of cursing him? It is a sudden idea of mine, and we must be quick, for joyous Grizel is drawing near, and this, you know, is the chapter in which her heart breaks.

It was Elspeth who opened the door to Grizel. "Does she know?" said Elspeth to herself, before either of them spoke.

"Does she know?" It was what Grizel was saying also.

"Oh, Elspeth, I am so glad! David has told me."

"She does know," Elspeth told herself, and she thought it was kind of Grizel to come so quickly. She said so.

"She doesn't know!" thought Grizel, and then these two kissed for the first time. It was a kiss of thanks from each.

"But why does she not know?" Grizel wondered a little as they entered the parlour, where Tommy was; he had been standing with his teeth knit since he heard the knock. As if in answer to the question, Elspeth said: "I have just broken it to Tommy. He has been in a few minutes only, and he is so surprised he can scarcely speak."

Grizel laughed happily, for that explained it. Tommy had not had time to tell her yet. She laughed again at Elspeth, who had thought she

TOMMY LOSES GRIZEL

had so much to tell and did not know half the story.

Elspeth begged Tommy to listen to the beautiful things Grizel was saying about David, but, truth to tell, Grizel scarcely heard them herself. She had given Tommy a shy, rapturous glance. She was wondering when he would begin. What a delicious opening when he shook hands! Suppose he had kissed her instead! Or, suppose he casually addressed her as darling! He might do it at any moment now! Just for once she would not mind though he did it in public. Perhaps as soon as this new remark of Elspeth's was finished, he meant to say: "You are not the only engaged person in the room, Miss Elspeth; I think I see another two!" Grizel laughed as if she had heard him say it. And then she ceased laughing suddenly, for some little duty had called Elspeth into the other room, and as she went out she stopped the movement of the earth.

These two were alone with their great joy.

Elspeth had said that she would be back in two minutes. Was Grizel wasting a moment when she looked only at him, her eyes filmy with love, the crooked smile upon her face so happy that it could not stand still? Her arms made a slight gesture towards him; her hands were open; she was giving herself to him. She could not see. For a fraction of time the space between them seemed to be annihilated. His arms were closing round her. Then she knew that neither of them had moved.

"Grizel!"

He tried to be true to her by deceiving her. It was the only way. "At last, Grizel," he cried, "at last!" and he put joyousness into his voice. "It has all come right, dear one!" he cried like an ecstatic lover. Never in his life had he tried so hard to deceive at the sacrifice of himself. But he was fighting something as strong as the instinct of self-preservation, and his usually expressionless face gave the lie to his joyous words. Loud above his voice his ashen face was speaking to her, and she cried in terror, "What is wrong?" Even then he attempted to deceive her, but suddenly she knew the truth.

"You don't want to be married!"

I think the room swam round with her. When it was steady again, "You did not say that, did you?" she asked. She was sure he had not said it. She was smiling again tremulously to show him that he had not said it.

"I want to be married above all else on earth," he said imploringly; but his face betrayed him still, and she demanded the truth, and he was forced to tell it.

A little shiver passed through her, that was all.

TOMMY LOSES GRIZEL

"Do you mean that you don't love me?" she said. "You must tell me what you mean."

"That is how others would put it, I suppose," he replied. "I believe they would be wrong. I think I love you in my own way; but I thought I loved you in their way, and it is the only way that counts in this world of theirs. It does not seem to be my world. I was given wings, I think, but I am never to know that I have left the earth until I come flop upon it with an arrow through them. I crawl and wriggle here, and yet" — he laughed harshly — "I believe I am rather a fine fellow when I am flying!"

She nodded. "You mean you want me to let you off?" she asked. "You must tell me what you mean." And as he did not answer instantly, "Because I think I have some little claim upon you," she said, with a pleasant smile.

"I am as pitiful a puzzle to myself as I can be to you," he replied. "All I know is that I don't want to marry anyone. And yet I am sure I could die for you, Grizel."

It was quite true. A burning house and Grizel among the flames, and he would have been the first on the ladder. But there is no such luck for you, Tommy.

"You are free," was what she said. "Don't look so tragic," she added, again with the pleasant smile. "It must be very distressing to you, but —

you will soon fly again." Her lips twitched tremulously. "I can't fly," she said.

She took the ring from her neck. She took it off its ribbon.

"I brought it," she said, "to let you put it on my finger. I thought you would want to do that," she said.

"Grizel," he cried, "can we not be as we have been?"

"No," she answered.

"It would all come right, Grizel. I am sure it would. I don't know why I am as I am; but I shall try to change myself. You have borne with me since we were children. Won't you bear with me for a little longer?"

She shook her head, but did not trust herself to speak.

"I have lost you," he said, and she nodded.

"Then I am lost indeed!" said he, and he knew it, too; but with a gesture of the hand she begged him not to say that.

"Without your love to help me —— " he began.

"You shall always have that," she told him with shining eyes, "always, always." And what could he do but look at her with the wonder and the awe that come to every man who, for one moment in his life, knows a woman well?

"You can love me still, Grizel!" His voice was shaky.

TOMMY LOSES GRIZEL

"Just the same," she answered, and I suppose he looked uplifted. "But you should be sorry," she said gravely, and it was then that Elspeth came back. She had not much exceeded her two minutes.

It was always terrible to Tommy not to have the feelings of a hero. At that moment he could not endure it. In a splendid burst of self-sacrifice he suddenly startled both Grizel and himself by crying, "Elspeth, I love Grizel, and I have just asked her to be my wife."

Yes, the nobility of it amazed himself, but bewitched him, too, and he turned gloriously to Grizel, never doubting but that she would have him still.

He need not have spoken so impulsively, nor looked so grand. She swayed for an instant and then was erect again. "You must forgive me, Elspeth," she said, "but I have refused him"; and that was the biggest surprise Tommy ever got in his life.

"You don't care for him!" Elspeth blurted out.

"Not in the way he cares for me," Grizel replied quietly, and when Elspeth would have said more she begged her to desist. "The only thing for me to do now, Elspeth," she said, smiling, "is to run away, but I want you first to accept a little wedding-gift from me. I wish you and David so much happiness; you won't refuse it, will you?"

Elspeth, still astounded, took the gift. It was a little garnet ring.

"It will have to be cut," Grizel said. "It was meant, I think, for a larger finger. I have had it some time, but I never wore it."

Elspeth said she would always treasure her ring, and that it was beautiful.

"I used to think it — rather sweet," Grizel admitted, and then she said good-bye to them both and went away.

CHAPTER XXIV

THE MONSTER

Tommy's new character was that of a monster. He always liked the big parts.

Concealed, as usual, in the garments that clung so oddly to him, modesty, generosity, indifference to applause and all the nobler impulses, he could not strip himself of them, try as he would, and so he found, to his scornful amusement, that he still escaped the public fury. In the two months that preceded Elspeth's marriage there was positively scarce a soul in Thrums who did not think rather well of him. "If they knew what I really am," he cried with splendid bitterness, "how they would run from me!"

Even David could no longer withhold the hand of fellowship, for Grizel would tell him nothing, except that, after all, and for reasons sufficient to herself, she had declined to become Mrs. Sandys. He sought in vain to discover how Tommy could be to blame. "And now," Tommy said grimly to Grizel, "our doctor thinks you have used me badly, and that I am a fine fellow to bear no resentment! Elspeth told me that he admires the gentle and manly dignity with which I submit to the blow, and I have no doubt that, as soon as I heard that, I made it more gentle and manly than ever!

"I have forbidden Elspeth," he told her, "to upbraid you for not accepting me, with the result that she thinks me too good to live! Ha, ha! what do you think, Grizel?"

It became known in the town that she had refused him. Everybody was on Tommy's side. They said she had treated him badly. Even Aaron was staggered at the sight of Tommy accepting his double defeat in such good part. "And all the time I am the greatest cur unhung," says Tommy. "Why don't you laugh, Grizel?"

Never, they said, had there been such a generous brother. The town was astir about this poor man's gifts to the lucky bride. There were rumours that among the articles was a silver coal-scuttle, but it proved to be a sugar-bowl in that pattern. Three bandboxes came for her to select from; somebody discovered who was on the watch, but may I be struck dead if more than one went back. Yesterday it was bonnets; to-day she is at Tilliedrum again, trying on her going-away dress. And she really was to go away in it, a noticeable thing, for in Thrums society, though they usually get a going-away dress, they are too canny to go away in it. The local shops were not ignored, but the

THE MONSTER

best of the trousseau came from London. "That makes the second box this week, as I'm a living sinner," cries the lady on the watch again. When boxes arrived at the station Corp wheeled them up to Elspeth without so much as looking at the label.

Ah, what a brother! They said it openly to their own brothers, and to Tommy in the way they looked at him.

"There has been nothing like it," he assured Grizel, "since Red Riding-hood and the wolf. Why can't I fling off my disguise and cry, 'The better to eat you with!'"

He always spoke to her now in this vein of magnificent bitterness, but Grizel seldom rewarded him by crying, "Oh, oh!" She might, however, give him a patient, reproachful glance instead, and it had the irritating effect of making him feel that perhaps he was under life-size, instead of over it.

"I daresay you are right," says Tommy, savagely.

"I said nothing."

"You don't need to say it. What a grand capacity you have for knocking me off my horse, Grizel!"

"Are you angry with me for that?"

"No; it is delicious to pick one's self out of the mud, especially when you find it is a baby you are picking up, instead of a brute. Am I a baby only, Grizel?"

"I think it is childish of you," she replied, "to say you are a brute."

"There is not to be even that satisfaction left to me! You are hard on me, Grizel."

"I am trying to help you. How can you be angry with me?"

"The instinct of self-preservation, I suppose. I see myself dwindling so rapidly under your treatment that soon there will be nothing of me left."

It was said cruelly, for he knew that the one thing Grizel could not bear now was the implication that she saw his faults only. She always went down under that blow with pitiful surrender, showing the woman suddenly, as if under a physical knouting.

He apologized contritely. "But, after all, it proves my case," he said, "for I could not hurt you in this way, Grizel, if I were not a pretty well-grown specimen of a monster."

"Don't," she said; but she did not seek to help him by drawing him away to other subjects, which would have been his way. "What is there monstrous," she asked, "in your being so good to Elspeth? It is very kind of you to give her all these things."

"Especially when by rights they are yours, Grizel!"

"No, not when you did not want to give them to me."

THE MONSTER

He dared say nothing to that; there were some matters on which he must not contradict Grizel now.

"It is nice of you," she said, "not to complain, though Elspeth is deserting you. It must have been a blow."

"You and I only know why," he answered. "But for her, Grizel, I might be whining sentiment to you at this moment."

"That," she said, "would be the monstrous thing."

"And it is not monstrous, I suppose, that I should let Gemmell press my hand under the conviction that, after all, I am a trump."

"You don't pose as one."

"That makes them think the more highly of me! Nothing monstrous, Grizel, in my standing quietly by while you are showing Elspeth how to furnish her house — I, who know why you have the subject at your finger-tips!"

For Grizel had given all her sweet ideas to Elspeth. Heigh-ho! how she had guarded them once, confiding them half reluctantly even to Tommy; half reluctantly, that is, at the start, because they were her very own, but once she was embarked on the subject talking with such rapture that every minute or two he had to beg her to be calm. She was the first person in that part of the world to think that old furniture need not be kept in the dark corners, and she knew where there was an oak bedstead that was looked upon as a disgrace, and where to obtain the dearest cupboards, one of them in use as the retiring-chamber of a rabbit-hutch, and stately clocks made in the town a hundred years ago, and quaint old-farrant lamps and cogeys and sand-glasses that apologized if you looked at them, and yet were as willing to be loved again as any old lady in a mutch. You will not buy them easily now, the people will not chuckle at you when you bid for them now. We have become so cute in Thrums that when the fender breaks we think it may have increased in value, and we preserve any old board lest the worms have made it artistic. Grizel, however, was in advance of her time. She could lay her hands on all she wanted, and she did, but it was for Elspeth's house.

"And the table-cloths and the towels and the sheets," said Tommy. "Nothing monstrous in my letting you give Elspeth them?"

The linen, you see, was no longer in Grizel's press.

"I could not help making them," she answered, "they were so longing to be made. I did not mean to give them to her. I think I meant to put them back in the press, but when they were made it was natural that they should want to have something to do. So I gave them to Elspeth."

THE MONSTER

"With how many tears on them?"

"Not many. But with some kisses."

"All which," says Tommy, "goes to prove that I have nothing with which to reproach myself!"

"No, I never said that," she told him. "You have to reproach yourself with wanting me to love you."

She paused a moment to let him say, if he dared, that he had not done that, when she would have replied instantly, "You know you did." He could have disabused her, but it would have been cruel, and so on this subject, as ever, he remained silent.

"But that is not what I have been trying to prove," she continued. "You know as well as I that the cause of this unhappiness has been — what you call your wings."

He was about to thank her for her delicacy in avoiding its real name, when she added, "I mean your sentiment," and he laughed instead.

"I flatter myself that I no longer fly, at all events," he said. "I know what I am at last, Grizel."

"It is flattery only," she replied with her old directness. "This thing you are regarding with a morbid satisfaction is not you at all."

He groaned. "Which of them all is me, Grizel?" he asked gloomily.

"We shall see," she said, "when we have got the wings off."

"They will have to come off a feather at a time."

"That," she declared, "is what I have been trying to prove."

"It will be a weary task, Grizel."

"I won't weary at it," she said, smiling.

Her cheerfulness was a continual surprise to him. "You bear up wonderfully well yourself," he sometimes said to her, almost reproachfully, and she never replied that, perhaps, that was one of her ways of trying to help him.

She is not so heartbroken, after all, you may be saying, and I had promised to break her heart. But, honestly, I don't know how to do it more thoroughly, and you must remember that we have not seen her alone yet.

She tried to be very little alone. She helped David in his work more than ever; not a person, for instance, managed to escape the bath because Grizel's heart was broken. You could never say that she was alone when her needle was going, and the linen became sheets and the like, in what was probably record time. Yet they could have been sewn more quickly; for at times the needle stopped and she did not know it. Once a bed-ridden old woman, with whom she had been sitting up, lay watching her instead of sleeping, and finally said: "What makes you sit staring at a cauld fire, and speaking to yoursel'?" And there was a strange day when she had been too long in

THE MONSTER

the Den. When she started for home she went in the direction of Double Dykes, her old home, instead.

She could bear everything except doubt. She had told him so, when he wondered at her calmness; she often said it to herself. She could tread any path, however drearily it stretched before her, so long as she knew whither it led, but there could be no more doubt. Oh, he must never again disturb her mind with hope! How clearly she showed him that, and yet they had perhaps no more than parted when it seemed impossible to bear for the next hour the desolation she was sentenced to for life. She lay quivering and tossing on the hearth-rug of the parlour, beating it with her fists, rocking her arms, and calling to him to give her doubt again, that she might get through the days.

"Let me doubt again!" Here was Grizel starting to beg it of him. More than once she got half-way to Aaron's house before she could turn; but she always did turn, with the words unspoken; never did Tommy hear her say them, but always that she was tranquil now. Was it pride that supported her in the trying hour? Oh, no, it was not pride. That is an old garment, which once became Grizel well, but she does not wear it now; she takes it out of the closet, perhaps, at times to look at it. What gave her strength when he was by was her promise to help him. It was not by asking for leave to dream herself that she could make him dream the less. All done for you, Tommy! It might have helped you to loosen a few of the feathers.

Sometimes she thought it might not be Tommy, but herself, who was so unlike other people; that it was not he who was unable to love, but she who could not be loved. This idea did not agitate her as a terrible thing; she could almost welcome it. But she did not go to him with it. While it might be but a fancy, that was no way to help a man who was overfull of them. It was the bare truth only that she wanted him to see, and so she made elaborate inquiries into herself, to discover whether she was quite unlovable. I suppose it would have been quaint, had she not been quite so much in earnest. She examined herself in the long mirror most conscientiously, and with a determinedly open mind, to see whether she was too ugly for any man to love. Our beautiful Grizel really did.

She had always thought that she was a nice girl, but was she? No one had ever loved her, except the old doctor, and he began when she was so young that perhaps he had been inveigled into it, like a father. Even David had not loved her. Was it because he knew her so well? What was it in women that made men love them? She asked it of David in such a way that he never

THE MONSTER

knew she was putting him to the question. He merely thought that he and she were having a pleasant chat about Elspeth, and, as a result, she decided that he loved Elspeth because she was so helpless. His head sat with uncommon pride on his shoulders while he talked of Elspeth's timidity. There was a ring of boastfulness in his voice as he paraded the large number of useful things that Elspeth could not do. And yet David was a sensible and careful man.

Was it helplessness that man loved in woman, then? It seemed to be Elspeth's helplessness that had made Tommy such a brother, and how it had always appealed to Aaron! No woman could be less helpless than herself, Grizel knew. She thought back and back, and she could not come to a time when she was not managing somebody. Women, she reflected, fall more or less deeply in love with every baby they see, while men, even the best of them, can look calmly at other people's babies. But when the helplessness of the child is in the woman, then other women are unmoved; but the great heart of man is stirred — woman is his baby. She remembered that the language of love is in two sexes — for the woman superlatives, for the man diminutives. The more she loves the bigger he grows, but in an ecstasy he could put her in his pocket. Had not Tommy taught her this? His little one, his child! Perhaps he really had loved her in the days when they both made believe that she was infantile; but soon she had shown with fatal clearness that she was not. Instead of needing to be taken care of, she had obviously wanted to take care of him: their positions were reversed. Perhaps, said Grizel to herself, I should have been a man.

If this was the true explanation, then, though Tommy, who had tried so hard, could not love her, he might be able to love — what is the phrase? — a more womanly woman, or, more popular phrase still, a very woman. Some other woman might be the right wife for him. She did not shrink from considering this theory, and she considered so long that I, for one, cannot smile at her for deciding ultimately, as she did, that there was nothing in it.

The strong like to be leaned upon and the weak to lean, and this irrespective of sex. This was the solution she woke up with one morning, and it seemed to explain not only David's and Elspeth's love, but her own, so clearly that in her desire to help she put it before Tommy. It implied that she cared for him because he was weak, and he drew a very long face.

"You don't know how the feathers hurt as they come out," he explained.

"But so long as we do get them out!" she said.

"Every other person who knows me thinks that

THE MONSTER

strength is my great characteristic," he maintained, rather querulously.

"But when you know it is not," said Grizel. "You do know, don't you?" she asked anxiously. "To know the truth about one's self, that is the beginning of being strong."

"You seem determined," he retorted, "to prevent my loving you."

"Why?" she asked.

"You are to make me strong in spite of myself, I understand. But, according to your theory, the strong love the weak only. Are you to grow weak, Grizel, as I grow strong?"

She had not thought of that, and she would have liked to rock her arms. But she was able to reply: "I am not trying to help you in order to make you love me; you know, quite well, that all that is over and done with. I am trying only to help you to be what a man should be."

She could say that to him, but to herself? Was she prepared to make a man of him at the cost of his possible love? This faced her when she was alone with her passionate nature, and she fought it, and with her fists clenched she cried: "Yes, yes, yes!"

Do we know all that Grizel had to fight? There were times when Tommy's mind wandered to excuses for himself; he knew what men were, and he shuddered to think of the might have been, had a girl who could love as Grizel did loved such a man as her father. He thanked his Maker, did Tommy, that he, who was made as those other men, had avoided raising passions in her. I wonder how he was so sure. Do we know all that Grizel had to fight?

They spoke much during those days of the coming parting, and she always said that she could bear it if she saw him go away more of a man than he had come.

"Then anything I have suffered or may suffer," she told him, "will have been done to help you, and perhaps in time that will make me proud of my poor little love-story. It would be rather pitiful, would it not, if I have gone through so much for no end at all?"

She spoke, he said, almost reproachfully, as if she thought he might go away on his wings, after all.

"We can't be sure," she murmured, she was so eager to make him watchful.

"Yes," he said, humbly but firmly, "I may be a scoundrel, Grizel, I am a scoundrel, but one thing you may be sure of, I am done with sentiment." But even as he said it, even as he felt that he could tear himself asunder for being untrue to Grizel, a bird was singing at his heart because he was free again, free to go out into the world and play as if it were but a larger den. Ah, if only Tommy could always have remained a boy!

Elspeth's marriage day came round, and I should like to linger in it, and show you Elspeth in her wedding-gown, and Tommy standing behind to catch her if she fainted, and Ailie weeping, and Aaron Latta rubbing his gleeful hands, and a smiling bridesmaid who had once thought she might be a bride. But that was a day in Elspeth's story, not in Tommy's and Grizel's. Only one incident in their story crept into that happy day. There were speeches at the feast, and the Rev. Mr. Dishart referred to Tommy in the kindliest way, called him "my young friend," quoted (inaccurately) from his book, and expressed an opinion, formed, he might say, when Mr. Sandys was a lad at school (cheers), that he had a career before him. Tommy bore it well, all except the quotation, which he was burning to correct, but sighed to find that it had set the dominies on his left talking about precocity. "To produce such a graybeard of a book at two and twenty, Mr. Sandys," said Cathro, "is amazing. It partakes, sir, of the nature of the miraculous; it's onchancey, by which we mean a deviation from the normal." And so on. To escape this kind of flattery (he had so often heard it said by ladies, who could say it so much better), Tommy turned to his neighbours on the right.

Oddly enough, they also were discussing deviations from the normal. On the table was a plant in full flower, and Ailie, who had lent it, was expressing surprise that it should bloom so late in the season.

"So early in its life, I should rather say," the doctor remarked after examining it. "It is a young plant, and in the ordinary course would not have come to flower before next year. But it is afraid that it will never see next year. It is one of those poor little plants that bloom prematurely because they are diseased."

Tommy was a little startled. He had often marvelled over his own precocity, but never guessed that this might be the explanation why he was in flower at twenty-two. "Is that a scientific fact?" he asked.

"It is a law of nature," the doctor replied gravely, and if anything more was said on the subject our Tommy did not hear it. What did he hear? He was a child again, in miserable lodgings, and it was sometime in the long middle of the night, and what he heard from his bed was his mother coughing away her life in hers. There was an angry knock, knock, knock, from somewhere near, and he crept out of bed to tell his mother that the people through the wall were complaining because she would not die more quietly; but when he reached her bed it was not his mother he saw lying there, but himself, aged twenty-four

THE MONSTER

or thereabouts. For Tommy had inherited his mother's cough; he had known it every winter, but he remembered it as if for the first time now.

Did he hear anything else? I think he heard his wings slipping to the floor.

He asked Ailie to give him the plant, and he kept it in his room very lovingly, though he forgot to water it. He sat for long periods looking at it, and his thoughts were very deep, but all he actually said aloud was, "There are two of us." Aaron sometimes saw them together, and thought they were an odd pair, and perhaps they were.

Tommy did not tell Grizel of the tragedy that was hanging over him. He was determined to save her that pain. He knew that most men in his position would have told her, and was glad to find that he could keep it so gallantly to himself. She was brave; perhaps some day she would discover that he had been brave also. When she talked of wings now, what he seemed to see was a green grave. His eyes were moist, but he held his head high. All this helped him.

Ah, well, but the world must jog along though you and I be damned. Elspeth was happily married, and there came the day when Tommy and Grizel must say good-bye. He was returning to London. His luggage was already in Corp's barrow, all but the insignificant part of it, which yet made a bulky package in its author's pocket, for it was his new manuscript, for which he would have fought a regiment, yes, and beaten them. Little cared Tommy what became of the rest of his luggage so long as that palpitating package was safe.

"And little you care," Grizel said, in a moment of sudden bitterness, "whom you leave behind, so long as you take it with you."

He forgave her with a sad smile. She did not know, you see, that this manuscript might be his last.

And it was the only bitter thing she said. Even when he looked very sorry for her, she took advantage of his emotion to help him only. "Don't be too sorry for me," she said calmly; "remember, rather, that there is one episode in a woman's life to which she must always cling in memory, whether it was a pride to her or a shame, and that it rests with you to make mine proud or shameful."

In other words, he was to get rid of his wings. How she harped on that!

He wanted to kiss her on the brow, but she would not have it. He was about to do it, not to gratify any selfish desire, but of a beautiful impulse that if anything happened she would have this to remember as the last of him. But she drew back almost angrily. Positively, she was putting it down to sentiment, and he forgave her even that.

But she kissed the manuscript. "Wish it luck," he had begged of her; "you were always so fond of babies, and this is my baby." So Grizel kissed Tommy's baby, and then she turned away her face.

CHAPTER XXV

MR. T. SANDYS HAS RETURNED TO TOWN

IT is disquieting to reflect that we have devoted so much paper (this is the third shilling's worth) to telling what a real biographer would almost certainly have summed up in a few pages. "Caring nothing for glory, engrossed in his work alone, Mr. Sandys, soon after the publication of the 'Letters,' sought the peace of his mother's native village, and there, alike undisturbing and undisturbed, he gave his life, as ever, to laborious days and quiet contemplation. The one vital fact in these six months of lofty endeavour is that he was making progress with the new book. Fishing and other distractions were occasionally indulged in, but merely that he might rise fresher next morning to a book which absorbed," etc.

One can see exactly how it should be done, it has been done so often before. And there is a deal to be said for this method. His book was what he had been at during nearly the whole of that time; comparatively speaking, the fishing and "other distractions" (a neat phrase) had got an occasional hour

T. SANDYS HAS RETURNED

only. But while we admire, we can't do it in that way. We seem fated to go on taking it for granted that you know the "vital facts" about Tommy, and devoting our attention to the things that the real biographer leaves out.

Tommy arrived in London with little more than ten pounds in his pockets. All the rest he had spent on Elspeth.

He looked for furnished chambers in a fashionable quarter, and they were much too expensive. But the young lady who showed them to him asked if it was *the* Mr. Sandys, and he at once took the rooms. Her mother subsequently said that she understood he wrote books, and would he deposit five pounds?

Such are the ups and downs of the literary calling.

The book, of course, was "Unrequited Love," and the true story of how it was not given to the world by his first publishers has never been told. They had the chance, but they weighed the manuscript in their hands as if it were butter, and said it was very small.

"If you knew how much time I have spent in making it smaller," replied Tommy, haughtily.

The madmen asked if he could not add a few chapters, whereupon, with a shudder, he tucked baby under his wing and flew away. That is how Goldie & Goldie got the book.

For one who had left London a glittering star, it was wonderful how little he brightened it by returning. At the club they did not know that he had been away. In society they seemed to have forgotten to expect him back.

He had an eye for them — with a touch of red in it; but he bided his time. It was one of the terrible things about Tommy that he could bide his time. Pym was the only person he called upon. He took Pym out to dinner and conducted him home again. His kindness to Pym, the delicacy with which he pretended not to see that poor old Pym was degraded and done for — they would have been pretty even in a woman, and we treat Tommy unfairly in passing them by with a bow.

Pym had the manuscript to read, and you may be as sure he kept sober that night as that Tommy lay awake. For when literature had to be judged, who could be so grim a critic as this usually lenient toper? He could forgive much, could Pym. You had run away without paying your rent, was it? Well, well, come in and have a drink. Broken your wife's heart, have you? Poor chap, but you will soon get over it. But if it was a split infinitive, "Go to the devil, sir."

"Into a cocked hat," was the verdict of Pym, meaning thereby that thus did Tommy's second work beat his first. Tommy broke down and wept.

T. SANDYS HAS RETURNED

Presently Pym waxed sentimental and confided to Tommy that he, too, had once loved in vain. The sad case of those who love in vain, you remember, is the subject of the book. The saddest of autobiographies, it has been called.

An odd thing, this, I think. Tearing home (for the more he was engrossed in mind the quicker he walked), Tommy was not revelling in Pym's praise; he was neither blanching nor smiling at the thought that he of all people had written as one who was unloved; he was not wondering what Grizel would say to it; he had even forgotten to sigh over his own coming dissolution (indeed, about this time the flower-pot began to fade from his memory). What made him cut his way so excitedly through the streets was this: Pym had questioned his use of the word "untimely" in chapter eight. And Tommy had always been uneasy about that word.

He glared at every person he passed, and ran into perambulators. He rushed past his chambers like one who no longer had a home. He was in the park now, and did not even notice that the Row was empty, that mighty round a deserted circus; management, riders, clowns, all the performers gone on their provincial tour, or nearly all, for a lady on horseback sees him, remembers to some extent who he is, and gives chase. It is our dear Mrs. Jerry.

"You wretch," she said, "to compel me to pursue you! Nothing could have induced me to do anything so unwomanly except that you are the only man in town."

She shook her whip so prettily at him that it was as seductive as a smile. It was also a way of gaining time while she tried to remember what it was he was famous for.

"I believe you don't know me!" she said, with a little shriek, for Tommy had looked bewildered. "That would be too mortifying. Please pretend you do!"

Her look of appeal, the way in which she put her plump little hands together, as if about to say her prayers, brought it all back to Tommy. The one thing he was not certain of was whether he had proposed to her.

It was the one thing of which she was certain.

"You think I can forget so soon," he replied reproachfully, but carefully.

"Then tell me my name," said she; she thought it might lead to his mentioning his own.

"I don't know what it is now. It was Mrs. Jerry once."

"It is Mrs. Jerry still."

"Then you did not marry him, after all?"

No wild joy had surged to his face, but when she answered yes, he nodded his head with gentle melancholy three times. He had not the smallest

"BUT MY FRIENDS STILL CALL ME MRS. JERRY," SHE SAID SOFTLY

T. SANDYS HAS RETURNED

desire to deceive the lady; he was simply an actor who had got his cue and liked his part.

"But my friends still call me Mrs. Jerry," she said softly. "I suppose it suits me somehow."

"You will always be Mrs. Jerry to me," he replied huskily. Ah, those meetings with old loves!

"If you minded so much," Mrs. Jerry said, a little tremulously (she had the softest heart, though her memory was a trifle defective), "you might have discovered whether I had married him or not."

"Was there no reason why I should not seek to discover it?" Tommy asked with tremendous irony, but not knowing in the least what he meant.

It confused Mrs. Jerry. They always confused her when they were fierce, and yet she liked them to be fierce when she re-met them, so few of them were.

But she said the proper thing. "I am glad you have got over it."

Tommy maintained a masterly silence. No wonder he was a power with women.

"I say I am glad you have got over it," murmured Mrs. Jerry again. Has it ever been noticed that the proper remark does not always gain in propriety with repetition?

It is splendid to know that right feeling still kept Tommy silent.

Yet she went on briskly as if he had told her

something: "Am I detaining you? You were walking so quickly that I thought you were in pursuit of someone."

It brought Tommy back to earth, and he could accept her now as an old friend he was glad to meet again. "You could not guess what I was in pursuit of, Mrs. Jerry," he assured her, and with confidence, for words are not usually chased down the Row.

But, though he made the sound of laughter, that terrible face which Mrs. Jerry remembered so well, but could not give a name to, took no part in the revelry; he was as puzzling to her as those irritating authors who print their jokes without a note of exclamation at the end of them. Poor Mrs. Jerry thought it must be a laugh of horrid bitterness, and that he was referring to his dead self or something dreadful of that sort, for which she was responsible.

"Please don't tell me," she said, in such obvious alarm that again he laughed that awful laugh. He promised, with a profound sigh, to carry his secret unspoken to the grave, also to come to her "At Home" if she sent him a card.

He told her his address, but not his name, and she could not send the card to "Occupier."

"Now tell me about yourself," said Mrs. Jerry, with charming cunning. "Did you go away?"

"I came back a few days ago only."

"Had you any shooting?" (They nearly

T. SANDYS HAS RETURNED

always threatened to make for a distant land where there was big game.)

Tommy smiled. He had never "had any shooting" except once in his boyhood, when he and Corp acted as beaters, and he had wept passionately over the first bird killed, and harangued the murderer.

"No," he replied; "I was at work all the time."

This, at least, told her that his work was of a kind which could be done out of London. An inventor?

"When are we to see the result?" asked artful Mrs. Jerry.

"Very soon. Everything comes out about this time. It is our season, you know."

Mrs. Jerry pondered while she said: "How too entrancing!" What did come out this month? Oh, plays! And whose season was it? The actor's, of course! He could not be an actor with that beard, but — ah, she remembered now!

"Are they really clever this time?" she asked roguishly — "for you must admit that they are usually sticks."

Tommy blinked at this. "I really believe, Mrs. Jerry," he said slowly, "it is you who don't know who I am!"

"You prepare the aristocracy for the stage, don't you?" she said plaintively.

"I!" he thundered.

"He had a beard," she said, in self-defence.

"Who?"

"Oh, I don't know! Please forgive me! I do remember, of course, who you are — I remember too well!" said Mrs. Jerry, generously.

"What is my name?" Tommy demanded.

She put her hands together again, beseechingly. "Please, please!" she said. "I have such a dreadful memory for names, but — oh, please!"

"What am I?" he insisted.

"You are the — the man who invents those delightful thingumbobs," she cried with an inspiration.

"I never invented anything, except two books," said Tommy, looking at her reproachfully.

"I know them by heart," she cried.

"One of them is not published yet," he informed her.

"I am looking forward to it so excitedly," she said at once.

"And my name is Sandys," said he.

"Thomas Sandys," she said, correcting him triumphantly. "How is that dear, darling little Agnes — Elspeth?"

"You have me at last," he admitted.

"'Sandys on Woman!'" exclaimed Mrs. Jerry, all rippling smiles once more. "Can I ever forget it!"

"I shall never pretend to know anything about

T. SANDYS HAS RETURNED

women again," Tommy answered dolefully, but with a creditable absence of vindictiveness.

"Please, please!" said the little hands again.

"It is a nasty jar, Mrs. Jerry."

"Please!"

"Oh that I could forget so quickly!"

"Please!"

"I forgive you, if that is what you want."

She waved her whip. "And you will come and see me?"

"When I have got over this. It needs — a little time." He really said this to please her.

"You shall talk to me of the new book," she said, confident that this would fetch him, for he was not her first author. "By the way, what is it about?"

"Can you ask, Mrs. Jerry?" replied Tommy, passionately. "Oh, woman, woman, can you ask?"

This puzzled her at the time, but she understood what he had meant when the book came out, dedicated to Pym. "Goodness gracious!" she said to herself as she went from chapter to chapter, and she was very self-conscious when she heard the book discussed in society, which was not quite as soon as it came out, for at first the ladies seemed to have forgotten their Tommy.

But the journals made ample amends. He had invented, they said, something new in literature, a story that was yet not a story, told in the form of essays which were no mere essays. There was no character mentioned by name, there was not a line of dialogue, essays only, they might say, were the net result, yet a human heart was laid bare, and surely that was fiction in its highest form. Fiction founded on fact, no doubt (for it would be ostrich-like to deny that such a work must be the outcome of a painful personal experience), but in those wise and penetrating pages Mr. Sandys called no one's attention to himself; his subject was an experience common to humanity, to be borne this way or that; and without vainglory he showed how it should be borne, so that those looking into the deep waters of the book (made clear by his pellucid style) might see, not the author, but themselves.

A few of the critics said that if the book added nothing to his reputation, it detracted nothing from it, but probably their pen added this mechanically when they were away. What annoyed him more was the two or three who stated that, much as they liked "Unrequited Love," they liked the "Letters" still better. He could not endure hearing a good word said for the "Letters" now.

The great public, I believe, always preferred the "Letters," but among important sections of it the new book was a delight, and for various reasons. For instance, it was no mere story. That got the thoughtful public. Its style, again, got the public which knows it is the only public that counts.

Society still held aloof (there was an African traveller on view that year), but otherwise everything was going on well, when the bolt came, as ever, from the quarter whence it was least expected. It came in a letter from Grizel, so direct as to be almost as direct as this: "I think it is a horrid book. The more beautifully it is written the more horrid it seems. No one was ever loved more truly than you. You can know nothing about unrequited love. Then why do you pretend to know? I see why you always avoided telling me anything about the book, even its title. It was because you knew what I should say. It is nothing but sentiment. You were on your wings all the time you were writing it. That is why you could treat me as you did. Even to the last moment you deceived me. I suppose you deceived yourself also. Had I known what was in the manuscript I would not have kissed it, I would have asked you to burn it. Had you not had the strength, and you would not, I should have burned it for you. It would have been a proof of my love. I have ceased to care whether you are a famous man or not. I want you to be a real man. But you will not let me help you. I have cried all day. GRIZEL."

Fury. Dejection. The heroic. They came in that order.

"This is too much!" he cried at first. "I can stand a good deal, Grizel, but there was once a worm that turned at last, you know. Take care, madam, take care. Oh, but you are a charming lady; you can decide everything for everybody, can't you! What delicious letters you write, something unexpected in everyone of them! There are poor dogs of men, Grizel, who open their letters from their loves knowing exactly what will be inside — words of cheer, words of love, of confidence, of admiration, which help them as they sit into the night at their work, fighting for fame that they may lay it at their loved one's feet. Discouragement, obloquy, scorn, they get in plenty from others, but they are always sure of her, — do you hear, my original Grizel? — those other dogs are always sure of her. Hurrah! Grizel, I was happy, I was actually honoured, it was helping me to do better and better, when you quickly put an end to all that. Hurrah, hurrah!"

I feel rather sorry for him. If he had not told her about his book it was because she did not and never could understand what compels a man to write one book instead of another. "I had no say in the matter; the thing demanded of me that I should do it, and I had to do it. Some must write from their own experience, they can make

T. SANDYS HAS RETURNED

nothing of anything else; but it is to me like a chariot that won't budge; I have to assume a character, Grizel, and then away we go. I don't attempt to explain how I write, I hate to discuss it; all I know is that those who know how it should be done can never do it. London is overrun with such, and everyone of them is as cock-sure as you. You have taken everything else, Grizel; surely you might leave me my books."

Yes, everything else, or nearly so. He put upon the table all the feathers he had extracted since his return to London, and they did make some little show, if less than it seemed to him. That little adventure in the park; well, if it started wrongly, it but helped to show the change in him, for he had determinedly kept away from Mrs. Jerry's house. He had met her once since the book came out, and she had blushed exquisitely when referring to it, and said: "How you have suffered! I blame myself dreadfully." Yes, and there was an unoccupied sofa near by, and he had not sat down on it with her and continued the conversation. Was not that a feather? And there were other ladies, and, without going into particulars, they were several feathers between them. How doggedly, to punish himself, he had stuck to the company of men, a sex that never interested him!

"But all that is nothing. I am beyond the pale. I did so monstrous a thing that I must die for it. What was this dreadful thing? When I saw you with that glove I knew you loved me, and that you thought I loved you, and I had not the heart to dash your joy. You don't know it, but that was the crime for which I must be exterminated, fiend that I am!"

Gusts of fury came at intervals all the morning. He wrote her appalling letters and destroyed them. He shook his fist and snapped his fingers at her, and went out for drink (having none in the house), and called a hansom to take him to Mrs. Jerry's, and tore round the park again and glared at everybody. He rushed on and on. "But the one thing you shall never do, Grizel, is to interfere with my work; I swear it, do you hear? In all else I am yours to mangle at your will, but touch it, and I am a beast at bay."

And still saying such things, he drew near the publishing offices of Goldie & Goldie, and circled round them, less like a beast at bay than a bird that is taking a long way to its nest. And about four of the afternoon what does this odd beast or bird or fish do but stalk into Goldie & Goldie's and order "Unrequited Love" to be withdrawn from circulation.

"Madam, I have carried out your wishes, and the man is hanged."

T. SANDYS HAS RETURNED

Not thus, but in words to that effect, did Tommy announce his deed to Grizel.

"I think you have done the right thing," she wrote back, "and I admire you for it." But he thought she did not admire him sufficiently for it, and he did not answer her letter, so it was the last that passed between them.

Such is the true explanation (now first published) of an affair that at the time created no small stir. "Why withdraw the book?" Goldie & Goldie asked of Tommy, but he would give no reason. "Why?" the public asked of Goldie & Goldie, and they had to invent several. The public invented the others. The silliest were those you could know only by belonging to a club.

I swear that Tommy had not foreseen the result. Quite unwittingly the favoured of the gods had found a way again. The talk about his incomprehensible action was the turning-point in the fortunes of the book. There were already a few thousand copies in circulation, and now many thousand people wanted them. Sandys, Sandys, Sandys! where had the ladies heard that name before? Society woke up, Sandys was again its hero; the traveller had to go lecturing in the provinces.

The ladies! Yes, and their friends, the men. There was a Tommy society in Mayfair that winter, nearly all of the members eminent or beautiful, and they held each other's hands. Both sexes were eligible, married or single, and the one rule was something about sympathy. It afterwards became the Souls, but those in the know still call them the Tommies.

They blackballed Mrs. Jerry (she was rather plump), but her married stepdaughter, Lady Pippinworth (who had been a Miss Ridge-Fulton), was one of them. Indeed, the Ridge-Fultons are among the thinnest families in the country.

T. Sandys was invited to join the society, but declined, and thus never quite knew what they did, nor can any outsider know, there being a regulation among the Tommies against telling. I believe, however, that they were a brotherhood, with sisters. You had to pass an examination in unrequited love, showing how you had suffered, and after that either the men or the women (I forget which) dressed in white to the throat, and then each got some other's old love's hand to hold, and you all sat on the floor and thought hard. There may have been even more in it than this, for one got to know Tommies at sight by a sort of careworn halo round the brow, and it is said that the House of Commons was several times nearly counted out because so many of its middle-aged members were holding the floor in another place.

Of course there were also the Anti-Tommies, who called themselves (rather vulgarly) the Tummies. Many of them were that shape. They held that, though you had loved in vain, it was no such mighty matter to boast of; but they were poor in argument, and their only really strong card was that Mr. Sandys was stoutish himself.

Their organs in the press said that he was a man of true genius, and slightly inclined to *embonpoint*.

This maddened him, but on the whole his return was a triumph, and despite thoughts of Grizel he was very, very happy, for he was at play again. He was a boy, and all the ladies were girls. Perhaps the lady he saw most frequently was Mrs. Jerry's stepdaughter. Lady Pippinworth was a friend of Lady Rintoul, and had several times visited her at the Spittal, but that was not the sole reason why Tommy so frequently drank tea with her. They had met first at a country house, where, one night after the ladies had retired to rest, Lady Pippinworth came stealing into the smoking-room with the tidings that there were burglars in the house. As she approached her room she had heard whispers, and then, her door being ajar, she had peeped upon the miscreants. She had also seen a pile of her jewellery on the table, and a pistol keeping guard on top of it. There were several men in the house, but that pistol cowed all of them save Tommy. "If we could lock them in!" someone suggested, but the key was on the wrong side of the door. "I shall put it on the right side," Tommy said pluckily, "if you others will prevent their escaping by the window"; and with characteristic courage he set off for her Ladyship's room. His intention was to insert his hand, whip out the key, and lock the door on the outside, a sufficiently hazardous enterprise; but what does he do instead? Locks the door on the inside, and goes for the burglars with his fists! A happy recollection of Corp's famous one from the shoulder disposed at once of the man who had seized the pistol; with the other gentleman Tommy had a stand-up fight in which both of them took and gave, but when support arrived, one burglar was senseless on the floor and T. Sandys was sitting on the other. Courageous of Tommy, was it not? But observe the end. He was left in the dining-room to take charge of his captives until morning, and by and by he was exhorting them in such noble language to mend their ways that they took the measure of him, and so touching were their family histories that Tommy wept and untied their cords and showed them out at the front door and gave them ten shillings each, and the one who begged for the honour of shaking hands with him also took his watch. Thus did Tommy and Lady Pippinworth become friends, but it was not this that sent him so often to her house to tea. She was a beautiful woman, with a reputation for having broken many hearts without damaging her own. He thought it an interesting case.

CHAPTER XXVI

GRIZEL ALL ALONE

IT was Tommy who was the favoured of the gods, you remember, not Grizel.

Elspeth wondered to see her, after the publication of that book, looking much as usual. "You know how he loved you now," she said, perhaps a little reproachfully.

"Yes," Grizel answered, "I know; I knew before the book came out."

"You must be sorry for him?"

Grizel nodded.

"But proud of him also," Elspeth said. "You have a right to be proud."

"I am as proud," Grizel replied, "as I have a right to be."

Something in her voice touched Elspeth, who was so happy that she wanted everyone to be happy. "I want you to know, Grizel," she said warmly, "that I don't blame you for not being able to love him; we can't help those things. Nor need you blame yourself too much, for I have often heard him say that artists must suffer in order to produce beautiful things."

"But I cannot remember," Elspeth had to admit, with a sigh, to David, "that she made any answer to that, except ' Thank you.' "

Grizel was nearly as reticent to David himself. Once only did she break down for a moment in his presence. It was when he was telling her that the issue of the book had been stopped.

"But I see you know already," he said. "Perhaps you even know why — though he has not given any sufficient reason to Elspeth."

David had given his promise, she reminded him, not to ask her any questions about Tommy.

"But I don't see why I should keep it," he said bluntly.

"Because you dislike him," she replied.

"Grizel," he declared, "I have tried hard to like him. I have thought and thought about it, and I can't see that he has given me any just cause to dislike him."

"And that," said Grizel, "makes you dislike him more than ever."

"I know that you cared for him once," David persisted, "and I know that he wanted to marry you——"

But she would not let him go on. "David," she said, "I want to give up my house, and I want you to take it. It is the real doctor's house of Thrums, and people in need of you still keep ringing me up of nights. The only door to your surgery is through my passage; it is I who should be in lodgings now."

"Do you really think I would, Grizel!" he cried indignantly.

"Rather than see the dear house go into another's hands," she answered steadily; "for I am determined to leave it. Dr. McQueen won't feel strange when he looks down, David, if it is only you he sees moving about the old rooms, instead of me."

"You are doing this for me, Grizel, and I won't have it."

"I give you my word," she told him, "that I am doing it for myself alone. I am tired of keeping a house, and of all its worries. Men don't know what they are."

She was smiling, but his brows wrinkled in pain. "Oh, Grizel!" he said, and stopped. And then he cried, "Since when has Grizel ceased to care for housekeeping?"

She did not say since when. I don't know whether she knew; but it was since she and Tommy had ceased to correspond. David's words showed her too suddenly how she had changed, and it was then that she broke down before him—because she had ceased to care for housekeeping.

But she had her way, and early in the new year David and his wife were established in their new home, with all Grizel's furniture, except such as was needed for the two rooms rented by her from Gavinia. She would have liked to take away the old doctor's chair, because it was the bit of him left behind when he died, and then for that very reason she did not. She no longer wanted him to see her always. "I am not so nice as I used to be, and I want to keep it from you," she said to the chair when she kissed it good-bye.

Was Grizel not as nice as she used to be? How can I answer, who love her the more only? There is one at least, Grizel, who will never desert you.

Ah, but was she?

I seem again to hear the warning voice of Grizel, and this time she is crying: "You know I was not."

She knew it so well that she could say it to herself quite calmly. She knew that, with whatever repugnance she drove those passions away, they would come back — yes, and for a space be welcomed back. Why does she leave Gavinia's blue hearth this evening, and seek the solitary Den? She has gone to summon them, and she knows it. They come thick in the Den, for they know the place. It was there that her mother was wont to walk with them. Have they been waiting for you

GRIZEL ALL ALONE

in the Den, Grizel, all this time? Have you found your mother's legacy at last?

Don't think that she sought them often. It was never when she seemed to have anything to live for. Tommy would not write to her, and so did not want her to write to him; but if that bowed her head, it never made her rebel. She still had her many duties. Whatever she suffered, so long as she could say, "I am helping him," she was in heart and soul the Grizel of old. In his fits of remorse, which were many, he tried to produce work that would please her. Thus, in a heroic attempt to be practical, he wrote a political article in one of the reviews, quite in the ordinary style, but so much worse than the average of such things that they would never have printed it without his name. He also contributed to a magazine a short tale,— he who could never write tales,— and he struck all the beautiful reflections out of it, and never referred to himself once, and the result was so imbecile that kindly people said there must be another writer of the same name. "Show them to Grizel," Tommy wrote to Elspeth, inclosing also some of the animadversions of the press, and he meant Grizel to see that he could write in his own way only. But she read those two efforts with delight, and said to Elspeth, "Tell him I am so proud of them."

Elspeth thought it very nice of Grizel to defend

the despised in this way (even Elspeth had fallen asleep over the political paper). She did not understand that Grizel loved them because they showed Tommy trying to do without his wings.

Then another trifle by him appeared, shorter even than the others; but no man in England could have written it except T. Sandys. It has not been reprinted, and I forget everything about it except that its subject was love. "Will not the friends of the man who can produce such a little masterpiece as this," the journals said, "save him from wasting his time on lumber for the reviews, and drivelling tales?" And Tommy suggested to Elspeth that she might show Grizel this exhortation also.

Grizel saw she was not helping him at all. If he would not fight, why should she? Oh, let her fall and fall, it would not take her farther from him! These were the thoughts that sent her into solitude, to meet with worse ones. She could not face the morrow. "What shall I do to-morrow?" She never shrank from to-day — it had its duties; it could be got through: but to-morrow was a never-ending road. Oh, how could she get through to-morrow?

Her great friend at this time was Corp; because he still retained his faith in Tommy. She could always talk of Tommy to Corp.

How loyal Corp was! He still referred to

GRIZEL ALL ALONE

Tommy as "him." Gavinia, much distressed, read aloud to Corp a newspaper attack on the political article, and all he said was, "He'll find a wy."

"He's found it," he went upstairs to announce to Grizel, when the praises of the "little masterpiece" arrived.

"Yes, I know, Corp," she answered quietly. She was sitting by the window where the plant was. Tommy had asked her to take care of it, without telling her why.

Something in her appearance troubled the hulking, blundering man. He could not have told what it was. I think it was simply this — that Grizel no longer sat erect in her chair.

"I'm nain easy in my mind about Grizel," he said that evening to Gavinia. "There's something queery about her, though I canna bottom 't."

"Yea?" said Gavinia, with mild contempt.

He continued pulling at his pipe, grunting as if in pleasant pain, which was the way Corp smoked.

"I could see she's no pleased, though he has found a wy," he said.

"What pleasure should she be able to sook out o' his keeping ding-ding-danging on about that woman?" retorted Gavinia.

"What woman?"

"The London besom that gae him the go-by."

TOMMY AND GRIZEL

"Was there sic a woman!" Corp cried.

"Of course there was, and it's her that he's aye writing about."

"Havers, Gavinia! It's Grizel he's aye writing about, and it was Grizel that gae him the go-by. It's town talk."

But whatever the town might say, Gavinia stuck to her opinion. "Grizel's no near so neat in her dressing as she was," she informed Corp, "and her hair is no aye tidy, and that bonnet she was in yesterday didna set her."

"I've noticed it," cried Corp. "I've noticed it this while back, though I didna ken I had noticed it, Gavinia. I wonder what can be the reason?"

"It's because nobody cares," Gavinia replied sadly. Trust one woman to know another!

"We a' care," said Corp, stoutly.

"We're a' as nothing, Corp, when he doesna care. She's fond o' him, man."

"Of course she is, in a wy. Whaur's the woman that could help it?"

"There's many a woman that could help it," said Gavinia, tartly, for the honour of her sex, "but she's no ane o' them." To be candid, Gavinia was not one of them herself. "I'm thinking she's terrible fond o' him," she said, "and I'm nain sure that he has treated her weel."

"Woman, take care; say a word agin him and I'll mittle you!" Corp thundered, and she desisted in fear.

But he made her re-read the little essay to him in instalments, and at the end he said victoriously, "You blethering crittur, there's no sic woman. It's just another o' his ploys!"

He marched upstairs to Grizel with the news, and she listened kindly. "I am sure you are right," she said; "you understand him better than any of them, Corp," and it was true.

He thought he had settled the whole matter. He was burning to be downstairs to tell Gavinia that these things needed only a man. "And so you'll be yoursel' again, Grizel," he said, with great relief.

She had not seen that he was aiming at her until now, and it touched her. "Am I so different, Corp?"

Not at all, he assured her delicately, but she was maybe no quite so neatly dressed as she used to be, and her hair wasna braided back so smooth, and he didna think that bonnet quite set her.

"Gavinia has been saying that to you!"

"I noticed it mysel', Grizel; I'm a terrible noticher."

"Perhaps you are right," she said, reflecting, after looking at herself for the first time for some days. "But to think of your caring, Corp!"

"I care most michty," he replied, with terrific earnestness.

"I must try to satisfy you, then," she said, smiling. "But, Corp, please don't discuss me with Gavinia."

This request embarrassed him, for soon again he did not know how to act. There was Grizel's strange behaviour with the child, for instance. "No, I won't come down to see him to-day, Corp," she had said; "somehow children weary me."

Such words from Grizel! His mouth would not shut and he could say nothing. "Forgive me, Corp!" she cried remorsefully, and ran downstairs, and with many a passionate caress asked forgiveness of the child.

Corp followed her, and for the moment he thought he must have been dreaming upstairs. "I wish I saw you wi' bairns o' your ain, Grizel," he said, looking on entranced; but she gave him such a pitiful smile that he could not get it out of his head. Deprived of Gavinia's counsel, and afraid to hurt Elspeth, he sought out the doctor and said bluntly to him, "How is it he never writes to Grizel? She misses him terrible."

"So," David thought, "Grizel's dejection is becoming common talk." "Damn him!" he said, in a gust of fury.

But this was too much for loyal Corp. "Damn you!" he roared.

But in his heart he knew that the doctor was a just man, and henceforth, when he was meaning to comfort Grizel, he was often seeking comfort for himself.

He did it all with elaborate cunning, to prevent her guessing that he was disturbed about her: asked permission to sit with her, for instance, because he was dull downstairs; mentioned as a ludicrous thing that there were people who believed Tommy could treat a woman badly, and waited anxiously for the reply. Oh, he was transparent, was Corp, but you may be sure Grizel never let him know that she saw through him. Tommy could not be blamed, she pointed out, though he did not care for some woman who perhaps cared for him.

"Exac'ly," said Corp.

And if he seemed, Grizel went on, with momentary bitterness, to treat her badly, it could be only because she had made herself cheap.

"That's it," said Corp, cheerfully. Then he added hurriedly, "No, that's no it ava. She's the last to mak' hersel' cheap." Then he saw that this might put Grizel on the scent. "Of course there's no sic woman," he said artfully, "but if there was, he would mak' it a' right. She mightna see how it was to be done, but kennin' what a crittur he is, she maun be sure he would find a wy. She would never lose hope, Grizel."

And then, if Grizel did not appease him instantly, he would say appealingly, "I canna think less o' him, Grizel; no, it would mak' me just terrible low. Grizel," he would cry sternly, "dinna tell me to think less o' that laddie."

Then, when she had reassured him, he would recall the many instances in which Tommy as a boy had found a way. "Did we ever ken he was finding it, Grizel, till he did find it? Many a time I says to mysel', says I, 'All is over,' and syne next minute that holy look comes ower his face, and he stretches out his legs like as if he was riding on a horse, and all that kens him says, 'He has found a wy.' If I was the woman (no that there is sic a woman) I would say to mysel', 'He was never beat,' I would say, 'when he was a laddie, and it's no likely he'll be beat when he's a man'; and I wouldna sit looking at the fire wi' my hands fauded, nor would I forget to keep my hair neat, and I would wear the frock that set me best, and I would play in my auld bonny wy wi' bairns, for says I to mysel', 'I'm sure to hae bairns o' my ain some day, and ——' "

But Grizel cried, "Don't, Corp, don't!"

"I winna," he answered miserably, "no, I winna. Forgive me, Grizel; I think I'll be stepping"; and then when he got as far as the door he would say, "I canna do 't, Grizel; I'm just terrible wae for the woman (if sic a woman there be), but I canna think ill o' him; you mauna speir it o' me."

He was much brightened by a reflection that

came to him one day in church. "Here have I been near blaming him for no finding a wy, and very like he doesna ken we want him to find a wy!"

How to inform Tommy without letting Grizel know? She had tried twice long ago to teach him to write, but he found it harder on the wrists than the heaviest luggage. It was not safe for him even to think of the extra twirl that turned an *n* into an *m*, without first removing any knick-knacks that might be about. Nevertheless, he now proposed a third set-to, and Grizel acquiesced, though she thought it but another of his inventions to keep her from brooding.

The number of words in the English tongue excited him, and he often lost all by not confining the chase to one, like a dog after rabbits. Fortunately, he knew which words he wanted to bag.

"Change at Tilliedrum!" "Tickets! show your tickets!" and the like, he much enjoyed meeting in the flesh, so to speak.

"Let's see 'Find a wy,' Grizel," he would say. "Ay, ay, and is that the crittur!" and soon the sly fellow could write it, or at least draw it.

He affected an ambition to write a letter to his son on that gentleman's first birthday, and so "Let's see what 'I send you these few scrapes' is like, Grizel." She assured him that this is not essential in correspondence, but all the letters he had ever heard read aloud began thus, and he got his way.

Anon Master Shiach was surprised and gratified to receive the following epistle: "My dear sir, I send you these few scrapes to tell you as you have found a way to be a year of age the morn. All tickets ready in which Gavinia joins so no more at present I am, sir, your obed^t father Corp Shiach."

The fame of this letter went abroad, but not a soul knew of the next. It said: "My dear Sir, I send you these few scrapes to tell you as Grizel needs cheering up. Kindly oblidge by finding a way so no more at present. I am sir your obed^t Servt Corp Shiach."

To his bewilderment, this produced no effect, though only because Tommy never got it, and he wrote again, more sternly, requesting his hero to find a way immediately. He was waiting restlessly for the answer at a time when Elspeth called on Grizel to tell her of something beautiful that Tommy had done. He had been very ill for nearly a fortnight, it appeared, but had kept it from her to save her anxiety. "Just think, Grizel; all the time he was in bed with bronchitis he was writing me cheerful letters every other day pretending there was nothing the matter with him. He is better now. I have heard about it from a Mrs. Jerry, a lady whom I knew in London, and who has nursed him in the kindest way." (But this same Mrs. Jerry had opened Corp's letters and destroyed them as of no importance.) "He would

GRIZEL ALL ALONE

never have mentioned it himself. How like him, Grizel! You remember, I made him promise before he went back to London that if he was ill he would let me know at once so that I could go to him, but he is so considerate he would not give me pain. He wrote those letters, Grizel, when he was gasping for breath."

"But she seemed quite unmoved," Elspeth said sadly to her husband afterwards.

Unmoved! Yes; Grizel remained apparently unmoved until Elspeth had gone, but then — the torture she endured! "Oh, cruel, cruel!" she cried, and she could neither stand nor sit; she flung herself down before the fire and rocked this way and that, in a paroxysm of woe. "Oh, cruel, cruel!"

It was Tommy who was cruel. To be ill, near to dying, apparently, and not to send her word! She could never, never have let him go had he not made that promise to Elspeth; and he kept it thus. Oh, wicked, wicked!

"You would have gone to him at once, Elspeth! You! Who are you, that talks of going to him as your right? He is not yours, I tell you; he is mine! He is mine alone; it is I who would go to him. Who is this woman that dares take my place by his side when he is ill!"

She rose to go to him, to drive away all others. I am sure that was what gave her strength to rise;

but she sank to the floor again, and her passion lasted for hours. And through the night she was crying to God that she would be brave no more. In her despair she hoped he heard her.

Her mood had not changed when David came to see her next morning, to admit, too, that Tommy seemed to have done an unselfish thing in concealing his illness from them. Grizel nodded, but he thought she was looking strangely reckless. He had a message from Elspeth. Tommy had asked her to let him know whether the plant was flourishing.

"So you and he don't correspond now?" David said, with his old, puzzled look.

"No," was all her answer to that. The plant, she thought, was dead; she had not, indeed, paid much attention to it of late; but she showed it to David, and he said it would revive if more carefully tended. He also told her its rather pathetic history, which was new to Grizel, and of the talk at the wedding which had led to Tommy's taking pity on it. "Fellow-feeling, I suppose," he said lightly; "you see, they both blossomed prematurely."

The words were forgotten by him as soon as spoken; but Grizel sat on with them, for they were like a friend — or was it an enemy? — who had come to tell her strange things. Yes, the doctor was right. Now she knew why Tommy had loved this plant. Of the way in which he would sit looking wistfully at it, almost nursing it, she had been told by Aaron; he had himself begged her to tend it lovingly. Fellow-feeling! The doctor was shrewder than he thought.

Well, what did it matter to her? All that day she would do nothing for the plant, but in the middle of the night she rose and ran to it and hugged it, and for a time she was afraid to look at it by lamplight, lest Tommy was dead. Whether she had never been asleep that night, or had awakened from a dream, she never knew, but she ran to the plant, thinking it and Tommy were as one, and that they must die together. No such thought had ever crossed his mind, but it seemed to her that she had been told it by him, and she lit her fire to give the plant warmth, and often desisted, to press it to her bosom, the heat seemed to come so reluctantly from the fire. This idea that his fate was bound up with that of the plant took strange possession of the once practical Grizel; it was as if some of Tommy's nature had passed into her to help her break the terrible monotony of the days.

And from that time there was no ailing child more passionately tended than the plant, and as spring advanced it began once more to put forth new leaves.

And Grizel also seemed glorified again. She was her old self. Dark shapes still lingered for her in the Den, but she avoided them, and if they tried to enter into her, she struggled with them and cast them out. As she saw herself able to fight and win once more, her pride returned to her, and one day she could ask David, joyously, to give her a present of the old doctor's chair. And she could kneel by its side and say to it, " You can watch me always; I am just as I used to be."

Seeing her once more the incarnation of vigor and content, singing gaily to his child, and as eager to be at her duties betimes as a morning in May, Corp grunted with delight, and was a hero for not telling her that it was he who had passed Tommy the word. For, of course, Tommy had done it all.

" Somebody has found a wy, Grizel! " he would say, chuckling, and she smiled an agreement.

" And yet," says he, puzzled, " I've watched, and you hinna haen a letter frae him. It defies the face o' clay to find out how he has managed it. Oh, the crittur! Ay, I suppose you dinna want to tell me what it is that has lichted you up again? "

She could not tell him, for it was a compact she had made with one who did not sign it. " I shall cease to be bitter and despairing and wicked, and try every moment of my life to be good and do

GRIZEL ALL ALONE

good, so long as my plant flourishes; but if it withers, then I shall go to him — I don't care what happens; I shall go to him."

It was the middle of June when she first noticed that the plant was beginning to droop.

CHAPTER XXVII

GRIZEL'S JOURNEY

NOTHING could have been less expected. In the beginning of May its leaves had lost something of their greenness. The plant seemed to be hesitating, but she coaxed it over the hill, and since then it had scarcely needed her hand; almost light-headedly it hurried into its summer clothes, and new buds broke out on it, like smiles, at the fascinating thought that there was to be a tomorrow. Grizel's plant had never been so brave in its little life when suddenly it turned back.

That was the day on which Elspeth and David were leaving for a fortnight's holiday with his relatives by the sea; for Elspeth needed and was getting special devotion just now, and Grizel knew why. She was glad they were going; it was well that they should not be there to ask questions if she also must set forth on a journey.

For more than a week she waited, and everything she could do for her plant she did. She watched it so carefully that she might have deceived herself into believing that it was standing

GRIZEL'S JOURNEY

still only, had there been no night-time. She thought she had not perhaps been sufficiently good, and she tried to be more ostentatiously satisfied with her lot. Never had she forced herself to work quite so hard for others as in those few days, and then when she came home it had drooped a little more.

When she was quite sure that it was dying, she told Corp she was going to London by that night's train. "He is ill, Corp, and I must go to him."

Ill! But how had he let her know?

"He has found a way," she said, with a tremulous smile. He wanted her to telegraph; but no, she would place no faith in telegrams.

At least she could telegraph to Elspeth and the doctor. One of them would go.

"It is I who am going," she said quietly. "I can't wait any longer. It was a promise, Corp. He loves me." They were the only words she said which suggest that there was anything strange about Grizel at this time.

Corp saw how determined she was when she revealed, incidentally, that she had drawn a sum of money out of the bank a week ago, "to be ready."

"What will folk say!" he cried.

"You can tell Gavinia the truth when I am gone," she told him. "She will know better than you what to say to other people." And that was some comfort to him, for it put the burden of invention upon his wife. So it was Corp who saw Grizel off. He was in great distress himself about Tommy, but he kept a courageous face for her, and his last words flung in at the carriage window were, "Now dinna be down-hearted; I'm nain down-hearted mysel', for we're very sure he'll find a wy." And Grizel smiled and nodded, and the train turned the bend that shuts out the little town of Thrums. The town vanishes quickly, but the quarry we howked it out of stands grim and red, watching the train for many a mile.

Of Grizel's journey to London there are no particulars to tell. She was wearing her brown jacket and fur cap because Tommy had liked them, and she sat straight and stiff all the way. She had never been in a train since she was a baby, except two or three times to Tilliedrum, and she thought this was the right way to sit. Always, when the train stopped, which was at long intervals, she put her head out at the window and asked if this was the train to London. Every station a train stops at in the middle of the night is the infernal regions, and she shuddered to hear lost souls clanking their chains, which is what a milk-can becomes on its way to the van; but still she asked if this was the train to London. When fellow-passengers addressed her, she was very modest and cautious in her replies. Sometimes a look of extraordinary happiness, of radiance, passed over her face, and

GRIZEL'S JOURNEY

may have puzzled them. It was part of the thought that, however ill he might be, she was to see him now.

She did not see him as soon as she expected, for at the door of Tommy's lodgings they told her that he had departed suddenly for the Continent about a week ago. He was to send an address by and by to which letters could be forwarded. Was he quite well when he went away? Grizel asked, shaking.

The landlady and her daughter thought he was rather peakish, but he had not complained.

He went away for his health, Grizel informed them, and he was very ill now. Oh, could they not tell her where he was? All she knew was that he was very ill. "I am engaged to be married to him," she said with dignity. Without this strange certainty that Tommy loved her at last, she could not have trod the road which faced her now. Even when she had left the house, where at their suggestion she was to call to-morrow, she found herself wondering at once what he would like her to do now, and she went straight to a hotel, and had her box sent to it from the station, and she remained there all day because she thought that this was what he would like her to do. She sat bolt upright on a cane chair in her bedroom, praying to God with her eyes open; she was begging Him to let Tommy tell her where he was, and promising to return home at once if he did not need her.

Next morning they showed her, at his lodgings,

two lines in a newspaper, which said that he was ill with bronchitis at the Hôtel Krone, Bad-Platten, in Switzerland.

It may have been an answer to her prayer, as she thought, but we know now how the paragraph got into print. On the previous evening the landlady had met Mr. Pym on the ladder of an omnibus, and told him, before they could be plucked apart, of the lady who knew that Mr. Sandys was ill. It must be bronchitis again. Pym was much troubled; he knew that the Krone at Bad-Platten had been Tommy's destination. He talked that day, and one of the company was a reporter, which accounts for the paragraph.

Grizel found out how she could get to Bad-Platten. She left her box behind her at the cloak-room of the railway station, where I suppose it was sold years afterwards. From Dover she sent a telegram to Tommy, saying: "I am coming. GRIZEL."

On entering the train at Calais she had a railway journey of some thirty hours, broken by two changes only. She could speak a little French, but all the use she made of it was to ask repeatedly if she was in the right train. An English lady who travelled with her for many hours woke up now and again to notice that this quiet, prim-looking girl was always sitting erect, with her hand on her umbrella, as if ready to leave the train at any moment. The lady pointed out some of the beauties of the scenery to her, and Grizel tried to listen. "I am afraid you are unhappy," her companion said at last.

"That is not why I am crying," Grizel said; "I think I am crying because I am so hungry."

The stranger gave her sandwiches and claret as cold as the rivers that raced the train; and Grizel told her, quite frankly, why she was going to Bad-Platten. She did not tell his name, only that he was ill, and that she was engaged to him, and he had sent for her. She believed it all. The lady was very sympathetic, and gave her information about the diligence by which the last part of Grizel's journey must be made, and also said: "You must not neglect your meals, if only for his sake; for how can you nurse him back to health if you arrive at Bad-Platten ill yourself? Consider his distress if he were to be told that you were in the inn, but not able to go to him."

"Oh!" Grizel cried, rocking her arms for the first time since she knew her plant was drooping. She promised to be very practical henceforth, so as to have strength to take her place by his side at once. It was strange that she who was so good a nurse had forgotten these things, so strange that it alarmed her, as if she feared that, without being able to check herself, she was turning into some other person.

The station where she alighted was in a hubbub of life; everyone seemed to leave the train here, and to resent the presence of all the others. They were mostly English. The men hung back, as if, now that there was business to be done in some foolish tongue, they had better leave the ladies to do it. Many of them seemed prepared, if there was dissension, to disown their womankind and run for it. They looked haughty and nervous. Such of them as had tried to shave in the train were boasting of it and holding handkerchiefs to their chins. The ladies were moving about in a masterful way, carrying bunches of keys. When they had done everything, the men went and stood by their sides again.

Outside the station buses and carriages were innumerable, and everybody was shouting; but Grizel saw that nearly all her fellow-passengers were hurrying by foot or conveyance to one spot, all desirous of being there first, and she thought it must be the place where the diligence started from, and pressed on with them. It proved to be a hotel where they all wanted the best bedroom, and many of them had telegraphed for it, and they gathered round a man in uniform and demanded that room of him; but he treated them as if they were little dogs and he was not the platter, and soon they were begging for a room on the fourth floor at the back, and swelling with triumph if they got it.

GRIZEL'S JOURNEY

The scrimmage was still going on when Grizel slipped out of the hotel, having learned that the diligence would not start until the following morning. It was still early in the afternoon. How could she wait until to-morrow?

Bad-Platten was forty miles away. The road was pointed out to her. It began to climb at once. She was to discover that for more than thirty miles it never ceased to climb. She sat down, hesitating, on a little bridge that spanned a horrible rushing white stream. Poets have sung the glories of that stream, but it sent a shiver through her. On all sides she was caged in by a ring of splendid mountains, but she did not give them one admiring glance (there is a special spot where the guide-books advise you to stop for a moment to do it); her one passionate desire was to fling out her arms and knock them over.

She had often walked twenty miles in a day, in a hill country too, without feeling tired, and there seemed no reason why she should not set off now. There were many inns on the way, she was told, where she could pass the night. There she could get the diligence next day. This would not bring her any sooner to him than if she waited here until to-morrow; but how could she sit still till to-morrow? She must be moving; she seemed to have been sitting still for an eternity. "I must not do anything rash," she told herself, carefully

"I must arrive at Bad-Platten able to sit down beside him the moment I have taken off my jacket — oh, without waiting to take off my jacket." She went into the hotel and ate some food, just to show herself how careful she had become. About three o'clock she set off. She had a fierce desire to get away from that heartless white stream and the crack of whips and the doleful pine woods, and at first she walked very quickly; but she never got away from them, for they marched with her. It was not that day, but the next, that Grizel thought anything was marching with her. That day her head was quite clear, and she kept her promise to herself, and as soon as she felt tired she stopped for the night at a village inn. But when she awoke very early next morning she seemed to have forgotten that she was to travel the rest of the way by diligence; for, after a slight meal, she started off again on foot, and she was walking all day.

She passed through many villages so like each other that in time she thought they might be the same. There was always a monster inn whence one carriage was departing as another drove up, and there was a great stone water-tank in which women drew their washing back and forward, and there was always a big yellow dog that barked fiercely and then giggled, and at the doors of painted houses children stood. You knew they were children by their size only. The one person she spoke to that day was a child who offered her a bunch of wild flowers. No one was looking, and Grizel kissed her and then hurried on.

The carriage passed and repassed her. There must have been a hundred of them, but in time they became one. No sooner had it disappeared in dust in front of her than she heard the crack of its whip behind.

It was a glorious day of sweltering sun; but she was bewildered now, and did not open the umbrella with which she had shielded her head yesterday. In the foreground was always the same white road, on both sides the same pine wood laughing with wild flowers, the same roaring white stream. From somewhere near came the tinkle of cow-bells. Far away on heights, if she looked up, were villages made of match-boxes. She saw what were surely the same villages if she looked down; or the one was the reflection of the other, in the sky above or in the valley below. They stood out so vividly that they might have been within arm's reach. They were so small that she felt she could extinguish them with her umbrella. Near them was the detestably picturesque castle perched upon a bracket. Everywhere was that loathly waterfall. Here and there were squares of cultivated land that looked like door-mats flung out upon the hillsides. The huge mountains raised their jagged heads through the snow, and were so sharp-edged that they might have been clipped out of cardboard. The sky was blue, without a flaw; but lost clouds crawled like snakes between heaven and earth. All day the sun scorched her, but the night was nipping cold.

From early morn till evening she climbed to get away from them, but they all marched with her. They waited while she slept. She woke up in an inn, and could have cried with delight because she saw nothing but bare walls. But as soon as she reached the door, there they all were, ready for her. An hour after she set off, she again reached that door; and she stopped at it to ask if this was the inn where she had passed the night. Everything had turned with her. Two squalls of sudden rain drenched her that day, and she forced her way through the first, but sought a covering from the second.

It was then afternoon, and she was passing through a village by a lake. Since Grizel's time monster hotels have trampled the village to death, and the shuddering lake reflects all day the most hideous of caravansaries flung together as with a giant shovel in one of the loveliest spots on earth. Even then some of the hotels had found it out. Grizel drew near to two of them, and saw wet halls full of open umbrellas which covered the floor and looked like great beetles. These buildings were too formidable, and she dragged herself past them. She came to a garden of hops and evergreens. Wet chairs were standing in the deserted walks, and here and there was a little arbour. She went into one of these arbours and sat down, and soon slid to the floor.

The place was St. Gian, some miles from Bad-Platten; but one of the umbrellas she had seen was Tommy's. Others belonged to Mrs. Jerry and Lady Pippinworth.

CHAPTER XXVIII

TWO OF THEM

WHEN Tommy started impulsively on what proved to be his only Continental trip he had expected to join Mrs. Jerry and her stepdaughter at Bad-Platten. They had been there for a fortnight, and "the place is a dream," Mrs. Jerry had said in the letter pressing him to come; but it was at St. Gian that she met the diligence and told him to descend. Bad-Platten, she explained, was a horror.

Her fuller explanation was that she was becoming known there as the round lady.

"Now, am I as round as all that?" she said plaintively to Tommy.

"Mrs. Jerry," he replied, with emotion, "you must not ask me what I think of you." He always treated her with extraordinary respect and chivalry now, and it awed her.

She had looked too, too round because she was in the company of Lady Pippinworth. Everyone seemed to be too round or too large by the side of that gifted lady, who somehow never looked too thin. She knew her power. When there were women in the room whom she disliked she merely went and stood beside them. In the gyrations of the dance the onlooker would momentarily lose sight of her; she came and went like a blinking candle. Men could not dance with her without its being said that they were getting stout. There is nothing they dislike so much, yet they did dance with her. Tommy, having some slight reason, was particularly sensitive about references to his figure, yet it was Lady Pippinworth who had drawn him to Switzerland. What was her strange attraction?

Calmly considered, she was preposterously thin, but men, at least, could not think merely of her thinness, unless, when walking with her, they became fascinated by its shadow on the ground. She was tall, and had a very clear, pale complexion and light-brown hair. Light brown, too, were her heavy eyelashes, which were famous for being black-tipped, as if a brush had touched them, though it had not. She made play with her eyelashes as with a fan, and sometimes the upper and lower seemed to entangle for a moment and be in difficulties, from which you wanted to extricate them in the tenderest manner. And the more you wanted to help her the more disdainfully she looked at you. Yet though she looked disdainful she also looked helpless. Now we have the secret of her charm.

This helpless disdain was the natural expression

of her face, and I am sure she fell asleep with a curl of the lip. Her scorn of men so maddened them that they could not keep away from her. "Damn!" they said under their breath, and rushed to her. If rumour is to be believed, Sir Harry Pippinworth proposed to her in a fury brought on by the sneer with which she had surveyed his family portraits. I know nothing more of Sir Harry, except that she called him Pips, which seems to settle him.

"They will be calling me the round gentleman," Tommy said ruefully to her that evening, as he strolled with her towards the lake, and indeed he was looking stout. Mrs. Jerry did not accompany them; she wanted to be seen with her trying stepdaughter as little as possible, and Tommy's had been the happy proposal that he should attend them alternately — "fling away my own figure to save yours," he had said gallantly to Mrs. Jerry.

"Do you mind?" Lady Pippinworth asked.

"I mind nothing," he replied, "so long as I am with you."

He had not meant to begin so near the point where they had last left off; he had meant to begin much farther back: but an irresistible desire came over him to make sure that she really did permit him to say this sort of thing.

Her only reply was a flutter of the little fans and a most contemptuous glance.

TWO OF THEM

"Alice," said Tommy, in the old way.

"Well?"

"You don't understand what it is to me to say Alice again."

"Many people call me Alice."

"But they have a right to."

"I supposed you thought you had a right to also."

"No," said Tommy. "That is why I do it."

She strolled on, more scornful and helpless than ever. Apparently it did not matter what one said to Lady Pippinworth; her pout kept it within the proprieties.

There was a magnificent sunset that evening, which dyed a snow-topped mountain pink. "That is what I came all the way from London to see," Tommy remarked, after they had gazed at it.

"I hope you feel repaid," she said, a little tartly.

"You mistake my meaning," he replied. "I had heard of these wonderful sunsets, and an intense desire came over me to see you looking disdainfully at them. Yes, I feel amply repaid. Did you notice, Alice, or was it but a fancy of my own, that when he had seen the expression on your face the sun quite slunk away?"

"I wonder you don't do so also," she retorted. She had no sense of humour, and was rather stupid; so it is no wonder that the men ran after her.

"I am more gallant than the sun," said he. "If

I had been up there in its place, Alice, and you had been looking at me, I could never have set."

She pouted contemptuously, which meant, I think, that she was well pleased. Yet, though he seemed to be complimenting her, she was not sure of him. She had never been sure of Tommy, nor, indeed, he of her, which was probably why they were so interested in each other still.

"Do you know," Tommy said, "what I have told you is really at least half the truth? If I did not come here to see you disdaining the sun, I think I did come to see you disdaining me. Odd, is it not, if true, that a man should travel so far to see a lip curl up?"

"You don't seem to know what brought you," she said.

"It seems so monstrous," he replied, musing. "Oh, yes, I am quite certain that the curl of the lip is responsible for my being here; it kept sending me constant telegrams; but what I want to know is, do I come for the pleasure of the thing or for the pain? Do I like your disdain, Alice, or does it make me writhe? Am I here to beg you to do it again, or to defy it?"

"Which are you doing now?" she inquired.

"I had hoped," he said with a sigh, "that you could tell me that."

On another occasion they reached the same point in this discussion, and went a little beyond

TWO OF THEM

it. It was on a wet afternoon, too, when Tommy had vowed to himself to mend his ways. "That disdainful look is you," he told her, "and I admire it more than anything in nature; and yet, Alice, and yet ―――"

"Well?" she answered coldly, but not moving, though he had come suddenly too near her. They were on a private veranda of the hotel, and she was lolling in a wicker chair.

"And yet," he said intensely, "I am not certain that I would not give the world to have the power to drive that look from your face. That, I begin to think, is what brought me here."

"But you are not sure," she said, with a shrug of the shoulder.

It stung him into venturing further than he had ever gone with her before. Not too gently, he took her head in both his hands and forced her to look up at him. She submitted without a protest. She was disdainful, but helpless.

"Well?" she said again.

He withdrew his hands, and she smiled mockingly.

"If I thought ―――" he cried with sudden passion, and stopped.

"You think a great deal, don't you?" she said. She was going now.

"If I thought there was any blood in your veins, you icy woman ―――"

"Or in your own," said she. But she said it a little fiercely, and he noticed that.

"Alice," he cried, "I know now. It is to drive that look from your face that I am here."

She courtesied from the door. She was quite herself again.

But for that moment she had been moved. He was convinced of it, and his first feeling was of exultation as in an achievement. I don't know what you are doing just now, Lady Pippinworth, but my compliments to you, and T. Sandys is swelling.

There followed on this exultation another feeling as sincere — devout thankfulness that he had gone no further. He drew deep breaths of relief over his escape, but knew that he had not himself to thank. His friends, the little sprites, had done it, in return for the amusement he seemed to give them. They had stayed him in the nick of time, but not earlier; it was quite as if they wanted Tommy to have his fun first. So often they had saved him from being spitted, how could he guess that the great catastrophe was fixed for to-night, and that henceforth they were to sit round him counting his wriggles, as if this new treatment of him tickled them even more than the other?

But he was too clever not to know that they might be fattening him for some very special feast, and his thanks took the form of a vow to need their help no more. To-morrow he would begin to climb the mountains around St. Gian; if he danced attendance on her dangerous Ladyship again, Mrs. Jerry should be there also, and he would walk circumspectly between them, like a man with gyves upon his wrists. He was in the midst of all the details of these reforms, when suddenly he looked at himself thus occupied, and laughed bitterly; he had so often come upon Tommy making grand resolves!

He stopped operations and sat down beside them. No one could have wished more heartily to be anybody else, or have had less hope. He had not even the excuse of being passionately drawn to this woman; he remembered that she had never interested him until he heard of her effect upon other men. Her reputation as a duellist, whose defence none of his sex could pass, had led to his wondering what they saw in her, and he had dressed himself in their sentiments and so approached her. There were times in her company when he forgot that he was wearing borrowed garments, when he went on flame, but he always knew, as now, upon reflection. Nothing seemed easier at this moment than to fling them aside; with one jerk they were on the floor. Obviously it was only vanity that had inspired him, and vanity was satisfied: the easier, therefore, to stop. Would you like to make the woman unhappy, Tommy?

You know you would not; you have somewhere about you one of the softest hearts in the world. Then desist; be satisfied that you did thaw her once, and grateful that she so quickly froze again. "I am; indeed I am," he responds. "No one could have himself better in hand for the time being than I, and if a competition in morals were now going on, I should certainly take the medal. But I cannot speak for myself an hour in advance. I make a vow, as I have done so often before, but it does not help me to know what I may be at before the night is out."

When his disgust with himself was at its height he suddenly felt like a little god. His new book had come into view. He flicked a finger at his reflection in a mirror. "That for you!" he said defiantly; "at least I can write; I can write at last!"

The manuscript lay almost finished at the bottom of his trunk. It could not easily have been stolen for one hour without his knowing. Just when he was about to start on a walk with one of the ladies, he would run upstairs to make sure that it was still there; he made sure by feeling, and would turn again at the door to make sure by looking. Miser never listened to the crispness of bank-notes with more avidity; woman never spent more time in shutting and opening her jewel-box.

"I can write at last!" He knew that, comparatively speaking, he had never been able to write before. He remembered the fuss that had been made about his former books. "Pooh!" he said, addressing them contemptuously.

Once more he drew his beloved manuscript from its hiding-place. He did not mean to read, only to fondle; but his eye chancing to fall on a special passage — two hours afterwards he was interrupted by the dinner-gong. He returned the pages to the box and wiped his eyes. While dressing hurriedly he remembered with languid interest that Lady Pippinworth was staying in the same hotel.

There were a hundred or more at dinner, and they were all saying the same thing: "Where have you been to-day?" "Really! but the lower path is shadier." "Is this your first visit?" "The glacier is very nice." "Were you caught in the rain?" "The view from the top is very nice." "After all, the rain lays the dust." "They give you two sweets at Bad-Platten and an ice on Sunday." "The sunset is very nice." "The poulet is very nice." The hotel is open during the summer months only, but probably the chairs in the dining-room and the knives and forks in their basket make these remarks to each other every evening throughout the winter.

Being a newcomer, Tommy had not been placed beside either of his friends, who sat apart "because," Mrs. Jerry said, "she calls me mamma, and I am not going to stand that." For some time he gave thought to neither of them; he was engrossed in what he had been reading, and it turned him into a fine and magnanimous character. When gradually her Ladyship began to flit among his reflections, it was not to disturb them, but because she harmonized. He wanted to apologize to her. The apology grew in grace as the dinner progressed; it was so charmingly composed that he was profoundly stirred by it.

The opportunity came presently in the hall, where it is customary after dinner to lounge or stroll if you are afraid of the night air. Or if you do not care for music, you can go into the drawing-room and listen to the piano.

"I am sure mamma is looking for you everywhere," Lady Pippinworth said, when Tommy took a chair beside her. "It is her evening, you know."

"Surely you would not drive me away," he replied with a languishing air, and then smiled at himself, for he was done with this sort of thing. "Lady Pippinworth," said he, firmly—it needs firmness when of late you have been saying "Alice."

"Well?"

"I have been thinking——" Tommy began.

"I am sure you have," she said.

"I have been thinking," he went on determinedly, "that I played a poor part this afternoon. I had no right to say what I said to you."

"As far as I can remember," she answered, "you did not say very much."

TWO OF THEM

"It is like your generosity, Lady Pippinworth," he said, "to make light of it; but let us be frank: I made love to you."

Anyone looking at his expressionless face and her lazy disdain (and there were many in the hall) would have guessed that their talk was of where were you to-day? and what should I do to-morrow?

"You don't really mean that?" her Ladyship said incredulously. "Think, Mr. Sandys, before you tell me anything more. Are you sure you are not confusing me with mamma?"

"I did it," said Tommy, remorsefully.

"In my absence?" she asked.

"When you were with me on the veranda."

Her eyes opened to their widest, so surprised that the lashes had no time for their usual play.

"Was that what you call making love, Mr. Sandys?" she inquired.

"I call a spade a spade."

"And now you are apologizing to me, I understand?"

"If you can in the goodness of your heart forgive me, Lady Pippinworth ———"

"Oh, I do," she said heartily, "I do. But how stupid you must have thought me not even to know! I feel that it is I who ought to apologize. What a number of ways there seem to be of making love, and yours is such an odd way!"

Now to apologize for playing a poor part is one

thing, and to put up with the charge of playing a part poorly is quite another. Nevertheless, he kept his temper.

"You have discovered an excellent way of punishing me," he said manfully, "and I submit. Indeed, I admire you the more. So I am paying you a compliment when I whisper that I know you knew."

But she would not have it. "You are so strangely dense to-night," she said. "Surely, if I had known, I would have stopped you. You forget that I am a married woman," she added, remembering Pips rather late in the day.

"There might be other reasons why you did not stop me," he replied impulsively.

"Such as?"

"Well, you — you might have wanted me to go on."

He blurted it out.

"So," said she slowly, "you are apologizing to me for not going on?"

"I implore you, Lady Pippinworth," Tommy said, in much distress, "not to think me capable of that. If I moved you for a moment, I am far from boasting of it; it makes me only the more anxious to do what is best for you."

This was not the way it had shaped during dinner, and Tommy would have acted wisely had he now gone out to cool his head. "If you moved me?" she repeated interrogatively; but, with the best intentions, he continued to flounder.

"Believe me," he implored her, "had I known it could be done, I should have checked myself. But they always insist that you are an iceberg, and am I so much to blame if that look of hauteur deceived me with the rest? Oh, dear Lady Disdain," he said warmly, in answer to one of her most freezing glances, "it deceives me no longer. From that moment I knew you had a heart, and I was shamed — as noble a heart as ever beat in woman," he added. He always tended to add generous bits when he found it coming out well.

"Does the man think I am in love with him?" was Lady Disdain's inadequate reply.

"No, no, indeed!" he assured her earnestly. "I am not so vain as to think that, nor so selfish as to wish it; but if for a moment you were moved ——"

"But I was not," said she, stamping her shoe.

His dander began to rise, as they say in the north; but he kept grip of politeness.

"If you were moved for a moment, Lady Pippinworth," he went on, in a slightly more determined voice, — "I am far from saying that it was so; but if——"

"But as I was not——" she said.

It was no use putting things prettily to her when she snapped you up in this way.

"You know you were," he said reproachfully.

"I assure you," said she, "I don't know what you are talking about, but apparently it is something dreadful; so perhaps one of us ought to go away."

As he did not take this hint, she opened a tattered Tauchnitz which was lying at her elbow. They are always lying at your elbow in a Swiss hotel, with the first pages missing.

Tommy watched her gloomily. "This is unworthy of you," he said.

"What is?"

He was not quite sure, but as he sat there misgivings entered his mind and began to gnaw. Was it all a mistake of his? Undeniably he did think too much. After all, had she not been moved? 'Sdeath!

His restlessness made her look up. "It must be a great load off your mind," she said, with gentle laughter, "to know that your apology was unnecessary."

"It is," Tommy said; "it is." ('Sdeath!)

She resumed her book.

So this was how one was rewarded for a generous impulse! He felt very bitter. "So, so," he said inwardly; also, "Very well, ve-ry well." Then he turned upon himself. "Serve you right," he said brutally. "Better stick to your books, Thomas, for you know nothing about women."

TWO OF THEM

To think for one moment that he had moved her! That streak of marble moved! He fell to watching her again, as if she were some troublesome sentence that needed licking into shape. As she bent impertinently over her book, she was an insult to man. All Tommy's interest in her revived. She infuriated him.

"Alice," he whispered.

"Do keep quiet till I finish this chapter," she begged lazily.

It brought him at once to the boiling-point.

"Alice!" he said fervently.

She had noticed the change in his voice. "People are looking," she said, without moving a muscle.

There was some subtle flattery to him in the warning, but he could not ask for more, for just then Mrs. Jerry came in. She was cloaked for the garden, and he had to go with her, sulkily. At the door she observed that the ground was still wet.

"Are you wearing your goloshes?" said he, brightening. "You must get them, Mrs. Jerry; I insist."

She hesitated. (Her room was on the third floor.) "It is very good of you to be so thoughtful of me," she said, "but ———"

"But I have no right to try to take care of you," he interposed in a melancholy voice. "It is true. Let us go."

"I sha'n't be two minutes," said Mrs. Jerry, in a flutter, and went off hastily for her goloshes, while he looked fondly after her. At the turn of the stair she glanced back, and his eyes were still begging her to hurry. It was a gracious memory to her in the after years, for she never saw him again.

As soon as she was gone he returned to the hall, and taking from a peg a cloak with a Mother Goose hood, brought it to Lady Pippinworth, who had watched her mamma trip upstairs.

"Did I say I was going out?" she asked.

"Yes," said Tommy, and she rose to let him put the elegant thing round her. She was one of those dangerous women who look their best when you are helping them to put on their cloaks.

"Now," he instructed her, "pull the hood over your head."

"Is it so cold as that?" she said, obeying.

"I want you to wear it," he answered. What he meant was that she never looked quite so impudent as in her hood, and his vanity insisted that she should be armed to the teeth before they resumed hostilities. The red light was in his eyes as he drew her into the garden where Grizel lay.

CHAPTER XXIX

THE RED LIGHT

It was an evening without stars, but fair, sufficient wind to make her Ladyship cling haughtily to his arm as they turned corners. Many of the visitors were in the garden, some grouped round a quartet of gaily attired minstrels, but more sitting in little arbours or prowling in search of an arbour to sit in; the night was so dark that when our two passed beyond the light of the hotel windows they could scarce see the shrubs they brushed against; cigars without faces behind them sauntered past; several times they thought they had found an unoccupied arbour at last, when they heard the clink of coffee-cups.

"I believe the castle dates from the fifteenth century," Tommy would then say suddenly, though it was not of castles he had been talking.

With a certain satisfaction he noticed that she permitted him, without comment, to bring in the castle thus and to drop it the moment the emergency had passed. But he had little other encouragement.

Even when she pressed his arm it was only as an intimation that the castle was needed.

"I can't even make her angry," he said wrathfully to himself.

"You answer not a word," he said in great dejection to her.

"I am afraid to speak," she admitted. "I don't know who may hear."

"Alice," he said eagerly, "what would you say if you were not afraid to speak?"

They had stopped, and he thought she trembled a little on his arm, but he could not be sure. He thought — but he was thinking too much again; at least, Lady Pippinworth seemed to come to that conclusion, for with a galling little laugh she moved on. He saw with amazing clearness that he had thought sufficiently for one day.

On coming into the garden with her, and for some time afterwards, he had been studying her so coolly, watching symptoms rather than words, that there is nothing to compare the man to but a doctor who, while he is chatting, has his finger on your pulse. But he was not so calm now. Whether or not he had stirred the woman, he was rapidly firing himself.

When next he saw her face by the light of a window, she at the same instant turned her eyes on him; it was as if each wanted to know correctly

THE RED LIGHT

how the other had been looking in the darkness, and the effect was a challenge.

Like one retreating a step, she lowered her eyes. "I am tired," she said. "I shall go in."

"Let us stroll round once more."

"No, I am going in."

"If you are afraid——" he said, with a slight smile.

She took his arm again. "Though it is too bad of me to keep you out," she said, as they went on, "for you are shivering. Is it the night air that makes you shiver?" she asked mockingly.

But she shivered a little herself, as if with a presentiment that she might be less defiant if he were less thoughtful. For a month or more she had burned to teach him a lesson, but there was a time before that when, had she been sure he was in earnest, she would have preferred to be the pupil.

Two ladies came out of an arbour where they had been drinking coffee, and sauntered towards the hotel. It was a tiny building, half concealed in hops and reached by three steps, and Tommy and his companion took possession. He groped in the darkness for a chair for her, and invited her tenderly to sit down. She said she preferred to stand. She was by the open window, her fingers drumming on the sill. Though he could not see her face, he knew exactly how she was looking.

TOMMY AND GRIZEL

"Sit down," he said, rather masterfully.

"I prefer to stand," she repeated languidly.

He had a passionate desire to take her by the shoulders, but put his hand on hers instead, and she permitted it, like one disdainful but helpless. She said something unimportant about the stillness.

"Is it so still?" he said in a low voice. "I seem to hear a great noise. I think it must be the beating of my heart."

"I fancy that is what it is," she drawled.

"Do you hear it?"

"No."

"Did you ever hear your own heart beat, Alice?"

"No."

He had both her hands now. "Would you like to hear it?"

She pulled away her hands sharply. "Yes," she replied with defiance.

"But you pulled away your hands first," said he.

He heard her breathe heavily for a moment, but she said nothing. "Yes," he said, as if she had spoken, "it is true."

"What is true?"

"What you are saying to yourself just now — that you hate me."

She beat the floor with her foot.

"How you hate me, Alice!"

"Oh, no."

THE RED LIGHT

"Yes, indeed you do."

"I wonder why," she said, and she trembled a little.

"I know why." He had come close to her again. "Shall I tell you why?"

She said "No," hurriedly.

"I am so glad you say No." He spoke passionately, and yet there was banter in his voice, or so it seemed to her. "It is because you fear to be told; it is because you had hoped that I did not know."

"Tell me why I hate you!" she cried.

"Tell me first that you do."

"Oh, I do, I do indeed!" She said the words in a white heat of hatred.

Before she could prevent him he had raised her hand to his lips.

"Dear Alice!" he said.

"Why is it?" she demanded.

"Listen!" he said. "Listen to your heart, Alice; it is beating now. It is telling you why. Does it need an interpreter? It is saying you hate me because you think I don't love you."

"Don't you?" she asked fiercely.

"No," Tommy said.

Her hands were tearing each other, and she could not trust herself to speak. She sat down deadly pale in the chair he had offered her.

"No man ever loved you," he said, leaning over her with his hand on the back of the chair. "You are smiling at that, I know; but it is true, Lady Disdain. They may have vowed to blow their brains out, and seldom did it; they may have let you walk over them, and they may have become your fetch-and-carry, for you were always able to drive them crazy; but love does not bring men so low. They tried hard to love you, and it was not that they could not love; it was that you were unlovable. That is a terrible thing to a woman. You think you let them try to love you, that you might make them your slaves when they succeeded; but you made them your slaves because they failed. It is a power given to your cold and selfish nature in place of the capacity for being able to be loved, with which women not a hundredth part as beautiful as you are dowered, and you have a raging desire, Alice, to exercise it over me as over the others; but you can't."

Had he seen her face then, it might have warned him to take care; but he heard her words only, and they were not at all in keeping with her face.

"I see I can't," was what she cried, almost in a whisper.

"It is all true, Alice, is it not?"

"I suppose so. I don't know; I don't care." She swung round in her chair and caught his sleeve. Her hands clung to it. "Say you love me now," she said. "I cannot live without your

THE RED LIGHT

love after this. What shall I do to make you love me? Tell me, and I will do it."

He could not stop himself, for he mistrusted her still.

"I will not be your slave," he said, through his teeth. "You shall be mine."

"Yes, yes."

"You shall submit to me in everything. If I say 'come,' you shall come to wheresoever it may be; and if I say 'stay,' and leave you for ever, you shall stay."

"Very well," she said eagerly. She would have her revenge when he was her slave.

"You can continue to be the haughty Lady Disdain to others, but you shall be only obedient little Alice to me."

"Very well." She drew his arm towards her and pressed her lips upon it. "And for that you will love me a little, won't you? You will love me at last, won't you?" she entreated.

He was a masterful man up to a certain point only. Her humility now tapped him in a new place, and before he knew what he was about he began to run pity.

"To humiliate you so, Alice! I am a dastard. I am not such a dastard as you think me. I wanted to know that you would be willing to do all these things, but I would never have let you do them."

"I am willing to do them."

"No, no." It was he who had her hands now. "It was brutal, but I did it for you, Alice — for you. Don't you see I was doing it only to make a woman of you? You were always adorable, but in a coat of mail that would let love neither in nor out. I have been hammering at it to break it only and free my glorious Alice. We had to fight, and one of us had to give in. You would have flung me away if I had yielded — I had to win to save you."

"Now I am lost indeed," he was saying to himself, even as it came rushing out of him, and what appalled him most was that worse had probably still to come. He was astride two horses, and both were at the gallop. He flung out his arms as if seeking for something to check him.

As he did so she had started to her feet, listening. It seemed to her that there was someone near them.

He flung out his arms for help, and they fell upon Lady Pippinworth and went round her. He drew her to him. She could hear no breathing now but his.

"Alice, I love you, for you are love itself; it is you I have been chasing since first love rose like a bird at my feet; I never had a passing fancy for any other woman; I always knew that somewhere in the world there must be you, and sometime this

THE RED LIGHT

starless night and you for me. You were hidden behind walls of ice; no man had passed them; I broke them down and love leaped to love, and you lie here, my beautiful, love in the arms of its lover."

He was in a frenzy of passion now; he meant every word of it; and her intention was to turn upon him presently and mock him, this man with whom she had been playing. Oh, the jeering things she had to say! But she could not say them yet; she would give her fool another moment — so she thought, but she was giving it to herself; and as she delayed she was in danger of melting in his arms.

"What does the world look like to you, my darling? You are in it for the first time. You were born but a moment ago. It is dark, that you may not be blinded before you have used your eyes. These are your eyes, dear eyes that do not yet know their purpose; they are for looking at me, little Alice, and mine are for looking into yours. I cannot see you; I have never seen the face of my love — oh, my love, come into the light that I may see your face."

They did not move. Her head had fallen on his shoulder. She was to give it but a moment, and then —— But the moment had passed and still her hair pressed his cheek. Her eyes were closed. He seemed to have found the way to woo her. Neither of them spoke. Suddenly they jumped apart. Lady Pippinworth stole to the door. They held their breath and listened.

It was not so loud now, but it was distinctly heard. It had been heavy breathing, and now she was trying to check it and half succeeding — but at the cost of little cries. They both knew it was a woman, and that she was in the arbour, on the other side of the little table. She must have been there when they came in.

"Who is that?"

There was no answer to him save the checked breathing and another broken cry. She moved, and it helped him to see vaguely the outlines of a girl who seemed to be drawing back from him in terror. He thought she was crouching now in the farthest corner.

"Come away," he said. But Lady Pippinworth would not let him go. They must know who this woman was. He remembered that a match-stand usually lay on the tables of those arbours, and groped until he found one.

"Who are you?"

He struck a match. They were those French matches that play an infernal interlude before beginning to burn. While he waited he knew that she was begging him, with her hands and with cries that were too little to be words, not to turn its light on her. But he did.

Then she ceased to cower. The girlish dignity

"I WOKE UP," SHE SAID

THE RED LIGHT

that had been hers so long came running back to her. As she faced him there was even a crooked smile upon her face.

"I woke up," she said, as if the words had no meaning to herself, but might have some to him.

The match burned out before he spoke, but his face was terrible. "Grizel!" he said, appalled; and then, as if the discovery was as awful to her as to him, she uttered a cry of horror and sped out into the night. He called her name again, and sprang after her; but the hand of another woman detained him.

"Who is this girl?" Lady Pippinworth demanded fiercely; but he did not answer. He recoiled from her with a shudder that she was not likely to forget, and hurried on. All that night he searched for Grizel in vain.

CHAPTER XXX

THE LITTLE GODS DESERT HIM

AND all next day he searched like a man whose eyes would never close again. She had not passed the night in any inn or village house of St. Gian; of that he made certain by inquiries from door to door. None of the guides had seen her, though they are astir so late and so early, patiently waiting at the hotel doors to be hired, that there seems to be no night for them — darkness only, that blots them out for a time as they stand waiting. At all hours there is in St. Gian the tinkle of bells, the clatter of hoofs, the crack of a whip, dust in retreat; but no coachman brought him news. The streets were thronged with other coachmen on foot looking into every face in quest of some person who wanted to return to the lowlands, but none had looked into her face.

Within five minutes of the hotel she might have been on any of half a dozen roads. He wandered or rushed along them all for a space, and came back. One of them was short and ended in the lake. All through that long and beautiful day this

THE LITTLE GODS DESERT HIM

miserable man found himself coming back to the road that ended in the lake.

There were moments when he cried to himself that it was an apparition he had seen and heard. He had avoided his friends all day; of the English-speaking people in St. Gian one only knew why he was distraught, and she was the last he wished to speak to; but more than once he nearly sought her to say, "Partner in my shame, what did you see? what did you hear?" In the afternoon he had a letter from Elspeth telling him how she was enjoying her holiday by the sea, and mentioning that David was at that moment writing to Grizel in Thrums. But was it, then, all a dream? he cried, nearly convinced for the first time, and he went into the arbour saying determinedly that it was a dream; and in the arbour, standing primly in a corner, was Grizel's umbrella. He knew that umbrella so well! He remembered once being by while she replaced one of its ribs so deftly that he seemed to be looking on at a surgical operation. The old doctor had given it to her, and that was why she would not let it grow old before she was old herself. Tommy opened it now with trembling hands and looked at the little bits of Grizel on it: the beautiful stitching with which she had coaxed the slits to close again; the one patch, so artful that she had clapped her hands over it. And he fell on his knees and kissed these little bits of

Grizel, and called her "beloved," and cried to his gods to give him one more chance.

"I woke up." It was all that she had said. It was Grizel's excuse for inconveniencing him. She had said it apologetically and as if she did not quite know how she came to be there herself. There was no look of reproach on her face while the match burned; there had been a pitiful smile, as if she was begging him not to be very angry with her; and then when he said her name she gave that little cry as if she had recognized herself, and stole away. He lived that moment over and over again, and she never seemed to be horror-stricken until he cried "Grizel!" when her recognition of herself made her scream. It was as if she had wakened up, dazed by the terrible things that were being said, and then, by the light of that one word "Grizel," suddenly knew who had been listening to them.

Did he know anything more? He pressed his hands harshly on his temples and thought. He knew that she was soaking wet, that she had probably sought the arbour for protection from the rain, and that, if so, she had been there for at least four hours. She had wakened up. She must have fallen asleep, knocked down by fatigue. What fatigue it must have been to make Grizel lie there for hours he could guess, and he beat his brow in anguish. But why she had come he could not

THE LITTLE GODS DESERT HIM

guess. "Oh, miserable man, to seek for reasons," he cried passionately to himself, "when it is Grizel — Grizel herself — you should be seeking for!"

He walked and ran the round of the lake, and it was not on the bank that his staring eyes were fixed.

At last he came for a moment upon her track. The people of an inn six miles from St. Gian remembered being asked yesterday by an English miss, walking alone, how far she was from Bad-Platten. She was wearing something brown, and her boots were white with dust, and these people had never seen a lady look so tired before; when she stood still she had to lean against the wall. They said she had red-hot eyes.

Tommy was in an einspänner now, the merry conveyance of the country and more intoxicating than its wines, and he drove back through St. Gian to Bad-Platten, where again he heard from Grizel, though he did not find her. What he found was her telegram from London: "I am coming. GRIZEL." Why had she come? why had she sent that telegram? what had taken her to London? He was not losing time when he asked himself distractedly these questions, for he was again in his gay carriage and driving back to the wayside inn. He spent the night there, afraid to go farther lest he should pass her in the darkness; for he had decided that, if alive, she was on this road. That she had walked all those forty miles uphill seemed certain, and apparently the best he could hope was that she was walking back. She had probably no money to enable her to take the diligence. Perhaps she had no money with which to buy food. It might be that while he lay tossing in bed she was somewhere near, dying for want of a franc.

He was off by morning light, and several times that day he heard of her, twice from people who had seen her pass both going and coming, and he knew it must be she when they said she rocked her arms as she walked. Oh, he knew why she rocked her arms! Once he thought he had found her. He heard of an English lady who was lying ill in the house of a sawmiller, whose dog (we know the dogs of these regions, but not the people) had found her prostrate in the wood, some distance from the highroad. Leaving his einspänner in a village, Tommy climbed down the mountain-side to this little house, which he was long in discovering. It was by the side of a roaring river, and he arrived only an hour too late. The lady had certainly been Grizel; but she was gone. The sawyer's wife described to him how her husband had brought her in, and how she seemed so tired and bewildered that she fell asleep while they were questioning her. She held her hands over her ears to shut out the noise of the river, which seemed to

THE LITTLE GODS DESERT HIM

terrify her. So far as they could understand, she told them that she was running away from the river. She had been sleeping there for three hours, and was still asleep when the good woman went off to meet her husband; but when they returned she was gone.

He searched the wood for miles around, crying her name. The sawyer and some of his fellow-workers left the trees they were stripping of bark to help him, and for hours the wood rang with "Grizel, Grizel!" All the mountains round took up the cry; but there never came an answer. This long delay prevented his reaching the railway terminus until noon of the following day, and there he was again too late. But she had been here. He traced her to that hotel whence we saw her setting forth, and the portier had got a ticket for her for London. He had talked with her for some little time, and advised her, as she seemed so tired, to remain there for the night. But she said she must go home at once. She seemed to be passionately desirous to go home, and had looked at him suspiciously, as if fearing he might try to hold her back. He had been called away, and on returning had seen her disappearing over the bridge. He had called to her, and then she ran as if afraid he was pursuing her. But he had observed her afterwards in the train.

So she was not without money, and she was on

her way home! The relief it brought him came to the surface in great breaths, and at first every one of them was a prayer of thankfulness. Yet in time they were triumphant breaths. Translated into words, they said that he had got off cheaply for the hundredth time. His little gods had saved him again, as they had saved him in the arbour by sending Grizel to him. He could do as he liked, for they were always there to succour him; they would never desert him — never. In a moment of fierce elation he raised his hat to them, then seemed to see Grizel crying "I woke up," and in horror of himself clapped it on again. It was but a momentary aberration, and is recorded only to show that, however remorseful he felt afterwards, there was life in our Tommy still.

The train by which he was to follow her did not leave until evening, and through those long hours he was picturing, with horrible vividness and pain, the progress of Grizel up and down that terrible pass. Often his shoulders shook in agony over what he saw, and he shuddered to the teeth. He would have walked round the world on his knees to save her this long anguish! And then again it was less something he saw than something he was writing, and he altered it to make it more dramatic. "I woke up." How awful that was! but in this new scene she uttered no words. Lady Pippinworth was in his arms when they heard a

THE LITTLE GODS DESERT HIM

little cry, so faint that a violin string makes as much moan when it snaps. In a dread silence he lit a match, and as it flared the figure of a girl was seen upon the floor. She was dead; and even as he knew that she was dead he recognized her. "Grizel!" he cried. The other woman who had lured him from his true love uttered a piercing scream and ran towards the hotel. When she returned with men and lanterns there was no one in the arbour, but there were what had been a man and a girl. They lay side by side. The startled onlookers unbared their heads. A solemn voice said, "In death not divided."

He was not the only occupant of the hotel reading-room as he saw all this, and when his head fell forward and he groaned, the others looked up from their papers. A lady asked if he was unwell.

"I have had a great shock," he replied in a daze, pulling his hand across his forehead.

"Something you have seen in your paper?" inquired a clergyman who had been complaining that there was no news.

"People I knew," said Tommy, not yet certain which world he was in.

"Dead?" the lady asked sympathetically.

"I knew them well," he said, and staggered into the fresh air.

Poor dog of a Tommy! He had been a total abstainer from sentiment, as one may say, for sixty

TOMMY AND GRIZEL

hours, and this was his only glass. It was the nobler Tommy, sternly facing facts, who by and by stepped into the train. He even knew why he was going to Thrums. He was going to say certain things to her; and he said them to himself again and again in the train, and heard her answer. The words might vary, but they were always to the same effect.

"Grizel, I have come back!"

He saw himself say these words, as he opened her door in Gavinia's little house. And when he had said them he bowed his head.

At his sudden appearance she started up; then she stood pale and firm.

"Why have you come back?"

"Not to ask your forgiveness," he replied hoarsely; "not to attempt to excuse myself; not with any hope that there remains one drop of the love you once gave me so abundantly. I want only, Grizel, to put my life into your hands. I have made a sorry mess of it myself. Will you take charge of what may be left of it? You always said you were ready to help me. I have come back, Grizel, for your help. What you were once willing to do for love, will you do for pity now?"

She turned away her head, and he went nearer her. "There was always something of the mother in your love, Grizel; but for that you would never

THE LITTLE GODS DESERT HIM

have borne with me so long. A mother, they say, can never quite forget her boy — oh, Grizel, is it true? I am the prodigal come back. Grizel, beloved, I have sinned and I am unworthy, but I am still your boy, and I have come back. Am I to be sent away?"

At the word "beloved" her arms rocked impulsively. "You must not call me that," she said.

"Then I am to go," he answered with a shudder, "for I must always call you that; whether I am with you or away, you shall always be beloved to me."

"You don't love me!" she cried. "Oh, do you love me at last!" And at that he fell upon his knees.

"Grizel, my love, my love!"

"But you don't want to be married," she said.

"Beloved, I have come back to ask you on my knees to be my wife."

"That woman ——"

"She was a married woman, Grizel."

"Oh, oh, oh!"

"And now you know the worst of me. It is the whole truth at last. I don't know why you took that terrible journey, dear Grizel, but I do know that you were sent there to save me. Oh, my love, you have done so much, will you do no more?"

And so on, till there came a time when his head

was on her lap and her hand caressing it, and she was whispering to her boy to look up and see her crooked smile again.

He passed on to the wedding. All the time between seemed to be spent in his fond entreaties to hasten the longed-for day. How radiant she looked in her bridal gown! "Oh, beautiful one, are you really mine? Oh, world, pause for a moment and look at the woman who has given herself to me!"

"My wife — this is my wife!" They were in London now; he was showing her to London. How he swaggered! There was a perpetual apology on her face; it begged people to excuse him for looking so proudly at her. It was a crooked apology, and he hurried her into dark places and kissed it.

Do you see that Tommy was doing all this for Grizel and pretending to her that it was for himself? He was passionately desirous of making amends, and he was to do it in the most generous way. Perhaps he believed when he seemed to enter her room saying, "Grizel, I have come back," that she loved him still; perhaps he knew that he did not love in the way he said; perhaps he saw a remorseful man making splendid atonement: but never should she know these things; tenderly as he had begun he would go on to the end. Here at last is a Tommy worth looking at, and he looked.

Yet as he drew near Thrums, after almost ex-

THE LITTLE GODS DESERT HIM

actly two days of continuous travel, many a shiver went down his back, for he could not be sure that he should find Grizel here; he sometimes seemed to see her lying ill at some wayside station in Switzerland, in France; everything that could have happened to her he conceived, and he moved restlessly in the carriage. His mouth went dry.

"Has she come back?"

The train had stopped for the taking of tickets, and his tremulous question checked the joy of Corp at sight of him.

"She's back," Corp answered in an excited whisper; and oh, the relief to Tommy! "She came back by the afternoon train; but I had scarce a word wi' her, she was so awid to be hame. 'I am going home,' she cried, and hurried away up the brae. Ay, and there's one queer thing."

"What?"

"Her luggage wasna in the van."

Tommy could smile at that. "But what sent her," he asked eagerly, "on that journey?"

Corp told him the little he knew. "But nobody kens except me and Gavinia," he said. "We pretend she gaed to London to see her father. We said he had wrote to her, wanting her to go to him. Gavinia said it would never do to let folk ken she had gaen to see you, and even Elspeth doesna ken."

"Is Elspeth back?"

"They came back yesterday."

Did David know the truth from Grizel? was what Tommy was asking himself now as he strode up the brae. But again he was in luck, for when he had explained away his abrupt return to Elspeth, and been joyfully welcomed by her, she told him that her husband had been in one of the glens all day. "He does not know that Grizel has come back," she said. "Oh," she exclaimed, "but you don't even know that she has been away! Grizel has been in London."

"Corp told me," said Tommy.

"And did he tell you why she had gone?"

"Yes."

"She came back an hour or two ago. Maggy Ann saw her go past. Fancy her seeing her father at last! It must have been an ordeal for her. I wonder what took place."

"I think I had better go and ask her," Tommy said. He was mightily relieved for Grizel's sake. No one need ever know now what had called her away except Corp and Gavinia, and even they thought she had merely been to London. How well the little gods were managing the whole affair! As he walked to Grizel's lodgings to say what he had been saying in the train, the thought came to him for a moment that as no one need ever know where she had been there was less reason why he should do this generous thing. But

THE LITTLE GODS DESERT HIM

he put it from him with lofty disdain. Any effect it had was to make him walk more firmly to his sacrifice, as if to show all ignoble impulses that they could find no home in that swelling breast. He was pleased with himself, was Tommy.

"Grizel, I have come back." He said it to the night, and bowed his head. He said it with head accompaniment to Grizel's lighted window. He said it to himself as he reached the door. He never said it again.

For Gavinia's first words were: "It's you, Mr. Sandys! Wherever is she? For mercy's sake, dinna say you've come without her!" And when he blinked at this, she took him roughly by the arm and cried, "Wherever's Grizel?"

"She is here, Gavinia."

"She's no here."

"I saw her light."

"You saw my light."

"Gavinia, you are torturing me. She came back to-day."

"What makes you say that? You're dreaming. She hasna come back."

"Corp saw her come in by the afternoon train. He spoke to her."

Gavinia shook her head incredulously. "You're just imagining that," she said.

"He told me. Gavinia, I must see for myself." She stared after him as he went up the stairs.

"You are very cruel, Gavinia," he said, when he came down. "Tell me where she is."

"May I be struck, Mr. Sandys, if I've seen or heard o' her since she left this house eight days syne." He knew she was speaking the truth. He had to lean against the door for support. "It canna be so bad as you think," she cried in pity. "If you're sure Corp said he saw her, she maun hae gone to the doctor's house."

"She is not there. But Elspeth knew she had come back. Others have seen her besides Corp. My God, Gavinia! what can have happened?"

In little more than an hour he knew what had happened. Many besides himself, David among them towards the end, were engaged in the search. And strange stories began to fly about like nightbirds; you will not search for a missing woman without rousing them. Why had she gone off to London without telling anyone? Had Corp concocted that story about her father to blind them? Had she really been as far as London? Have you seen Sandys? — he's back. It's said Corp telegraphed to him to Switzerland that she had disappeared. It's weel kent Corp telegraphed. Sandys came at once. He is in a terrible state. Look how white he is aneath that lamp. What garred them telegraph for him? How is it he is in sic a state? Fond o' her, was he? Yea, yea,

THE LITTLE GODS DESERT HIM

even after she gave him the go-by. Then it's a weary Sabbath for him, if half they say be true. What do they say? They say she was queer when she came back. Corp doesna say that. Maybe no; but Francie Crabb does. He says he met her on the station brae and spoke to her, and she said never a word, but put up her hands like as if she feared he was to strike her. The Dundas lassies saw her frae their window, and her hands were at her ears as if she was trying to drown the sound o' something. Do you mind o' her mother? They say she was looking terrible like her mother.

It was only between the station and Gavinia's house that she had been seen, but they searched far afield. Tommy, accompanied by Corp, even sought for her in the Den. Do you remember the long, lonely path between two ragged little dykes that led from the Den to the house of the Painted Lady? It was there that Grizel had lived with her mamma. The two men went down that path, which is oppressed with trees. Elsewhere the night was not dark, but, as they had known so well when they were boys, it is always dark after evenfall in the Double Dykes. That is the legacy of the Painted Lady. Presently they saw the house — scarcely the house, but a lighted window. Tommy remembered the night when as a boy, Elspeth crouching beside him, he had peered in fearfully at that corner window on Grizel and her mamma, and the shuddersome things he had seen. He shuddered at them again.

"Who lives there now?" he asked.

"Nobody. It's toom."

"There is a light."

"Some going-about body. They often tak' bilbie in toom houses, and that door is without a lock; it's keepit close wi' slipping a stick aneath it. Do you mind how feared we used to be at that house?"

"She was never afraid of it."

"It was her hame."

He meant no more than he said, but suddenly they both stopped dead.

"It's no possible." Corp said, as if in answer to a question. "It's no possible," he repeated beseechingly.

"Wait for me here, Corp."

"I would rather come wi' you."

"Wait here!" Tommy said almost fiercely, and he went on alone to that little window. It had needed an effort to make him look in when he was here before, and it needed a bigger effort now. But he looked.

What light there was came from the fire, and whether she had gathered the logs or found them in the room no one ever knew. A vagrant stated afterwards that he had been in the house some days before and left his match-box in it.

THE LITTLE GODS DESERT HIM

By this fire Grizel was crouching. She was comparatively tidy and neat again; the dust was gone from her boots, even. How she had managed to do it no one knows, but you remember how she loved to be neat. Her hands were extended to the blaze, and she was busy talking to herself.

His hand struck the window heavily, and she looked up and saw him. She nodded, and put her finger to her lips as a sign that he must be cautious. She had often, in the long ago, seen her mother signing thus to an imaginary face at the window — the face of the man who never came.

Tommy went into the house, and she was so pleased to see him that she quite simpered. He put his arms round her, and she lay there with a little giggle of contentment. She was in a plot of heat.

"Grizel! Oh, my God!" he said, "why do you look at me in that way?"

She passed her hand across her eyes, like one trying to think.

"I woke up," she said at last. Corp appeared at the window now, and she pointed to him in terror. Thus had she seen her mother point, in the long ago, at faces that came there to frighten her.

"Grizel," Tommy entreated her, "you know who I am, don't you?"

She said his name at once, but her eyes were on

the window. "They want to take me away," she whispered.

"But you must come away, Grizel. You must come home."

"This is home," she said. "It is sweet."

After much coaxing, he prevailed upon her to leave. With his arm round her, and a terrible woe on his face, he took her to the doctor's house. She had her hands over her ears all the way. She thought the white river and the mountains and the villages and the crack of whips were marching with her still.

CHAPTER XXXI

"THE MAN WITH THE GREETIN' EYES"

For many days she lay in a fever at the doctor's house, seeming sometimes to know where she was, but more often not, and night after night a man with a drawn face sat watching her. They entreated, they forced him to let them take his place; but from his room he heard her moan or speak, or he thought he heard her, or he heard a terrible stillness, and he stole back to listen; they might send him away, but when they opened the door he was there, with his drawn face. And often they were glad to see him, for there were times when he alone could interpret her wild demands and soothe those staring eyes.

Once a scream startled the house. Someone had struck a match in the darkened chamber, and she thought she was in an arbour in St. Gian. They had to hold her in her bed by force at times; she had such a long way to walk before night, she said.

She would struggle into a sitting posture and put her hands over her ears.

TOMMY AND GRIZEL

Her great desire was not to sleep. "I should wake up," she explained fearfully.

She took a dislike to Elspeth, and called her "Alice."

These ravings, they said to each other, must have reference to what happened to her when she was away, and as they thought he knew no more of her wanderings than they, everyone marvelled at the intuition with which he read her thoughts. It was he who guessed that the striking of matches somehow terrified her; he who discovered that it was a horrid roaring river she thought she heard, and he pretended he heard it too, and persuaded her that if she lay very still it would run past. Nothing she said or did puzzled him. He read the raving of her mind, they declared admiringly, as if he held the cipher to it.

"And the cipher is his love," Mrs. McLean said, with wet eyes. In the excitement of those days Elspeth talked much to her of Tommy's love for Grizel, and how she had refused him, and it went round the town with embellishments. It was generally believed now that she really had gone to London to see her father, and that his heartless behaviour had unhinged her mind.

By David's advice, Corp and Gavinia did not contradict this story. It was as good as another, he told them, and better than the truth.

But what was the truth? they asked greedily.

"THE MAN WITH THE EYES"

"Oh, that he is a noble fellow," David replied grimly.

They knew that, but——

He would tell them no more, however, though he knew all. Tommy had made full confession to the doctor, even made himself out worse than he was, as had to be his way when he was not making himself out better.

"And I am willing to proclaim it all from the market-place," he said hoarsely, "if that is your wish."

"I daresay you would almost enjoy doing that," said David, rather cruelly.

"I daresay I should," Tommy said, with a gulp, and went back to Grizel's side. It was not, you may be sure, to screen him that David kept the secret; it was because he knew what many would say of Grizel if the nature of her journey were revealed. He dared not tell Elspeth, even; for think of the woe to her if she learned that it was her wonderful brother who had brought Grizel to this pass! The Elspeths of this world always have some man to devote himself to them. If the Tommies pass away, the Davids spring up. For my own part, I think Elspeth would have found some excuse for Tommy. He said so himself to the doctor, for he wanted her to be told.

"Or you would find the excuse for her in time," David responded.

"Very likely," Tommy said. He was humble enough now, you see. David could say one thing only which would rouse him, namely, that Grizel was not to die in this fever; and for long it seemed impossible to say that.

"Would you have her live if her mind remains affected?" he asked; and Tommy said firmly, "Yes."

"You think, I suppose, that then you would have less for which to blame yourself!"

"I suppose that is it. But don't waste time on me, Gemmell, when you have her life to save, if you can."

Well, her life was saved, and Tommy's nursing had more to do with it than David's skill. David admitted it; the town talked of it. "I aye kent he would find a wy," Corp said, though he had been among the most anxious. He and Aaron Latta were the first admitted to see her, when she was able once more to sit in a chair. They had been told to ask her no questions. She chatted pleasantly to them, and they thought she was quite her old self. They wondered to see Tommy still so sad-eyed. To Ailie she spoke freely of her illness, though not of what had occasioned it, and told her almost gleefully that David had promised to let her sew a little next week. There was one thing only that surprised Ailie. Grizel had said that as soon as she was a little stronger she was going home.

"THE MAN WITH THE EYES"

"Does she mean to her father's house?" Ailie asked.

This was what started the report that, touched no doubt by her illness, Grizel's unknown father had, after all, offered her a home. They discovered, however, what Grizel meant by home when, one afternoon, she escaped, unseen, from the doctor's house, and was found again at Double Dykes, very indignant because someone had stolen the furniture.

She seemed to know all her old friends except Elspeth, who was still Alice to her. Seldom now did she put her hands over her ears, or see horrible mountains marching with her. She no longer remembered, save once or twice when she woke up, that she had ever been out of Thrums. To those who saw her casually she was Grizel — gone thin and pale and weak intellectually, but still the Grizel of old, except for the fixed idea that Double Dykes was her home.

"You must not humour her in that delusion," David said sternly to Tommy; "when we cease to fight it we have abandoned hope."

So the weapon he always had his hand on was taken from Tommy, for he would not abandon hope. He fought gallantly. It was always he who brought her back from Double Dykes. She would not leave it with any other person, but she came away with him.

"It's because she's so fond o' him," Corp said.

But it was not. It was because she feared him, as all knew who saw them together. They were seen together a great deal when she was able to go out. Driving seemed to bring back the mountains to her eyes, so she walked, and it was always with the help of Tommy's arm. "It's a most pitiful sight," the people said. They pitied him even more than her, for though she might be talking gaily to him and leaning heavily on him, they could see that she mistrusted him. At the end of a sweet smile she would give him an ugly, furtive look.

"She's like a cat you've forced into your lap," they said, "and it lies quiet there, ready to jump the moment you let go your grip."

They wondered would he never weary. He never wearied. Day after day he was saying the same things to her, and the end was always as the beginning. They came back to her entreaty that she should be allowed to go home as certainly as they came back to the doctor's house.

"It is a long time, you know, Grizel, since you lived at Double Dykes — not since you were a child."

"Not since I was a child," she said as if she quite understood.

"Then you went to live with your dear, kind doctor, you remember. What was his name?"

"THE MAN WITH THE EYES"

"Dr. McQueen. I love him."

"But he died, and he left you his house to live in. It is your home, Grizel. He would be so grieved if he thought you did not make it your home."

"It is my home," she said proudly; but when they returned to it she was loath to go in. "I want to go home!" she begged.

One day he took her to her rooms in Corp's house, thinking her old furniture would please her; and that was the day when she rocked her arms joyously again. But it was not the furniture that made her so happy; it was Corp's baby.

"Oh, oh!" she cried in rapture, and held out her arms; and he ran into them, for there was still one person in Thrums who had no fear of Grizel.

"It will be a damned shame," Corp said huskily, "if that woman never has no bairns o' her ain."

They watched her crooning over the child, playing with him for a long time. You could not have believed that she required to be watched. She told him with hugs that she had come back to him at last; it was her first admission that she knew she had been away and a wild hope came to Tommy that along the road he could not take her she might be drawn by this little child.

She discovered a rent in the child's pinafore and must mend it at once. She ran upstairs, as a matter of course, to her work-box, and brought down a needle and thread. It was quite as if she was at home at last.

"But you don't live here now, Grizel," Tommy said, when she drew back at his proposal that they should go away; "you live at the doctor's house."

"Do I, Gavinia?" she said beseechingly.

"Is it here you want to bide?" Corp asked, and she nodded her head several times.

"It would be so much more convenient," she said, looking at the child.

"Would you take her back, Gavinia," Tommy asked humbly, "if she continues to want it?"

Gavinia did not answer.

"Woman!" cried Corp.

"I'm mortal wae for her," Gavinia said slowly, "but she needs to be waited on hand and foot."

"I would come and do the waiting on her hand and foot, Gavinia," Tommy said.

And so it came about that a week afterwards Grizel was reinstalled in her old rooms. Every morning when Tommy came to see her she asked him, icily how Alice was. She seemed to think that Alice, as she called her, was his wife. He always replied, "You mean Elspeth," and she assented, but only, it was obvious, because she feared to contradict him. To Corp and Gavinia she would still say passionately, "I want to go home!" and probably add fearfully, "Don't tell him."

Yet though this was not home to her, she seemed

"THE MAN WITH THE EYES"

to be less unhappy here than in the doctor's house, and she found a great deal to do. All her old skill in needlework came back to her, and she sewed for the child such exquisite garments that she clapped her hands over them.

One day Tommy came with a white face and asked Gavinia if she knew whether a small brown parcel had been among the things brought by Grizel from the doctor's house.

"It was in the box sent after me from Switzerland," he told her, "and contained papers."

Gavinia had seen no such package.

"She may have hidden it," he said, and they searched, but fruitlessly. He questioned Grizel gently, but questions alarmed her, and he desisted.

"It does not matter, Gavinia," he said, with a ghastly smile; but on the following Sunday, when Corp called at the doctor's house, the thought "Have they found it?" leaped in front of all thought of Grizel. This was only for the time it takes to ask a question with the eyes, however, for Corp was looking very miserable.

"I'm sweer to say it," he announced to Tommy and David, "but it has to be said. We canna keep her."

Evidently something had happened, and Tommy rose to go to Grizel without even asking what it was. "Wait," David said, wrinkling his eyebrows, "till Corp tells us what he means by that. I knew it might come, Corp. Go on."

"If it hadna been for the bairn," said Corp, "we would hae tholed wi' her, however queer she was; but wi' the bairn I tell you it's no mous. You'll hae to tak' her awa'."

"Whatever she has been to others," Tommy said, "she is always an angel with the child. His own mother could not be fonder of him."

"That's it," Corp replied emphatically. "She's no the mother o' him, but there's whiles when she thinks she is. We kept it frae you as long as we could."

"As long as she is so good to him ——" David began.

"But at thae times she's not," said Corp. "She begins to shiver most terrible, as if she saw fearsome things in her mind, and syne we see her looking at him like as if she wanted to do him a mischief. She says he's her brat; she thinks he's hers, and that he hasna been well come by."

Tommy's hands rose in agony, and then he covered his face with them.

"Go on, Corp," David said hoarsely; "we must have it all."

"Sometimes," Corp went on painfully, "she canna help being fond o' him, though she thinks she shouldna hae had him. I've heard her saying, 'My brat!' and syne birsing him closer to her, as

"THE MAN WITH THE EYES"

though her shame just made him mair to her. Women are so queer about thae things. I've seen her sitting by his cradle, moaning to hersel', 'I did so want to be good! It would be sweet to be good!' and never stopping rocking the cradle, and a' the time the tears were rolling down."

Tommy cried, "If there is any more to tell, Corp, be quick."

"There's what I come here to tell you. It was no langer syne than jimply an hour. We thocht the bairn was playing at the gavle-end, and that Grizel was up the stair. But they werena, and I gaed straight to Double Dykes. She wasna there, but the bairn was, lying greetin' on the floor. We found her in the Den, sitting by the burn-side, and she said we should never see him again, for she had drowned him. We're sweer, but you'll need to tak' her awa'."

"We shall take her away," David said, and when he and Tommy were left together he asked: "Do you see what it means?"

"It means that the horrors of her early days have come back to her, and that she is confusing her mother with herself."

David's hands were clenched. "That is not what I am thinking of. We have to take her away; they have done far more than we had any right to ask of them. Sandys, where are we to take her to?"

"Do even you grow tired of her?" Tommy cried.

David said between his teeth: "We hope there will soon be a child in this house, also. God forgive me, but I cannot bring her back here."

"She cannot be in a house where there is a child!" said Tommy, with a bitter laugh. "Gemmell, it is Grizel we are speaking of! Do you remember what she was?"

"I remember."

"Well, where are we to send her?"

David turned his pained eyes full on Tommy.

"No!" Tommy cried vehemently.

"Sandys," said David, firmly, "that is what it has come to. They will take good care of her." He sat down with a groan. "Have done with heroics," he said savagely, when Tommy would have spoken. "I have been prepared for this; there is no other way."

"I have been prepared for it, too," Tommy said, controlling himself; "but there is another way: I can marry her, and I am going to do it."

"I don't know that I can countenance that," David said, after a pause. "It seems an infernal shame."

"Don't trouble about me," replied Tommy, hoarsely; "I shall do it willingly."

And then it was the doctor's turn to laugh. "You!" he said with a terrible scorn as he looked

"THE MAN WITH THE EYES"

Tommy up and down. "I was not thinking of you. All my thoughts were of her. I was thinking how cruel to her if some day she came to her right mind and found herself tied for life to the man who had brought her to this pass."

Tommy winced and walked up and down.

"Desire to marry her gone?" asked David, savagely.

"No," Tommy said. He sat down. "You have the key to me, Gemmell," he went on quietly. "I gave it to you. You know I am a man of sentiment only; but you are without a scrap of it yourself, and so you will never quite know what it is. It has its good points. We are a kindly people. I was perhaps pluming myself on having made an heroic proposal, and though you have made me see it just now as you see it, as you see it I shall probably soon be putting on the same grand airs again. Lately I discovered that the children who see me with Grizel call me 'the Man with the Greetin' Eyes.' If I have greetin' eyes it was real grief that gave them to me; but when I heard what I was called it made me self-conscious, and I have tried to look still more lugubrious ever since. It seems monstrous to you, but that, I believe, is the kind of thing I shall always be doing. But it does not mean that I feel no real remorse. They were greetin' eyes before I knew it, and though I may pose grotesquely as a fine fellow for finding Grizel a home where there is no child and can never be a child, I shall not cease, night nor day, from tending her. It will be a grim business, Gemmell, as you know, and if I am Sentimental Tommy through it all, why grudge me my comic little strut?"

David said, "You can't take her to London."

"I shall take her to wherever she wants to go."

"There is one place only she wants to go to, and that is Double Dykes."

"I am prepared to take her there."

"And your work?"

"It must take second place now. I must write; it is the only thing I can do. If I could make a living at anything else I would give up writing altogether."

"Why?"

"She would be pleased if she could understand, and writing is the joy of my life — two reasons."

But the doctor smiled.

"You are right," said Tommy. "I see I was really thinking what a fine picture of self-sacrifice I should make sitting in Double Dykes at a loom!"

They talked of ways and means, and he had to admit that he had little money. But the new book would bring in a good deal, David supposed.

"The manuscript is lost," Tommy replied, crushing down his agitation.

"Lost! When? Where?"

"THE MAN WITH THE EYES"

"I don't know. It was in the bag I left behind at St. Gian, and I supposed it was still in it when the bag was forwarded to me here. I did not look for more than a month. I took credit to myself for neglecting my manuscript, and when at last I looked it was not there. I telegraphed and wrote to the innkeeper at St. Gian, and he replied that my things had been packed at his request in presence of my friends there, the two ladies you know of. I wrote to them, and they replied that this was so, and said they thought they remembered seeing in the bottom of the bag some such parcel in brown paper as I described. But it is not there now, and I have given up all hope of ever seeing it again. No, I have no other copy. Every page was written half a dozen times, but I kept the final copy only."

"It is scarcely a thing anyone would steal."

"No; I suppose they took it out of the bag at St. Gian, and forgot to pack it again. It was probably flung away as of no account."

"Could it have been taken out on the way here?"

"The key was tied to the handle so that the custom officials might be able to open the bag. Perhaps they are fonder of English manuscripts than one would expect, or more careless of them."

"You can think of no other way in which it might have disappeared?"

"None," Tommy said; and then the doctor faced him squarely.

"Are you trying to screen Grizel?" he asked. "Is it true, what people are saying?"

"What are they saying?"

"That she destroyed it. I heard that yesterday, and told them your manuscript was in my house, as I thought it was. Was it she?"

"No, no. Gavinia must have started that story. I did look for the package among Grizel's things."

"What made you think of that?"

"I had seen her looking into my bag one day. And she used to say I loved my manuscripts too much ever to love her. But I am sure she did not do it."

"Be truthful, Sandys. You know how she always loved the truth."

"Well, then, I suppose it was she."

After a pause the doctor said: "It must be about as bad as having a limb lopped off."

"If only I had been offered that alternative!" Tommy replied.

"And yet," David mused, better pleased with him, "you have not cried out."

"Have I not! I have rolled about in agony, and invoked the gods, and cursed and whimpered; only I take care that no one shall see me."

"And that no one should know poor Grizel had done this thing. I admire you for that, Sandys."

"THE MAN WITH THE EYES"

"But it has leaked out, you see," Tommy said; "and they will all be admiring me for it at the wedding, and no doubt I shall be cocking my greetin' eyes at them to note how much they are admiring."

But when the wedding-day came he was not doing that. While he and Grizel stood up before Mr. Dishart, in the doctor's parlour, he was thinking of her only. His eyes never left her, not even when he had to reply "I do." His hand pressed hers all the time. He kept giving her reassuring little nods and smiles, and it was thus that he helped Grizel through.

Had Mr. Dishart understood what was in her mind he would not have married them. To her it was no real marriage; she thought they were tricking the minister, so that she should be able to go home. They had rehearsed the ceremony together many times, and oh, she was eager to make no mistake.

"If they were to find out!" she would say apprehensively, and then perhaps giggle at the slyness of it all. Tommy had to make merry with her, as if it was one of his boyish plays. If he was overcome with the pain of it, she sobbed at once and wrung her hands.

She was married in gray silk. She had made the dress herself, as beautifully as all her things were made. Tommy remembered how once, long ago, she had told him, as a most exquisite secret, that she had decided on gray silk.

Corp and Gavinia and Ailie and Aaron Latta were the only persons asked to the wedding, and when it was over, they said they never saw anyone stand up by a woman's side looking so anxious to be her man; and I am sure that in this they did Tommy no more than justice.

It was a sad day to Elspeth. Could she be expected to smile while her noble brother did this great deed of sacrifice? But she bore up bravely, partly for his sake, partly for the sake of one unborn.

The ring was no plain hoop of gold; it was garnets all the way round. She had seen it on Elspeth's finger, and craved it so greedily that it became her wedding-ring. And from the moment she had it she ceased to dislike Elspeth, and pitied her very much, as if she thought happiness went with the ring. "Poor Alice!" she said when she saw Elspeth crying at the wedding, and having started to go away with Tommy, she came back to say again, "Poor, poor Alice!"

Corp flung an old shoe after them.

CHAPTER XXXII

TOMMY'S BEST WORK

AND thus was begun a year and a half of as great devotion as remorseful man ever gave to woman. When she was asleep and he could not write, his mind would sometimes roam after abandoned things; it sought them in the night as a savage beast steals forth for water to slake the thirst of many days. But if she stirred in her sleep they were all dispelled; there was not a moment in that eighteen months when he was twenty yards from Grizel's side.

He would not let himself lose hope. All the others lost it. "The only thing you can do is to humour her," even David was reduced in time to saying; but Tommy replied cheerily, "Not a bit of it." Every morning he had to begin at the same place as on the previous morning, and he was always as ready to do it, and as patient, as if this were the first time.

"I think she is a little more herself to-day," he would say determinedly, till David wondered to hear him.

"She makes no progress, Sandys."

"I can at least keep her from slipping back."

And he did, and there is no doubt that this was what saved Grizel in the end. How he strove to prevent her slipping back! The morning was the time when she was least troubled, and had he humoured her then they would often have been easy hours for him. But it was the time when he tried most doggedly, with a gentleness she could not ruffle, to teach her the alphabet of who she was. She coaxed him to let her off those mental struggles; she turned petulant and sulky; she was willing to be good and sweet if he would permit her to sew or to sing to herself instead, or to sit staring at the fire: but he would not yield; he promised those things as the reward, and in the end she stood before him like a child at lessons.

"What is your name?" The catechism always began thus.

"Grizel," she said obediently, if it was a day when she wanted to please him.

"And my name?"

"Tommy." Once, to his great delight, she said, "Sentimental Tommy." He quite bragged about this to David.

"Where is your home?"

"Here." She was never in doubt about this, and it was always a pleasure to her to say it.

"Did you live here long ago?"

TOMMY'S BEST WORK

She nodded.

"And then did you live for a long time somewhere else?"

"Yes."

"Where was it?"

"Here."

"No, it was with the old doctor. You were his little housekeeper; don't you remember? Try to remember, Grizel; he loved you so much."

She tried to think. Her face was very painful when she tried to think. "It hurts," she said.

"Do you remember him, Grizel?"

"Please let me sing," she begged, "such a sweet song!"

"Do you remember the old doctor who called you his little housekeeper? He used to sit in that chair."

The old chair was among Grizel's many possessions that had been brought to Double Dykes, and her face lit up with recollection. She ran to the chair and kissed it.

"What was his name, Grizel?"

"I should love to know his name," she said wistfully.

He told her the name many times, and she repeated it docilely.

Or perhaps she remembered her dear doctor quite well to-day, and thought Tommy was some one in need of his services.

"He has gone into the country," she said, as she had so often said to anxious people at the door; "but he won't be long, and I shall give him your message the moment he comes in."

But Tommy would not pass that. He explained to her again and again that the doctor was dead, and perhaps she would remember, or perhaps, without remembering, she said she was glad he was dead.

"Why are you glad, Grizel?"

She whispered, as if frightened she might be overheard: "I don't want him to see me like this." It was one of the pathetic things about her that she seemed at times to have some vague understanding of her condition, and then she would sob. Her tears were anguish to him, but it was at those times that she clung to him as if she knew he was trying to do something for her, and that encouraged him to go on. He went over, step by step, the time when she lived alone in the doctor's house, the time of his own coming back, her love for him and his treatment of her, the story of the garnet ring, her coming to Switzerland, her terrible walk, her return; he would miss out nothing, for he was fighting for her. Day after day, month by month, it went on, and to-morrow, perhaps, she would insist that the old doctor and this man who asked her so many questions were one. And Tommy argued with her until he had driven that notion out, to make way for another, and then he fought it, and so on and on all round the circle of her delusions, day by day and month by month.

She knew that he sometimes wrote while she was asleep, for she might start up from her bed or from the sofa, and there he was, laying down his pen to come to her. Her eyes were never open for any large fraction of a minute without his knowing, and immediately he went to her, nodding and smiling lest she had wakened with some fear upon her. Perhaps she refused to sleep again unless he promised to put away those horrid papers for the night, and however intoxicating a point he had reached in his labours, he always promised, and kept his word. He was most scrupulous in keeping any promise he made her, and one great result was that she trusted him implicitly. Whatever others promised, she doubted them.

There were times when she seemed to be casting about in her mind for something to do that would please him, and then she would bring pieces of paper to him, and pen and ink, and tell him to write. She thought this very clever of her, and expected to be praised for it.

But she might also bring him writing materials at times when she hated him very much. Then there would be sly smiles, even pretended affection, on her face, unless she thought he was not looking, when she cast him ugly glances. Her intention was to trick him into forgetting her so that she might talk to herself or slip out of the room to the Den, just as her mother had done in the days when it was Grizel who had to be tricked. He would not let her talk to herself until he had tried endless ways of exorcising that demon by interesting her in some sort of work, by going out with her, by talking of one thing and another till at last a subject was lit upon that made her forget to brood.

But sometimes it seemed best to let her go to the Den, she was in such a quiver of desire to go. She hurried to it, so that he had to stride to keep up with her; and he said little until they got there, for she was too excited to listen. She was very like her mother again; but it was not the man who never came that she went in search of — it was a lost child. I have not the heart to tell of the pitiful scenes in the Den while Grizel searched for her child. They always ended in those two walking silently home, and for a day or two Grizel would be ill, and Tommy tended her, so that she was soon able to hasten to the Den again, holding out her arms as she ran.

"She makes no progress," David said.

"I can keep her from slipping back," Tommy still replied. The doctor marvelled, but even he did not know the half of all her husband did for Grizel. None could know half who was not there by night. Here, at least, was one day ending placidly, they might say when she was in a tractable mood,— so tractable that she seemed to be one of themselves,— and Tommy assented brightly, though he knew, and he alone, that you could never be sure the long day had ended till the next began.

Often the happiest beginning had the most painful ending. The greatest pleasure he could give her was to take her to see Elspeth's baby girl, or that sturdy rogue, young Shiach, who could now count with ease up to seven, but swayed at eight, and toppled over on his way to ten; or their mothers brought them to her, and Grizel understood quite well who her visitors were, sometimes even called Elspeth by her right name, and did the honours of her house irreproachably, and presided at the tea-table, and was rapture personified when she held the baby Jean (called after Tommy's mother), and sat gaily on the floor, ready to catch little Corp when he would not stop at seven. But Tommy, whom nothing escaped, knew with what depression she might pay for her joy when they had gone. Despite all his efforts, she might sit talking to herself, at first of pleasant things and then of things less pleasant. Or she stared at her reflection in the long mirror and said: "Isn't she sweet!" or "She is not really sweet, and she did so want to be good!" Or instead of that she would suddenly go upon her knees and say, with clasped hands, the childish prayer, "Save me from masterful men," which Jean Myles had told Tommy to teach Elspeth. No one could have looked less masterful at those times than Tommy, but Grizel did not seem to think so. And probably they had that night once more to search the Den.

"The children do her harm; she must not see them again," he decided.

"They give her pleasure at the time," David said. "It lightens your task now and then."

"It is the future I am thinking of, Gemmell. If she cannot progress, she shall not fall back. As for me, never mind me."

"Elspeth is in a sad state about you, though! And you can get through so little work."

"Enough for all our wants." (He was writing magazine papers only.)

"The public will forget you."

"They have forgotten me."

David was openly sorry for him now. "If only your manuscript had been saved!"

"Yes; I never thought the little gods would treat me so scurvily as that."

"Who?"

"Did I never tell you of my little gods? I so often emerged triumphant from my troubles, and so undeservedly, that I thought I was especially looked after by certain tricky spirits in return for the entertainment I gave them. My little gods, I called

TOMMY'S BEST WORK

them, and we had quite a bowing acquaintance. But you see at the critical moment they flew away laughing."

He always knew that the lost manuscript was his great work. "My seventh wave," he called it; "and though all the conditions were favourable," he said, "I know that I could run to nothing more than little waves at present. As for rewriting that book, I can't; I have tried."

Yet he was not asking for commiseration. "Tell Elspeth not to worry about me. If I have no big ideas just now, I have some very passable little ones, and one in particular that ——" He drew a great breath. "If only Grizel were better," that breath said, "I think Tommy Sandys could find a way of making the public remember him again."

So David interpreted it, and though he had been about to say, "How changed you are!" he did not say it.

And Tommy, who had been keeping an eye on her all this time, returned to Grizel. As she had been through that long year, so she was during the first half of the next; and day by day and night by night he tended her, and still the same scenes were enacted in infinite variety, and still he would not give in. Everything seemed to change with the seasons, except Grizel, and Tommy's devotion to her.

Yet you know that she recovered, ever afterwards to be herself again; and though it seemed to come in the end as suddenly as the sight may be restored by the removal of a bandage, I suppose it had been going on all the time, and that her reason was given back to her on the day she had strength to make use of it. Tommy was the instrument of her recovery. He had fought against her slipping backward so that she could not do it; it was as if he had built a wall behind her, and in time her mind accepted that wall as impregnable and took a forward movement. And with every step she took he pushed the wall after her, so that still if she moved it must be forward. Thus Grizel progressed imperceptibly as along a dark corridor towards the door that shut out the light, and on a day in early spring the door fell.

Many of them had cried for a shock as her only chance. But it came most quietly. She had lain down on the sofa that afternoon to rest, and when she woke she was Grizel again. At first she was not surprised to find herself in that room, nor to see that man nodding and smiling reassuringly; they had come out of the long dream with her, to make the awakening less abrupt.

He did not know what had happened. When he knew, a terror that this could not last seized him. He was concealing it while he answered her puzzled questions. All the time he was telling

TOMMY'S BEST WORK

her how they came to be there, he was watching in agony for the change.

She remembered everything up to her return to Thrums; then she walked into a mist.

"The truth," she begged of him, when he would have led her off by pretending that she had been ill only. Surely it was the real Grizel who begged for the truth. She took his hand and held it when he told her of their marriage. She cried softly, because she feared that she might again become as she had been; but he said that was impossible, and smiled confidently, and all the time he was watching in agony for the change.

"Do you forgive me, Grizel? I have always had a dread that when you recovered you would cease to care for me." He knew that this would please her if she was the real Grizel, and he was so anxious to make her happy for evermore.

She put his hand to her lips and smiled at him through her tears. Hers was a love that could never change. Suddenly she sat up. "Whose baby was it?" she asked.

"I don't know what you mean, Grizel," he said uneasily.

"I remember vaguely," she told him, "a baby in white whom I seemed to chase, but I could never catch her. Was it a dream only?"

"You are thinking of Elspeth's little girl, perhaps. She was often brought to see you."

"Has Elspeth a baby?" She rose to go exultantly to Elspeth.

"But too small a baby, Grizel, to run from you, even if she wanted to."

"What is she like?"

"She is always laughing."

"The sweet!" Grizel rocked her arms in rapture and smiled her crooked smile at the thought of a child who was always laughing. "But I don't remember her," she said. "It was a sad little baby I seemed to see."

CHAPTER XXXIII

THE LITTLE GODS RETURN WITH A LADY

GRIZEL's clear, searching eyes, that were always asking for the truth, came back to her, and I seem to see them on me now, watching lest I shirk the end.

Thus I can make no pretence (to please you) that it was a new Tommy at last. We have seen how he gave his life to her during those eighteen months, but he could not make himself anew. They say we can do it, so I suppose he did not try hard enough; but God knows how hard he tried.

He went on trying. In those first days she sometimes asked him, "Did you do it out of love, or was it pity only?" And he always said it was love. He said it adoringly. He told her all that love meant to him, and it meant everything that he thought Grizel would like it to mean. When she ceased to ask this question he thought it was because he had convinced her.

They had a honeymoon by the sea. He insisted upon it with boyish eagerness, and as they walked on the links or sat in their room he would exclaim ecstatically: "How happy I am! I wonder if there were ever two people quite so happy as you and I!"

And if he waited for an answer, as he usually did, she might smile lightly and say: "Few people have gone through so much."

"Is there any woman in the world, Grizel, with whom you would change places?"

"No, none," she said at once; and when he was sure of it, but never until he was sure, he would give his mind a little holiday; and then, perhaps, those candid eyes would rest searchingly upon him, but always with a brave smile ready should he chance to look up.

And it was just the same when they returned to Double Dykes, which they added to and turned into a comfortable home — Tommy trying to become a lover by taking thought, and Grizel not letting on that it could not be done in that way. She thought it was very sweet of him to try so hard — sweeter of him than if he really had loved her, though not, of course, quite so sweet to her. He was a boy only. She knew that, despite all he had gone through, he was still a boy. And boys cannot love. Oh, who would be so cruel as to ask a boy to love?

That Grizel's honeymoon should never end was his grand ambition, and he took elaborate precautions against becoming a matter-of-fact husband. Every morning he ordered himself to gaze at her with rapture, as if he had wakened to the glorious thought that she was his wife.

"I can't help it, Grizel; it comes to me every morning with the same shock of delight, and I begin the day with a song of joy. You make the world as fresh and interesting to me as if I had just broken like a chicken through the egg-shell." He rose at the earliest hours. "So that I can have the longer day with you," he said gaily.

If when sitting at his work he forgot her for an hour or two he reproached himself for it afterwards, and next day he was more careful. "Grizel," he would cry, suddenly flinging down his pen, "you are my wife! Do you hear me, madam? You hear, and yet you can sit there calmly darning socks! Excuse me," he would say to his work, "while I do a dance."

He rose impulsively and brought his papers nearer her. With a table between them she was several feet away from him, which was more, he said, than he could endure.

"Sit down for a moment, Grizel, and let me look at you. I want to write something most splendiferous to-day, and I am sure to find it in your face. I have ceased to be an original writer; all the purple patches are cribbed from you."

He made a point of taking her head in his

hands and looking long at her with thoughts too deep for utterance; then he would fall on his knees and kiss the hem of her dress, and so back to his book again.

And in time it was all sweet to Grizel. She could not be deceived, but she loved to see him playing so kind a part, and after some sadness to which she could not help giving way, she put all vain longings aside. She folded them up and put them away like the beautiful linen, so that she might see more clearly what was left to her and how best to turn it to account.

He did not love her. "Not as I love him," she said to herself,—"not as married people ought to love; but in the other way he loves me dearly." By the "other way" she meant that he loved her as he loved Elspeth, and loved them both just as he had loved them when all three played in the Den.

"He would love me if he could." She was certain of that. She decided that love does not come to all people, as is the common notion; that there are some who cannot fall in love, and that he was one of them. He was complete in himself, she decided.

"Is it a pity for him that he married me? It would be a pity if he could love some other woman, but I am sure he could never do that. If he could love anyone it would be me, we both want it so much. He does not need a wife, but he needs someone to take care of him — all men need that; and I can do it much better than any other person. Had he not married me he never would have married; but he may fall ill, and then how useful I shall be to him! He will grow old, and perhaps it won't be quite so lonely to him when I am there. It would have been a pity for him to marry me if I had been a foolish woman who asked for more love than he can give; but I shall never do that, so I think it is not a pity.

"Is it a pity for me? Oh, no, no, no!

"Is he sorry he did it? At times, is he just a weeny bit sorry?" She watched him, and decided rightly that he was not sorry the weeniest bit. It was a sweet consolation to her. "Is he really happy? Yes, of course he is happy when he is writing; but is he quite contented at other times? I do honestly think he is. And if he is happy now, how much happier I shall be able to make him when I have put away all my selfish thoughts and think only of him."

"The most exquisite thing in human life is to be married to one who loves you as you love him." There could be no doubt of that. But she saw also that the next best thing was the kind of love this boy gave to her, and she would always be grateful for the second best. In her prayers she thanked God for giving it to her, and promised Him to try to merit it; and all day and every day she kept her promise. There could not have been a brighter or more energetic wife than Grizel. The amount of work she found to do in that small house which his devotion had made so dear to her that she could not leave it! Her gaiety! Her masterful airs when he wanted something that was not good for him! The artfulness with which she sought to help him in various matters without his knowing! Her satisfaction when he caught her at it, as clever Tommy was constantly doing! "What a success it has turned out!" David would say delightedly to himself; and Grizel was almost as jubilant because it was so far from being a failure. It was only sometimes in the night that she lay very still, with little wells of water on her eyes, and through them saw one — the dream of woman — whom she feared could never be hers. That boy Tommy never knew why she did not want to have a child. He thought that for the present she was afraid; but the reason was that she believed it would be wicked when he did not love her as she loved him. She could not be sure — she had to think it all out for herself. With little wells of sadness on her eyes, she prayed in the still night to God to tell her; but she could never hear His answer.

She no longer sought to teach Tommy how he should write. That quaint desire was abandoned from the day when she learned that she had

THE LITTLE GODS RETURN

destroyed his greatest work. She had not destroyed it, as we shall see; but she presumed she had, as Tommy thought so. He had tried to conceal this from her to save her pain, but she had found it out, and it seemed to Grizel, grown distrustful of herself, that the man who could bear such a loss as he had borne it was best left to write as he chose.

"It was not that I did not love your books," she said, "but that I loved you more, and I thought they did you harm."

"In the days when I had wings," he answered, and she smiled. "Any feathers left, do you think, Grizel?" he asked jocularly, and turned his shoulders to her for examination.

"A great many, sir," she said, "and I am glad. I used to want to pull them all out, but now I like to know that they are still there, for it means that you remain among the facts not because you can't fly, but because you won't."

"I still have my little fights with myself," he blurted out boyishly, though it was a thing he had never meant to tell her, and Grizel pressed his hand for telling her what she already knew so well.

The new book, of course, was "The Wandering Child." I wonder whether any of you read it now? Your fathers and mothers thought a great deal of that slim volume, but it would make little stir in an age in which all the authors are trying who can say "damn" loudest. It is but a reverie about a child who is lost, and his parents' search for him in terror of what may have befallen. But they find him in a wood singing joyfully to himself because he is free; and he fears to be caged again, so runs farther from them into the wood, and is running still, singing to himself because he is free, free, free. That is really all, but T. Sandys knew how to tell it. The moment he conceived the idea (we have seen him speaking of it to the doctor), he knew that it was the idea for him. He forgot at once that he did not really care for children. He said reverently to himself, " I can pull it off," and, as was always the way with him, the better he pulled it off the more he seemed to love them.

"It is myself who is writing at last, Grizel," he said, as he read it to her.

She thought (and you can guess whether she was right) that it was the book he loved rather than the children. She thought (and you can guess again) that it was not his ideas about children that had got into the book, but hers. But she did not say so; she said it was the sweetest of his books to her.

I have heard of another reading he gave. This was after the publication of the book. He had gone into Corp's house one Sunday, and Gavinia was there reading the work to her lord and master, while little Corp disported on the floor. She read

THE LITTLE GODS RETURN

as if all the words meant the same thing, and it was more than Tommy could endure. He read for her, and his eyes grew moist as he read, for it was the most exquisite of his chapters about the lost child. You would have said that no one loved children quite so much as T. Sandys. But little Corp would not keep quiet, and suddenly Tommy jumped up and boxed his ears. He then proceeded with the reading, while Gavinia glowered and Corp senior scratched his head.

On the way home he saw what had happened, and laughed at the humour of it, then grew depressed, then laughed recklessly. "Is it Sentimental Tommy still?" he said to himself, with a groan. Seldom a week passed without his being reminded in some such sudden way that it was Sentimental Tommy still. "But she shall never know!" he vowed, and he continued to be half a hero.

His name was once more in many mouths. "Come back and be made of more than ever!" cried that society which he had once enlivened. "Come and hear the pretty things we are saying about you. Come and make the prettier replies that are already on the tip of your tongue; for oh, Tommy, you know they are! Bring her with you if you must; but don't you think that the nice, quiet country with the thingumbobs all in bloom would suit her best? It is essential that you should run up to see your publisher, is it not? The men have dinners for you if you want them, but we know you don't. Your yearning eyes are on the ladies, Tommy; we are making up theatre-parties of the old entrancing kind; you should see our new gowns; please come back and help us to put on our cloaks, Tommy; there is a dance on Monday—come and sit it out with us. Do you remember the garden-party where you said—— Well, the laurel walk is still there; the beauties of two years ago are still here, and there are new beauties, and their noses are slightly tilted, but no man can move them; ha, do you pull yourself together at that? We were always the reward for your labours, Tommy; your books are move one in the game of making love to us; don't be afraid that we shall forget it is a game; we know it is, and that is why we suit you. Come and play in London as you used to play in the Den. It is all you need of women; come and have your fill, and we shall send you back refreshed. We are not asking you to be disloyal to her, only to leave her happy and contented and take a holiday."

He heard their seductive voices. They danced around him in numbers, for they knew that the more there were of them the better he would be pleased; they whispered in his ear and then ran away looking over their shoulders. But he would not budge.

HE HEARD THEIR SEDUCTIVE VOICES. THEY DANCED AROUND HIM
IN NUMBERS

THE LITTLE GODS RETURN

There was one more dangerous than the rest. Her he saw before the others came and after they had gone. She was a tall, incredibly slight woman, with eyelashes that needed help, and a most disdainful mouth and nose, and she seemed to look scornfully at Tommy and then stand waiting. He was in two minds about what she was waiting for, and often he had a fierce desire to go to London to find out. But he never went. He played the lover to Grizel as before — not to intoxicate himself, but always to make life sunnier to her; if she stayed longer with Elspeth than the promised time, he became anxious and went in search of her. "I have not been away an hour!" she said, laughing at him, holding little Jean up to laugh at him. "But I cannot do without you for an hour," he answered ardently. He still laid down his pen to gaze with rapture at her and cry, "My wife!"

She wanted him to go to London for a change, and without her, and his heart leaped into his mouth to prevent his saying No; yet he said it, though in the Tommy way.

"Without you!" he exclaimed. "Oh, Grizel, do you think I could find happiness apart from you for a day? And could you let me go?" And he looked with agonized reproach at her, and sat down, clutching his head.

"It would be very hard to me," she said softly; "but if the change did you good ——"

"A change from you! Oh, Grizel, Grizel!"

"Or I could go with you?"

"When you don't want to go!" he cried huskily. "You think I could ask it of you!"

He quite broke down, and she had to comfort him. She was smiling divinely at him all the time, as if sympathy had brought her to love even the Tommy way of saying things. "I thought it would be sweet to you to see how great my faith in you is now," she said.

This was the true reason why generous Grizel had proposed to him to go. She knew he was more afraid than she of Sentimental Tommy, and she thought her faith would be a helping hand to him, as it was.

He had no regard for Lady Pippinworth. Of all the women he had dallied with, she was the one he liked the least, for he never liked where he could not esteem. Perhaps she had some good in her, but the good in her had never appealed to him, and he knew it, and refused to harbour her in his thoughts now; he cast her out determinedly when she seemed to enter them unbidden. But still he was vain. She came disdainfully and stood waiting. We have seen him wondering what she waited for; but though he could not be sure, and so was drawn to her, he took it as acknowledgment of his prowess and so was helped to run away.

To walk away would be the more exact term,

THE LITTLE GODS RETURN

for his favourite method of exorcising this lady was to rise from his chair and take a long walk with Grizel. Occasionally if she was occupied (and a number of duties our busy Grizel found to hand!) he walked alone, and he would not let himself brood. Someone had once walked from Thrums to the top of the Law and back in three hours, and Tommy made several gamesome attempts to beat the record, setting out to escape that willowy woman, soon walking her down and returning in a glow of animal spirits. It was on one of these occasions, when there was nothing in his head but ambition to do the fifth mile within the eleven minutes, that he suddenly met her Ladyship face to face.

We have now come to the last fortnight of Tommy's life.

CHAPTER XXXIV

A WAY IS FOUND FOR TOMMY

THE moment for which he had tried to prepare himself was come, and Tommy gulped down his courage, which had risen suddenly to his mouth, leaving his chest in a panic. Outwardly he seemed unmoved, but within he was beating to arms. "This is the test of us!" all that was good in him cried as it answered his summons.

They began by shaking hands, as is always the custom in the ring. Then, without any preliminary sparring, Lady Pippinworth immediately knocked him down; that is to say, she remarked, with a little laugh: "How very stout you are getting!"

I swear by all the gods that it was untrue. He had not got very stout, though undeniably he had got stouter. "How well you are looking!" would have been a very ladylike way of saying it, but his girth was best not referred to at all. Those who liked him had learned this long ago, and Grizel always shifted the buttons without comment.

A WAY IS FOUND FOR TOMMY

Her malicious Ladyship had found his one weak spot at once. He had a reply ready for every other opening in the English tongue, but now he could writhe only.

Who would have expected to meet her here? he said at last feebly. She explained, and he had guessed it already, that she was again staying with the Rintouls; the castle, indeed, was not half a mile from where they stood.

"But I think I really came to see you," she informed him, with engaging frankness.

It was very good of her, he intimated stiffly; but the stiffness was chiefly because she was still looking in an irritating way at his waist.

Suddenly she looked up. To Tommy it was as if she had raised the siege. "Why aren't you nice to me?" she asked prettily.

"I want to be," he replied.

She showed him a way. "When I saw you steaming towards the castle so swiftly," she said, dropping badinage, "the hope entered my head that you had heard of my arrival."

She had come a step nearer, and it was like an invitation to return to the arbour. "This is the test of us!" all that was good in Tommy cried once more to him.

"No, I had not heard," he replied, bravely if baldly. "I was taking a smart walk only."

"Why so smart as that?"

He hesitated, and her eyes left his face and travelled downward.

"Were you trying to walk it off?" she asked sympathetically.

He was stung, and replied in words that were regretted as soon as spoken: "I was trying to walk you off."

A smile of satisfaction crossed her impudent face.

"I succeeded," he added sharply.

"How cruel of you to say so, when you had made me so very happy! Do you often take smart walks, Mr. Sandys?"

"Often."

"And always with me?"

"I leave you behind."

"With Mrs. Sandys?"

Had she seemed to be in the least affected by their meeting it would have been easy to him to be a contrite man at once; any sign of shame on her part would have filled him with desire to take all the blame upon himself. Had she cut him dead, he would have begun to respect her. But she smiled disdainfully only, and stood waiting. She was still, as ever, a cold passion, inviting his warm ones to leap at it. He shuddered a little, but controlled himself and did not answer her.

"I suppose she is the lady of the arbour?" Lady Pippinworth inquired, with mild interest.

A WAY IS FOUND FOR TOMMY

"She is the lady of my heart," Tommy replied valiantly.

"Alas!" said Lady Pippinworth, putting her hand over her own.

But he felt himself more secure now, and could even smile at the woman for thinking she was able to provoke him.

"Look upon me," she requested, "as a deputation sent north to discover why you have gone into hiding."

"I suppose a country life does seem exile to you," he replied calmly, and suddenly his bosom rose with pride in what was coming. Tommy always heard his finest things coming a moment before they came. "If I have retired," he went on windily, "from the insincerities and glitter of life in town," — but it was not his face she was looking at, it was his waist, — "the reason is obvious," he rapped out.

She nodded assent without raising her eyes.

Yet he still controlled himself. His waist, like some fair tortured lady of romance, was calling to his knighthood for defence, but with the truer courage he affected not to hear. "I am in hiding, as you call it," he said doggedly, "because my life here is such a round of happiness as I never hoped to find on earth, and I owe it all to my wife. If you don't believe me, ask Lord or Lady

Rintoul, or any other person in this countryside who knows her."

But her Ladyship had already asked, and been annoyed by the answer.

She assured Tommy that she believed he was happy. "I have often heard," she said musingly, "that the stout people are the happiest."

"I am not so stout," he barked.

"Now I call that brave of you," said she, admiringly. "That is so much the wisest way to take it. And I am sure you are right not to return to town after what you were; it would be a pity. Somehow it"—and again her eyes were on the wrong place—"it does not seem to go with the books. And yet," she said philosophically, "I daresay you feel just the same?"

"I feel very much the same," he replied warningly.

"That is the tragedy of it," said she.

She told him that the new book had brought the Tommy Society to life again. "And it could not hold its meetings with the old enthusiasm, could it," she asked sweetly, "if you came back? Oh, I think you act most judiciously. Fancy how melancholy if they had to announce that the society had been wound up, owing to the stoutness of the Master."

Tommy's mouth opened twice before any words could come out. "Take care!" he cried.

"Of what?" said she, curling her lip.

A WAY IS FOUND FOR TOMMY

He begged her pardon. "You don't like me, Lady Pippinworth," he said, watching himself, "and I don't wonder at it; and you have discovered a way of hurting me of which you make rather unmerciful use. Well, I don't wonder at that, either. If I am — stoutish, I have at least the satisfaction of knowing that it gives you entertainment, and I owe you that amend and more." He was really in a fury, and burning to go on — "For I did have the whip-hand of you once, madam," etc., etc.; but by a fine effort he held his rage a prisoner, and the admiration of himself that this engendered lifted him into the sublime.

"For I so far forgot myself," said Tommy, in a glow, "as to try to make you love me. You were beautiful and cold; no man had ever stirred you; my one excuse is that to be loved by such as you was no small ambition; my fitting punishment is that I failed." He knew he had not failed, and so could be magnanimous. "I failed utterly," he said, with grandeur. "You were laughing at me all the time; if proof of it were needed, you have given it now by coming here to mock me. I thought I was stronger than you, but I was ludicrously mistaken, and you taught me a lesson I richly deserved; you did me good, and I thank you for it. Believe me, Lady Pippinworth, when I say that I admit my discomfiture, and remain your very humble and humbled servant."

Now was not that good of Tommy? You would think it still better were I to tell you what part of his person she was looking at while he said it.

He held out his hand generously (there was no noble act he could not have performed for her just now), but, whatever her Ladyship wanted, it was not to say good-bye. "Do you mean that you never cared for me?" she asked, with the tremor that always made Tommy kind.

"Never cared for you!" he exclaimed fervently. "What were you not to me in those golden days!" It was really a magnanimous cry, meant to help her self-respect, nothing more; but it alarmed the good in him, and he said sternly: "But of course that is all over now. It is only a sweet memory," he added, to make these two remarks mix.

The sentiment of this was so agreeable to him that he was half thinking of raising her hand chivalrously to his lips when Lady Pippinworth said:

"But if it is all over now, why have you still to walk me off?"

"Have you never had to walk me off?" said Tommy, forgetting himself, and, to his surprise, she answered, "Yes."

"But this meeting has cured me," she said, with dangerous graciousness.

"Dear Lady Pippinworth," replied Tommy, ar-

A WAY IS FOUND FOR TOMMY

dently, thinking that his generosity had touched her, "if anything I have said ——"

"It is not so much what you have said," she answered, and again she looked at the wrong part of him.

He gave way in the waist, and then drew himself up. "If so little a thing as that helps you ——" he began haughtily.

"Little!" she cried reproachfully.

He tried to go away. He turned. "There was a time," he thundered.

"It is over," said she.

"When you were at my feet," said Tommy.

"It is over," she said.

"It could come again!"

She laughed a contemptuous No.

"Yes!" Tommy cried.

"Too stout," said she, with a drawl.

He went closer to her. She stood waiting disdainfully, and his arms fell.

"Too stout," she repeated.

"Let us put it in that way, since it pleases you," said Tommy, heavily. "I am too stout." He could not help adding, "And be thankful, Lady Pippinworth, let us both be thankful, that there is some reason to prevent my trying."

She bowed mockingly as he raised his hat. "I wish you well," he said, "and these are my last words to you"; and he retired, not without distinction. He retired, shall we say, as conscious of his waist as if it were some poor soldier he was supporting from a stricken field. He said many things to himself on the way home, and he was many Tommies, but all with the same waist. It intruded on his noblest reflections, and kept ringing up the worst in him like some devil at the telephone.

No one could have been more thankful that on the whole he had kept his passions in check. It made a strong man of him. It turned him into a joyous boy, and he tingled with hurrahs. Then suddenly he would hear that jeering bell clanging, "Too stout, too stout." "Take care!" he roared. Oh, the vanity of Tommy!

He did not tell Grizel that he had met her Ladyship. All she knew was that he came back to her more tender and kind, if that were possible, than he had gone away. His eyes followed her about the room until she made merry over it, and still they dwelt upon her. "How much more beautiful you are than any other woman I ever saw, Grizel!" he said. And it was not only true, but he knew it was true. What was Lady Pippinworth beside this glorious woman? what was her damnable coldness compared to the love of Grizel? Was he unforgivable, or was it some flaw in the making of him for which he was not responsible? With clenched hands he asked himself these questions. This love that all his books were about—

A WAY IS FOUND FOR TOMMY

what was it? Was it a compromise between affection and passion countenanced by God for the continuance of the race, made beautiful by Him where the ingredients are in right proportion, a flower springing from a soil that is not all divine? Oh, so exquisite a flower! he cried, for he knew his Grizel. But he could not love her. He gave her all his affection, but his passion, like an outlaw, had ever to hunt alone.

Was it that? And if it was, did there remain in him enough of humanity to give him the right to ask a little sympathy of those who can love? So Tommy in his despairing moods, and the question ought to find some place in his epitaph, which, by the way, it is almost time to write.

On the day following his meeting with Lady Pippinworth came a note from Lady Rintoul inviting Grizel and him to lunch. They had been to Rintoul once or twice before, but this time Tommy said decisively, "We sha'n't go." He guessed who had prompted the invitation, though her name was not mentioned in it.

"Why not?" Grizel asked. She was always afraid that she kept Tommy too much to herself.

"Because I object to being disturbed during the honeymoon," he replied lightly. Their honeymoon, you know, was never to end. "They would separate us for hours, Grizel. Think of it! But, pooh! the thing is not to be thought of.

Tell her Ladyship courteously that she must be mad."

But though he could speak thus to Grizel, there came to him tempestuous desires to be by the side of the woman who could mock him and then stand waiting.

Had she shown any fear of him all would have been well with Tommy; he could have kept away from her complacently. But she had flung down the glove, and laughed to see him edge away from it. He knew exactly what was in her mind. He was too clever not to know that her one desire was to make him a miserable man; to remember how he had subdued and left her would be gall to Lady Pippinworth until she achieved the same triumph over him. How confident she was that he could never prove the stronger of the two again! What were all her mockings but a beckoning to him to come on? "Take care!" said Tommy between his teeth.

And then again horror of himself would come to his rescue. The man he had been a moment ago was vile to him, and all his thoughts were now heroic. You may remember that he had once taken Grizel to a seaside place; they went there again. It was Tommy's proposal, but he did not go to flee from temptation; however his worse nature had been stirred and his vanity pricked, he was too determinedly Grizel's to fear that in any

A WAY IS FOUND FOR TOMMY

fierce hour he might rush into danger. He wanted Grizel to come away from the place where she always found so much to do for him, so that there might be the more for him to do for her. And that week was as the time they had spent there before. All that devotion which had to be planned could do for woman he did. Grizel saw him planning it and never admitted that she saw. In the after years it was sweet to her to recall that week and the hundred laboriously lover-like things Tommy had done in it. She knew by this time that Tommy had never tried to make her love him, and that it was only when her love for him revealed itself in the Den that desire to save her pride made him pretend to be in love with her. This knowledge would have been a great pain to her once, but now it had more of pleasure in it, for it showed that even in those days he had struggled a little for her.

We must hasten to the end. Those of you who took in the newspapers a quarter of a century ago know what it was, but none of you know why he climbed the wall.

They returned to Thrums in a week. They had meant to stay longer, but suddenly Tommy wanted to go back. Yes, it was Lady Pippinworth who recalled him, but don't think too meanly of Tommy. It was not that he yielded to one of those fierce desires to lift the gauntlet;

he had got rid of them in fair fight when her letter reached him, forwarded from Thrums. "Did you really think your manuscript was lost?" it said. That was what took Tommy back. Grizel did not know the reason; he gave her another. He thought very little about her that day. He thought still less about Lady Pippinworth. How could he think of anything but it? She had it, evidently she had it; she must have stolen it from his bag. He could not even spare time to denounce her. It was alive — his manuscript was alive, and every moment brought him nearer to it. He was a miser, and soon his hands would be deep among the gold. He was a mother whose son, mourned for dead, is knocking at the door. He was a swain, and his beloved's arms were outstretched to him. Who said that Tommy could not love?

The ecstasies that came over him and would not let him sit still made Grizel wonder. "Is it a book?" she asked; and he said it was a book — such a book, Grizel! When he started for the castle next morning, she thought he wanted to be alone to think of the book. "Of it and you," he said; and having started, he came back to kiss her again; he never forgot to have an impulse to do that. But all the way to the Spittal it was of his book he thought, it was his book he was kissing. His heart sang within him, and the songs were sonnets

A WAY IS FOUND FOR TOMMY

to his beloved. To be worthy of his beautiful manuscript — he prayed for that as lovers do; that his love should be his, his alone, was as wondrous to him as to any of them.

But we are not noticing what proved to be the chief thing. Though there was some sun, the air was shrewd, and he was wearing the old doctor's coat. Should you have taken it with you, Tommy? It loved Grizel, for it was a bit of him; and what, think you, would the old doctor have cared for your manuscript had he known that you were gone out to meet that woman? It was cruel, no, not cruel, but thoughtless, to wear the old doctor's coat.

He found no one at the Spittal. The men were out shooting, and the ladies had followed to lunch with them on the moors. He came upon them, a gay party, in the hollow of a hill where was a spring suddenly converted into a wine-cellar; and soon the men, if not the ladies, were surprised to find that Tommy could be the gayest of them all. He was in hilarious spirits, and had a gallantly forgiving glance for the only one of them who knew why his spirits were hilarious. But he would not consent to remain to dinner. "The wretch is so hopelessly in love with his wife," Lady Rintoul said, flinging a twig of heather at him. It was one of the many trivial things said on that occasion and long remembered; the only person who afterwards professed her inability to remember what Tommy said to her that day, and she to him, was Lady Pippinworth. "And yet you walked back to the castle with him," they reminded her.

"If I had known that anything was to happen," she replied indolently, "I should have taken more note of what was said. But as it was, I think we talked of our chance of finding white heather. We were looking for it, and that is why we fell behind you."

That was not why Tommy and her Ladyship fell behind the others, and it was not of white heather that they talked. "You know why I am here, Alice," he said, as soon as there was no one but her to hear him.

She was in as great tension at that moment as he, but more anxious not to show it. "Why do you call me that?" she replied, with a little laugh.

"Because I want you to know at once," he said, and it was the truth, "that I have no vindictive feelings. You have kept my manuscript from me all this time, but, severe though the punishment has been, I deserved it, yes, every day of it."

Lady Pippinworth smiled.

"You took it from my bag, did you not?" said Tommy.

"Yes."

"Where is it, Alice? Have you got it here?"

"No."

A WAY IS FOUND FOR TOMMY

"But you know where it is?"

"Oh, yes," she said graciously, and then it seemed that nothing could ever disturb him again. She enjoyed his boyish glee; she walked by his side listening airily to it.

"Had there been a fire in the room that day I should have burned the thing," she said without emotion.

"It would have been no more than my deserts," Tommy replied cheerfully.

"I did burn it three months afterwards," said she, calmly.

He stopped, but she walked on. He sprang after her. "You don't mean that, Alice!"

"I do mean it."

With a gesture fierce and yet imploring, he compelled her to stop. "Before God, is this true?" he cried.

"Yes," she said, "it is true"; and, indeed, it was the truth about his manuscript at last.

"But you had a copy of it made first. Say you had!"

"I had not."

She seemed to have no fear of him, though his face was rather terrible. "I meant to destroy it from the first," she said coldly, "but I was afraid to. I took it back with me to London. One day I read in a paper that your wife was supposed to have burned it while she was insane. She was insane, was she not? Ah, well, that is not my affair; but I burned it for her that afternoon."

They were moving on again. He stopped her once more.

"Why have you told me this?" he cried. "Was it not enough for you that I should think she did it?"

"No," Lady Pippinworth answered, "that was not enough for me. I always wanted you to know that I had done it."

"And you wrote that letter, you filled me with joy, so that you should gloat over my disappointment?"

"Horrid of me, was it not!" said she.

"Why did you not tell me when we met the other day?"

"I bided my time, as the tragedians say."

"You would not have told me," Tommy said, staring into her face, "if you had thought I cared for you. Had you thought I cared for you a little jot——"

"I should have waited," she confessed, "until you cared for me a great deal, and then I should have told you. That, I admit, was my intention."

She had returned his gaze smilingly, and as she strolled on she gave him another smile over her shoulder; it became a protesting pout almost when she saw that he was not accompanying her.

A WAY IS FOUND FOR TOMMY

Tommy stood still for some minutes, his hands, his teeth, every bit of him that could close, tight clenched. When he made up on her, the devil was in him. She had been gathering a nosegay of wild flowers. "Pretty, are they not?" she said to him. He took hold of her harshly by both wrists. She let him do it, and stood waiting disdainfully; but she was less unprepared for a blow than for what came.

"How you love me, Alice!" he said in a voice shaking with passion.

"How I have proved it!" she replied promptly.

"Love or hate," he went on in a torrent of words, "they are the same thing with you. I don't care what you call it; it has made you come back to me. You tried hard to stay away. How you fought, Alice! but you had to come. I knew you would come. All this time you have been longing for me to go to you. You have stamped your pretty feet because I did not go. You have cried, 'He shall come!' You have vowed you would not go one step of the way to meet me. I saw you, I heard you, and I wanted you as much as you wanted me; but I was always the stronger, and I could resist. It is I who have not gone a step towards you, and it is my proud little Alice who has come all the way. Proud little Alice!—but she is to be my obedient little Alice now."

His passion hurled him along, and it had its

effect on her. She might curl her mouth as she chose, but her bosom rose and fell.

"Obedient?" she cried, with a laugh.

"Obedient!" said Tommy, quivering with his intensity. "Obedient, not because I want it, for I prefer you as you are, but because you are longing for it, my lady — because it is what you came here for. You have been a virago only because you feared you were not to get it. Why have you grown so quiet, Alice? Where are the words you want to torment me with? Say them! I love to hear them from your lips. I love the demon in you — the demon that burned my book. I love you the more for that. It was your love that made you do it. Why don't you scratch and struggle for the last time? I am half sorry that little Alice is to scratch and struggle no more."

"Go on," said little Alice; "you talk beautifully." But though her tongue could mock him, all the rest of her was enchained.

"Whether I shall love you when you are tamed," he went on with vehemence, "I don't know. You must take the risk of that. But I love you now. We were made for one another, you and I, and I love you, Alice — I love you and you love me. You love me, my peerless Alice, don't you? Say you love me. Your melting eyes are saying it. How you tremble, sweet Alice! Is that your way of saying it? I want to hear you say it. You

A WAY IS FOUND FOR TOMMY

have been longing to say it for two years. Come, love, say it now!"

It was not within this woman's power to resist him. She tried to draw away from him, but could not. She was breathing quickly. The mocking light quivered on her face only because it had been there so long. If it went out she would be helpless. He put his hands on her shoulders, and she was helpless. It brought her mouth nearer his. She was offering him her mouth.

"No," said Tommy, masterfully. "I won't kiss you until you say it."

If there had not been a look of triumph in his eyes, she would have said it. As it was, she broke from him, panting. She laughed next minute, and with that laugh his power fell among the heather.

"Really," said Lady Pippinworth, "you are much too stout for this kind of thing." She looked him up and down with a comic sigh. "You talk as well as ever," she said condolingly, "but heigh-ho, you don't look the same. I have done the best I could for you for the sake of old times, but I forgot to shut my eyes. Shall we go on?"

And they went on silently, one of them very white. "I believe you are blaming me," her Ladyship said, making a face, just before they overtook the others, "when you know it was your own fault for "— she suddenly rippled — " for not waiting until it was too dark for me to see you!"

They strolled with some others of the party to the flower-garden, which was some distance from the house, and surrounded by a high wall studded with iron spikes and glass. Lady Rintoul cut him some flowers for Grizel, but he left them on a garden-seat — accidentally, everyone thought afterwards in the drawing-room when they were missed; but he had laid them down, because how could those degraded hands of his carry flowers again to Grizel? There was great remorse in him, but there was a shrieking vanity also, and though the one told him to be gone, the other kept him lagging on. They had torn him a dozen times from each other's arms before he was man enough to go.

It was gloaming when he set off, waving his hat to those who had come to the door with him. Lady Pippinworth was not among them; he had not seen her to bid her good-bye, nor wanted to, for the better side of him had prevailed — so he thought. It was a man shame-stricken and determined to kill the devil in him that went down that long avenue — so he thought.

A tall, thin woman was standing some twenty yards off, among some holly-trees. She kissed her hand mockingly to him, and beckoned and laughed when he stood irresolute. He thought he heard her cry, " Too stout!" He took some fierce steps

A WAY IS FOUND FOR TOMMY

towards her. She ran on, looking over her shoulder, and he forgot all else and followed her. She darted into the flower-garden, pulling the gate to after her. It was a gate that locked when it closed, and the key was gone. Lady Pippinworth clapped her hands because he could not reach her. When she saw that he was climbing the wall she ran farther into the garden.

He climbed the wall, but, as he was descending, one of the iron spikes on the top of it pierced his coat, which was buttoned to the throat, and he hung there by the neck. He struggled as he choked, but he could not help himself. He was unable to cry out. The collar of the old doctor's coat held him fast.

They say that in such a moment a man reviews all his past life. I don't know whether Tommy did that; but his last reflection before he passed into unconsciousness was "Serves me right!" Perhaps it was only a little bit of sentiment for the end.

Lady Disdain came back to the gate, by and by, to see why he had not followed her. She screamed and then hid in the recesses of the garden. He had been dead for some time when they found him. They left the gate creaking in the evening wind. After a long time a terrified woman stole out by it.

CHAPTER XXXV

THE PERFECT LOVER

Tommy has not lasted. More than once since it became known that I was writing his life I have been asked whether there ever really was such a person, and I am afraid to inquire for his books at the library lest they are no longer there. A recent project to bring out a new edition, with introductions by some other Tommy, received so little support that it fell to the ground. It must be admitted that, so far as the great public is concerned, Thomas Sandys is done for.

They have even forgotten the manner of his death, though probably no young writer with an eye on posterity ever had a better send-off. We really thought at the time that Tommy had found a way.

The surmise at Rintoul, immediately accepted by the world as a fact, was that he had been climbing the wall to obtain for Grizel the flowers accidentally left in the garden, and it at once tipped the tragedy with gold. The newspapers, which were in the middle of the dull season, thanked

THE PERFECT LOVER

their gods for Tommy, and enthusiastically set to work on him. Great minds wrote criticisms of what they called his life-work. The many persons who had been the first to discover him said so again. His friends were in demand for the most trivial reminiscences. Unhappy Pym cleared £11 10s.

Shall we quote? It is nearly always done at this stage of the biography, so now for the testimonials to prove that our hero was without a flaw. A few specimens will suffice if we select some that are very like many of the others. It keeps Grizel waiting, but Tommy, as you have seen, was always the great one; she existed only that he might show how great he was. "Busy among us of late," says one, "has been the grim visitor who knocks with equal confidence at the doors of the gifted and the ungifted, the pauper and the prince, and twice in one short month has he taken from us men of an eminence greater perhaps than that of Mr. Sandys; but of them it could be said their work was finished, while his sun sinks tragically when it is yet day. Not by what his riper years might have achieved can this pure spirit now be judged, and to us, we confess, there is something infinitely pathetic in that thought. We would fain shut our eyes, and open them again at twenty years hence, with Mr. Sandys in the fulness of his powers. It is not to be. What he might have become is hidden from us; what he was we know. He was little more than a stripling when he 'burst upon the town' to be its marvel — and to die; a 'marvellous boy' indeed; yet how unlike in character and in the nobility of his short life, as in the mournful yet lovely circumstances of his death, to that other Might-Have-Been who 'perished in his pride.' Our young men of letters have travelled far since the days of Chatterton. Time was when a riotous life was considered part of their calling — when they shunned the domestic ties and actually held that the consummate artist is able to love nothing but the creations of his fancy. It is such men as Thomas Sandys who have exploded that pernicious fallacy. . . .

"Whether his name will march down the ages is not for us, his contemporaries, to determine. He had the most modest opinion of his own work, and was humbled rather than elated when he heard it praised. No one ever loved praise less; to be pointed at as a man of distinction was abhorrent to his shrinking nature; he seldom, indeed, knew that he was being pointed at, for his eyes were ever on the ground. He set no great store by the remarkable popularity of his works. 'Nothing,' he has been heard to say to one of those gushing ladies who were his aversion, 'nothing will so certainly perish as the talk of the town.' It may be so, but if so, the greater the pity that he has gone

THE PERFECT LOVER

from among us before he had time to put the coping-stone upon his work. There is a beautiful passage in one of his own books in which he sees the spirits of gallant youth who died too young for immortality haunting the portals of the Elysian Fields, and the great shades come to the portal and talk with them. We venture to say that he is at least one of these."

What was the individuality behind the work? They discussed it in leading articles and in the correspondence columns, and the man proved to be greater than his books. His distaste for admiration is again and again insisted on and illustrated by many characteristic anecdotes. He owed much to his parents, though he had the misfortune to lose them when he was but a child. "Little is known of his father, but we understand that he was a retired military officer in easy circumstances. The mother was a canny Scotchwoman of lowly birth, conspicuous for her devoutness even in a land where it is everyone's birthright, and on their marriage, which was a singularly happy one, they settled in London, going little into society, the world forgetting, by the world forgot, and devoting themselves to each other and to their two children. Of these Thomas was the elder, and as the twig was early bent so did the tree incline. From his earliest years he was noted for the modesty which those who remember his boyhood in Scotland (whither the children went to an uncle on the death of their parents) still speak of with glistening eyes. In another column will be found some interesting recollections of Mr. Sandys by his old schoolmaster, Mr. David Cathro, M.A., who testifies with natural pride to the industry and amiability of his famous pupil. 'To know him,' says Mr. Cathro, 'was to love him.'"

According to another authority, T. Sandys got his early modesty from his father, who was of a very sweet disposition, and some instances of this modesty are given. They are all things that Elspeth did, but Tommy is now represented as the person who had done them. "On the other hand, his strong will, singleness of purpose, and enviable capacity for knowing what he wanted to be at were a heritage from his practical and sagacious mother." "I think he was a little proud of his strength of will," writes the R.A. who painted his portrait (now in America), "for I remember his anxiety that it should be suggested in the picture." But another acquaintance (a lady) replies: "He was not proud of his strong will, but he liked to hear it spoken of, and he once told me the reason. This strength of will was not, as is generally supposed, inherited by him; he was born without it, and acquired it by a tremendous effort. I believe I am the only person to whom he confided this, for he shrank from talk about himself, looking upon

THE PERFECT LOVER

it as a form of that sentimentality which his soul abhorred."

He seems often to have warned ladies against this essentially womanish tendency to the sentimental. "It is an odious onion, dear lady," he would say, holding both her hands in his. If men in his presence talked sentimentally to ladies he was so irritated that he soon found a pretext for leaving the room. "Yet let it not be thought," says One Who Knew Him Well, "that because he was so sternly practical himself he was intolerant of the outpourings of the sentimental. The man, in short, reflected the views on this subject which are so admirably phrased in his books, works that seem to me to found one of their chief claims to distinction on this, that at last we have a writer who can treat intimately of human love without leaving one smear of the onion upon his pages."

On the whole, it may be noticed, comparatively few ladies contribute to the obituary reflections, "for the simple reason," says a simple man, "that he went but little into female society. He who could write so eloquently about women never seemed to know what to say to them. Ordinary tittle-tattle from them disappointed him. I should say that to him there was so much of the divine in women that he was depressed when they hid their wings." This view is supported by Clubman, who notes that Tommy would never join in the somewhat free talk about the other sex in which many men indulge. "I remember," he says, "a man's dinner at which two of those present, both persons of eminence, started a theory that every man who is blessed or cursed with the artistic instinct has at some period of his life wanted to marry a barmaid. Mr. Sandys gave them such a look that they at once apologized. Trivial, perhaps, but significant. On another occasion I was in a club smoking-room when the talk was of a similar kind. Mr. Sandys was not present. A member said, with a laugh, 'I wonder for how long men can be together without talking gamesomely of women?' Before any answer could be given Mr. Sandys strolled in, and immediately the atmosphere cleared, as if someone had opened the windows. When he had gone the member addressed turned to him who had propounded the problem and said, 'There is your answer — as long as Sandys is in the room.'"

"A fitting epitaph, this, for Thomas Sandys," says the paper that quotes it, "if we could not find a better. Mr. Sandys was from first to last a man of character, but why when others falter was he always so sure-footed? It is in the answer to this question that we find the key to the books, and to the man who was greater than the books. He was the Perfect Lover. As he died seeking flowers for her who had the high honour to be his wife, so he had always lived. He gave his affection to her, as

THE PERFECT LOVER

our correspondent Miss (or Mrs.) Ailie McLean shows, in his earliest boyhood, and from this, his one romance, he never swerved. To the moment of his death all his beautiful thoughts were flowers plucked for her; his books were bunches of them gathered to place at her feet. No harm now in reading between the lines of his books and culling what is the common knowledge of his friends in the north, that he had to serve a long apprenticeship before he won her. For long his attachment was unreciprocated, though she was ever his loyal friend, and the volume called 'Unrequited Love' belongs to the period when he thought his life must be lived alone. The circumstances of their marriage are at once too beautiful and too painful to be dwelt on here. Enough to say that, should the particulars ever be given to the world, with the simple story of his life, a finer memorial will have been raised to him than anything in stone, such as we see a committee is already being formed to erect. We venture to propose as a title for his biography, 'The Story of the Perfect Lover.'"

Yes, that memorial committee was formed; but so soon do people forget the hero of yesterday's paper that only the secretary attended the first meeting, and he never called another. But here, five and twenty years later, is the biography, with the title changed. You may wonder that I had the heart to write it. I do it, I have sometimes pretended to myself, that we may all laugh at the stripling of a rogue, but that was never my reason. Have I been too cunning, or have you seen through me all the time? Have you discovered that I was really pitying the boy who was so fond of boyhood that he could not with years become a man, telling nothing about him that was not true, but doing it with unnecessary scorn in the hope that I might goad you into crying: "Come, come, you are too hard on him!"

Perhaps the manner in which he went to his death deprives him of these words. Had the castle gone on fire that day while he was at tea, and he perished in the flames in a splendid attempt to save the life of his enemy (a very probable thing), then you might have felt a little liking for him. Yet he would have been precisely the same person. I don't blame you, but you are a Tommy.

Grizel knew how he died. She found Lady Pippinworth's letter to him, and understood who the woman was; but it was only in hopes of obtaining the lost manuscript that she went to see her. Then Lady Pippinworth told her all. Are you sorry that Grizel knew? I am not sorry — I am glad. As a child, as a girl, and as a wife, the truth had been all she wanted, and she wanted it just the same when she was a widow. We have a right to know the truth; no right to ask anything else from God, but the right to ask that.

THE PERFECT LOVER

And to her latest breath she went on loving Tommy just the same. She thought everything out calmly for herself; she saw that there is no great man on this earth except the man who conquers self, and that in some the accursed thing which is in all of us may be so strong that to battle with it and be beaten is not altogether to fail. It is foolish to demand complete success of those we want to love. We should rejoice when they rise for a moment above themselves, and sympathize with them when they fall. In their heyday young lovers think each other perfect; but a nobler love comes when they see the failings also, and this higher love is so much more worth attaining to that they need not cry out though it has to be beaten into them with rods. So they learn humanity's limitations, and that the accursed thing to me is not the accursed thing to you; but all have it, and from this comes pity for those who have sinned, and the desire to help each other springs, for knowledge is sympathy, and sympathy is love, and to learn it the Son of God became a man.

And Grizel also thought anxiously about herself, and how from the time when she was the smallest girl she had longed to be a good woman and feared that perhaps she never should. And as she looked back at the road she had travelled, there came along it the little girl to judge her. She came trembling, but determined to know the truth, and she looked at Grizel until she saw into her soul, and then she smiled, well pleased.

Grizel lived on at Double Dykes, helping David in the old way. She was too strong and fine a nature to succumb. Even her brightness came back to her. They sometimes wondered at the serenity of her face. Some still thought her a little stand-offish, for, though the pride had gone from her walk, a distinction of manner grew upon her and made her seem a finer lady than before. There was no other noticeable change, except that with the years she lost her beautiful contours and became a little angular — the old maid's figure, I believe it is sometimes called.

No one would have dared to smile at Grizel become an old maid before some of the young men of Thrums. They were people who would have suffered much for her, and all because she had the courage to talk to them of some things before their marriage-day came round. And for their young wives who had tidings to whisper to her about the unborn she had the pretty idea that they should live with beautiful thoughts, so that these might become part of the child.

When Gavinia told this to Corp, he gulped and said, "I wonder God could hae haen the heart."

"Life's a queerer thing," Gavinia replied, sadly

THE PERFECT LOVER

enough, " than we used to think it when we was bairns in the Den."

He spoke of it to Grizel. She let Corp speak of anything to her because he was so loyal to Tommy.

"You've given away a' your bonny things, Grizel," he said, "one by one, and this notion is the bonniest o' them a'. I'm thinking that when it cam' into your head you meant it for yoursel'."

Grizel smiled at him.

"I mind," Corp went on, "how when you was little you couldna see a bairn without rocking your arms in a waeful kind o' a way, and we could never thole the meaning o't. It just comes over me this minute as it meant that when you was a woman you would like terrible to hae bairns o' your ain, and you doubted you never should."

She raised her hand to stop him. "You see, I was not meant to have them, Corp," she said. "I think that when women are too fond of other people's babies they never have any of their own."

But Corp shook his head. "I dinna understand it," he told her, "but I'm sure you was meant to hae them. Something's gane wrang."

She was still smiling at him, but her eyes were wet now, and she drew him on to talk of the days when Tommy was a boy. It was sweet to Grizel to listen while Elspeth and David told her of the thousand things Tommy had done for her when

TOMMY AND GRIZEL

she was ill, but she loved best to talk with Corp of the time when they were all children in the Den. The days of childhood are the best.

She lived so long after Tommy that she was almost a middle-aged woman when she died.

And so the Painted Lady's daughter has found a way of making Tommy's life the story of a perfect lover, after all. The little girl she had been comes stealing back into the book and rocks her arms joyfully, and we see Grizel's crooked smile for the last time.